A SCORE TO SETTLE

J C Johns

A Score to Settle

By J C Johns

ONE

THE WEATHER MATCHED GABRIEL LEE'S MOOD as he drove his eight-year-old Nissan over yet another hill. He had been driving for three hours and the drizzle had started annoying him within the first ten minutes. Not quite enough to have the wipers on full, but slightly too much for just intermittent.

He was driving through rolling hills with fields, farmland and the occasional whiff of muck-spreading, like so much of England. Each time he crested another hill, he gazed forward in the hope that he was driving towards a brighter sky, with the chance of a break in the monotony. And every time, his stomach sank a little further as the dream was dashed and he just saw more of the same stretching out before him.

If the sky was clear and blue, the scenery would be lush and he could gaze across England's green and pleasant land. But the drizzle somehow leached all life and colour out of the countryside until it became grey. Everywhere, just miles and miles of grey.

As he reached the top of the latest hill, he finally saw his destination listed on a road sign: 'Porlington 11'. His spirit briefly lifted as he realised he could be there within twenty minutes. Then it crashed back down again as he saw the motorhome trundling along the road half a mile in front of him, straddling the white lines in the centre so no other vehicle would get by in either direction.

'Must be lovely to be in one of those,' he thought to himself. 'Relative comfort, a bed in the back for if you get tired, a fridge full of beer just three feet behind you for when you get bored of driving, and miles of open road in front of you. Mostly because all the traffic is stuck behind you.'

Gabriel did not suffer fools gladly, and he considered most people who drove motorhomes (or dragged caravans behind their medium-sized cars for a cheap weekend away in a field somewhere) to be fools. He thought those people who drove motorhomes and towed small cars behind them even stranger. Caravans dragging cars just seemed wrong.

With that thought, he perceived a slight increase in the intensity of the drizzle and caught up with the motorhome at the same moment. Gabriel duly dropped his speed to the 32 miles per hour the motorhome was limping along at and resigned himself to not reaching Porlington for at least another hour as there wasn't a chance he'd be able to get past the behemoth in front of him on these windy roads. His satnav was telling him he was on an A road with a 60mph speed limit. If only.

Gabriel was 30 years old and currently going through a rather acrimonious divorce from Shelley Cole. She had always refused to take his surname as she preferred her own and thought if people said 'Shelley Lee' too quickly her entire persona and self-worth would be reduced to sounding like a stammer. Not wishing to be associated with a speech impediment, she stuck to using Cole. He suspected it also had a lot to do with the fact her father was the founder and proprietor of Cole's—a chain of grocery stores with no less than five branches now across a 25-mile range of small towns which had so far managed to fend off the competition from the larger supermarket chains. Well, she was welcome to inherit her little empire, she certainly wouldn't have a clue how to run it once the old man died. Gabriel wondered how long she would still want to be associated with the name once it became synonymous with failure.

It was down to Shelley that he had chosen Porlington to move to. They had been driving back from a wedding a few years back and decided to have a pleasant Sunday afternoon drive through the countryside on a more circuitous route than was perhaps advisable with the hangover from hell and as they had driven through Porlington, Shelley had commented, 'Dear God, look at this ghastly little place. So provincial. It's bound to be full of small-minded little people. I'd be happy to never come here again.'

Somewhere she had vowed never to return to sounded like the perfect place to move to.

Porlington turned out to be quite a large town once he began researching it. It had a population of around 150,000 the last time someone bothered to count, two multiplex cinemas, several clubs based around the River Dent catering to vessels from kayaks up to motorboats, and it was on the edge of the Dent Forest, which the river ran through.

More importantly for Gabriel, there was a reasonable musical life, with two amateur orchestras drawn from Porlington and the surrounding area, an operatic society in neighbouring Summerton, a locally-renowned philately society over the hill in Moleshine, and a good selection of pubs and clubs claiming to have regular live music.

Gabriel played a number of instruments, some to a pretty high standard. Oboe was his first study, but he also dabbled pretty well with piano and guitar. In recent times, he had occasionally guest conducted the local orchestra and found he had quite a penchant for it. The reviews in the local paper had always been kind and had certainly favoured him over the principal conductor who was far too academic and old-fashioned, despite only being in his mid-forties. Well, they'd just have to cope without Gabriel now. He was venturing into new pastures, albeit grey ones with lots of drizzle.

His car was packed up with the few things he had managed to claim as his own from his and Shelley's house, along with a few boxes of old sheet music which she had insisted he took or she would burn in the back garden. Probably with an effigy of him sat atop.

He'd persuaded her to let him take enough money from the joint account to pay for a deposit and two months' rent on a small flat not too far from Porlington town centre, just so she could get rid of him. As Gabriel gazed at the back of the motorhome trundling along in front of him, he wondered how long it would be before Shelley moved the boyfriend she'd been hiding from him for over a year into his house and his bed.

'Finally!' he said out loud as the motorhome indicated left, slowed down to a near-stop and gradually eased its ridiculous mass into a drizzle-soaked field for the owners to begin a weekend of staring at rain through the windows whilst playing endless rounds of backgammon. Gabriel accelerated back to a sensible speed and realised nearly fifty minutes had passed since he saw the promise of Porlington in eleven miles on that road sign.

Just as he began to wonder if a zero had fallen off the end of that sign and he was doomed to several more hours in the car, he rounded a corner and saw civilisation in front of him, confirmed by a sign saying, 'Welcome to Porlington'.

As he crossed the border into his new home, he had no idea that within a few months he would witness the first part of a murder.

TWO

S ANDRA'S VOICE BOOMED ACROSS THE CHURCH hall as the orchestra were setting chairs out before the rehearsal.

'Michael! Michael! We've had an email from somebody wanting to join the orchestra.'

'What do they play?' came back the gruff reply from Michael Fordington, conductor of the Porlington Philharmonia. This was barked without him even lifting his head out of the large chest of music he was rifling through, trying to find the conductor score for the Overture from The Marriage of Figaro.

Sandra unsuccessfully attempted to battle her way through chairs to reach the back of the hall where she could command Michael's full attention.

'Betty, you're really not helping by putting the chairs so close together, how are people supposed to reach where they need to be if the chairs resemble interlocking Roman shields?!' Sandra bellowed as she tried to plough through the second violin section, dragging five plastic chairs in her wake.

Betty Brannon just looked up and smiled. That's about all Betty ever did these days. Since reaching eighty and surviving not one but two strokes (and varicose veins), she now just smiled and shrugged her shoulders as her sole method of communication. Frankly, the most useful thing she did in the orchestra was setting the chairs out (and she was pretty inept at that). Her violin playing was non-existent. Mind, that was true of most of the second violins. Betty waited for Sandra to finish thundering her way through, then calmly put the chairs right back where she had put them before, smiling throughout.

'Michael, did you hear what I said?' Sandra demanded when she eventually reached the back of the hall, having managed to carve a path of destruction through the chairs and knock over a bass trombone en route.

'...left the damn piece in here somewhere, I know we've done it in the last few years. What fool has been messing around with this music...?' came a mumbled reply from within the chest.

'MICHAEL!'

The boom of Sandra's tenor echoed around the church hall for a good few seconds after she emitted the foghorn-like battle cry. The room fell so silent you could almost hear the sound of eyebrows raising as people paused from setting up and looked over to see what had rattled Sandra so early in the evening.

Michael emerged from the chest, red-faced from the exertion of extracting himself. 'What is it, woman? Can't you see I'm trying to find a score? If I don't find it, we'll have to play through something by Vaughan Williams again, or whatever we can find on the top here!'

'I've been trying to tell you, we've had an email from someone wanting to join the orchestra.'

'Yes, I heard you the first time. What do they play?'

11

Sandra gave no sign that he had, indeed, already asked this question as, since then, she had been forced to set sail across the floor like an icebreaker forging its way through a glacier and her mood was going downhill rapidly.

'Oboe,' she replied.

'Well we don't need another oboe. We've already got two.' And with that, he disappeared back into the chest.

'For heaven's sake, man, get back up here.' Sandra's patience was running out as she hauled Michael's not inconsiderable frame by his collar from the chest, before he took up permanent residence in it and turned feral. 'He conducts too…'

'So what? We have a conductor too, in case you hadn't noticed my presence here for the last thirty years.'

'Yes, but we have been saying for a while that if we had somebody else around who could conduct, it would ease the pressure on you a bit. We could go away more often instead of being tied to a fifteen-mile radius all the time so you can get back to conduct everything.'

'I'm not giving up my concerts!' shrieked Michael. By now, the throng of orchestra members milling around had given up listening in and gone back to their weekly default setting of ignoring Michael and Sandra having yet another one of their spats. 'I didn't start this orchestra just for some whippersnapper to swan in and take it over!'

'Look, you stubborn oaf, Doctor Fry has been telling you for some time that you need to take it easier and think of your health…'

'And you think interrupting me trying to find a score for tonight's rehearsal to tell me that I'm being replaced will do anything to help that?!'

Michael was now beginning to turn a new shade lying somewhere between vermillion and puce, and flecks of spittle were appearing in the corners of his mouth, just waiting to be hurled forth into Sandra's face at any moment the next time he hit a particularly plosive consonant. As such, she thought discretion might be the better part of valour.

'Fine, but we're going to continue discussing this later. The workload is too much for you to cope with on your own. You promised me once you hit seventy you would start scaling back so we could have more time together.'

A timid voice came from the podium. 'Michael? Sandra? Ahem, is this what you're looking for...?' Debbie Greer peered cautiously over the conductor stand to the back of the hall where Michael and Sandra turned towards her in their most menacing fashion. Undeterred, she pushed through the fear and in an ever-rising voice continued, 'Is it the Mozart you were after? I heard you mention it last week so I dug it out of the chest and put it on your stand before you got here. Didn't you notice it?'

By this time, the pitch of her voice was passing into territory where only canines would hear it and her eyes had tripled in size. Debbie had learned this technique many years before to avoid the bullying she had encountered most of her life. Look as cute and innocent as possible and people might just find enough compassion to stop screaming at you.

No such luck on this occasion.

'WHY would you do that?' screamed Michael. The spittle flecks all took flight on his first word, which was issued with a diaphragm lift so forceful that Pavarotti would have been proud. They landed several rows further forward, mostly on an unsuspecting bassoon player whose back was turned. 'I've been searching in this damn chest for twenty minutes! What possessed you to move my music?!'

In a not particularly disguised mumbling, a brave soul from the percussion section uttered, 'Well she is the orchestra librarian so it's her music really…' Michael and Sandra were used to ignoring the percussion section.

'I… I… just thought it might be helpful if it was on your stand so it was one less thing for you to worry about,' Debbie said, reaching the point where her bottom lip was beginning to quiver.

'I don't know why she comes every week just to take this abuse from them,' mumbled Doris the tea-lady as she pushed through the empty brass section chairs with her crate of paraphernalia, hoping the noise of clattering chairs and stands wouldn't cause her quip to be missed.

Michael and Sandra reached the podium, leaving the orchestra seating behind them looking ever more like a recently-ploughed field.

'There you are, dear. That's the score you were looking for, isn't it?' Sandra offered in an attempt to calm Michael down before the rehearsal started, lest he take out his frustrations on the players even more than usual.

'I suppose. Although it would be far more help if it was where it was supposed to be,' Michael grumbled.

'What, like not on your music stand?' was heard to drift over from the percussion section.

Michael realised it was 7:30pm. He took to the podium like an executioner takes to a scaffold and surveyed his victims. His heart sank. 'What's all this mess? There are chairs everywhere! Why aren't you all sat there ready to begin—we're going to be late.' He didn't mention the large number of players still missing, which he always took as a personal affront.

Eyes rolled behind him and the players shuffled into position, muttering to one another. Sandra took up her position as leader, next to the podium, sitting with a ramrod straight back, her eyes wandering over the orchestra, daring anybody to continue talking now that she was ready to start.

Once they were seated, the principal oboe gave an A for everyone to tune to. A few bothered, some others just sounded their strings without actually listening to the sound produced or making any adjustments. Most did nothing.

As silence fell, Michael announced they would start with the Mozart. He waited for people to find their scores and place them on their stands. Once there was absolute silence in the room, he started his usual pre-conducting ritual. With both feet firmly planted on his podium (which raised his height by three whole inches), he closed his eyes and put his head back, slowly shook his hands and inhaled deeply through his nostrils. Once he had filled his lungs, he paused for dramatic effect before slowly breathing out throw the narrowest aperture he could make with his lips.

A percussionist was heard to say to his neighbour (and anyone else listening in the otherwise silent room), 'Who does he think he is? Bernstein?' After years of practice, Michael ignored this, as he ignored all sarcasm directed at him.

He gradually opened his eyes, gazed around the room, looked at the score on his stand, slowly picked up his baton, opened the score to the first page and placed his hands in the air in front of him. The musicians had learned long ago not to bother picking up their instruments until this point in the choreography, otherwise their arms would be exhausted before a note had even been played.

Giving a single upbeat, Michael started flapping on the podium. Over the years, the players had individually settled on the word 'flapping' in their heads, all independently from one another. Occasionally, it could be called waving, or perhaps flailing. In slower pieces, flopping seemed more appropriate and the definition for his attempts at conducting faster pieces could be described as thrashing (or, if beating in two, threshing). But a good overall description for Michael Fordington's gyrations with a baton would be flapping.

The strings and bassoons burst into life on the first downbeat, before realising the upbeat tempo bore no resemblance to the speed at which Michael was actually going to take the overture. Hauling their tempo back like a jockey pulling on a horse's reins, they eventually landed back with Michael just in time for the rest of the orchestra to crash in. As the music progressed, both the tempo and the orchestra's collective will to live slowly dwindled at an approximately parallel rate.

Hiding at the back of the hall, Doris looked at the tea-making facilities she had just finished removing from the large plastic box and leaned over to Gertie, the wife of one of the viola players who came along to help with tea each week. 'You know, Gert, they say that the Marriage of Figaro Overture is the perfect length of time to boil an egg. Judging by the speed he's taking this tonight, there'll be time for the chicken to lay it too. They're never going to be on time for the break, don't put the urn on just yet.' With a saturnine glance at the players, she wandered outside to sit on the bench where the passing traffic would drown out the orchestra and she could consider how her life had reached this point.

THREE

D<small>EAR</small> G<small>ABRIEL</small>,

Many thanks for your email to the Porlington Philharmonia. As I'm sure you understand, most orchestras, especially one of our standing, will already have a full woodwind complement. However, in the event of one of our oboe / cor anglais players being unable to attend a rehearsal, I shall keep your details on file, in case we require you to stand in for them. I shall be in touch at the appropriate time should we wish to extend you this opportunity.

In the meantime, I note that your previous email says you have some conducting experience. For some time, the committee of the Porlington Philharmonia have been considering allowing a young person to get some experience conducting the orchestra and extending the opportunity to learn under our conductor Michael Fordington. If this is something you would like to apply to be considered for, please forward us a full curriculum vitae complete with references and a short personal statement (three or four pages perhaps) on why you would like to work with us and what benefits you could bring us. Whilst, at 30 years old, you can't really be considered a young person, we would still consider accepting an application from you.

With my very best wishes,

Sandra F

'Well, that email is about as rude and passive-aggressively narcissistic as one could get,' thought Gabriel as he scanned through his usual round of early-morning mail.

In amongst the various pieces of junk mail, unwanted marketing and an email from Shelley asking if he had appointed a solicitor for the divorce proceedings yet, it seemed like a relative ray of sunshine. Clearly, she was going to be her usual difficult self about the separation and go all out to get everything she could, whilst attempting to heap the maximum amount of humiliation upon him, all the while seemingly forgetting that it was her who had committed adultery. In a former time, she would have been taken outside the town limits and stoned. But in modern-day England, this was perceived as a badge of honour and, somehow, she was regarded as the injured party.

Well, perhaps this opportunity with the Porlington Philharmonia might help to take his mind off things. A quick glance at their website showed that they were clearly the weaker of the two local orchestras, but also had a far higher opinion of themselves than the Fawlham Symphony Orchestra eight miles away. But this one was closer. Within walking distance, in fact (he was hoping more like staggering distance if he could find some drinking buddies amongst the brass section for post-rehearsal imbibing).

Gabriel was aware that it was always difficult moving to a new area and not knowing anybody. Whilst studying for his degree in music technology at the University of West London, he had met Shelley, they had fallen madly in love after several nights of wild passion and their whirlwind romance had resulted in him moving to her home town upon graduation, where he knew nobody except her. Her family (her father in particular) were quick to exploit this.

'Didn't you ever fancy doing a real degree, boy?' he would ask Gabriel. Usually followed by, 'Never fancied a proper university? Didn't you get the grades at A Level?' Coming from a man who left school at 15 with no qualifications and who hadn't sat a single exam in his life, Gabriel always thought this was a bit rich. Although he couldn't dispute the fact that Mr Cole had forged a quite decent life for himself with a successful business and multiple houses dotted around the UK and Spain. He suspected most of those were mortgaged and mortgaged again and more akin to tax write-offs than property investments.

Within a matter of weeks, Shelley's father had Gabriel working a menial job in one of his slightly-less-than-medium-sized stores, earning only a fraction above minimum wage. Shelley and Gabriel were speedily moved out to one of the aforementioned properties (a very modest two-bedroom terrace, although from the way Mr Cole constantly went on about it, you'd think he'd bought them Buckingham Palace).

All thoughts of music were gradually stamped out of Gabriel over time and he came to accept that the best he could expect from life would be becoming a mid-level manager in a chain of stores nobody who lived thirty miles or more away had ever heard of. Granted, it was a regular income with a house attached, although the moderately high rent for said house appeared to be taken in its entirety from Gabriel's wages, with none of the burden shouldered by Shelley.

Of course, once she informed him they were getting married and demanded the society wedding of the decade, full of more friends than a family could possibly have, his pay-packet also appeared to decrease by an alarming rate to pay for 'his half of the wedding' as her father put it. Mr Cole was happy to pay for his little darling to have the day of her life, as long as Gabriel met him half-way and put in an equivalent share. Naturally, this was not reflected in the guest list, as only those family and friends on Gabriel's side who were pre-approved by the Coles could be invited. There had briefly been a question mark over his grandmother, as she was Irish and this made them nervous for some reason. His (entirely false) claim that in her youth she had been on a date with Gerry Adams and was still in touch with a lot of people from 'back then' sealed her invitation, albeit grudgingly, and with a lot of furtive looks in her direction throughout the day.

Gabriel decided to put all thoughts of the past out of his head as he spent too long dwelling on them and today was the start of a new chapter. He had persuaded the local music shop to give him a trial run as a sales assistant and he was due to start at 9am. He gulped down the rest of his coffee and headed out the door to walk across town to the small industrial unit which would be his new place of work. At least it was music related and not full of

21

groceries. He sincerely hoped there would be nothing 'organic' or 'locally produced' (ground of which he was fairly sure), although whilst the signs in his father-in-law's shops claimed these things, he knew full well they were total claptrap.

Porlington Pianos was a small, family-run business. Gabriel thought it was a bit much to make such an issue of being a local family firm when the owner had admitted to him they had only relocated here five years ago after their previous venture had run into difficulties.

Neil King was a large, jovial type who seemed friendly enough on first meeting, although the rather chunky, old-fashioned hearing aids did cause Gabriel to wonder how much music Neil could hear. Susan, Neil's wife, seemed lovely, although a little timid. The trio were completed by Grant, their son, who was unmarried, in his mid-40s and still lived at home with his parents. Gabriel wasn't entirely sure he trusted him, but he couldn't quite figure out why.

He knocked on the door at 8:50am and waited. After several more attempts at knocking, Neil showed up to let him in. 'Sorry, m'dear, didn't hear you knocking.'

Gabriel thought about recommending Neil turned his hearing aids on, but thought that might be too forward on his first morning.

'We've been hugely successful over recent times and have now expanded into the next property,' Neil yelled over his shoulder as he led Gabriel through a veritable Aladdin's Cave, stacked high with old sheet music, keyboards that would have been out-of-date ten years ago and more guitar paraphernalia than you could shake a semiquaver at.

They went on a whirlwind tour of two units that had a single doorway knocked through, with Neil pointing out the main items of interest. There weren't many. When they arrived back in the main shop area after twenty minutes, Gabriel ventured what he thought was a pertinent question, 'So, erm, where are the pianos…?'

'What pianos?' Neil asked, at a volume just ever-so-slightly above that which would normally be acceptable for everyday conversation.

'Well, it's called Porlington Pianos. But you have no pianos…'

'My dear chap, nobody wants pianos anymore! Keyboards. That's what they want. We're the only shop in the area who has contracts with both Yamaha and Casio.'

Gabriel didn't think it politically wise to point out they were the only music shop in the area. 'Have you ever had pianos?'

Neil continued without missing a beat. 'No, of course not! Keyboards, guitars and drum kits. That's the future. All the parents want now is something cheap that little Johnny or Jemima can beat to death in the cheapest plastic available to mankind, so it's disposable. If they make it to grade 3, they can worry about real instruments then.'

'So why, if you've only been here for five years and you've never stocked pianos, is it called Porlington Pianos?'

'Image, dear boy! Didn't they teach you anything on that fancy degree course of yours?' Neil was now gesticulating wildly. He had clearly wanted to be some sort of showman in an earlier chapter of his life and felt that all the world was indeed his stage. Shame it was to an audience of one, who was singularly unimpressed. 'If we claim to be the most high-end shop in the area, all the middle class luvvies will come flooding to us and accept whatever rubbish we serve them up. Pianos take up space. In my showroom, that is. And modern houses don't have space for them—nobody wants a piano any more. We're hardly likely to have a Benjamin Grosvenor come out of this area! They're all happy with keyboards which will be hammered for six months, then left to gather dust and eventually thrown away to make space for the drum kit that we'll talk them into once little Johnny is bored with the keyboard.'

Gabriel wondered if anybody called Johnny had ever crossed the threshold of this shop.

'So, let me put you in the capable hands of my son, Grant. He'll tell you what you'll be doing today.'

And with that, Grant appeared from the shadows. Gabriel was sure his feet didn't move and he just glided, with a smarmy appearance and rubbing his hands together in glee. Or conniving dastardliness.

'Good morning, Gabriel. If you'd like to follow me. Apologies, I would shake your hand, but I've just used alcohol gel. I don't like germs, and some of the little horrors we get in here are riddled with them. Their children are no better.' With that utterance, Grant emitted a bark that Gabriel assumed was his version of laughter. It was in three parts, the last of which shifted into his falsetto register which gave him an immensely effeminate appearance. Grant's fingernails appeared far too manicured for Gabriel's liking.

'So, you'll be on the tills today while I do a stock check. Ma and Pa will take care of dealing with the customers, we just need you to ring up items on the till and take payment. Are you familiar with taking card payments?'

24

'Err, yes. I've worked in retail for some years now.' Gabriel had a sinking feeling in his stomach again, which gave him flashbacks of being stuck behind that caravan last week. This was going to be no better than working for his father-in-law, just with different products.

'Excellent.'

More hand rubbing. Yup, this guy was a rather podgy Montgomery Burns.

'Then I shall leave you to it. Everything has a barcode, so just scan and take their filthy lucre. If there are any technical questions about a product, just refer them to one of those who understand these things.'

Gabriel attempted not to take offence. He failed, but didn't let it show, all the time wondering what he had gotten himself into.

The morning passed without incident. Or customers. Every now and again, Neil, Susan and Grant occasionally flitted through the shop section like phantoms moving from one part of a haunted castle to another. If Neil or Grant passed through, Gabriel attempted to look busy, although he had nothing to do. If Susan drifted through, he gave her a smile and received a wry, sad smile in return. At 11:30am, she brought him the weakest coffee he had ever drunk in his life, topped up with milk and sugar, neither of which he took. He smiled and thanked her. She offered no conversation other than another smile, which fell from her lips in the same way the life must have fallen from her eyes decades before.

Gabriel wasn't entirely sure what the lunchtime arrangements were, or when he was supposed to take a break. As it was nearly 4pm, he was pondering heading into the warehouse next door to ask about this when the bell above the door rang.

A quiet, mousey girl in her mid-twenties walked into the shop, looking around nervously. Like trapdoor spiders pouncing on their prey, all three of the King family suddenly appeared from nowhere to fawn over her and ask what she wanted. When she said that she wanted some violin strings, you could visibly see them all deflate and refer her to Gabriel at the tills, before moving away back into the shadows to wait for the next victim to touch one of the strands of their web.

It suddenly occurred to Gabriel that these people were like the Sowerberrys from Oliver Twist (with Grant fulfilling the role of Noah Claypole); they had hoped for the sale of a coffin, but all the customer wanted was a wreath.

The girl walked over to the counter and gave a nervous smile to Gabriel.

'Hello, I'm, erm, after some spare strings for my violin.'

'Hi. Well, we have a great selection on sale here today.' All those years of working for Mr Cole had taught him to improvise with the best of them. 'Just let me have a look at what we've got. Do you have any preference as to manufacturer or gauge?' He had no idea what he was saying, it just sounded like the thing you should ask when attempting to sell somebody a set of violin strings.

'Oh, I'm not sure. I just need a spare set in case one goes. I'm starting with a new orchestra tomorrow night and want to be prepared, just in case.'

'No problem, I'm sure we have some excellent ones here somewhere.'

Gabriel wasn't sure at all. He turned and looked at the display behind him which was full of guitar strings. Probably couldn't palm her off with those. A violinist would probably know the difference (a guitarist probably wouldn't...). The display also appeared to have a large selection of varying sizes of 'Air Guitar Strings' which were empty cellophane bags with cardboard tops attempting to be funny. He suspected that was Grant's doing. He also suspected that the joke only needed a few of these, not the forty or so he could see on display. Gabriel wondered if they'd ever sold a single one.

'Sorry, it's my first day. I'm not sure where we keep the violin strings. Could you excuse me for just one moment, please?'

'Of course. Take your time, I'm not in a rush.'

Gabriel hurried back to the warehouse to find it empty. It briefly occurred to him that the family might be sleeping underground in coffins, before he thought to check the kitchenette on the other side of the shop. Sure enough, Susan was in there, boiling a kettle.

'Sorry to interrupt you, but where do we keep the violin strings?' Gabriel enquired. Susan didn't respond, she just held up a cup and raised her eyebrows in what appeared to be an enquiry as to whether he would care for another coffee. 'No, thanks. I'm trying to limit my caffeine intake.' Her eyebrows slowly fell, followed by the rest of her face, and eventually the empty cup. 'But perhaps later this afternoon...?' he asked, just out of guilt at seeing her dwindling countenance.

Susan's face lit up and she patted him on the arm, before taking his hand and walking him through to the shop. She knelt down under the counter and pulled out two cases of violin strings, placing them on the countertop and smiling at Gabriel before wandering back to the kitchenette.

'Sorry,' he said to the girl in front of him.

27

'It's okay, you said it was your first day,' she replied, with a small, coquettish smile forming at the corner of her mouth.

'Do you want a full set of all four strings?' Gabriel asked.

'Probably best. I think mine are all okay, but you never know if one might snap.'

'Or if you need to slice some cheese,' he quipped.

The silence that followed felt to Gabriel like eternity was gobbling up his entire universe, filled only with the sound of distant wind and tumbleweeds slowly blowing through the shop.

'Err, yes. Or that,' the girl said.

Gabriel turned away so she couldn't see his face turning bright crimson. Why had he tried to be funny? He wasn't good with girls. He wasn't confident like so many of his friends at university. He couldn't flirt. For heaven's sake, he was still technically married! Although he was pretty confident that ship had sailed when Shelley had started sleeping around. He wasn't even sure how long that had been going on for, or just how many men there had been. Or if it had been limited to just the last few months, or if it had been going on since they first got together and he was just the fool that had fallen for all her lies. He'd always suspected that when he was away, when she hadn't replied to his messages, that she'd been with somebody else. And why were thoughts of Shelley flooding his head now, when he was trying to be nice to this girl and put her at ease? He attempted to pull himself together.

'Okay, so, erm, this is a full set of reasonable quality strings. Should be good as spares.' He had no idea if they were or not, but it seemed like the right thing to say.

'You've got an E string, an A string, a D string and a…'
Oh dear God, there was no going back. His mouth had engaged and he couldn't stop now, no matter how much he wished for the ground to swallow him up, or the rapture, or good old-fashioned spontaneous combustion. '… a G string…'

She laughed. Thank God, she laughed. He attempted to laugh, but it came out more as a whimper.

'Good to know. Thanks for clarifying that for me.' She seemed remarkably unfazed at his complete idiocy. He handed the pack of strings over like they were radioactive and he couldn't wait to get rid of them. Then he remembered he needed to put them through the system.

'Sorry, I just need to, erm, scan them.' She handed them back and he noticed she was slightly flushed too. Probably nothing to the tomato red that he must have been. He could feel his face giving off more heat than the face of the sun. The beep of the till jolted them both back to reality. 'That'll be £39.95 please.'

'Sorry, how much?' she replied.

'The till says £39.95.' He could feel his face increasing in temperature again.

'Oh, that's quite a lot more than I normally pay online.'

'Oh. Sorry, I have no idea how much they cost, but they look like our cheapest set.'

She paused and considered this. After a few moments, she handed over her card. 'That'll be fine. I suppose a good set of reliable strings is worth paying for.'

Gabriel was utterly humiliated as he was sure this set really wasn't premium in any way except the price tag. He just hoped she wouldn't figure that out. The others in the case had fancier packaging so he was sure they'd cost more.

'Contactless okay…?'

'I'm pretty sure that's over the contactless limit.'

'Sorry, of course it is.' He handed the card back. 'If you could just pop your card into the machine and enter your PIN.' At that moment, he saw Grant glide through with his perfectly and disturbingly manicured nails. His gaze appeared to pass right through Gabriel's soul, as though he was judging him for being the blithering idiot he was currently portraying.

The girl complied with his request and the till informed him the transaction had been completed. He suddenly felt the need to attempt to somehow haul the situation back to his advantage, at least to the point where he wasn't utterly humiliated.

'So which orchestra are you joining?' he asked as he handed the strings over in a small Porlington Pianos bag with the receipt neatly tucked inside.

That seemed to break the ice and she appeared to relax a little.

'The Porlington Philharmonia. I moved here last year and wanted to join an orchestra to get back into playing, but I haven't got around to it until now.'

Gabriel's heart suddenly leapt. Here was common ground, just waiting to be shared.

'Oh really? They've just asked me to be their assistant conductor.' Suddenly he felt like less of a buffoon and felt he may have some kudos again.

'Nice! I always had a bit of a thing for conductors…' The girl's voice suddenly trailed off as she realised what she had said. At least her face was now matching the glowing red that Gabriel's was.

They both laughed nervously.

'I'm sorry, shall we start this again? I'm Gabriel. I'm the idiot who just started working in the music shop and is overcharging you for violin strings.'

The girl laughed. Eventually, she looked up and met his eyes, extending her hand.

'Hi. I'm Lauren. I'm the idiot who is so nervous about playing in an orchestra that she decided to buy a second pair of overpriced strings just in case she snapped several in her first rehearsal back for years.'

They shook hands and laughed.

'Well, Lauren, it's a pleasure to meet you. I'll look forward to hearing you on Thursday evening and I hope I don't take any tempos too fast that I cause you to snap a G string. Or any other string.'

Her hand slipped away as she laughed even harder.

'I'll look forward to the challenge, Maestro.'

And with that, Lauren and her bag of violin strings was gone from the shop. As she disappeared into the gloom of the late afternoon air, Gabriel suddenly realised his heart was racing, but for reasons other than humiliation.

FOUR

THE FOLLOWING THURSDAY ARRIVED AND Gabriel felt pensive as he stood outside the Porlington Methodist church hall, waiting to go in. Secretly, he was loitering in the hope of seeing Lauren so they could walk in together. Safety in numbers, and all that. Since their disastrous encounter over violin strings, he'd found his thoughts kept drifting towards her. When he was shopping yesterday, as he walked down each aisle he'd found himself casually wondering if she'd like Italian food or Mexican or whatever he was passing by.

It had reached 7:20pm, so he thought he better go in and introduce himself as there was still no sign of her.

As he walked into the hall, he heard all the usual sounds you'd associate with an amateur orchestra— chairs being scraped into position, music stands being assembled (then disassembled, then reassembled and so on, as you need a degree in mechanical engineering to understand how those things actually work), a low hum of chatter, all accompanied by just a faint whiff of Sudocrem. He was never sure if it was the church halls that caused that last part, or just the propensity of amateur orchestras to have an unusually high number of old people.

Glancing around, he noticed this orchestra certainly hit that demographic. It would appear that his presence would lower the average age by several decades.

He suddenly became aware that someone had locked their radar onto him and they were heading in at an alarmingly fast rate.

'Hello, I'm Sandra. Who might you be?'

'Hi, I'm Gabriel. We emailed about...'

'Of course we did. Welcome to our jolly band of musicians.' Looking around, he didn't see much jollity. 'We're delighted to be able to offer you a trial run to see if you fit our requirements.'

Gabriel thought this might not be the time to point out that he really did consider this arrangement to be the other way around.

'Let me introduce you to our conductor, Michael Fordington.'

Sandra whisked Gabriel away to the back of the hall where a large man was bent double over an even larger chest.

'Michael, this is the young man I told you... Michael. MICHAEL!'

The large frame slowly extricated itself from the chest, which appeared to contain a random selection of single sheets of music.

'Mmm, what? I'm just trying to find... Oh. Who's this?' Michael's demeanour suddenly became colder as his beady eyes landed on Gabriel, and he appeared to grow an inch or two.

'This is Gabriel Flee, the young man I told you about, who emailed us.'

'Actually, it's Lee…' Gabriel pointed out in his most polite and deferential tone.

'What? I didn't realise he was actually coming tonight. I don't have anything for him to do in this concert. Why is he here?' Michael barked at Sandra.

'I'm so sorry, Mr Flee, would you give us just one moment?' Sandra said, with a smile so false it barely reached the edges of her mouth, let alone her eyes.

Gabriel wondered what to do next. They were both stood there just staring at him. He decided that the onus was on him to step away for a moment, rather than the two of them. As he was walking to the front of the church hall, where people were still coming in, he heard Michael say, 'What did he say his name was? Lee? What sort of name is Lee Flee?'

Gabriel was on the verge of turning around to correct them on the matter of his name once again when he noticed Lauren had arrived and he decided his name was no longer terribly important. He clambered over chairs and sidestepped a strange, elderly woman with an inane grin on her face that appeared to be aimed in his direction. She also appeared to be pushing a row of chairs rather randomly into the middle of the hall.

'Hey Lauren. How's the G string holding out?' he heard himself say as he reached her at the back. Not only did he immediately realise what had come out of this mouth, but he simultaneously realised the volume at which he had said it. A lady carrying a large plastic box of tea-making equipment gasped and said, 'Well I never!' before moving on her way.

Lauren heard the statement before she realised it was him saying it and initially she took a short intake of breath before recognising him. She apparently also saw the look

34

of abject despair on his face that ensued as she just laughed at him.

'Well that's certainly something I've never been asked at my first rehearsal with a new orchestra! Are you sure you should be asking women that in your position as conductor?!' Lauren said in a rather quiet sotto voce.

A passing percussionist who was wheeling a timpani through the crowd heard this and was heard to exclaim, 'A new conductor?! Praise be, the day has finally come! Has the old fart finally... Oh. He's still here. Damn.' The rest of the statement was lost as he weaved his way through instrument cases, taking care to knock over as many cello cases as possible, letting out a short giggle as each one hit the floor and glaring at Michael who was still at the back of the hall, having a rather heated discussion with Sandra, both of them with gritted teeth.

'Oh my God, I am so sorry, Lauren, I'm normally so in control. I have no idea what keeps coming out of my mouth.'

'Don't worry, it's fine. I've had worse said to me. Although you might not want to say things like that on the podium,' she replied.

'I'm not entirely sure I'm going to make it to the podium. The conductor appears not to have received the memo saying that I'd be joining this lot tonight,' Gabriel replied, with a glance towards Michael and Sandra, both of whom were several shades redder than when he had left them.

'Don't worry, love,' said a middle-aged lady who was stood nearby with a violin case. 'I'm sure it'll work out. This isn't exactly the first time this has happened.' Her words didn't hold much comfort for Gabriel.

'Hello, I'm Jane. Are you coming to join us?' she continued, shifting her attention to Lauren.

'Yes. Well, I hope so. I was told to prepare some pieces to audition, but I'm not sure who to speak to…' Lauren replied.

'Ah, you got the standard email. Don't worry about it. I've never known anybody have to audition yet. We're just grateful for anybody who turns up who can play. Can you play?

'I did my grade 8 in school, but that was a while ago.'

'In that case, you're already over-qualified. Come and sit with me, I'll look after you.'

And with that, Lauren was ushered away from Gabriel before he had the opportunity to make any more inappropriate comments. Strangely, as she disappeared into the melee of the orchestra wrestling with chairs, stands and cases, he suddenly felt like the sun had passed behind a cloud. He wasn't quite sure what to do next, so he stood at the back, smiling inanely at anyone who walked past him, receiving a number of quizzical looks in return as people hurried past him like he had leprosy.

With that, he realised Sandra and Michael were stood next to him, both with fixed smiles on their faces that appeared so tense he feared their faces might actually shatter.

'My apologies for the misunderstanding, Mr Flee,' Sandra started.

'It's Lee. Gabriel Lee,' Gabriel interjected once again.

'If you say so. Michael and I have discussed this and agreed that…'

'Look, boy, this isn't exactly my idea,' Michael interrupted. 'But Sandra here thinks that we should give you a chance. I've got nothing for you to do tonight as we have a concert in three weeks and the programme is set already. I've been rehearsing it all for months, so it wouldn't be proper… appropriate… it just wouldn't be cricket for you to step in with one of the pieces now, as you won't have had time to learn it.' Gabriel saw Sandra's eyes imperceptibly roll as she thought he wasn't watching. 'So here's the thing. I'm happy for you to sit in on the rehearsal tonight and for the next few weeks and learn how things are run around here. Then we can maybe discuss something for the next concert after that. Mmm?'

Gabriel mumbled his appreciation in what he hoped was a conciliatory tone whilst doing his very best not to let his face display his true thoughts. He had already decided this would be a total waste of time and, if not for Lauren's presence here, he would already be on his way back to his flat.

'Right, well if you'd care to take a seat anywhere you like—just here would be fine—then you can watch how I run things this evening.'

And with that, Michael and Sandra were gone. Gabriel eased uncomfortably into a chair which had less legroom than a budget flight out of Stansted, and settled in for what he was sure would be one of the most boring nights of his life.

He was wrong.

Michael had lumbered up onto the podium and appeared to be going through some pre-rehearsal ritual where he was leaning his head back with his eyes shut and inhaling loudly through his nostrils. Sandra was sat next to him in the leader position, watching his every move. Everybody else was still continuing their conversations.

Michael eventually came back to terra firma and announced to the orchestra they were going to begin. An

A was commanded from the principal oboe and the most lacklustre attempt at tuning Gabriel had ever witnessed ensued. Once this racket had died down, Michael addressed his spectators.

'This evening, we will be learning two new pieces, which I have just decided we will be adding to the concert.'

Gabriel considered how only a few moments before, Michael had informed him that he had been rehearsing everything in the programme for months. He heard audible groans from the orchestra, punctuated by a voice that sounded like it came from the percussion section saying, 'What a surprise!' Whilst this was heard by everyone in the room, Michael chose to ignore it for some reason, but needed an outlet for his frustration. He picked on a cellist who was clearly autistic and still trying to get their cello absolutely in perfect tune. 'Johnathan, will you PLEASE stop fiddling with your instrument?! I'm trying to talk here!'

'Sor... sorry, Michael, I was just trying to tune...'

'I don't care if you're trying to build the pyramids, do it silently!' boomed back the response. 'I have decided to add Ravel's *Bolero* and...' Gabriel missed what the second piece Michael announced was as the first one garnered a chorus of disapproval from the violas, cellos, basses and percussion. He definitely heard the word 'off' following something else from numerous people.

'My snare drum is in for repair that night...' was heard to drift across from the percussion.

'I'm sure you will agree that this will be an excellent programme that people will flock to hear,' Michael said. The collective expressions from the orchestra implied they thought otherwise.

'So, if you'd all like to open your scores for...'

With that, the doors burst open and a rakish young man walked through, announcing in a loud voice, 'Don't worry, everyone, I'm here. As you were.'

Henry James was the principal trumpet of the Porlington Philharmonia. He was 28 years old and had the body of a Greek god. Unfortunately, he also had the mind of a Greek goat. Utterly charming, debonair, and with an opinion of himself so high it required an oxygen mask, he considered himself to be the lady-slayer of Porlington and the surrounding areas. This wasn't entirely true. In fact, it wasn't even remotely accurate.

He sauntered to the front and shimmied his way through the orchestra to take up his place in the brass section. He paused as he passed the principal oboe.

'Hello, Allegra,' he said, just a little too loudly, flashing his most winning smile. Most of the women in the orchestra melted as he did so, with more than a few faint sighs. The men just rolled their eyes.

Allegra di Rossi was the principal oboe and, as her name suggested, was of Italian descent with a beauty that would make Helen of Troy feel inadequate and require ongoing therapy for body perception issues. Her large brown eyes slowly lifted from her score to discern which trivial mortal had interrupted her serene existence. The thing about Allegra was that everything appeared to move in slow motion—to all intents and purposes, her body moved at a rate approximately half the speed of the rest of the world. Her hand gradually rose from her lap to delicately brush her flawless jet-black hair from covering her right eye; as her finger caressed the lock of hair aside, said lock appeared to hang in mid-air for a moment before gravity took the weakest of holds on it and it floated to its new position.

The men of the orchestra had no idea their jaws had slowly fallen open as they were reminded of her presence amongst them, as the women gazed upon her with an equal mix of wonder, jealousy and secret contempt.

'Henry,' came back the response, uttered in a whisper so delicate it was near inaudible. No emotion flickered across her face. No mere man could even guess at what thoughts might have been passing through her utterly brilliant mind. The closest thing to a professional musician the orchestra had, Allegra had gained first class honours from the Royal Academy of Music before deciding she wanted another career and becoming a paediatric surgeon. Nobody could quite guess her age as she had accomplished so much, but still looked 25.

She was also Henry's Achilles heel. He could never understand why she displayed not the slightest bit of attention in him when they were clearly the two most beautiful people in the orchestra and were obviously destined to produce beautiful babies. Or at least practise the act of creating them on a regular basis.

'So, Allegra, are you busy on Saturday evening?' he uttered with a cheeky wink.

'No,' she replied, as the wind caught her hair and flared it out around her perfectly formed shoulders (yes, they were indoors, but every person present was convinced they saw that happen).

'You. Me. That new little Italian restaurant that has opened on Ambrose Place. What do you say?' Henry ventured with a twinkle in his eye.

'Call me once you reach puberty, Henry.' And with that, her gaze descended in tiny increments back to the score on the music stand in front of her, clearly indicating his audience with her was at an end.

Flushed and slightly stammering under his breath, he barged through music stands to take up his position at the back.

'Can we PLEASE turn to the Dvorak and make a start?!' bellowed Michael from the podium, clearly irritated by this interruption. This elicited no response whatsoever from the orchestra, with the sole exception of Sandra who was sat in the leader position with her violin under her chin(s) and ready to go. The women were still pondering Henry's jawline whilst the men were internally (and, in the case of a couple of viola players, externally) drooling over Allegra. All were lost in their own thoughts.

'NOW!' boomed Michael, attempting to rescue some semblance of consciousness from the sea of blank faces in front of him.

Music was rustled. Instruments were picked up (although not placed into playing position just yet). More eyes were rolled and Michael started his usual pre-flapping ritual. As it neared it's inevitable and long-awaited end, the lower strings eased their instruments into position whilst the horns waited to see if they would even reach the fourth bar for their entry and the upper woodwind decided they probably wouldn't be needed for bar six for a while as Michael would probably tell the cellos off for something and make them repeat a couple of notes over and over again.

Gabriel watched in fascination from the back of the hall for the next hour as Dvorak's 9th Symphony was mutilated into something aurally resembling a flock of geese being slowly fed into a wood chipper. He watched

Lauren sitting in the violins, trying her hardest to blend in and keep her head when all around her were losing theirs.

FIVE

THE ALARM WENT OFF AT PRECISELY 7AM. Sandra gazed at Michael next to her in bed and wondered exactly how they had ended up at this place in their lives. She had been awake for nearly an hour, but knew better than to leave the bed after she stirred, lest she wake him and face the intolerable outburst that would no doubt follow.

Strangely, he could be woken by the slightest breath out of place, or a mere foot being placed on the floor on the opposite side of the bed, and yet the constant, rasping 'WAA WAA WAA' of the alarm clock didn't even begin to rouse him from his slumber. For a man she considered to be so in tune with music and sound, she did wonder how he could be so oblivious to the blindingly obvious and yet painfully aware of the irrelevant minutiae in life. This observation wasn't necessarily limited to their sleeping and waking habits.

They had met many years before, in another orchestra, in another town, in another age. Him, the bright young conductor full of promise and with the potential to be the next Leonard Bernstein; her, the slightly younger violinist with ideas of going off to the bright lights of a major city and being a full-time musician under the leadership of one so brilliant as him.

In those early days, he hadn't even noticed her. Of course, since then, he always insisted he had, but she knew the truth. She was just any other faceless string player in a sea of faces eager to sit in front of the great maestro and learn from him, hanging on his every word and memorising every syllable that dripped from his mouth. To him, she had been nothing more than a tiny fish in a larger shoal—never noticed as an individual, a face that he probably wouldn't even recall if they had bumped into each other on the street. She was abundantly aware that her role in those early days was just to fill a seat and make the best possible sound she could on her violin for the genius that stood in front of her.

The sad truth was that she had always known he would never amount to much. In those early days, he was spoken about in such hushed tones by certain people; he was revered by many and portrayed as such a rising young talent (although 'young' might be a stretch as he was a considerable way into his 30s even then). But Sandra had seen many 'young' things come and go in that particular orchestra. Some went on to achieve a moderate level of local fame, before blending into the mediocre and being quickly forgotten. Others appeared once or twice, never to be seen again. There was one particular young man who appeared for a while and, in the brief period he was with them, dazzled everyone. London-trained, with an immense professional pedigree behind him, but still in his early 30s, who believed in the principle of rule-by-comedy rather than rule-by-fear. Nobody ever knew much about him, other than he'd been through a messy divorce and needed some time out of the rat-race to recover. After about a year, he moved on, once said recovering had been achieved, never to be seen again, but sorely missed. And then Michael had arrived.

The problem was, he immediately followed real genius, which put his arrogant and rather bombastic nature into stark relief. He, of course, was blissfully unaware of this, and just assumed the stance he had always taken towards conducting and running an orchestra was the correct one. Most people in that orchestra had never warmed to him, and considered him a difficult man who didn't inspire the players he stood in front of. He never realised that his predecessor had inspired genuine admiration in a way he could never achieve.

Sandra had always been inspired by genius, but at the same time was slightly terrified of it. She had sat there playing her violin under all the previous conductors, scratching along every week with whatever score was placed in front of her. Michael's predecessor had filled her with awe, but this meant she could barely breathe when he was conducting, or talking to the orchestra, or making his usual jokes, or doing whatever it was he did that made everybody in front of him achieve more than they could ever believe possible.

But when Michael came along, his somewhat cumbersome and unfounded narcissistic ways seemed somehow like a breath of fresh air to her. He didn't notice her any more than those who came before him, but his obvious flaws made this maestro seem somehow slightly more human, and therefore approachable. That he couldn't conduct, or even hold a basic rehearsal together, didn't seem to matter to Sandra. His many faults made him seem just human enough that she could consider him someone with whom she could have a conversation, perhaps even build a friendship.

That was 34 years ago. For the first two years, Michael never spoke to her, and she was sure he hadn't even noticed her. Mind, he never really spoke to anyone except when he needed something, so she tried not to take it personally. Then Sandra agreed to serve on the committee, after a schism amongst the previous committee, resulting in departures, accusations, hurt feelings and general all-round pointless kerfuffle. She couldn't even remember what it was all about now.

Being on the committee was something of a poisoned chalice. Whilst one would imagine the members would have some say, it became quickly apparent that this wasn't the case. They were there as lackies and rubber-stampers. Mind, that suited Sandra, who wasn't really interested in politics or planning, and had only agreed as a favour to the chairman. He was a big, gruff fellow with a huge RAF moustache, having been a Wing Commander or something, and was not the sort of person one declined a request from.

Michael had an honorary and non-voting position on the committee, but, realistically, he was the power hiding in the shadows. He informed the chairman of everything he wanted to happen, and this was railroaded through at the next available meeting. Votes weren't even held. It was simply a case of the committee members being informed, then the minutes stating they had unanimously agreed. The principle of dictatorship was alive and well.

After two years of suffering through interminably boring committee meetings, the music librarian for the orchestra died somewhat unexpectedly. He was a tuba player in the orchestra (Sandra always considered the tuba an odd instrument to have taken up), so was rarely needed and spent the hours he wasn't playing organising the music. He was a farmer for his day job. Turns out being kicked in the chest by a mule and landing face first in a pile of diarrhetic mule droppings can cause broken ribs to pierce the heart and lungs, topped off by drowning in something unspeakable. Apparently, the mule was sick of tuba practice. Understandably.

Anyhow, it meant the orchestra was without a librarian. Sandra was asked by the chairman if she would take the role on. Despite her misgivings about falling foul of a disgruntled equus asinus x equus caballus, she couldn't really say no to the chairman's twitching moustache and agreed before she could think it through.

Suddenly, Michael knew her name. And he talked to her. Well, talked *at* her. He informed her of the pieces she would need to hire from the local library, and then expected them within a few days, despite the library usually needing several weeks to source the material.

For some reason, Michael always insisted on coming with her to collect the music. However, he was noticeably absent on the occasions she had to return scores, which she suspected was something to do with the librarian who suffered from high blood pressure screaming every time that there were some parts missing and inflicting exorbitant penalty fees. Sandra was initially terrified by this, but eventually became desensitised.

Then one night, the unthinkable happened. The committee grew a backbone and there was a coup d'état. What started out as a perfectly normal and banal committee meeting suddenly descended into chaos when one brave soul asked if they could have a vote on some minor point of order. The chairman couldn't understand why they suddenly wanted to waste time with voting, but realised there was some hostility in the room, so eventually agreed. That was his first mistake.

As soon as the members were asked to vote, a majority voted against. It wasn't even an important point—something about whether there should be a choice of biscuits in the break at rehearsals rather than just digestives. The chairman was outraged at this clear undermining of his power and ranted for around ten minutes, railing against the 'loony left do-gooders' and the Labour Party. Quite what they had to do with digestives, Sandra never did figure out. This rant was his second mistake.

At the end of his tirade, a committee member (who was referred to as Brutus for years to come) stood up and said he found the way the chairman spoke to the committee to be inappropriate and bullying, calling for a vote of no confidence. This was seconded by someone almost immediately and the vote narrowly succeeded. It was clearly pre-planned, but the chairman then made his third mistake, which was to threaten to resign. Brutus stood and immediately accepted the resignation (which hadn't actually been tendered, only threatened), but it was clear the chairman's time was at an end. He stormed from the house, his moustache twitching so hard it looked like a stoat's tail flailing in the throes of an epileptic fit.

He was barely out of the door when someone tabled a motion nominating Brutus as the new chairman. As before, this was seconded and successfully voted on before all those outside of the coup's inner circle knew what had hit them. Brutus stood dramatically (even more full of his own self-importance than the Wing Commander) and began a rambling tirade about removing the old guard and, suddenly, Michael's position as conductor was on the table. Apparently, Brutus had a new person in mind, who he considered would take the orchestra in a better direction—this was passed with the same speed as the previous motions and Michael found himself out of a position, with everyone in the room staring silently at him, waiting for him to leave.

'Sandra, are you coming?' he asked quietly. She suddenly remembered that they had come from the library after picking up some scores late that afternoon and she was his lift.

'Erm, yes, of course Michael. Right away,' she had mumbled, quickly gathering her notepad, pen and handbag, before leaving with him and beginning the drive back to his house.

The drive was horrible. The silence lay like a lead weight in the car, and Sandra wasn't sure what was louder—Michael's breathing, her heartbeat or the fan belt in her engine that kept slipping. Around half-way into the 30-minute journey, a sound somewhere between a sob and a yelp suddenly emitted from Michael's cavernous chest and Sandra became aware he was shaking in the passenger seat, silently racked with inaudible sobbing. She pulled over into a country lay-by and put her arms around him. He shook in her embrace for at least ten minutes, still unable to allow himself to let any real sound out in case it opened the floodgates and actual wailing ensued.

Eventually, he began to calm down and the racking spasms gradually subsided. She didn't know what to say, so continued to hold him, more as a conversation-avoidance tactic than anything else. After a while, he lifted his tear-stained face from her shoulder and looked at her. Without a word being said, they fell into a passionate kiss. To this day, she still had no idea how this had happened as he had never shown the slightest affection towards her, but all of a sudden she found herself putting her seat back and feeling him clamber on top of her.

Around three minutes later, it was over. He felt he had found a new ally, and she had fallen utterly in love. He never did find out that it was her first time.

Decades later, she found herself still waking up next to him. She looked at him and heard his snoring next to her. She remembered how he had taken months to recover from the hurt of that night before one day announcing to her that they were starting the Porlington Philharmonia. He had chosen Porlington as it was about the only town in the area that didn't have an orchestra, so he felt he wouldn't have any competition. The problem was, it also didn't have any spare musicians as those who could play already travelled to other orchestras in nearby towns and villages.

They had struggled for years but eventually built the group up from a few decrepit string players to something resembling a chamber orchestra (a grand title for a string octet plus two flutes and a bassoon). Eventually, they managed to entice in some other unsuspecting victims and, over time, they had grown to be almost a real orchestra. Granted, they still needed to spend a fortune on hiring in local semi-professionals for some positions, but Michael thought this gave the orchestra gravitas as the semi-professionals wished to play with them. Truth was, they didn't; they just wanted the money, and the other surrounding orchestras were sufficiently talented that they didn't need to buy in extras.

The clock read 7:20, and she realised she had been lost in thought for a long time. It was time for him to wake up, otherwise he would be even more grumpy than normal. As usual, she was the fall guy—she swung her legs out of the bed and stood up, her nightie falling back into position as she stretched. The sound of flannelette rustling woke Michael.

'Mmm? What..? Why are you making all that noise?! It's the middle of the night!'

'No, dear, we've overslept. It's time to get up. I'll go and make you some coffee,' Sandra replied. As she walked out of the bedroom and headed down the stairs to the kitchen, she heard him burp, fart, curse and fart again. In any other man, it would have been an age thing, but he'd always had that particular wake-up ritual.

SIX

AS GABRIEL WALKED INTO PORLINGTON PIANOS at 8:45am, he saw Michael driving past in a rather beaten-up old car, heading out of the town on the Summerton Road. He waved, but was either ignored or not seen, he wasn't sure which. Gabriel was still attempting to gather his thoughts about the carnage that was the rehearsal he had attended the previous night.

Grant was behind the counter, studying his ludicrously effeminate nails.

'Good morning, Maestro. How were your first steps on the road to world domination last night?' he asked Gabriel as he noticed him entering the shop.

'I think it's fair to say I won't be impressing an audience anytime soon,' Gabriel replied.

'It's not about impressing the audience, dear boy. It's about impressing all the beautiful ladies in the orchestra. Did you wow them? Did you… make them bend to your musical will?'

Gabriel was sure he saw Grant's eyes half-close as he uttered this rather disturbing question.

'MOTHER! What are you doing?!' Grant bellowed as Susan walked into the shop, carrying two large boxes. She was so startled, the top box looked like it might fall off at any moment.

'Here, let me help you with those,' Gabriel said, rushing to Susan's aid. As he removed the top box and saw her face, she gave him one of her wan smiles, whilst her eyes screamed both depression and repression. He gave her a really big smile in the knowledge that it would probably be the nicest thing to happen to her that day. Susan shuffled through the shop and into the door that led into the warehouse.

'Oh for God's sake, those are supposed to be in here,' Grant muttered angrily before following Susan out through the door.

Gabriel placed the box he had taken onto the counter, intending to deal with it later.

The last couple of days had passed by with virtually no customers and no excitement. He was beginning to realise that Porlington Pianos was not a hub of excitement, and he was beginning to question how they stayed afloat, let alone how they could afford to take him on as a member of staff. Still, he was happy to ride this particular gravy train as long as it was rolling along. Even if it meant having to deal with Grant and Neil, whilst trying not to think about how miserable Susan was, and wondering what the two men in her life had done to her over the years to cause her to be that way. Still, it was better than having to deal with his ex-father-in-law on a daily basis.

By lunchtime, he had sorted several deliveries, sold a ¾ size violin to a very stroppy parent who needed it *today* for her daughter who was clearly going to be the next Nigel Kennedy, despite being only six years old, and rearranged the air guitar strings into gauge order. At least, that's what he told a somewhat bemused Grant as he

53

floated back through the shop on one of his numerous appearances.

Gabriel found his thoughts drifting to Lauren. At the end of the rehearsal the previous night, she had been mobbed by the other violinists, with Jane doing her best to guide her through the thronging crowd who were eager to see the first new string section member since Old Testament times. Jane had ushered Lauren past him towards the safety of the outside world before they had a chance to speak again; the thought of another snatched conversation was all that had kept him in that godawful rehearsal for so long, even if he probably would have stuffed it up with talk of G strings again. However, as she was shuffled past him, Lauren did manage to make eye contact with him and give him a shy smile. He was sure he had seen a twinkle in her eye, although he could have dreamt that. He was still gazing after her when Allegra had walked past him.

'Lovely to see some new blood here, I hope you'll both stick around,' she had said, although he was so oblivious to anybody else as his gaze followed Lauren out of the door that he hadn't made eye contact with Allegra and had only managed to murmur, 'Yeah... thanks...' as he continued to watch the door in case Lauren walked back in.

This morning, he didn't even remember the incident, or the throwaway comment from a percussionist who was pushing a timpani past and couldn't believe any man hadn't noticed Allegra di Rossi had graced him with conversation— 'Right, this one's gay then...'

For the first time since the separation, Gabriel realised he might actually be ready to close the book on his previous life with Shelley. The more he thought about it, the more he realised the feeling he had was relief at being shot of his ex-wife and her family. Perhaps it was time to start the process of escape. Once he had realised Shelley was sleeping with somebody else, he knew there would never be any notion of going back, but now he felt a lightness at the prospect of having it all over with and in the past.

Nothing was happening in the shop, so he ran a search on his phone for local solicitors. There was a surprisingly long list, all of whom appeared to deal with virtually every aspect of law, and none of which stood out as the firm he would need to go up against Mr Cole—it was clear in Gabriel's mind that he wouldn't be divorcing Shelley, but her father.

Susan walked through the shop with her head down, bearing a cup of something that claimed to be tea. As she placed it on the counter in front of him, gave him another pathetic smile and went to move off, the words tumbled out of his mouth before he realised his lack of tact.

'Susan, can I ask you a question?'

She looked up at him, startled that somebody would ask her something that required a response, rather than just barking orders at her. She smiled and nodded.

'Who would be the best firm of solicitors around here to talk to about a rather tricky divorce? I think I'm going to need a Rottweiler, not just your average family law firm.'

Susan stared intently at Gabriel and blinked several times. He suddenly realised this was not an appropriate conversation to have begun with this person in his place of work.

A steely look placed itself firmly into Susan's gaze and, for the first time since he had met her, Gabriel saw real strength in this woman.

'Oh, that's easy, my dear. You want to talk to Anthea Sweeney. She works at Tallon Grey over on East Street. Tell her I sent you. Lovely woman, as long as she's on your side. God help the people on the other side, though.'

And with that, Susan was gone, leaving Gabriel wondering just what had happened. This apparently downtrodden woman had in-depth knowledge of local divorce solicitors, and the look of one who had an axe just waiting to be wielded. She suddenly leapt about a million points in Gabriel's estimation and made him wonder just what went on in her head, where her husband and son couldn't hear. A smile slowly spread across his face as he realised Susan may just have more power than he had previously credited her with, and he liked it.

Gabriel ran a quick search and found Tallon Grey. On his lunch break, he rang the office and booked an appointment with Anthea for 5:30 that evening.

After a nondescript afternoon, with not a single customer or any reason to actually be at work, he found himself in the waiting area of what looked like a small firm of lawyers. A tall, slightly overweight man hurried through Reception, yelling into his phone, 'I don't care what they found on his person when they brought him in, he's my client and you talked to him without my permission. I'll be down in fifteen minutes and I want a word with the desk sergeant about abuse of power.'

Another mousey little woman drifted through the office, saying hello to everyone and asking the bored-looking receptionist for files on the Hamilton case.

After about ten minutes, a smiley face appeared next to him and asked, 'Mr Lee? I'm Anthea Sweeney. Would you like to come through to my office?' He dutifully followed.

Once they were seated and he had declined her offer of coffee, she jumped straight in. 'How lovely to meet you. I can't wait to see you in action.'

His startled expression was apparently more obvious than he realised, as she laughed from the other side of the desk.

'Oh, I'm sorry. That wasn't the best opening, was it?! I saw you at the rehearsal last night. I play cello in the Porlington Philharmonia.'

The situation began to make a bit more sense. He looked at the quite tall lady who was sat opposite him and decided he liked her. She had kind eyes, and an easy smile that put him at ease.

'I heard a vicious rumour you were our new assistant conductor. I can't believe Michael finally agreed to let somebody else take the reins on something. Do you have any idea what you'll be doing yet? Please say you're going to be conducting something in the next concert—it's already painfully long and if I have to look at him puffing away for the whole thing, I'll either die of boredom or stab him through the eye with my bow.'

Gabriel decided he liked this woman.

'Actually, I've been told there is nothing for me in the next concert, as you've been rehearsing everything for months and Michael doesn't want to upset the finely-tuned balance,' he ventured, more as a test to see what came next.

'Oh, poppycock,' she replied. 'He just threw two new pieces at us the other night and he couldn't accurately conduct a lightning bolt to his cranium, let alone an orchestra. Is there really no way you could do *something* in the concert..?'

Gabriel found he really was warming to Anthea and her brutal honesty.

'I'm pretty sure Sandra and Michael would have something to say if I tried to push too hard at this stage.'

'But is that a good enough reason not to at least try? Consider it a mercy mission for the orchestra and the audience,' Anthea replied.

'Well, I'm not sure it's really worth me coming back again...'

'Oh, you must! Please don't leave us all alone with no glimmer of hope!' she pleaded, before adjusting her position in her chair, gradually fading the smile down to a more business-like position. 'Anyway, enough of my petty woes, you came in to talk to me about something. What can I help you with?' she asked, her gaze turning to steel and piercing his very core before he could realise.

'Erm, well, I need a solicitor for my divorce. Susan King recommended you and said to mention her.'

'Did she now?' Anthea asked. Without him realising, she had adjusted her position to be leaning forward, with her elbows on the table and her fingers pointed together under her chin. Gabriel now felt he was being eyed up by a lioness surveying the prey she was going to take home to her cubs as dinner.

'Mrs King and I do go way back. Lovely lady. How do you know her?'

'I moved here recently and I'm working for the Kings at Porlington Pianos,' he stammered, now feeling like he wasn't the client, but was under interrogation.

'Ha. Good luck. Don't get too attached to the place,' she said, without further elaboration. 'Susan is a client of mine and she wouldn't admit that to just anyone, so I'm assuming she trusts you. That kind of recommendation goes a long way with me,' she offered, without any further clarification.

'Might I ask what branch of law you specialise in..?' Gabriel ventured, feeling both brave and apprehensive at the same time.

'I mostly work in family law, corporate and financial law, and criminal law,' Anthea replied. 'In most firms, one would specialise in one field, but in a place as small as Porlington, the firms aren't big enough to allow us that luxury. I primarily serve as an officer of the court in those capacities, but I work across most fields, depending on what our clients need. I get things done. Simple as that.' Again, no further explanation was offered.

'Well, Susan recommended you and I need a divorce,' Gabriel said.

'Okay, well you better tell me all about it.'

Gabriel went through the story for nearly an hour and a half. It felt like twenty minutes, but he didn't realise quite how much anger was pent up, and how much detail he went into, probably quite needlessly. Once he had finished and stopped to draw breath, Anthea finished taking notes and looked up at him.

'So you've had a pretty rough ride then,' Anthea said. 'I am sorry to hear how awful life has been for you, and I promise we will do our very best to help you as much as we can. As far as routes forward go, I would say that the divorce itself is an easy enough matter. Adultery is always a no-brainer to a court. Your real problem is going to be trying to secure a reasonable settlement—I suspect the word amicable won't be applied to this after the event, judging from what you've said about your father-in-law. Let's take the easy part first.

'There are five options which constitute grounds for divorce in the UK. Adultery, desertion, unreasonable behaviour, both of you agreeing to divorce after a period of separation of two years, or one of you applying to the court after a separation of five years without the need for the other party's consent. In this instance, I would strongly advise you go for adultery. It hasn't been long enough for the two of you to agree a two-year separation, although I'm sure Shelley and her family would love to have that option open to them.

'Now, it sounds like she has already consulted with solicitors, so I'm quite sure they're preparing a suit for unreasonable behaviour against you...'

'What?! How on earth could they do that?!' Gabriel spluttered. He began to raise the first in a long list of objections before Anthea calmed him down by holding her hands up in surrender.

'I know, I know. I'm not saying that divorce is easy, or fair, Gabriel. However, in my experience, the party who has caused the injury usually feel they have something to prove in addition to getting what they want. If they can tell their family and friends that they divorced you, it exonerates them and makes them feel more socially acceptable. In most instances, that isn't the case. Simply put, why should they get to cause you pain, then paint you as the bad guy?'

Gabriel nodded his agreement. He was beginning to feel like this woman might actually be on his side. Not that anyone wouldn't be on his side, he was the victim, but he somehow felt like he had to prove his victimhood to this complete stranger.

'Now, these things usually stay in hiatus until both parties agree a way forward or one party pulls the trigger on the firing pistol. She is unlikely to do that, as her solicitor will be pointing out that she doesn't have much of a leg to stand on. No matter how badly she might want rid of you, in the first two years, she is the one who has to prove unreasonable behaviour on your part and her solicitor will be advising her that you could counter-sue for divorce on grounds of adultery. Courts don't like adultery. It rather trumps everything else, and it opens the possibility for you to dump your legal costs on her.'

Gabriel couldn't agree more.

'So, I'm going to ask you some more questions, then make a suggestion or two. First, you've explained the situation very clearly, and I really am sorry for what you've been through. What you haven't told me is why you decided to come and see me today. What's changed in your life that you decided to ring my secretary today and ask for an immediate appointment?'

Gabriel found himself on the back foot without a solid answer—he hadn't really had time to think this through. He blurted out the first thing that came into his head, which turned out to be the most honest one.

'Well, I've met this girl...'

'Okay soldier, let me stop you right there. Bear in mind that I have to be honest about anything that you tell me and I can't lie, so think very carefully about the answer you give next. Have you had sex with this woman? And I'm assuming you mean a woman, not a girl?'

'Of course I mean a woman!' Gabriel exclaimed, a little too loudly. He took a second to catch his breath.

61

'And no, nothing has happened. I meant exactly what I said—I've met a woman. Nothing more. No date, no kissing, no physical contact. I'm pretty sure she thinks I'm a complete imbecile. It just got me thinking that it would be nice to have some options without feeling like I'm cheating on my wife. I mean ex-wife.'

'Okay, good,' Anthea replied. 'That's a relief. At the moment, you are technically still married and that would be classed as adultery, regardless of the fact Shelley committed that act first.'

Gabriel found Anthea's use of Shelley's name somewhat grating. He began to realise he preferred to think of her as his ex-wife, rather than Shelley. This all seemed somehow easier if she was a concept rather than a person whom he had once loved. The realisation that he just used the words 'once loved' in his head rather than 'loved' made him pause for a moment. Perhaps this wasn't going to be so ghastly after all.

'You okay there, Skippy?' Anthea asked.

He laughed. 'Yeah, I'm fine. It's just a lot to process.'

'I know this is difficult. And, frankly, I couldn't care less what you do, within legal boundaries. From what you've said, you deserve some happiness. But it is my job to prepare you for every eventuality, and warn you about possible pitfalls that might jeopardise your position further down the road.'

'Thanks, I appreciate that,' he replied.

'I would strongly suggest that we pre-empt anything they're planning. If you've held out this long, they won't be expecting you to take the initiative. I suspect they have a suit drawn up whereby she suggests she will begin proceedings based on your unreasonable behaviour, as she really doesn't have any other grounds at this point, and she certainly won't want a suit launched against her. Do you think her father would go so far as to have you watched or followed?'

That concept hadn't even occurred to Gabriel, and it took him aback. Whilst it wouldn't occur to Shelley, her father was a different matter and it was entirely possible that Mr Cole would do something underhand like that behind Shelley's back.

'I don't know,' he said, honestly.

'Okay, well, let's not do anything silly just yet, eh? Live the single life, don't be seen doing anything that could be used against you. I would suggest that we get a suit filed suing her for divorce on grounds of adultery as quickly as possible. With the recent changes in the law, you can also name the person with whom she committed that act, which I would suggest you do. Once the court has that on record, you are still technically married, but if you decide to begin a new relationship after the court has been notified of her adultery, they won't hold a new relationship against you quite as badly.'

Gabriel liked the sound of this. Moral high ground suddenly became quite appealing. And he began to feel the clutches of all the Cole family slowly loosening their perceived grip on him.

'The other misconception that people come in here with is that the injured party will somehow do better in a divorce case. I'm going to be honest, the UK has a no-fault principle underlying divorce cases. Regardless of the reasons *why* a divorce is being granted, the court will generally prefer to split assets and liabilities in a 50/50 way, unless there is a good reason not to. So if you have any notions that you might take 80% of the Cole family fortune...'

'No, that's not it at all. I just want to be shot of them. I just want my freedom back,' Gabriel said.

'Okay, well, let's not be too hasty here. I've seen people sign away far too much in the past because they want to escape. I'm going to advise you not to do that. If the court sees that you are suing her for divorce on grounds of adultery, but you are being fair with marital assets and a potential settlement, things are far more likely to go through quickly and according to that basis. Remember, if she wants more, she has to prove she is entitled to it, by which I mean a pre-nuptial agreement. How much you both contributed to the marriage and its assets isn't really a concern here. The court will want a quick and easy settlement, dividing everything as evenly as possible. The lack of children helps a great deal here.'

Gabriel hadn't even considered that aspect, but he supposed she was right.

'Here's what I suggest. Let me draw up some initial papers for you to look at, applying for a divorce. We'll include a financial settlement offer, which gives you the high ground from the start. They'd need some very good reasons to successfully challenge all this. Just a couple of last questions for you.'

'Okay…'

'Did you ever sacrifice a goat in the back garden against her will, whilst making her watch?'

'What?! Why would I do such a thing?' Gabriel asked, suddenly as confused as he'd ever been in his life.

'Just answer the question, Mr Lee.'

'No, of course I didn't!'

'Good. Did you ever hit her, physically restrain her, shove her, force her to have sex against her will, or perform any act of aggression, violence or sexual misconduct against her or anybody else?'

'No!' Gabriel could feel his heart rate rising at being interrogated in this way.

'Are you sure, Mr Lee? Think very carefully, as I can only help you if you've been honest with me.'

'Absolutely not! I've never harmed anyone or forced someone to do anything they didn't want to!'

'Have you ever lied to a court, an officer of the court, a police officer, or committed any act of fraud or deception?'

'Why are you asking me these horrible things? Of course I haven't!' He was beginning to look at the door and calculating a method of escape from the building.

'Good. Now that I've panicked you, is there anything else you wish to tell me that might come back to bite us in the bum in the future with this case? I don't like being bitten in the bum, no matter how hard Mr Sweeney tries every Friday evening.' Gabriel saw the twinkle had returned to Anthea's eye. He felt a sense of relief again.

'No. Obviously, I can't sum up an entire relationship in just an hour or two, but I can promise you I've never done any of those things, or anything else that might be used against me in that way. I loved her and always tried to do my best for our relationship.'

'Good,' Anthea said, fixing him with a steely gaze. 'Then if you're happy to instruct me, I will do my very best to get you the best possible deal I can. And I do love a good bitch fight.'

Gabriel laughed. 'I'm glad to hear it. My ex-wife can be quite a bitch.'

'Oh, when you come to next week's rehearsal, look for the old man on the double bass on your far right. That's

Mr Sweeney. Ask him how much of a bitch I can be,' Anthea replied with an ever-growing twinkle.

'I might just do that. I sympathise with him,' Gabriel ventured, feeling braver than he did before.

'Good. And please convince that bloody useless Fordington man to step off his podium and stop flapping at us every week. It would be great to have some new vitality in the orchestra. I know he won't give you anything in this concert, but please do push to get something to do in the next one, just to give us all a reason to go on living.'

'I will do my best, Mrs Sweeney. But I can't promise I'll persuade Michael and Sandra to agree.'

'Don't worry about them, my dear. Just take things slowly and do what you can. Mr Sweeney and I have some sway around the place, so we'll try to smooth things over for you to do a bit more. Now, I'm afraid I have about a hundred forms for you to fill in, which will probably constitute one of the most boring 30 minutes of your life.'

SEVEN

CONCERT DAY HAD ARRIVED. GABRIEL HAD spent the last three weeks living a life of relative drudgery, but it was at least more interesting than his marriage had been.

Each weekday, he trudged into Porlington Pianos and spent the day utterly bored, just watching Susan moping about the place, counting down the minutes until she could make everyone coffee again whilst Grant floated through the shop with his nails looking more manicured each day, emitting his silly, high-pitched giggle with his piggy eyes sneering at Gabriel through very grubby glasses.

Neil was hardly ever to be seen and Gabriel had taken up a new game in his mind—wondering where Neil was and what he was up to. Yesterday, Gabriel had imagined him hidden away in a secret office breaking codes for GCHQ. The day before, he had decided Neil must be in a secret underground vault, counting his secret stash of gold doubloons that he had uncovered in a former life as a pirate. He suspected the truth was far less interesting.

Unfortunately, life in Porlington was (so far) as dull as Shelley had predicted several years before. He met virtually nobody in the shop as there were hardly any customers, and one couldn't really form much of a bond with people who only came in once in a blue moon. Whilst he had attended every orchestra rehearsal for the last three weeks, he still hadn't really had a meaningful conversation with many people. He suspected they were all looking at him wondering who this man was who turned up every week and just sat at the back, as he still hadn't been introduced to them. The tea ladies eyed him with suspicion. Anthea hadn't been at the two rehearsals since their meeting in her office, due to a heavy cold.

And then there was Lauren. Gabriel so wanted to talk to her, but she usually arrived slightly late and had to rush in to take her place in the orchestra as things were just beginning. During the break, she was surrounded by other violinists, clearly protective of their new member (the only one who didn't remember flared trousers the first time around). Jane Lazenby was very good at looking after Lauren and shuffling her away from any string player who looked like they might scare her away with banality. At the end of rehearsals, Lauren usually got ushered out by Jane before any of the orchestra could scare their newest (and youngest, and probably most talented) violin player away.

They had managed one brief conversation during a break when everyone else had foolishly turned away from Lauren momentarily. Gabriel had found out that she was a teacher, currently educating Year 3 children in Porlington Primary. It occurred to him that this town loved its alliteration.

And then Henry James had swooped in to whisk Lauren away to the other side of the room, asking her if she had joined a local gym yet and if she'd like to go to his with him. Gabriel had felt a brief sense of both panic and jealousy. Then he remembered what Anthea had said about not getting involved with anyone until the divorce proceedings were properly underway. He had watched from afar as Lauren laughed at something Henry had said, and Gabriel realised that he never had any chance with someone like her when there were people like Henry in the world.

'I really wouldn't worry about it. Most girls realise pretty quickly what an idiot he is. She looks like she's just humouring him,' said a voice from over Gabriel's shoulder.

He turned and saw Allegra smiling at him. Suddenly he found himself unable to speak as he saw her beauty for the first time.

'Henry knows he has a certain level of beauty,' she continued, pretending to ignore his unexpected breathlessness. She was probably used to this reaction. 'However, he tries too hard and he doesn't have the social skills to back up the façade.'

Gabriel somehow found his voice. 'To be fair, it's quite a façade,' he said, looking enviously at the trumpeter's perfectly coiffed hair and scarily white teeth, atop a frame that belonged more in Hollywood than Porlington.

'Some girls might think so. But us women don't fall for looks alone so easily. Most of us fell afoul of boys like him when we were in our early twenties and have long since realised we need a bit more substance. Or at least an IQ higher than a somewhat lecherous lizard.'

Gabriel laughed, perhaps a little too loudly. 'Well, I'm not sure I've got much more to offer, and I don't even have that façade working in my favour,' he admitted somewhat sheepishly.

'Don't be too hard on yourself. I've seen the way she looks at you. She certainly doesn't humour you the way she's currently doing to him. Turn around and look at them.' Gabriel did so, while Allegra continued to talk behind him. 'See the way she looks at him and smiles, then after about twenty seconds, gets bored and her gaze starts to drift.'

Gabriel watched, but wasn't sure he saw anything other than her glancing away, then looking back at Henry. He was sure he saw her bite her bottom lip in a beautifully coquettish way as she gazed up at Henry.

'Just wait a moment,' Allegra whispered in Gabriel's ear. He wasn't entirely sure what he was waiting for. 'Just a moment more…'

Then it happened. Henry had been talking for some time, although they were too far away for Gabriel to hear what he was talking about. Lauren's gaze did falter from the Narcissus in front of her, and drifted across the room. It found Gabriel and she appeared to forget Henry was even talking to her. Her eyes warmed and the faintest smile appeared in the corner of her mouth.

Henry must have asked her a question just at that moment as her attention shifted quickly back to him and she started talking, before he interrupted her and his monologue began again.

'See, I told you. She looks at you a lot. You really should talk to her, or at least arrange to meet her away from here.'

Gabriel turned back to Allegra and asked, 'How on earth do you do that? Read people so well.'

'One learns to in my line of work. I'm a paediatric surgeon, so I have to make quick assessments of both the tiny humans with whom I work, and their parents, who can very often mask the underlying problem, or at least project their own ridiculous internet research onto my patient. And after all the Henrys and Henriettas I've known in my life, one learns to read people pretty quickly.'

Gabriel wondered how he had never noticed this woman before. 'Gabriel Lee,' he said, holding out his hand.

She took it and smiled at him. 'Allegra di Rossi. Principal oboe and professional people-watcher.'

They both smiled. He hadn't noticed the jealous glares heading his way from every man in the room. Nor had he noticed that the members of the orchestra had, for the first time, seen him as more than just a faceless person who sat at the back of rehearsals. After all, if Allegra was talking and laughing with him, he must be someone important. Nor, while he was distracted by Allegra, did he notice that Lauren had seen the two of them smiling at each other and the brief look of something approaching jealousy pass across her face.

That was all a couple of weeks ago and he now found himself stood in St Saviour's-on-the-Wall Church on the outskirts of Porlington. The Methodist church the orchestra rehearsed in was far too small to hold both an orchestra and an audience, so on concert days, they all decamped to St Saviour's. It was a big place, with hideous lighting that belonged more in a multi-storey car park than a place of worship. It was cold, as most Anglican churches are, with two church wardens who both looked like they were sucking a lemon through an old sock and clearly resented having to give up their precious Saturday afternoon to host an orchestra.

Michael wasn't helping. He was barking at them that there weren't enough matching chairs for the orchestra. The church wardens weren't giving an inch and were heard to tell him that's all the chairs they had, and this hadn't changed in all the years they had been playing there.

Sandra swept in and tried to steer Michael's oversized frame away from an argument, with a question about where the percussion should set up. A percussionist was heard to say, 'The Cock and Bottle round the corner, perhaps..?' This was ignored by both Michael and Sandra. Gabriel stared at the two of them and wondered how on earth these two had come to be together, and how they didn't kill each other.

Sandra noticed Betty Brannon trying to set chairs out. 'NO, Betty! Why would you put the horns there? You know the timpani set up on that dais and the horns don't like to be in front of them.'

Betty looked up and smiled her usual, inane smile, before going back to setting the chairs out exactly as she had before Sandra had yelled at her.

Gabriel saw Anthea walking in with her cello, looking like she was on the mend from her cold. She was followed by a tall man, walking purposefully forwards clutching a double bass. Anthea saw Gabriel and diverted in his direction.

'Hello Gabriel, how are you?'

'Good, thanks, Mrs Sweeney. Are you over your cold?'

'Please, call me Anthea. Can't stand formality. Unless I don't like someone. But you're okay,' she quickly added as she saw the look of panic cross his face.

'This is Mr Sweeney, my husband,' she said, gesturing to the man hugging the double bass behind her. He appeared older, but with a surprising youthfulness and exactly the same twinkle in his eye that Anthea had.

'Please, call me Rupert,' he corrected, holding out his hand whilst managing to clutch the double bass between his elbows.

'Hi, I'm Gabriel. It's a pleasure.'

'So Anthea tells me you've come to usher in the new era with the orchestra. New start. Clean slate. Taking Michael out at dawn and shooting him.'

'Ha, not quite,' Gabriel laughed. 'Although I hear similar sentiments from several orchestra members,' he continued in a surprisingly uncircumspect manner.

Anthea laughed. 'Please do have him taken out and shot at dawn. Or dusk. Anytime would do, really.'

A percussionist appeared out of nowhere, pushing a timpani. 'Happy to help…'

'Has he told you what you'll be doing in the next concert yet?' Anthea enquired.

'No, he hasn't really spoken to me. I'm hoping I might get a bit of warning before Thursday's rehearsal as I'd like to spend some time on the score.'

'Oh don't bother with that, lad,' Rupert chimed in. 'He hasn't looked at a score before the first rehearsal in all the years I've known him. And it shows. Ooh, there's Dicky.' And with that, Rupert was gone, lugging his double bass up towards the stage at a surprisingly brisk speed.

'I'm sure things will settle down once today is over,' Anthea said. 'He's always a nightmare coming up to concerts.'

'I hope you're right. It would be nice to feel like I had some reason for turning up. I've got no idea if I've even got a seat for tonight. Do you think I should buy a ticket?'

'You will do no such thing! Don't worry, there'll be plenty of seats. Just look like you belong and nobody will question you. Avoid the old woman that looks like the

Bride of Chucky. That's Frenella. Vile little woman, with an annoyingly high-pitched laugh. She likes to think of herself as the guardian of the gates at concerts and she's in charge of tickets. She's married to one of the brass players. She'll appear at 6:45 and plonk herself behind her table in front of the main entrance, staring at everyone who walks through the door and daring them to not approach her to show a ticket or buy one from her. Just use a different entrance and don't make eye contact with her if she notices you.'

'Thanks, I'll bear that in mind. Anything else I should know?'

'Lots of things, my dear, but I don't have time to teach you all of them before this painful rehearsal starts. By the way, I've got your paperwork drawn up. Sorry I haven't been around the last couple of weeks. Damn cold. Anyway, if you want to pop in this week and sign it, we can get things rolling with the divorce. Catch the bitch ex-wife on the back foot, eh?'

'That sounds great. Should I make an appointment with your secretary?'

'No, don't bother. Just pop in when you finish at the King's little music shop one afternoon. I usually just catch up on paperwork after 4pm, so I should be around. I've got one or two nice little barbs in the initial motion that should unsettle them, but I'm saving the real gold just in case we need it in court. I'm hoping it won't come to it though. I suspect the shock of being served with papers first (and with no warning) where you name her as an adulteress will throw them into such a state of shock they won't know what to do. You're actually giving her exactly what she wants, but certainly not in the way she wanted it, which will put her in a quandary. People tend to panic

74

at that stage and show their hand. If not all, then at least a few cards. And we'll be waiting for them.'

Gabriel realised he was feeling just a little excited at this prospect, and was relishing the idea of getting the upper hand for possibly the first time in all the years he had known Shelley and her monstrous father.

'You're on. I'll be in on Monday!'

'That's the spirit, soldier. It's not going to be an easy ride, but drawing first blood always feels good and shows the other side you're not going to be walked over. Now, I have to get onto the stage in order to pretend I know what I'm doing, or I give a flying furbee about this bloody awful concert. Are you coming to the Cock and Bottle for something to eat between rehearsal and concert?'

'Erm, I hadn't really given it much thought. Figured I'd work the rest of the day out while I'm sat here during the rehearsal with nothing to do.'

'Well, that's settled then. You can come round the corner with Mr Sweeney and myself. They do a particularly excellent pie and mash, although the rest of the selection is also good.'

'Okay, you've won me over,' Gabriel relented. And with that, Anthea disappeared up onto the stage.

2pm hit and Michael strode onto his little podium (at three inches high, it didn't seem like much of a podium…) and started his usual pre-flapping ritual. The orchestra just carried on talking. Sandra glared in vain at all those around her, but they had clearly sat through this too many times before.

Eventually, Sandra tapped her bow on her stand just loudly enough to gain most people's attention. She kept tapping it in the hope the percussion section would stop talking amongst themselves. After nearly a minute, she gave up. Shortly after that, they stopped talking, just to make the point.

Michael surveyed the orchestra. 'Marriage of Figaro Overture,' he exclaimed. There was some rustling as people opened the correct piece of music, and he started flapping.

The next two hours were taken up with playing through the various pieces in the first half. Figaro Overture. Tchaikovsky Violin Concerto, with some local violinist who was ex-military taking the solo. He wasn't dreadful, but only about two notches up from that. Michael kept stopping for no apparent reason, so what should have been 43 minutes' worth of music somehow got spread across nearly two hours. He would just stop, complain at the strings (but not about anything specific), lose his place, get corrected by someone in the orchestra, lose his temper, and make them start from about four pages prior to the point he said wasn't right.

There was a brief break where there was the promise of cake in the Lady Chapel, until they all flooded in there to realise the church wardens had thrown the cake away as the Lady Chapel apparently wasn't a cafeteria and they felt great disrespect had been shown by bringing food and drink (orange squash) into it. A somewhat disgruntled orchestra filtered out into the rest of the church to sit and be bored for 15 minutes, while Sandra attempted to stop Michael blasting the church wardens, who couldn't actually be found.

After a short while, everyone drifted back into position to endure Ravel's *Bolero*, the Dvorak *9th Symphony* and the Radetsky *March*, with multiple stops which appeared to achieve nothing other than wearing down the players' will to live.

Gabriel sat in the church and played Angry Birds on his phone, whilst questioning the life choices that had landed him here this afternoon and trying not to obviously stare at Lauren.

Part way through the Dvorak, he noticed Anthea looking utterly bored and rolling her eyes every 17 bars or so. Her desk partner looked like she had slipped into a comatose state with her eyes utterly dead but her fingers still somehow playing her cello.

A couple of desks behind them, he saw Rupert and a young lad (presumably the aforementioned Dicky) on their double basses. Gabriel was in the process of wondering what a single bass was when he realised Rupert wasn't actually watching his music; he was just staring at the lad next to him for an inordinately long amount of time. Picture a double bass player with their head hard to the left, just staring. Dicky seemed to be a very nice, wholesome young lad of about 20. He was hurling himself into the music and playing the bass very enthusiastically. And Rupert was just staring at him, his hands moving on automatic, with his mouth slightly open. Gabriel expected a faint dribble to ooze from the corner of Rupert's mouth at any moment. Neither of them were watching Michael.

Things eventually ground to a halt. Even the percussion section had lost enough of their collective will to live and no witty barbs were forthcoming. Every member of the orchestra looked like they desperately needed a very strong drink or three as they slowly filtered away from their seats. They appeared to have visibly aged over the course of the nearly four-hour rehearsal.

Anthea and Rupert headed over in Gabriel's direction. They placed their instruments on the pews near him and rolled their eyes.

'I don't have the words,' Rupert said, whilst glancing around to see where Dicky was.

'Kill me now,' Anthea countered. 'Did you enjoy that? Learn much from the great Maestro?' she enquired of Gabriel.

'It was certainly different to anything I've experienced before,' he replied. 'Is it always like this?'

'Oh yes,' they both replied in unison.

'Does he realise this concert is going to be about three weeks long?'

'Not at all,' Anthea said in a resigned manner. 'We've all tried to talk to him about how stupidly long these concerts are, but he won't listen. He doesn't even notice the audience disappearing as the concerts go on. And you haven't heard him waffle on between numbers yet. That's quite the experience.'

With that, the side door they had all used as the entrance burst open and a wizened old woman burst into the church. She was probably best described as handsome. Although the look in her eye would be more accurately determined as fearsome. She marched up to Michael and barked, 'Have you had your tablets today? You know what happens when you don't have your tablets. How is your blood pressure feeling? Any dizziness or light-headed spells?'

The remaining members of the orchestra in the performance area of the church shrank back into the walls like cockroaches disappearing when you turn the lights on. Other than Michael, the only person who remained steadfastly rooted to their spot was Sandra, although she looked distinctly uncomfortable.

'Of course I've had my bloody pills, woman,' Michael replied in a gruff voice.

'You say that every time, but on most occasions, you don't. Do you want your children to have to bury their father in the next month?' came back the reply from the severe-looking woman.

'Who on earth is that?' Gabriel enquired of the Sweeneys.

'And WHY didn't you call me during the break to let me know how things were going?' demanded the woman, who was now going a slightly strange shade of crimson.

'For God's sake, I'm busy, I've had a rehearsal to run!' Michael hurled back at her.

Sandra attempted to interrupt the conversation. 'He has been very busy, Elizabeth. The demands of this programme are…' Her voice tailed off as the woman appeared to freeze, other than her head slowly turning towards Sandra with the most disdainful and piercing glare Gabriel had ever seen.

'I. Beg. Your. Pardon?' the woman slowly spat at Sandra in the most controlled *sotto voce* Gabriel had ever heard. Gritted teeth and everything.

He missed the reply and the rest of the conversation as it dropped to a whisper.

Rupert finally broke the silence amongst their small group and answered Gabriel's question. 'Oh, that's Elizabeth. She's Michael's wife.'

EIGHT

GABRIEL, ANTHEA AND RUPERT HAD DECAMPED to the Cock and Bottle round the corner from St Saviour's, along with most of the orchestra. The brass section were at the bar, ordering multiple pints per person and several chasers. The old brass player adage of 'never do a gig sober' appeared to be alive and well.

Gabriel ordered a burger with all the trimmings and a coke, whilst Anthea and Rupert ordered superfood salads. With two pints of London Pride each. Dicky had joined them, wanting only a tiramisu and a tonic water.

'Hello, I'm Richard. Lovely to meet you. I hear you're going to be taking over and rescuing us all,' he said.

'Not quite. I don't think I'm ever going to be allowed to... I'm sorry, what the hell just happened?!' Gabriel shifted his gaze to Anthea and Rupert as the duty adults at the table.

'Hasn't anybody given you the story?!' Rupert asked, with genuine shock on his face. 'Surely somebody has filled you in?'

Gabriel just stared, open-mouthed at them all. 'I thought Michael and Sandra were married?' he spluttered.

'Okay, my dear. You clearly haven't been briefed,' Anthea interjected before Gabriel exploded out of sheer curiosity. 'Michael is married to Elizabeth. They have three children, two boys and a girl. All now married, with children of their own. Their eldest grandchild is in her twenties.'

Gabriel interrupted, still confused. 'But Michael and Sandra… at rehearsals…'

Rupert picked up the tale. 'Yes, they've been together for donkey's years. It's an honest mistake.'

'But… but… what the…'

Anthea rescued him. 'Okay, I'll make this simple for you. Michael and Elizabeth are married. But Sandra is his mistress. It's been going on since before any of us were involved with the orchestra.'

'But Sandra has his surname?! What the…'

'No she doesn't,' Rupert said gently. 'How exactly did she sign her email to you?'

'Sandra Fordington!' Gabriel said, his voice rising to near screaming pitch.

'Would you like to check that?' Anthea asked in her most deferential tone.

'For God's sake, I'm sure that's what it said,' Gabriel insisted. He scrolled back through his emails on his phone. He eventually found it and realised it was signed 'Sandra F'. 'Well what the hell..?'

Rupert placed his hand on Gabriel's in a friendly, but ever-so-slightly unnerving manner. Dicky / Richard just sipped his tonic water.

'Sandra's surname is Finley. She signs herself as Sandra F so it has the appearance of having his surname,' Rupert said.

'So… What…?! I don't understand! Gabriel spluttered.

Anthea decided to put Gabriel out of his misery.

'Right. Michael and Elizabeth have been somewhat happily married for many years. They have children. At some point, quite a long time ago, Michael and Sandra started having an affair. Nobody is quite sure how it happened, or when. It predates pretty much all of us, and we all made the same mistake for a long time in the beginning. Sandra likes to think she's his wife, and he usually stays with her after each Thursday rehearsal before going back to Elizabeth the next day. Are you with me so far?'

'Does Elizabeth know?!' Gabriel asked.

'My dear boy, of course she knows,' Rupert replied, picking up the story. 'It's been going on for so long that's beyond question. There are even rumours that once upon a time she joined in, although these have never been substantiated. Where would she think he is every Thursday evening?'

Richard looked up from his ever-dwindling tiramisu. 'All a bit strange, if you ask me.'

Rupert laughed just a little too loudly. Anthea smiled and looked back to Gabriel.

'Don't try to understand it, Twinkle. None of us do.' Gabriel believed her.

'So does Elizabeth turn up to every concert and just put up with seeing the two of them together?' he asked.

'Usually,' Rupert said. 'You'll quite often see Elizabeth and Sandra talking in the corner. Probably commiserating over what an absolute sod he is. I think that, deep down, they're quite good friends in a very strange, somewhat disturbing sort of way.'

Gabriel's mind was racing. He thought his life was complicated, but this all seemed beyond anything he could imagine. And everyone seemed okay with it.

'Dicky, how's the pudding?' Rupert asked, smiling a touch too hard.

'S'not bad. Hopefully enough sugar to get me through this disaster of a concert tonight before I pop off to see one of my girls after.'

Gabriel felt sure he saw Rupert's face drop a bit. Anthea noticed it too, but just smirked and turned away so nobody else noticed.

'Haven't you got some of your kids down this weekend, Rupert?' Richard asked.

'Good God, no!' came back the reply. 'Haven't got any of the ghastly creatures until next weekend. I'm free to do what I like this week...'

Gabriel decided to be brave and ask a personal question of Anthea, 'How many children do you have?'

'None,' she quickly answered. 'Mr Sweeney, on the other hand, has seven. None by me. Really not a children kind of person.'

'Seven?!' Gabriel realised the question came out just a little too loud.

'Yes, seven. By four different mothers. He was quite the rogue in his youth.'

'I like to think of it as spreading the love,' Rupert countered.

'More like being a slut. Nothing new there then,' Richard muttered.

Anthea laughed and turned back to Gabriel. 'So, any more questions about our glorious leader?'

'More, I suspect, than could be answered before you lot need to get back to do something useful.'

They all realised it was gone 7pm and they should probably go to change and get ready for the concert. Richard stood and headed for the bathroom. 'I'll just... erm... use the facilities,' said Rupert, hurriedly, before following Richard into said facilities.

Gabriel looked at Anthea, somewhat quizzically.

'Oh, those boys!' she exclaimed. 'Right, I need to slip into my concert dress. Don't get your hopes up, it's the same one I use every time, and nothing is on display. Like the rest of the orchestra. You'll be glad about that when you see us all in action later.'

Gabriel thought that he wouldn't mind seeing a bit more of Lauren. Or possibly Allegra, despite being slightly terrified of her beauty.

Once the others had returned from the toilets a minute or two later, they all headed back round the corner to the church. Anthea, Rupert and Richard all disappeared to get changed, and Gabriel found himself at a loose end. He was very glad to have walked in with them, as he could see Frenella sat at the front desk, her somewhat undersized but ludicrously prominent teeth looking for someone to devour with their disturbingly pronounced overbite. He slipped by her before she could challenge him and steal his soul. He went to look for somewhere to sit. There were many options, as only about five people had turned up to be in the audience so far. He went to sit behind a couple of people talking about half-way up the aisle.

He was already seated before he realised one of those people was Sandra, talking to two other people in the same row.

'Well, of course, it's always lovely to play Italian music. Such a wonderful sound. I lived in Italy for a year back in my youth,' he overhead her saying.

He wondered how she would have fitted in wherever she was in Italy. She wasn't exactly a classic beauty. And Italians weren't known for their respect for the English, basically because the Italians just did everything better. Art, food, music, beauty, style, life in general. He simply couldn't imagine Sandra existing in such a climate.

After listening to the conversation witter on for a while, he realised the church was beginning to fill up a bit. He guessed at around 75 people. Unfortunately, the church could hold around 400, so it felt like an empty barn by the time Sandra had taken her position as leader and Michael eventually took to the podium. For the first overture, he made no introduction, just stood there and breathed through his nose in the most ridiculously pretentious manner, before shaking himself and flapping his arms. Eventually he looked at the orchestra and raised his hands to begin the concert.

And thus began one of the most interminably boring nights of Gabriel's life. At some point during the Dvorak 9th Symphony, he seriously considered using his dreadful A5 folded programme (with no useful information at all) to inflict death by a thousand cuts on himself. Although the paper it was printed on more closely resembled toilet roll, so unlikely to provide the desired effect. He counted down the minutes until the end. When he reached the end of the countdown and realised he hadn't begun at a high enough figure, he started again. And when he reached the end of that, he tried again.

He found himself people-watching. Betty just sat there and smiled, barely touching her violin. Henry sat there, beautifully poised and waiting for his opportunity, just itching to take his top off and show his stunning body to the adoring audience. Allegra contributed occasionally, but still all without breaking a sweat. Jane was sat next to Lauren and looked very intent playing her violin. Lauren just looked like a vision and Gabriel wished he could be playing along with them, or at least conducting. His thoughts drifted to the next concert—would he be allowed to conduct something? What would it be? When was it?

Eventually, after several hours of musical torture, the ordeal was at an end. Michael took multiple bows, always walking off in between and then walking back on again, regardless of whether the orchestra or audience wanted him to or not.

He realised he was sat across the aisle from Elizabeth (how could he have missed that until this point?). She sat there in abject silence and he noticed that not only was nobody from the orchestra brave enough to approach her and talk to her, pretty much everybody looked down at the floor as they filed past her. She sat on the end of the aisle looking as though she was cast in stone, with the occasional rising and falling of the fur coat around her shoulders being the only visible signs of life.

After a minute or so, Sandra walked up to her and started telling her how well she thought it went and what a delight Michael's conducting had been. Elizabeth's expression barely changed as she surveyed Sandra— Gabriel wondered what was really going on behind her eyes. Hatred? Acceptance? Relief at getting rid of him for one whole day every week? Or was she just biding her time until she could plunge a dagger into Sandra and end a lifetime of being a cuckquean under its original definition? Or, perhaps more disturbingly, it's more modern usage?

Gabriel's opining came to an abrupt halt as a rather unfortunate event occurred. The orchestra were filing down the central passageway of the church in an effort to escape, but just as Jane was walking Lauren past them, Jane's voice carried just a little too loudly.

'Thank the Lord that's over. How on earth we got through that stupidly long programme and all stayed together despite that useless old oaf flapping his arms at us I will never know. It wouldn't be so bad if any of his gestures actually *meant* something in terms of conducting...' She stopped herself as she realised who she was walking past.

Elizabeth barely showed a reaction and Gabriel wondered if she had even heard. Sandra, on the other hand, rounded on Jane and Lauren, suddenly bright red as she hissed at them, 'Who do you think you are? You should be grateful to even have the privilege of watching him conduct, let alone being able to learn from him!' It occurred to Gabriel that she might not have realised which one of them said it. 'Have you no gratitude that he gives up his time every week for the likes of you, to try and help you improve your pathetic musical abilities? What do you think it's like for him having to work with people with no talent?'

Gabriel noticed Anthea, Rupert and Richard behind Jane and Lauren, frozen in time, waiting to see how this resolved. Anthea looked genuinely concerned, her face appearing to show an internal struggle as to whether to wade in to try and rescue the situation or not. Rupert smirked at Richard like a schoolboy and Richard just rolled his eyes, clearly waiting to get past the women so he could get to whichever young beauty he was wooing that night.

'And why do you think it's acceptable to criticise other people when the two of you played so terribly tonight? I could hear you behind me, sniggering at times; I could hear you were ignoring my bowings in the score throughout the Dvorak, thinking you know better; I could hear all the bad intonation on the top notes throughout. My God, the two of you couldn't even play in tune with each other, let alone the rest of the section. I'll be splitting you up this Thursday and one of you will be going into the 2nds!'

Jane had gone a bright shade of vermillion and was taking a sharp intake of breath, ready to hit back when Lauren put her hand to her mouth, tears forming in the corners of her eyes, before running down the church and out the doors at the back. Gabriel desperately wanted to run after her, but he was hemmed in by Sandra and Jane on his left, blocking his exit, and a row of geriatrics in the pew on his right, appearing to all still be asleep. Or dead.

Somehow, Elizabeth had managed to find enough room and she just slipped out of her seat, slowly gliding down the aisle without saying a word.

Jane was about to blast Sandra about the same time as Anthea was about to interrupt to calm the situation down (if that were possible), when a percussionist barged through the lot of them pushing a timpani on a small trolley, scattering them like pins in a bowling alley.

'Mind yer backs, coming through, nothing to see here. Let a poor percussionist through after his soul was broken by bloody Bolero tonight...'

This appeared to break the tension. Anthea swept forwards and grabbed Jane by the arm.

'Jane! It's been so long since we caught up. How are the kids?' she was heard to say as she dragged her towards the back of the church, leaving Sandra with nobody to round on. Rupert and Richard were quite literally running the other way.

Gabriel realised Sandra had locked her targets onto him. 'Ah, Mr Flee,' she began, her teeth still gritted. He thought it best not to choose this moment to correct her again on his name. 'I trust you will be with us this Thursday? We will begin rehearsing our Christmas programme and you will be delighted to know that Michael has agreed to let you conduct one of the pieces.' He found he wasn't delighted at all. The thickness of this woman's hide would put a rhinoceros to shame. She had switched from attempting to ingratiate herself with Elizabeth to spitting venom at Jane and Lauren to informing him about Michael's wishes (which he was no longer convinced she had a right to represent) within a few seconds. Her eyes appeared quite dead and Gabriel realised he'd never seen any sort of life or kindness in them. He found himself wondering what had happened to her that had made her this way when he realised he should probably respond, as all grateful serfs should when their feudal lord has granted them some favour.

'That's very kind of him. Which piece will it be?' he asked.

Sandra's exterior appeared to drop a considerable number of degrees, landing somewhere between quite frosty and nuclear winter.

'I hardly think that's important, Mr Flee. I'm surprised you're not more grateful.'

'I'm sorry, I didn't mean to be rude, I just meant it would be nice to be able to prepare the piece before Thursday.'

'You will be informed as to what you are doing and given the score on Thursday. At which point, you will be expected to conduct the first part of the rehearsal.' Sandra went to move away to find another victim.

'Sorry, erm, you mean I won't have any time for score preparation? Just half an hour at the start while Michael does something else would be really helpful.'

'I thought you were trained? Michael doesn't need any time to prepare scores! Can't you read music?'

Gabriel thought to himself that it was because he *was* trained that he would require the time to fully prepare the piece of music, but he suspected that wouldn't go very far with Sandra at the moment. Perhaps discretion might be the better route.

'Of course, whatever you think best.' He wanted to scream at her, 'What kind of idiots are you that think the pathetic rehearsal technique and lack of preparation makes for a good concert?!' but he thought better of it. His thoughts were too preoccupied with where Lauren was and what sort of state she would be in, and he just wanted to escape Sandra in order to find her.

'That's settled then. We will see you on Thursday.' And with that, Sandra was gone, sailing off into the distance, like the Dover to Calais ferry. She gravitated immediately towards Michael, fawning over him as though he were Bernstein reincarnated. Despite him having strangely large eyebrows, the similarities ended there.

Gabriel ran out of the church and looked around to see where Lauren had gone. He searched all around the churchyard, but there was no sign of her. After 20 minutes of looking, he was on the verge of giving up when Anthea appeared behind him.

'We're going for a post-apocalypse drink at the Cock and Bottle. Do come and join us,' she said.

'To be honest, Anthea, I'm done for the night. I think I'm just going to go home and have one of the beers in my fridge.' He thought it best not to tell his divorce solicitor that beer was the only thing he had in his fridge, other than a half-empty squeezy bottle of mayonnaise and a couple of sachets of UHT milk he'd swiped the last time he went to Burger King.

'Okay sweetie. If you change your mind, you know where we are. And I hope we'll be seeing you on Thursday. In the meantime, pop in on Monday and let's get those divorce papers signed so we can get things rolling.'

He assured her that he would call by the office on Monday, then he headed out of the churchyard and up the hill to the car park. As he reached the top, he looked out and surveyed the lights of the town he now called home. Had things gone differently tonight, he would have been looking at them and enjoying his new-found freedom, but he somehow felt trapped yet again in a situation which wasn't his fault but made him feel constricted.

Gabriel walked to the back of the car park to find his car when he realised there was someone sat in the car a few empty spaces over from his, with the door slightly ajar and the light on. He realised the person in there was shaking, racked with sobs.

He went up to the car to check they were okay and saw it was Lauren, her face blotchy and her eyes red from crying. He quickly went to the driver's door and gently pulled it open. She started and looked at him with genuine fear in her eyes.

'Hey, I come in peace,' he began. 'I don't know what the hell just happened back there, but I wanted to say I thought you did great tonight.' Gabriel found all thoughts of G strings and flirting had left his mind and he just wanted to take this beautiful girl in his arms and hug her until the racking sobs stopped.

'I'm… I'm so sorry. I don't normally get emotional like this. I must look such a… a state,' Lauren tried to say.

'You look pretty damn good to me.'

She looked at him and pouted, with a cynical look in her eyes.

'Honestly, you've always looked pretty damn good to me. If it's not too inappropriate, could I give you a hug?' he asked. 'You look like you need one.'

She slowly climbed out of her car and stood in front of him. He took her in his arms and held her, feeling her soften and begin to cry again. Afterwards, he had no idea how long he had stood there, just holding her. The sobs eventually subsided, and she held him back. He felt like he never wanted her to let him go, but after a while, she slipped out of his grasp and started to wipe her face.

'My mother always told me I got emotional far too easily. She said it was one of my worst qualities.'

'Really?' he replied. 'I think it makes you human. I quite like that.' That set her off crying again, and Gabriel realised he didn't have a clue what to say to her that might make things better. 'I wish I knew something I could say or do that would make you feel better,' he offered, weakly.

Lauren stood back from him slightly and stared at him. 'You seem nice. I've always thought you seemed nice.

You've been kind to me since we met, and not many people are kind to me.'

Gabriel couldn't believe that. Who couldn't be kind to such a beautiful and vulnerable creature?

'Would you like to come back to mine?' she asked.

Gabriel looked at her in utter bemusement. He wasn't the kind of person who got propositioned by someone he didn't really know. And he wasn't sure this was even a proposition. It could just mean coffee. He felt his throat go dry and his palms go sweaty as his mind tried to work out what he should do.

'I could do with someone to just hug me tonight,' Lauren said, as though sensing his confusion.

Gabriel swallowed hard and looked at her. 'Yes, of course I would.'

They held each other for a few more moments, as they both tried to calm themselves down, before climbing into their cars. He followed her about two miles out of the town to a small two-bedroomed terrace. After they both parked and reached the front door, he followed her upstairs.

NINE

G ABRIEL WOKE TO THE SOUND OF THE ALARM clock going off at 8am. After a moment, he realised it wasn't his alarm clock and he sat up in the bed. The room smelled unfamiliar and the surroundings weren't his.

He looked down at the pillow next to his to see a note.

'Good morning!

Thank you for an amazing day yesterday. I haven't felt able to open up to anyone like that in years. Thanks for listening and not judging me.

It's 7am and I've snuck out as I have to go to work. You know where the coffee machine is, and I've left you a croissant and a pain au chocolat in the kitchen. I reset the alarm so you should have time to finish them, drink your coffee and get to work, as you slept right through the first alarm! If you'd rather have something else, feel free to go through my kitchen.

Have a good day and call me later.

Lauren x'

The last two days came flooding back to him. On Saturday night, after the concert, they had gone back to her place. They had gone upstairs and she started crying again. Gabriel had held her while he waited for her to

94

calm down. They had found themselves curled up in her bed in just their underwear, with her quietly whimpering and they fell asleep in each other's arms.

He woke first the following morning and found his arms were still wrapped protectively around her, despite his left arm having no feeling in it due to having spent the night under her neck. She eventually stirred and turned towards him, greeting him with the most beautiful smile he had ever seen.

'Good morning,' she had whispered quietly.

'Hello you. How did you sleep?'

'Really well. That's the best nights' sleep I've had in a long time. Thank you.'

They had slowly gathered themselves together and he used the shower after her, painfully aware he only had his clothes from the previous night. She lent him a cow-print dressing gown which emasculated virtually every fibre of his being, although she laughed every time she saw him in it so he embraced the situation and attempted to have a normal morning with her whilst wearing the monstrosity.

They sat on her sofa and watched cooking programmes for the rest of the morning and after he had driven them to his place a while later in last night's clothes, he quickly changed into something suitable for a Sunday afternoon. After this, they went for a long walk around the nearby park and found themselves sat on a bench as they talked for hours about each other. He told her about Shelley and his looming divorce. She told him about her stern mother who always put her down, and her father who essentially sounded like a decent bloke, but just went out to work in a biscuit factory for as many hours as he could manage, then tried to avoid his wife as much as possible when he returned home.

The one saving grace her mother had was that she pushed Lauren to achieve the best she could academically. She was always encouraged in the things that might help this, so was made to attend ballet classes, encouraged to draw and paint, pushed into various musical instruments until she eventually settled on the violin, which she appeared to have a natural aptitude for. She had considered going away to study music, but this was quickly dismissed by her mother, who wanted far higher things for her daughter. They eventually compromised on teaching, although Lauren said her mother had always considered this far too ordinary and would have preferred law or medicine.

Lauren had kept the violin up after leaving school, as she genuinely enjoyed it. She had played in the university orchestra and said she was enjoying playing with the Porlington Philharmonia, even if it was somewhat different to what she had expected.

Gabriel tactfully avoided all talk of the incident with Sandra the previous night as he didn't want to upset her again. He asked about her father, as she hadn't mentioned him much.

'He was a nice guy. Always gentle. But he would never stand up to my mother, even for my sake, which made him seem weak in my eyes. He seemed to think that she knew best, and was happy to let her rule our house. Even when she hit me if I got less than an A in an assignment, he never intervened.'

'That seems a bit harsh, but I suppose once you got to secondary school things must have eased,' he offered.

'That was during my A levels.'

Gabriel sat on the park bench, stunned by what he was hearing. His rather boring childhood seemed idyllic in comparison to what Lauren had suffered. He began to understand why, when she escaped to university, she rarely went home.

'They must have been proud when you got a 2:I for your biochemistry degree though?'

'They never found out,' she said, with a sad look in her eyes. 'They both died within two months of each other in my final year. Cancer. What are the odds? She went first, and Dad had a new lease of life for a week or two, but then I realised he was behaving strangely. When I confronted him, he admitted he'd been diagnosed in the last few weeks of her life, but he felt he had to concentrate on supporting her.' A flash of anger passed across Lauren's face. 'I wish he'd done something sooner; if they could have saved him, or given him more time, I'd have had the chance to get to know him out of her shadow.'

Gabriel reached his arms around her and held her again. There were no tears this time; he guessed she had already cried most of her tears for her parents. A sad sigh slipped out of her body and she sat up on the bench.

'Is that a duck pond over there? Let's go see!'

And, with that, she was up and heading towards the pond. He was surprised at the sudden change of tone, not sure if it was her covering her emotions, or if she could just switch between states that easily. He ran after her.

They found an ice cream stall which also sold duck food. The man serving them took great care in telling them one must never feed bread to ducks, swans or any other bird. The food he sold was a specially formulated blend of wheat, maize and fish meal and floated for longer without doing damage to the birds. It also seemed very

97

expensive at £2.50 for a tiny little plastic pot of food that he poured out of a bag he must have bought at a pet store (probably for less than £2.50 for the entire bag).

As they walked away from the ice cream vendor towards the ducks, Gabriel commented, 'You know, we could have bought an entire loaf for 80p and fed every duck for two miles…'

'Gabriel Lee!' (Lauren had no idea how grateful he was that she got it right and didn't think 'Flee' was any part of his name.) 'I am disgusted with you! How could you consider bloating out those poor little duckies, so they can't swallow properly nutritious food? Do you want them to contract angel-wing? You can damn well pay the £2.50 for something that will do them some good and stop complaining! Cheapskate!' she said, with the corners of her mouth turned up in an involuntarily teasing smirk.

He looked at her with some surprise that her knowledge of wildfowl was so all-encompassing.

'Erm, no problem. Glad to be of service. You seem to know a great deal about the subject.'

'I was part of the Conservationist Society in Sixth Form.'

'You'll be telling me you're a vegetarian next…' Gabriel regretted saying this the second the word 'vegetarian' was out of his mouth and he saw the steely look in her eye. For such a delicate person, she was surprisingly feisty.

'And what if I am?' Lauren demanded.

'Nothing! No problem at all!' he cried in self-defence.

'Good!'

After throwing a few pellets to the ducks who seemed remarkably unappreciative of his somewhat considerable investment in nutritious food for their benefit, he asked, 'So *are* you a vegetarian…?'

'Yes, of course I am!' came back the reply, in a tone that didn't suggest any criticism of her position on this topic would work in his favour.

'Great… Good for you… Go veggies…!' he replied in an ever-weakening and really quite pathetic voice that tailed off into silence.

After a minute or two of silent duck-feeding had passed, Lauren decided she'd had her fun and should let him off the hook. 'Of course, I don't judge anybody else for killing poor little animals and devouring their rotting corpses.'

Gabriel's heart sank and his eyes followed. Lauren saw this and realised she might have gone too far. 'I'm joking, you silly boy. It's fine. If you want to eat steak and chicken, I'm not going to stop you or preach at you. Oh wait, I probably will do the latter, but it doesn't worry me. I make my life choices, you make yours. I expect people to respect mine, but I respect theirs too. But I draw the line at you bringing panda steaks round to mine to cook.'

The laugh that came out of Gabriel's mouth and nostrils was possibly the most high-pitched sound he had ever emitted, but it was more from relief than finding it funny.

'All the duck food has gone,' he said as he looked at the empty carton in his hand.

'Well, best we go shopping and buy something for you to cook me tonight then.'

'I've never cooked vegetarian before. I wouldn't know where to begin!'

'It's easy,' Lauren said with a serious expression. 'We'll go shopping and buy fake meat. You cook it pretty much the same way you cook butchered, murdered meat.'

It occurred to Gabriel that whilst she was toying with him, she might have a point. 'And what aisle do I find fake meat in?' he asked, in all seriousness. This was a whole new world to him.

'It's generally in the freezer section. There are a couple of brand names that I can show you that should give you a head start. If you want to be really in with the cool kids (by which I mean all us vegetarians), you need to understand the shorthand though.'

'This seems far more complicated than I first thought...'

'Right, fake chicken is called fricken. Fake beef is called feef. With me so far?'

'I think so,' he said, nervously.

'Fake lamb is famb and fake pork is fork.'

'Okay...'

'Do you know what fake duck is?'

Gabriel paused and flushed, not entirely sure what to respond. 'Erm...'

'It's fake duck. Be careful with that one.'

He laughed as they headed back to his car, arm in arm.

Later that night, after eating a meal of fricken in korma sauce with almond rice and naan bread whilst watching X Factor on television, they found themselves on the wrong side of nearly three bottles of wine between them. They'd spent the evening holding hands watching mostly talentless people mutilating their chosen songs and hearing phrases such as, 'you've come so far on your journey', 'you're so brave choosing such a hard song' and, at one point, 'your great uncle who died on Tuesday would be so proud…' despite said great uncle living on another continent and having had no real contact with the family in several years. They began to feel drowsy during the late-night talk show that followed and eventually, Lauren said, 'Well, I guess we better head upstairs then.'

Gabriel wasn't quite sure what to do. Anthea had advised against this, but he was signing the papers tomorrow, and he was pretty sure Shelley would be doing exactly the same thing with whichever man she had ensnared most recently. 'Sure,' he replied, nervously.

They headed up to her bedroom and fell into bed, in a night that proved far more athletic than the previous one.

TEN

MONDAY PLODDED ALONG IN A RATHER boring fashion. Gabriel survived his day at Porlington Pianos, managing not to upset anyone and not to make any huge mistakes on the till. At 5pm, he left and headed to see Anthea.

'Well, that was a load of old crap on Saturday, wasn't it?' were the first words out of her mouth as Gabriel took his seat in her office. 'Mr Sweeney was moaning about it all weekend.'

'It wasn't all bad,' Gabriel muttered in an attempt to be diplomatic. 'There were some good moments…'

'Name one,' came back the stern response.

'The meal at the Cock and Bottle was quite good fun…'

Anthea laughed. Gabriel found her brutal honesty refreshing. There was no edge to her, no agenda. Anything less than positive that she said was said because it was accurate and there was no malign intent behind it.

Gabriel thought he'd try to find a few things out. 'So nobody has told me what's next. I'm assuming I might get a chance to conduct something, but I have no idea when the next concert is.'

'That would be our Christmas Extravaganza. Known amongst the orchestra as our Christmas Mutilation. There'll be the usual round of a couple of Leroy Anderson pieces, a chunk of Nutcracker, a few godawful pieces that Michael thinks audiences will like (which they won't) which bear no links to Christmas at all, topped off by a couple of carols which nobody will sing along to and the orchestra will hack through at the quickest speed possible in order to get to the pub. Any of those tickle your fancy?'

'I could probably have predicted all of that if I'd thought about it. What do you think he'll let me do?'

'Lord only knows. Something very short and inconsequential, I expect.'

'Tell me honestly, Anthea, is there really any point in me bothering to continue with this?' he asked.

'I'd say it's in your best interests to carry on.'

'Why?'

'Because you're the first glimmer of hope we've had in years and if you quit now, I will personally destroy your divorce case and ensure you walk away with nothing.'

Gabriel looked at her and realised her face wasn't giving anything away, but there wasn't the usual twinkle in her eye. He began to feel somewhat nervous.

'Okay, well, I'll turn up on Thursday and see what Michael has to say…'

'Good boy. You do that. And how did your weekend with Lauren pan out…?'

Gabriel felt like a rabbit caught in oncoming headlights, not quite sure which way to jump. He spluttered as he tried to think what words would get him out of the impending interrogation.

'Don't worry Sunbeam, I'm not cross with you,' Anthea said in a way that led him to believe she wasn't entirely being truthful. 'I'm just looking out for your best interests.'

'It was a bit of a surprise to me too. How did you know?!'

'Mr Sweeney and I were enjoying a rare pint of ale in the Park Pub on Sunday afternoon and we saw the two of you walking by, arm in arm.'

'Oh…' Busted.

'I'm guessing you found her after the concert on Saturday and spent the weekend consoling her?' The twinkle in Anthea's eye was momentarily back.

'Something like that. I didn't go looking for her, I saw her crying in her car when I went back to mine.' It was almost true. He *had* given up looking for her when he returned to his car and everything he just said was technically accurate.

'Well I hope you made sure that girl had a very large drink when you got back to whichever house you returned to together. The way Sandra spoke to her was completely unacceptable, although I suspect it was aimed more at Jane. Lord knows Sandra will have had the most enormous whisky once she got home.'

This surprised Gabriel. 'I saw her rather more as a red wine or sherry woman.'

'Oh heavens no. After rehearsals, and especially after concerts, she'll knock back the largest single malt you've ever seen. Neat. No ice. Must be half a tumbler. Quite often after concerts, she'll get through three or four, although she insists it's only ever one. Personally, I think it's the stress of having to see Elizabeth at concerts. Anyway, you're here to talk about your divorce.' And with that, she was all business again. 'Here are the papers which I've drawn up. You need to read through them and check you're happy. I can tell you now that the highlights are as follows:

'We're divorcing your wife on grounds of adultery. This will immediately give you some power back in the eyes of the court. It won't really give you any more leverage in terms of claiming assets because, as we've previously discussed, each party in a case not involving children is pretty much entitled to 50% each, regardless of circumstances. However, by drawing first blood, it will immediately prejudice the court ever so slightly against her and in your favour. We may need that further down the road if her father and his team of hack solicitors decide to play silly beggars.

'On that subject, do try to limit the amount you're seen in public with Lauren for the next few weeks. Once this gets filed and they are served with the papers, all hell is likely to break loose. They can't do a thing about it, but I wouldn't want to throw away one of our best cards—your fidelity as opposed to her infidelity—by them photographing you and claiming in court that the only reason you're seeking a divorce is because you want to set up shop with your new girlfriend.

Gabriel agreed with her, cross with himself that he'd lasted several weeks managing to avoid Lauren (not even intervening when Henry swooped in on her in the break at rehearsal) but suddenly things had become complicated just when he needed them to be easy.

Anthea continued, 'Recent changes to the law mean that you can name the other party with whom she committed adultery. This is a fairly new thing and it's entirely up to you. It won't achieve anything in particular, but it could make you feel better and it could potentially put a strain on any new relationship she has. Depends how much you want to twist the knife.'

'Can I ask a question?' Gabriel enquired.

'Of course.'

'How many additional pages am I allowed to list the number of people I suspect her of committing adultery with?'

Anthea laughed very loudly. 'I'm guessing that means you don't want to name just one person then? That actually works in our favour, as I can tweak the wording to reflect her adultery with numerous, unnamed partners.'

She clattered away on her keyboard. 'Oh, do read through everything while I'm adjusting. I'll print out a new copy and show you the changes I've made.'

Gabriel spent ten minutes reading through the entire writ before giving his acceptance. Anthea printed out a new copy with some tweaks and pointed these out to him.

'That all seems pretty accurate to me,' he said.

'Great. If you just sign on the last page, we can get this filed at the County Court tomorrow. Here, have a pen.'

With that, Gabriel realised the moment had come to sign a document that would end his marriage. Whilst he knew he would be signing something today, it came as quite a shock that it would be this. Years of planning went into the marriage and he knew the date and time of it way in advance. But he was suddenly being presented with the article to end it and he hadn't had any real warning.

'Oh, I didn't realise I'd be doing this today.'

'Yes you did, I told you what you'd be coming in to sign.'

'Well, yes, but I don't think it had quite registered until now.'

'Don't worry, my dear, this isn't the final thing you'll sign. This is just to start the ball rolling. After this, there will be lots of toing and froing for a few months and eventually there will be a final agreement which you'll have to sign. That will go off and a decree nisi will be issued. Some weeks after that, a decree absolute will be issued, and then you'll be free. You have time to adjust to that final signature.'

Gabriel paused and took a breath, looking at the line on which he had to sign.

Anthea reached across her desk and gently smiled at him, not just with her mouth, but with her eyes.

'Do you want to go back to a life with Shelley?'

'No, of course not,' came back the instant reply.

'Would you ever trust her again?'

'No.'

'Do you want to be free of it all so that you can move on with your life, meet someone new and be happy?'

Her questions made him realise just how free he had felt this weekend, and how much he wanted Shelley, her father, and their whole former life to be gone from his existence.

He took the pen she had handed him, took a deep breath, reflected on what he was doing (reaching the conclusion it was absolutely the right and only option) and signed his name on the line. On Anthea's prompting, he added a date next to it.

'Okay, I'll get this to my secretary and have one of our legal executives go down to file this in the morning. You okay?'

'I think so,' he replied. He was still in a state of shock. Then the wave of relief hit him. 'Actually, I'm better than okay. I'm taking charge.'

'That's the spirit, Tiger. You just remember this feeling when the bananas hit the fan over the next few months. And they will. But remember how you feel right now and remember that when that decree absolute hits your doormat, you will feel like this again.'

Gabriel left Anthea's office walking tall with his head held high. No matter how the next few months went with the inevitable mud-slinging, he got to put Shelley on the back foot and put a dent in her sense of self-importance and self-justification. And he knew the exact shade of puce that her father would turn when he found out. Gabriel's smile grew even further. He reached for his phone and dialled Lauren's number.

'Hey. How are you? Good. I've just signed my divorce application papers and I feel like celebrating. Fancy a drink tonight? Great. How about the Italian on Ambrose Place? Fantastic. I'll pick you up at 7:30.'

ELEVEN

GABRIEL AND LAUREN SAT IN *NESSUN DORMA* waiting for their main courses to arrive. They'd both gone for the tomato, mozzarella and basil starter (Gabriel had attempted to appear sympathetic to her affliction as a vegetarian by not ordering something with a rotting corpse involved as an entrée, although this courtesy hadn't extended to the main course and he was now waiting for veal in a white wine sauce—he suspected there was no vegetarian version of this; 'feal' just didn't seem likely). The tomatoes had been infused with oregano and just the right amount of extra virgin olive oil, which had put him in a remarkably good mood.

Said mood was also helped by the Montepulciano he was glugging down in copious quantities. When he had arrived at Lauren's, she had insisted on driving so he could have a drink on the day he signed the beginning of his divorce. She sat there sipping her sparkling water, finding his oncoming inebriation amusing.

'It all went well then?' she asked.

'It did, thanks. I had a brief moment of doubt when I actually had to sign, but I got over it pretty quickly.'

'I think that's to be expected when you're closing a chapter on such a huge part of your life. Even if you knew it was coming and despite knowing it was the right thing to do, it still can't be easy to finalise something so… permanently.' She was staring at him intently, waiting to see his reaction.

'Quite. But I felt such a huge sense of relief once I'd done it, I don't know what I was worrying about.'

Lauren appeared to visibly relax as he said this. Gabriel guessed it must be hard for the new girlfriend (although he wasn't sure that was what she was, this was all still so new) to hear about his wife. Ex-wife.

'Anthea and Rupert saw us on Sunday in the park, you know.'

'Oh? Did she disapprove?' Lauren seemed nervous again.

'Actually, I don't think she did. I rather got the impression that she was pleased for both of us.'

'Could this impact on the divorce?'

'She told me to be careful, so for the next couple of weeks, I think we should limit how much we're seen in public. She suggested my ex-father-in-law might go to the extreme of having me followed and photographed. That hadn't even occurred to me, but I wouldn't put it past him once they get over the shock of me taking the first step.'

'What makes you think I want to see you again over the next couple of weeks?' Lauren asked.

He looked up, suddenly concerned that he might have assumed too much. Then he saw the coquettish look in her eye, and the smile dancing around the corner of her mouth, and realised she had assumed they would continue to see each other.

'Well, who could resist such a catch?' he ventured.

110

'Do you really want me to answer that?'

With that, his veal and her gnocchi salsa rosa arrived. 'For the beautiful couple,' the Italian waiter said, with a wide smile as he laid their plates in front of them. They both looked down at their plates in an attempt to hide the blushing they were experiencing.

The food was exquisite. They could tell this was a real Italian family enterprise, as they had both been to rural Italy in the past. This wasn't just a chain churning out the same recipes with bland food. These dishes consisted of hearty Italian ingredients, prepared in a way only the Italians could manage. The restaurant was decked out to match the food, and they could believe they were on holiday in Puglia, grabbing a meal at the local trattoria before returning to their trullo in the southern Italian summer heat. Ironic, as it was November in England and the temperature outside was approximately six degrees.

'Oh my god, I think we need to come here more often,' Gabriel mumbled through mouthfuls of his vitello alla crema.

'Not for a while, as you're worried about your stalker ex-father-in-law.'

'Oh god.' Gabriel was crestfallen as it dawned on him this might be the last meal of the condemned man. At least for a while. 'Say it isn't so...'

'Your divorce, your rules. Ask Anthea when we can come here again.'

Gabriel was genuinely welling up at the thought of not being able to return for the foreseeable. This food was divine.

'I'll bribe her. Or threaten to take each section where the cellos have semiquavers at double speed in whatever I'm allowed to conduct one day.'

111

Lauren laughed. Gabriel didn't. He appeared to have traded one hell for another.

'So tell me, how did you end up becoming a teacher after getting a biochemistry degree and basically being a genius?' he asked, hoping she would lead the conversation for a while so he could savour every mouthful of seasoned dead calf in cream, white wine, shallots and mushrooms without having to speak.

Lauren appeared not to notice his plot. She continued to place one gnocchi at a time into her mouth, where it appeared to dissolve with just the slightest breath. Her sentences were only briefly interrupted by this.

'I was never sure of what I wanted to do. When I was a teenager, I knew I wanted to get away from my mother, and university seemed the best opportunity. I'd always enjoyed science at school, so that fell into place pretty easily. The problem was, because I was effectively running away from home and using the best opportunity that was available, I didn't really have an endgame. I'd considered all the obvious options—research, the oil and petrochemical industry, cosmetics, and so on, but none of them really appealed. I think it was after my father died that I realised what I really wanted to do was help kids who didn't know what to do with their lives. I was still one myself really. I finished my degree, signed up for a PGCE and that's how I've found myself in teaching.'

'Do you enjoy it?' Gabriel asked, hoping for a longer answer so he could masticate the veal even more slowly and feel the flavours encompassing his mouth and throat.

'Yes, I do. We have a lot of troubled kids at my school. Broken homes, single-parent families with large numbers of children by different fathers, traveller communities, and so on. I enjoy seeing them each day, but I particularly enjoy looking back at each child at the end of term and realising how far they've come, both academically and as a person, since the last term. Except for Rob. He makes no progress. Hopeless child, hopeless parents. I've tried everything, but nothing works. If anything, he goes backwards each week and I expect by Easter he will have resigned from the human race to become a housebrick. I'll keep trying though.'

Gabriel went to ask more about Rob, in the hope it would keep her talking so he could disappear into his little world of veal ecstasy when she got in first.

'So tell me more about your life. Why did you choose the path you ended up on?'

He realised he wasn't going to be able to duck out of this one, and he'd have to commit to a slightly longer answer whilst not enjoying his food. It occurred to him that in a year's time, he wouldn't even remember this meal, but he desperately hoped Lauren would still be in his life. Hopefully as the major part of it. He put down his knife and fork, and committed to the conversation, allowing himself the occasional mouthful just to savour the work that the maestros in the kitchen had done.

He talked about his pretty bland life—normal parents, normal home life, normal upbringing in the Home Counties (whatever normal was these days). He recalled how his parents had told him early on that he had to choose just one or two hobbies, but pursue them to the best ability he could. He was allowed to dabble with a few things at a time until he worked out which ones he liked best. As a young child, he did the usual round of a term of piano, a term of football, a term of violin, a term of trampolining, and so on. The family already owned a piano, inherited from a great grandparent, and the school

113

loaned instruments. Football and trampolining required no outlay other than kit he already possessed for P.E. at school. His parents were fine with him dabbling for a while as long as no outlay was required other than for the lessons themselves. They were by no means a poor family, nor were they rich, just happily middle-class with a father who worked in banking and a mother who was a schoolteacher. Gabriel had always assumed they took this stance in his early years to teach him the value of things.

One day, the local music service had sent a team of instrumental teachers into his school to do a mini-concert in a recruitment drive for music lessons. He'd sat and listened to them playing as an ensemble, but there was something about the haunting sound of the oboe that resonated deep within him and moved him in a way the other instruments didn't. Gabriel went home that evening and told his parents he had decided on his main extra-curricular focus. They agreed to support him and he borrowed one of the school oboes for the next two years, having lessons each week with the tutor he had heard playing in that ensemble.

After two years, he had made remarkable progress and gained a distinction in his Grade 3 oboe exam, quite the feat for a nine-year-old. His parents were very proud and agreed to buy him his own oboe as he had shown such commitment and attainment. By the time he was 14, he had gained a merit at Grade 8 and was on his third oboe, by now a beautiful Patricola Rigoletto Rosewood oboe. His parents had supported him as he showed such dedication and bought him a very fine instrument on which to take his Grade 8. Naturally, they had also supported him in other activities—it turned out he quite a penchant for rugby and chess—but all other hobbies had paled in comparison with his love of the oboe.

'Of course, my oboe isn't a patch on the Fossati that Allegra has, but she took it much further than me and is a far superior player,' he explained to Lauren, who flinched ever so slightly at the mention of Allegra's name. Gabriel had imbibed far too much Montepulciano to notice.

'I guess it was a useful lesson to learn as a child—if you're going to do something, do it to the best of your abilities; find what you really enjoy and stick with it, no matter what.'

He finally managed the last few mouthfuls of his veal, wishing there was more and giving serious consideration to ordering another one, even though his stomach was objecting to having so much rich food crammed into it.

As the plates were cleared, he admitted one of his biggest failings. 'Of course, the oboe also became my weakness. I put so much time into practising that I let the rest of my studies slip. I managed reasonable grades at GCSE, less so at A Level. Whilst I was desperate to go to a conservatoire to study properly, my academic grades just didn't survive. I ended up having to settle for a Music Technology degree and that's where I met my beloved and soon-to-be ex-wife. I coasted through the course and the easiest option was to follow her back to where she came from and do as I was told.' Gabriel was a long way down the road to being drunk and was being hopelessly honest. 'She seemed to offer me the best options I could hope for in life, although she despised music and didn't encourage me at all.'

'Did you ever love her?' Lauren asked, whilst declining a dessert to the hovering waitress.

115

'I think I did. Looking back now, I'm not so sure, but I suppose I must have at the time and I'm just being jaded in the light of starting divorce proceedings. I'm able to see now that she definitely wasn't the right match for me, but she appeared to be my only option. I don't know when I decided to just settle, as I'd always been so focused before.' His voice trailed off. He excused himself and went to the toilet, as the Montepulciano had completed its journey from taste buds to bladder. When he came back, he found Lauren with her coat on, having paid the bill. He went to object, but she wouldn't hear of it.

'You've had a tough day. This is my treat.'

He began to voice a complaint, when he noticed the look in her eye implied the lady wasn't for turning. Whilst he knew it was a brave new world and people split bills, he was still old-school enough that he found the concept of letting a woman buy him dinner grated against his sense of propriety; not in a sexist way, but in the sense that he wanted her to feel special and treated.

'Mr Lee, you can continue to object, or I can give you a lift home. I should warn you that the first option involves a somewhat substantial walk.'

'Okay, if you insist,' he slurred, realising that he might have had just a touch too much fine wine.

'I think you better stay at mine tonight too, as you'll need your car in the morning.'

He certainly wasn't going to object.

On the drive home, Gabriel voiced his concerns with whether it was worth him turning up to Thursday's orchestra rehearsal.

'Oh you've got to come!' Lauren said. 'I need some company!'

116

'I won't get anywhere near you with Jane guarding you,' he mumbled from the passenger seat.

'She's not that bad. I think she's just trying to make sure I keep coming back each week as they need the help.'

'Anthea said something interesting today. She implied there was some history between Sandra and Jane and she thought Sandra's outburst on Saturday wasn't really aimed at you.'

'Oh…?'

'Seems to make sense to me. Why would she want to have a go at you? She doesn't seem the type to be threatened by someone younger.'

'I suppose so.'

Gabriel recounted the gist of what Anthea had told him before finding himself being helped out of the car and shepherded into Lauren's place. He didn't even notice that she had gently placed him on the sofa, and he was softly snoring by the time she came back with a blanket. Lauren smiled as she gently removed his clothes down to his underwear, placing his head on a cushion, covering him with the blanket and kissing his forehead before turning out the light and heading to her bed.

TWELVE

THURSDAY EVENING ARRIVED, WITH GABRIEL finding himself back at Porlington Methodist at 7pm, against his better judgement and wondering if there would be any point in him turning up this week. As he walked into the church at 7:10pm, he was barged out of the way by Megan Sims, principal horn.

'Sorry, coming through. Hot flush alert. Need some cool air…' she apologised as she pushed past and disappeared into the cold November night.

A percussionist drove a timpani into Gabriel's lower back heading in the opposite direction. 'Sorry, love, wide load coming through.' Gabriel hopped out of the way. 'Between me and Menopausal Megan, you really are standing in the worst spot imaginable.' The percussionist stopped and looked at Gabriel. 'I thought you were supposed to be our new conductor?'

'So did I,' Gabriel countered, rolling his eyes before catching himself and thinking this probably wasn't terribly professional behaviour.

'Ah, is Michael doing his usual trick of keeping you around but leaving you out in the cold?'

'Apparently that's the place to be, although I don't have hot flushes which require Arctic temperatures.'

The percussionist barked a short laugh before continuing to shove his kettle drum up the aisle.

'Hello stranger,' came the quiet utterance from behind Gabriel.

'Hello you,' he replied as he recognised Lauren's voice.

'I wasn't sure you'd come back.'

'Neither was I.'

'Well, I'm glad you did. Has the hangover passed?'

Gabriel didn't wish to remember Monday night. Or Tuesday morning. To be honest, he didn't really remember much of Monday night. But the following morning was burned into his memory. He had found himself waking up on an unfamiliar sofa, in only his boxers, with a half-filled washbowl of vomit on the floor next to his face that he could only assume was his. Despite his pounding headache, he had staggered into the kitchen, blissfully unaware that he was still only in his underwear and not considering that there may be someone in there who might not wish to see this.

Mercifully, the only thing in Lauren's kitchen that was out of the ordinary was a note she had left for him on the worktop.

'Hope you're feeling better than I expect you will. I had to shoot to work early, but please help yourself to anything you can find in the kitchen. Including cleaning products for my washing-up bowl, which judging by the sounds I heard from upstairs last night, will need some serious disinfecting.

'I've got some school stuff on over the next couple of evenings, but I hope I'll see you at rehearsal on Thursday. Feel free to text me if you're bored at work today. I'll reply when I can.

119

'Lauren x'

Gabriel felt utterly ashamed and was trying to ignore the churning in his stomach. He hadn't been in this state since university. Shelley would never have tolerated it. And then it hit him that he was standing in a beautiful woman's kitchen in just his underwear, reading a note that asked him to talk to her later that day and hoping she'd see him later in the week. The fact he had thrown up and only managed to sleep on her couch didn't really seem to matter right now. He was utterly convinced that Shelley would be of the opinion that he would never find a woman again now that she had disposed of him, expecting him to live out his days in a monastery somewhere, contemplating how he was never really good enough for her.

Sod that.

He drank a whole litre of orange juice followed by two cups of coffee from Lauren's pod machine, which were surprisingly good. He thought it might not be the best idea to drive anywhere for a few hours, so he opted for a shower and then, somewhat grudgingly, to stagger into work by foot, wearing the same clothes as yesterday. Neil wasn't in today (probably off being a secret agent, or parachuting over the Great Wall of China). Grant came over to talk a few minutes after Gabriel arrived before noticing the same clothes and apparently smelling something unpleasant, despite Gabriel's best efforts to use a number of Lauren's incomprehensible bathroom products to mask the odour of shame.

Susan just smiled, patted his arm and plied him with dreadful coffee.

After a couple of days of detoxing and copious numbers of showers back at his place, he felt he had exorcised the demon drink from his system by Thursday evening.

He looked at Lauren. 'Yeah, sorry about that. I didn't realise how much I'd had to drink.'

'It's fine, you needed to after kicking off your divorce. I was glad to help. Disappointed you weren't in a fitter state to celebrate in other ways, but happy that you managed to forget about all the rubbish for a while.'

Gabriel was about to apologise again when Jane came through the door with Menopausal Megan.

'Really? Magnets?' she was heard to say.

'Oh God, yes. They're the greatest things I ever bought.' Megan replied. 'You just clamp one on the inside of your knickers, with the other on the outside. Works wonders. Massively reduces hot flushes and helps to regulate all your movements. You never get the control back, but you can at least predict when disaster is looming. Mostly.'

Gabriel thought to himself that she must have clearly forgotten to install these magic magnets tonight after the way she charged past him earlier. Her face was still flushed and she was sweating just ever so slightly all across her face and forehead.

'Where can I get them?' Jane asked.

'I've got several sets. All my friends want to try them. I'll bring some for you next week. Tell you what, try this set for the first half of the rehearsal.' And with that, Megan reached into her trousers and underwear and hoiked out two objects that looked like pebbles. 'You put the big one on the inside, against you, and the smaller one fits into the groove but on the other side of your underwear. Please tell me you're wearing underwear...?'

Jane laughed. 'Yes, I'm wearing underwear.'

121

Megan apparently had no shame and just pulled Jane's trousers forward. 'You're barely wearing underwear. I haven't worn something that skimpy since I was in my twenties. You'll need something larger than that once you finish menopause. It'll be just like being a child in nappies again, believe me. We've both had kids; we gave birth to our pelvic floors.' And with that, Megan reached into Jane's trousers—and presumably underwear—to attach the magnets.

Once the destruction of Jane's dignity was complete, they walked up the aisle with Jane taking Lauren's arm to lead her to her seat; she didn't even acknowledge Lauren or Gabriel's presence, but continued to listen to Megan.

'Now, you must try MoodModerator. It's a natural therapy that stops you being a complete bitch. But don't tell anyone you're taking it, because it's still fun to be a bitch, but with you in control of it. It's got fenugreek, grape seed, ginseng and...' Gabriel missed the end of the list of ingredients as the women moved out of earshot, with Lauren shooting him an apologetic glance over her shoulder.

A voice boomed over Gabriel's shoulder. 'Ah, Mr Flee. I have decided to let you conduct a piece in the Christmas concert.' Michael's frame loomed over Gabriel.

A piece. The use of the singular made Gabriel think he might never have any meaningful role in this orchestra, but at least it was a start.

'That's great, Michael. Thanks very much.' He saw Michael noticeably bristle, causing him to wonder if he should have referred to him as Mr Fordington, or Maestro.

Michael pretended all was well with the world. 'I did a set of variations on a theme of 'Joy to the World' some years ago which the orchestra always enjoy. I will allow you to conduct this.'

Gabriel suspected the orchestra probably didn't enjoy this, but this didn't seem the moment to point that out. 'Sounds fantastic,' he heard himself saying.

'Excellent. I'll bring it for you next week and you can start the rehearsal.'

Gabriel's heart sank with the realisation that he'd have nothing to do tonight. He had hoped to impress Lauren with his conducting prowess this evening, in order to make up for Monday's vomiting incident. A few seconds later, he realised what Michael had just said.

'Erm, how can I start the rehearsal with it if you'll only be giving me the score a few moments before? I won't have time to prepare it...'

'Well just read the score in front of you. Why do you need to prepare anything?' Michael asked, clearly confused.

'But I won't know the tempo to take it at, and I won't have had a chance to mark cues to bring instruments in,' he began to object, just as Sandra appeared behind him.

'Is there a problem?' she asked.

'I was just saying that I could do with a week to prepare the score for...' Gabriel didn't get any further.

'I just told you,' Michael interrupted, 'Read the score in front of you and conduct. I've never needed to prepare anything in my life.' Gabriel didn't like to point out that this was clearly evident in last week's concert.

'That's settled then,' Sandra said in a rather abrupt fashion. 'Michael, a word...?'

And with that, they were gone. Doris the tea lady walked past. 'Don't worry dear, you really won't need to prep. The orchestra know it inside out and they're used to ignoring the conductor. You could stand there painting a watercolour and the piece would go swimmingly.'

'That's not really the point…' he began to object.

'It's a shame he's given you that. The orchestra hate that arrangement of his.'

What was left of Gabriel's sense of hope plummeted through the floor.

A loud bark from the podium brought the orchestra to attention. 'Right. The Christmas concert. We'll be doing the usual carols…' There was a collective groan.

'Nobody will sing along, it'll be like we're sacrificing Santa Claus. Again,' was heard to drift from the percussion.

'And, of course, we'll be doing the suite from Nutcracker…'

Henry James, who was unusually present at the start of a rehearsal, was heard to say, 'Why in the name of Nureyev's nether-regions must we do Nutcracker again? We've murdered it for years! Can't we do something else for a change? Even Swan Lake would be a welcome break.'

It was like Michael hadn't even heard this, or the resounding chorus of agreement from the orchestra.

'…added in will be various festive pieces, including Lehár's "Gold and Silver Waltz", Mozart's "Overture" from *The Marriage of Figaro*, Strauss's "Blue Danube" and other Christmas works.' Gabriel failed to understand what any of these had to do with Christmas. Michael reeled off a few more pieces and finished the list with, 'And our new deputy conductor will be conducting my ever-popular arrangement of "Variations on Joy to the World".'

Gabriel was expecting the orchestra to begin a riot at this point, but the stunned silence that followed surprised him. Gradually, the entire orchestra (except Sandra) turned their heads to look at him hiding in the back row. Lauren smiled. The others portrayed a look of bewilderment tinged with just the slightest hint of hope.

Sandra cut this off very quickly by demanding an A from the principal oboe. Allegra gradually turned her head in slow motion to look at Sandra with an inscrutable look before reaching down in a lackadaisical fashion to pick up her oboe. After a faint sigh, she placed the double reed in between her lips and 440MHz sang throughout the room. Nearly 30% of the orchestra sounded their instruments to check their tuning, which was an improvement on previous weeks.

Gabriel found his mouth was dry after having 36 people staring at him (as that was the sum total of those who had bothered to turn up tonight), so he stood and walked through the back doors to the entrance foyer where the kitchen was, in order to get a glass of water.

'Where could I find a glass and a tap for drinking water?' he enquired of Doris.

'Hold on, my dear. Let me fetch that for you.'

Gabriel drained it in three gulps.

'So, you're finally going to get to do something. You must be excited,' Doris stated, her voice laden with sarcasm.

'I'm not sure excited is the word. Relieved that my bothering to turn up every week might not be a total waste of time, perhaps,' he responded.

'Are you any good?'

'Depends on your definition of good.' The sounds of Lehár being mutilated drifted through the glass doors. 'I reckon I could get a better sound than this though.' Gabriel had lost all sense of decorum and long since given up on attempting to be diplomatic.

'Ha. I reckon even I could get a better sound than this. I'm Doris, this is Gertie.'

Gabriel said hello and saw a sharp intellect behind Doris's eyes, and virtually nothing behind Gertie's. 'So what brings you both to this orchestra every week?'

'My son plays viola. That's him in the red jumper.' Gabriel peered through the glass and saw a man in his forties staring intently at his music, moving in a robotic fashion, his brow furrowed. 'See the old man next to him?' she asked. 'That's Gertie's husband.' The man looked like he had been old when David Lloyd George was Prime Minister. A thick handlebar moustache did nothing to hide the gaunt face and glassy expression. He was barely moving beyond the occasional twitch. Gabriel looked at Doris, who checked to see Gertie was looking away before shaking her head in a manner that implied he shouldn't any questions before silently mouthing the word 'Alzheimer's' at him. Gertie just stared through the glass, a look of rapturous love on her face.

Gabriel and Doris chatted for a while, mostly about her son, David, who was, in her words, 'a bit special.' Gabriel shot him a glance and realised they probably didn't have much of a clue about autism when David was in school, but he'd probably be diagnosed within a heartbeat these days.

The door swung back and Menopausal Megan barged through. 'Sorry, sorry! I had a thimble of tea earlier and my bladder can't cope! This is what I get for giving up my magnets to help someone else. Don't mind me!'

Gabriel's eyes followed Megan through the kitchenette and out the door to where the toilets were. Doris got up and closed the door so the din from the orchestra didn't interrupt their conversation.

'I mean, it's nice to still have David living at home, but I do hope that one day he might meet a nice girl and settle down. I'd quite like my freedom back. I haven't really had that since my husband died ten years ago, Doris continued.

'Oh, I'm sorry for your loss,' Gabriel said.

'Don't be, I'm not. He was awful. Any man who can...'

'He's not right, that one,' suddenly burst from Gertie.

Doris rolled her eyes. 'Who's that, Gert?' she asked, otherwise unperplexed at being interrupted.

'That man.'

'Which one, love?'

'Him that runs the corner shop down on Coronation Avenue. He's... foreign...'

Menopausal Megan came back through, having emptied her apparently tiny bladder. 'He's not foreign, Gertie, he's Welsh,' she said.

'He's not Welsh. Not with skin that dark.'

'He's third-generation Welsh after his great grandparents emigrated here last century. He's got a thicker Welsh accent than Tom Jones,' Megan said before attempting to sneak back into the rehearsal quietly. She failed, crashing into chairs all the way back to her seat, mumbling, 'Sorry!' at every opportunity and walking as though her bladder had filled up again and needed emptying already.

Doris closed the door behind her again.

'Well, he's not right.' Gertie was apparently still on her high horse. 'I reckon he's, you know, one of them…'

'Here we go,' Doris muttered under her breath. 'I don't think he is, Gert. He's married and has children. All of whom are training to be doctors.'

'No, he's not right. I went in there the other day and he was wearing purple. I mean, what grown man wears purple? Only one who… you know…'

Gabriel quickly glanced at his shirt cuffs to check and felt a surprisingly strong sense of relief at seeing they were blue.

'It's his wife and children I feel sorry for. They must have no idea. Those kids will never amount to anything with a father who…' Gertie's voice trailed off and she went back into hibernation, staring at her husband through the window.

Doris seized the opportunity to shift away from this line of conversation. 'Right, better get the urn up to temperature.' She tweaked a dial on the rusty old urn and began to fill the rows of mugs with far too much milk. Gabriel realised this was why the tea and coffee was so dreadful each week.

He stared at the orchestra through the windows, who were being subjected to one of Michael's tirades about their playing not being good enough. Anthea looked at him in despair and silently mouthed the words, 'Help us,' with a resigned expression on her face reserved only for those trapped in a particularly unpleasant circle of Hell, aware their fate is an eternal one with no prospect of escape.

After a few minutes, Michael announced it was time for the break. Jane shot to her feet to usher Lauren up the aisle, immediately regretting it as her metal music stand got caught in the magnetic field emanating from her underwear, sticking itself to her and sending music and pencils flying in all directions. She tried in vain to remove it but just made it worse, leaving her looking like she had turned into a giant magnetic paper clip holder with a nervous twitch, by now knocking nearby music stands and chairs flying as she flailed in her vain attempts to detach herself.

'Hold on, dear, I'm on my way to rescue you. Forgot to warn you about that!' came Megan's battle cry across the orchestra. 'Just bear with, I'm trying not to wet myself en route.'

Gabriel glanced over at Rupert and Richard in the double bass section who looked like they were already wetting themselves with laughter. Henry James was shrieking a particularly effeminate, high-pitched laugh as he filmed the whole debacle. Betty Brannon was attempting to rescue the chairs as they flew away, placing them back in their correct positions before Jane knocked them away again, her screams now turning into sobs. That strange, enigmatic smile never left Betty's face as she set the chairs up like skittles just waiting to be knocked over again. Debbie Greer, the librarian, was cowering behind Michael's music stand, trying to escape to the safe place in her head. Allegra glided away from the scene, seemingly unaware of the carnage being wreaked around her.

Michael stared in bewilderment and Sandra had gone a deep shade of vermilion. Anthea dashed over to grab Lauren before marching her up the aisle to deposit her with Gabriel.

'There you go, dear. Have a chat to Twinkletoes here while Jane is otherwise occupied. It's about time you both got to have a conversation with another person without being dragged away by Jane, set upon by Henry and his raging libido, or ignored because nobody knows who you are.'

THIRTEEN

O NCE MEGAN HAD DISENTANGLED JANE FROM all metalwork in her immediate vicinity, things had returned to a rather dull level. Gabriel had suspected that was the most exciting thing to happen within the Porlington Philharmonia for decades. He had chatted with Lauren for a while, before Michael had called them all back to continue mutilating music. Jane spent the rest of the evening looking utterly traumatised, a situation not helped by Megan's attempts at calming her down ('Don't worry, dear, it's only a music stand, it's not like you had a prolapse or anything!'). At the end of the rehearsal, Jane hadn't even attached herself to Lauren, choosing just to pack up her violin in record time and flee the scene.

'Don't worry, dear, you get the hang of them!' Megan called after her, much to Rupert and Richard's amusement. Even Anthea gave up trying to suppress a smirk.

An utterly boring weekend followed for Gabriel, as Lauren told him she would be away visiting friends from university until late Sunday. His disappointment must have been evident as the last thing she said to him before

131

leaving Thursday's rehearsal was, 'Don't worry, I'll be back by next week. Then we can see each other again.'

However, the following week she found herself snowed under with work and couldn't free up any time in the evenings. Apparently, Christmas was a busy time of year and she had to organise the school carol concert on top of all her normal work. She kept texting him each evening though, so he didn't think she was trying to avoid him.

Life at Porlington Pianos did nothing to improve his mood. The Kings continued to freak him out in their own special little ways and he still couldn't reconcile the tiny number of customers who came into the shop with the ever-burgeoning amount of deliveries they had. During one of his brief appearances, Neil assured him they were stocking up for the Christmas rush. 'There's no time of year quite like it! Parents will buy so much for their darling little children without any thought to the longevity of such an investment. It's like it's Christmas!' Gabriel thought this a strange thing to say as it actually *was* Christmas.

When Gabriel took his lunch break on Wednesday, he saw he had a voicemail from Anthea. He escaped out the back to listen.

'Hello, my little ray of sunshine. Anthea here. I've heard back from your wife's solicitors. Any chance you could pop in after work to have a chat through their response? I'll expect you around 5:30. Lots of love, see you later.'

He felt his stomach knot. He had no regrets about starting the divorce process, nor did he wish to pause it. But this sudden interruption of his new life to deal with something from his old one jarred him and made him realise he was going through a traumatic time. Much as he liked to pretend it wasn't happening, and exist in the brave new world in which he found himself, he realised it would be some time before he could officially cut all ties with the past and move on completely.

He was shown into Anthea's office by her mousey secretary a little after 5:30pm, having declined her offer of tea or coffee. He sat down opposite Anthea and waited for the worst.

'Okay, so we drew first blood—we always knew they wouldn't like this and would get their knickers in a knot. And boy, have they.'

Gabriel gulped and wished he'd asked for a glass of water as his mouth now felt as dry as the Sahara.

'I've had a letter from your father-in-law's solicitor. Fortunately for us, the man appears to be an idiot. I'm guessing he's been used by your father-in-law's company for decades and this just got added to the list of things he's expected to sort.'

'Ah, you must mean Martin Brady.'

'The very same.'

'The two of them play golf together several times a week. Martin has dealt with all the company legal stuff since time immemorial. Utterly boring man, but his specialism is company law, not family.'

'Okay, well that helps us in some senses and could work against us in others. Useful to know, so I can plan for an unexpected attack on the financial front.'

'I expect Shelley's father just rang him out of habit. He tends to fix most things that get thrown at him, and I wouldn't be too sure his morals are entirely scrupulous.'

'I'll be investigating him then,' Anthea muttered, furiously scribbling notes.

'So what have they said?' Gabriel asked, dreading the answer.

Anthea put down her pen, picked up the two pieces of paper stapled together with single-sided printing on them, adorned with Martin Brady's letterhead, and began.

'They've taken the somewhat unusual step of contacting us direct at a stage so early it's practically premature. That smacks of desperation. I checked with the court this afternoon and they haven't even acknowledged service of documents yet. They technically have eight days to do that. As we filed last Tuesday, the court will allow 48 hours for them to be served, which leaves us to assume they received the papers on Thursday. This means they have to acknowledge service and state whether they agree or disagree with the divorce by this coming Tuesday. The fact they've written to me implies we caught them on the back foot and they want more information before they decide which way to go.

'Of course, we don't have to respond by Tuesday. We have up to 28 days to reply to their letter, so I'd suggest riding it out until the end of next week, thus forcing their hand.

'They've basically said that they are surprised at your application for divorce on grounds of adultery. After the hassle she's given you regarding getting the divorce rolling, this is a rather stupid tactic, as we can prove that they were expecting this. What may be harder to prove is that she has been sleeping with someone else.'

'What?!' Gabriel exploded. 'She openly admitted it to me!'

'I know, but one person's word against the other doesn't make for a solid legal argument, even though we only need balance of probabilities, not proof beyond reasonable doubt. Of course, that counts against her as much as it counts against us.

'The short version of the letter (and I've made a copy for you to take away and read properly) is that they are threatening to countersue for divorce on grounds of unreasonable behaviour.'

Gabriel found himself having to fight the urge to scream.

'However, there are several things that work in our favour within this. First, you have assured me that there are no such grounds and I'm inclined to believe you. Secondly, they haven't stated what those grounds are. This is just a vague threat. If there was anything to worry about, they'd be launching it at us from the earliest opportunity, which leads me to believe they're just trying to buy time and provoke a response from us. Thirdly, this idiot solicitor has said they intend to make an application for ancillary relief.'

'What's that?' Gabriel asked.

'Something that hasn't existed since 2010, which means they can't apply for it.'

Gabriel found himself relaxing and feeling just a glimmer of hope.

'Prior to 2010, it meant one party seeking financial relief from the other. Now I'm pretty sure that she isn't wanting for anything whilst living in one of Daddy's spare houses, so they'd have one hell of a time trying to prove this to a judge. I'm also convinced that you aren't leading a playboy lifestyle at her expense. Your existence, and please pardon my candour, seems pretty modest.'

'You could say that,' Gabriel replied, remembering he needed to find a bit extra for the gas bill that month now that the cold temperatures had hit and the heating was on more.

'If they try to file a petition in this format, they would be laughed out of court. The Family Procedure Rules 2010 dispensed with the term "ancillary relief" and redubbed it "application for a financial order". I don't intend to point out their mistake. Whilst White v White 2001 might still give us some issues, I'm pretty sure a judge will take a very dim view of a solicitor not being current with the law.'

Gabriel's head was spinning.

'The short version of this is as follows: they have to show their hand by Tuesday. We don't have to do anything for another 26 days, allowing time for communication of documents. I'm inclined to recommend that we just sit tight and wait for their next move. Even if they are stupid enough to try to counterclaim for unreasonable behaviour, adultery trumps pretty much everything. Although we might need to consider how we're going to prove this.'

Gabriel found he was quite happy with this turn of events. They obviously had the Coles rattled and despite the threatening letter, they didn't have to do anything except sit back and wait, as they would be forced to show their hand first.

'So, what happens now?' he asked.

'We wait, dear boy. We wait.'

FOURTEEN

GABRIEL ARRIVED AT THURSDAY'S REHEARSAL at 6:40pm, hoping to get as much time as possible with the promised score before having to flap in front of the orchestra whilst sight-reading.

The church was locked up.

He desperately hoped Michael was one of those annoying people who turned up early to everything, but his experiences of the last few months were giving him a sense of impending doom. He fiddled with his baton case as he waited for someone to turn up, hopefully with the score from which he was about to make his first impression on the orchestra.

At 6:55, Anthea and Rupert pulled into the car park to the side of the church, with Classic FM blasting from their car. They parked, extracted their instruments and headed over to the front door. Rupert pulled out a key and unlocked.

'Hello snookums. How are you?' Anthea asked, greeting him with a peck on the cheek. She wasn't very different outside of work, but there was a noticeable change and he wondered to what extent the two lives were actually separate, or how much was an act. Or if she was schizophrenic. Or just that utterly professional.

'Not bad, thanks. I'm dreading tonight, though. I can't believe Michael isn't giving me any time with the conductor score to prepare.'

Rupert chimed in, whilst trying to manhandle several locks at once, 'I wouldn't worry, old chap. We've played that godawful arrangement so many times that we could blast through it in our sleep.' He continued to wrestle with the Chubb lock, the Yale lock, and every other lock short of a canal lock. Gabriel wondered if the people who had designed the vaults in the Bank of England had made it as secure as Porlington Methodist Church.

As Rupert began to swear under his breath, Anthea put her hand on Gabriel's arm.

'Don't worry, my dear, I promise you that the orchestra are on your side. Anyone who isn't Michael is welcome in their eyes. You could hang one of the 2nd violinists and the rest of the band would cheer. Actually, that would be for several reasons,' she said with a somewhat distant smile.

Rupert's swearing grew louder and Gabriel worried that the residents in the care home over the road might be startled if he got much louder.

They eventually gained access. Gabriel stood by the entranceway as Rupert and Anthea swung into action, setting out chairs.

'Erm, can I do anything…?' he asked.

'Best not,' Rupert replied, shoving a stack of five chairs across the wooden floor, seemingly oblivious to the faint scratches he was causing on it. 'We're used to how things should be placed. You'll just mess it up.'

'I thought Betty set the chairs out?' Gabriel countered.

'Oh no,' Anthea interjected. 'Betty just faffs. We do the real work, then she shuffles a couple around, after which the players put them back where we put them in the first place. Nobody has the heart to tell her she's a silly old bat and should leave well alone. One doesn't say that to a woman who has had a stroke.'

Gabriel felt a pang of sympathy for Betty, and realised that Rupert and Anthea were the real backbone of the orchestra—they did the heavy lifting but let other people take the credit, so those individuals felt valued. His solicitor and her husband both shot up at least fifty points in his estimation at that moment.

With that, Richard walked in, his double bass slung in its case on his back, making him resemble the largest snail in the world.

'Ah, Dicky. Come and give me a hand, would you?' Rupert cried.

Richard was about to retort with some smutty comment when he saw Gabriel stood in front of him and he watered his response down to, 'Sure.' Rupert looked slightly crestfallen at the lack of banter, as did Richard, but Gabriel didn't feel he knew either of them well enough yet to say he really wasn't bothered and actually quite enjoyed a bit of banter.

By 7:07pm the chairs were set out, waiting for bodies to fill them. One or two people began to drift in, all wrapped up warm in winter coats and scarves, instrument cases in hand.

Betty walked through the door at 7:11pm. As soon as she saw other human beings, her face lit up with an inane smile. She set her scarf, coat and violin case on a chair nearby and started to shuffle chairs around.

'Oh for…'

'RUPERT!' Anthea scolded under her breath.

'Sorry, dear…' came the response.

'Just got to pop outside to take a call from a girl…' Richard mumbled, his shoulder-length hair flowing behind him as he hurriedly exited the vicinity with his phone gradually reaching his left ear.

At 7:14pm, Michael and Sandra entered the building. They were arguing. Everyone already in there noticed and either ignored this or rolled their eyes. Gabriel thought it best not to interrupt until the temperature between the two of them had simmered down to a rolling boil.

By 7:22, this hadn't happened, and Gabriel's level of panic surpassed whatever disagreement was occurring between Michael and his mistress. He walked up to the two of them.

'Hello, Michael. Do you have the score for "Joy to the World"?' he asked.

Time froze. Michael and Sandra both stopped, mid-argument, and turned their heads towards Gabriel, astounded that someone had interrupted them. Who would have the nerve? Their mouths gradually fell open and they just stared. For a long time.

Gabriel decided to stand his ground and stared directly at Michael, raising his eyebrows after a few seconds to request a response to his perfectly reasonable question.

He was sure he heard Sandra hiss very quietly before she moved slowly away to seethe elsewhere. Michael's face colour passed through several shades in a short space of time before he swallowed and took out his music case. 'I do,' came the response, through gritted teeth. 'Here you go.' Never before had three words been uttered with so much contempt or with such hostility.

Gabriel wondered if it was worth ramming the score he had just been handed down Michael's throat before fleeing the scene, but concluded there were too many witnesses. He took the music, thanked Michael and beat a hasty retreat to the back of the church where he hoped to get as many seconds as possible with this score before having to look like he was in charge of an orchestra.

As scores went, this one was a disaster. Handwritten, no sense of layout or spacing, with several sections illegible. He hoped the orchestra had better scores—he was wrong. He started on the first page and scanned through quickly, deciding there was nothing untoward with this arrangement and it should be fairly simple to conduct. His relief felt palpable. After all, how difficult could it be to conduct Handel? Although it wasn't actually Handel who wrote the original tune, nobody quite knew who it was. Musicologists had suggested the American Lowell Mason had written it in 1836 for some time, until 1986 when it was proved the tune had already existed in 1833. Still probably not by Handel, though. Someone, somewhere, had thought it a good idea to base their tune on various bits of Handel's *Messiah*, but had never signed their name to it, so nobody would ever know who it really was.

Gabriel suspected Michael would take full credit for it, if given the opportunity. He no doubt considered his version far superior to any predecessors. The further Gabriel scanned through the score, the more he realised this couldn't be further from the truth.

The orchestra drifted in. Henry put in an unusually early appearance, sauntering to the brass section with a swagger normally only seen displayed by one of the Gallagher brothers. 'Hello, chaps. Ready to squeak some

141

notes?' he enquired of them. The elderly trombone section just looked at him; Gabriel couldn't work out if their expressions were rooted in contempt, pity or confusion.

Allegra glided in next. She sailed across the floor, leaving barely a ripple in her wake, before sighing into her seat and putting her oboe together, turning her back on Henry before he had a chance to talk to her.

Menopausal Megan crashed through the door, staggering up the aisle with the gait of one who had been knocking back gin since 10am. Gabriel was quite sure she hadn't been, she just walked that way, probably due to her only moving her legs from the knees down, in the hope that clamping together her upper thighs would stop the waterfall from her miniscule bladder. Lauren snuck in, only to be grabbed by Jane and dragged to their usual places.

At 7:31pm, Michael tore himself away from Sandra, his face like thunder. This was unusually late for him to begin a rehearsal. Gabriel was unsure whether he should take to the podium, so held back. This turned out to be a wise move, as Michael took his usual position, with Sandra shifting uncomfortably into position beside him. The two of them refused to look at each other.

Michael began his pre-rehearsal dance routine, not that anybody paid any attention. After a sharp intake of breath and leaving his head back for a worrying amount of time without breathing, he eventually exhaled and lowered his eyes to survey the people in front of him. Hush gradually fell.

'Tonight, we continue our work towards Christmas. We'll be looking at "The Blue Danube" and the Lehár again tonight. But first, I am delighted to introduce our assistant conductor, Mr Flee. He will be conducting the

"Joy to the World" variations this year.' The orchestra went to groan. Gabriel heard the intake of breath and the start of one or two low notes from various voice boxes, before they caught themselves and realised it probably wasn't the done thing to complain about the new conductor. He might turn out to be bearable. 'He will be taking the first part of tonight's rehearsal.'

With that, Michael stepped off the podium. Grudgingly. One foot lingered on it, as though he was attached by one of Menopausal Megan's magic magnets. Perhaps it was just a sense of not wishing to give up any control. Either way, Gabriel nervously walked up to the stand, his hands clammy, his throat dry and his hands shaking.

'Good evening, everyone. Might I say what a pleasure it is to work with you all. And can I add my thanks for a great concert the other week, I really enjoyed listening to you all.'

Later, Gabriel swore blind that a tumbleweed rolled through the room at that point, as the sea of faces in front of him remained utterly blank. One or two folk looked slightly confused at being told they were good, or that somebody had enjoyed listening to them. A couple more had expressions that suggested they thought he was lying, which of course he was. Most just sat there and waited for something to happen.

'I'm Gabriel. Gabriel Lee. That's LEE, no "F" at the start of it.'

Again, more blank expressions—they appeared unsure as to whether a verbal, or even facial, response was required.

'So, could we take "Joy to the World" from the top, please? I think perhaps it's best if we just play through, then talk about it.' He felt like a lone voice in the wilderness. He might as well have been reciting Tolstoy to the Elgin Marbles for all the reaction he was getting. 'Okay, I'll be conducting in four. I'll give you two beats in, so you can get the tempo. I'll do this in the concert too.'

A few of the orchestra stared slightly more intently at him and inclined their head, as though listening to an alien speaking a language not of this world. Nobody made any notes.

'Okay, ready…?' He raised his hands, his baton poised in his right hand, ready for action.

Eventually, most of the orchestra picked up their instruments, most of them simultaneously rolling their eyes.

The faintest cough came from Allegra's direction. Gabriel looked at her, noticing her hair flaring in the wind again (despite being indoors). Presumably the same wind that drifted the tumbleweed through a moment before.

How could he be so stupid? He was an oboe player! How could he forget tuning? He'd just assumed this had already happened.

'Er, could we get an A please?' he asked in Allegra's direction. She slowly put the instrument to her lips and blew. A beautiful sound flowed out, quickly ruined by everybody else playing rather randomly. Some attempted to lock in to what Allegra was playing. Fewer made any attempt to adjust their instrument to be in tune with her note. Henry hadn't even picked up his trumpet, he was just staring at Allegra, as though he may wither away to nothing if he didn't get a date with her sometime soon.

Eventually, silence fell, and Gabriel felt most eyes were on him.

'Okay, so two beats in. Three, four…'

As soon as he had said the last number, he realised every eye left him, never to return again. They looked at their scores and played.

'Played' was perhaps not the best choice of word. 'Mutilated' might come closer. 'Destroyed' or 'annihilated' could also have been used, but seemed a little harsh. Granted, it was a truly appalling arrangement, with no sense of thematic writing on Michael's part, but they weren't even attempting to play well. Or accurately.

Gabriel stopped conducting and held his hands up. Nobody was watching him, so this made no difference and the bandwagon thundered on regardless.

'Right, strings, let's just have a look at that last section…' He might as well have been yelling into a storm for all the difference it made. The noise didn't abate.

'OKAY!' he yelled at the top of his voice. The sound died a slow and painful death over at least ten seconds, as though someone had removed the batteries. Betty was still scratching something out on her violin until her desk partner nudged her. The orchestra looked up at Gabriel in bemusement, not understanding why he had stopped.

'Strings, can we just go over that last section again. Actually, I mean the section several pages back. There don't appear to be any bar numbers or rehearsal marks in this score, so can we go from the section where the trombones had the tune.' More blank looks. He stepped down to look at Sandra's score, much to her horror. '1st violins, that's the middle system on the third page, second bar in. 2nd violins…' He moved over to look at one of their scores. 'That's the second system down on page three, fourth bar…' He moved his way around the string section until he had established where they should all be going from.

'On my cue... three, four...' His baton went down on the next beat, but nobody played anything. 'Can we try that again, please?' The same thing happened. 'Why aren't you playing?' he asked, beginning to get exasperated.

'Sorry, *where* do you want us to go from?' asked a brave 2nd violinist.

'I just *said* where you should all be... Never mind.' He repeated the process, with Sandra looking ever more piqued each time he looked at her score.

'Why are you starting part way through the piece?' she hissed under her voice.

Gabriel's patience was running out, so he didn't even attempt to reply quietly. 'Because we need to go over the section that fell apart,' he said in a voice that everyone in the room could hear. A high-pitched giggle came from Henry's direction. Anthea and Rupert smiled at him, with an expression of rapture that the promised saviour had finally arrived. Lauren's eyes smiled at him although her sense of self-preservation didn't allow this smile to spread to her lips. Allegra winked at him. Sandra went purple. And Gabriel couldn't even look behind him to see what on earth Michael was doing, but he did permit himself a glance at the percussion section who were clearly watching Michael's every move with looks of glee across their faces at his evident discomfort.

'That's not how we do things around here,' Sandra spat at a volume nobody could miss.

'Well it's how I rehearse. Now, do you all know where you are? Good. Just the strings please. Three, four...'

146

A deafening blast came from the trombone section, obliterating the strings.

'Sorry, just the strings please,' Gabriel said in the kindest voice he could muster, having to suppress the ever-rising urge to scream.

'But we've got the tune,' objected an elderly trombone player.

'I know that, but the strings separated quite badly in this bit, so I'd like to hear them on their own. And again. Three, four...'

The trombones leapt into action again, blasting out the violin line instead of the melody they actually had.

'STOP! Sorry, trombones, can you please *not* play? I only want the strings to play, so I can hear them without any distractions.'

'But we were playing the violin line that time.'

'I KNOW!' Gabriel paused to let his voice drop back to its normal octave. 'But I would like to hear the string lines, played *only* by the strings. Not by trombones. Please could you not play for a minute or two until I ask you to again.' He noticed they were going a similar shade to Sandra. Oh wait, a quick glance at Sandra showed she had gone an even richer shade of purple.

'And *why* do you want the strings to play without anyone else?' she demanded.

'Because you got it wrong, and this is how rehearsals work.' Any shred of patience he had was now long gone. 'Strings. Only strings. Please. Three, four...'

The sound that followed made Gabriel think the strings on the instruments were still inside the cat from which they came. He stopped them after only three bars.

'Good first effort. Can we try that again please? Could you listen to one another to make sure you're all blending?

And could you please watch me to see where my beat is as it went a bit awry.'

He started it again and found it wasn't much better.

'Perhaps just one last time. And…'

There was a marginal improvement as they realised they were going to have to get this together.

Gabriel stopped them again. 'Sandra, we appear to have bows going in all sorts of directions; can you clarify what the bowing is at the start of this section please?'

Sandra looked like she was going to explode with rage. Menopausal Megan looked like she was going to explode with mirth. The trombones looked like they were going to explode with boredom if they didn't get to play something soon. Anything. Even if it wasn't what they were supposed to be playing.

'The violins should be following what I'm doing with my bowing and making appropriate notes,' Sandra said in a voice so quiet it was almost inaudible.

Gabriel wasn't sure how to respond. He gently said, 'Very well. But your bowing was different that time to the first…'

Anthea leapt to her feet to head off the oncoming storm. 'Ladies and Gentlemen, this seems to be an opportune time to take our break.' It was twenty minutes too early, which sent Doris and Gertie into a frenzy out in the kitchen. 'Can we please show our appreciation for our new deputy conductor?' There was a surprisingly large round of applause. When Gabriel thought about this moment afterwards, he decided approximately a third of the orchestra clapped very enthusiastically, another third clapped politely and the remainder sat there unable to decide if they were bewitched, bothered or bewildered.

148

They all stood and drifted towards the kitchen where Doris was in a state of panic.

Michael and Sandra were notable by their absence during the break as everybody talked just a little too loudly to mask the shouting that was occurring between the two of them outside in an attempt to stop it drifting in. Gabriel was swamped by violinists thanking him for taking the time to go over a section they had always struggled with. It occurred to him that he hadn't really had the opportunity to go over it, but they seemed grateful. The trombones glowered at him from afar.

After ten minutes, when only eight people had managed to get a drink, Michael suddenly appeared on the podium in the church, barking at everyone to get back in to continue the rehearsal. Gabriel's time this evening was clearly at an end, as Michael announced they were doing *The Blue Danube*. The orchestra slowly filed back in, muttering and swearing. Rupert caught Gabriel's elbow as he passed him.

'Don't worry, old chap. You did marvellously. Some people just don't like change. And others feel threatened. If you want my advice, sit at the back during the rest of the rehearsal, to show willing, but as soon as Michael finishes, scarper and run for the hills. You probably don't want to get caught by him or Sandra tonight. Don't worry, we'll put in some good words with the people who matter.'

Gabriel felt crestfallen. He felt like this entire evening had been a disaster and a waste of his time, and now he was being advised to leave before he had a chance to speak to Lauren, whom he hadn't seen properly since last week.

'It's good advice, pumpkin,' Anthea said as she followed Rupert back in to the church. 'Suck it up, come back next week and continue exactly where you left off. And don't expect Rome to be built in a day. Or even a century.' She gave him an unexpected peck on the cheek before walking back to her seat to await her fate.

Gabriel's rebellious side made him stay out in the kitchen with Doris and Gertie for a while, helping to do the drying up. After a while, he went back in to sit in the back row and listen to the remainder of the rehearsal. He watched the percussion looking bored with nothing to do, playing on their phones. Presumably they all had a group chat going, as they occasionally chuckled at exactly the same moment.

As Michael finished the final chords of Silent Night, Gabriel slipped out of the door and into the night, messaging Lauren to ask if she fancied meeting up that weekend.

FIFTEEN

A FTER LAUREN RESPONDED LATER THAT NIGHT, inviting him around over the weekend, Gabriel found himself sat on her sofa on Saturday night, drinking cheap Chardonnay, eating mediocre Chinese food and watching X Factor. He didn't mind any of this, as he got to spend time with her, both of them yelling criticism at the television every time one of the contestants hit a dodgy note (which was far more frequently these days than he remembered in the earlier series).

Eventually the conversation turned to that week's rehearsal.

'WHY?! Why on earth did I put myself through that?' he asked, incredulously.

Lauren giggled. As Gabriel just stared at her with his best crestfallen look (it didn't require much acting), she burst into all-out hysterics, unable to stop tears forming in the corners of her eyes.

'I'm sorry, I shouldn't laugh,' she said, before squealing approximately an octave higher than a moment ago. 'I wish I'd seen the look on your face, but I was glued to Sandra, trying to guess what colour she'd turn next. I just enjoy watching her suffer.'

Gabriel found himself at a loss for words. He still couldn't fathom how a rehearsal had gone so spectacularly badly.

'Do you think they're likely to get any better by the concert? It's only a couple of weeks away.'

'I doubt it,' Lauren replied, barely able to contain her laughter. 'They certainly never got any better for the last concert.'

Gabriel buried his face in his hands, partly in mock horror, mostly in real despair.

'Stop complaining and finish this spring roll for me, I'm stuffed.' He obliged and took the food from her plate.

Between mouthfuls of over-crispy pastry and undercooked bean sprouts, he asked a question that had been bothering him.

'I've got a bit of a problem,' he began.

'I know, I play violin for them.'

'No, not the orchestra. I wouldn't limit that by calling it a *bit* of a problem...'

'Fair point.'

They both winced as a contestant on the television hit a particularly unsavoury note.

'Anthea and Rupert have sent me friend requests on Facebook.'

'Okay. Big deal,' Lauren replied, waiting to hear what the judges would make of the vocally-challenged imbecile who was trying to cover their lack of singing technique with wild hip thrusts and ludicrous facial expressions.

'I'm just not sure if it's terribly professional to have your solicitor as a friend on Facebook.'

'Is Rupert your solicitor?' she enquired.

'Well, no...'

'So there's no problem there then. When did you and Anthea meet for the first time?'

'The first time we spoke was in her office in my first divorce meeting. Although she spent the first couple of minutes talking about the orchestra rehearsal the week before.'

'So you'd already been in a social situation together before you instructed her as your solicitor?'

'Yes, but I didn't talk to her.'

'I wouldn't worry about it. The two of you are in an orchestra together; it's reasonable you'd have some sort of social interaction.'

'I suppose so. I'm just a bit worried that it might prejudice my divorce case.'

'How could it?' Lauren asked, turning away from the television to fix him with a firm stare. 'And do you think that Anthea would put you in that position? To be fair, you're getting divorced. You're not running for President of the United States, where everything you do and every message you send is under scrutiny. How could your ex-wife, or her solicitors, object to you and your solicitor being friends on Facebook when you have a pre-existing social connection?'

Gabriel realised that Lauren always referred to Shelley as his ex-wife, never by name.

'I guess you're right. I'm just a bit nervous about all this, as I don't want to give them anything to use against me.'

'Like I said, do you think Anthea would put you in that position?'

'No, she wouldn't. She might be a tad eccentric, but she's good at her job. She always seems several steps ahead of me when we talk about the divorce.'

'So stop worrying. Here, have your last chicken ball and drink the rest of your wine. I want to open a new bottle.' With that, as he opened his mouth to object, she shoved the aforementioned deep-fried, battered poultry product into his mouth, ensuring a few seconds of his inability to communicate whilst trying to chew. 'Give me your phone,' she commanded. As he chomped away, trying to regain the ability to talk, he rolled his eyes and obliged.

Lauren opened Facebook, found his pending friend requests and sniggered.

'You've got half the orchestra waiting here! Why haven't you accepted all of these?!'

Gabriel swallowed the last of the chicken and spluttered, 'I didn't know if it would be the right thing! What if Michael or Sandra took offence...?'

'Do you really think either of those dinosaurs are on any form of social media?!'

'I guess not,' he said, trying not to choke on a final piece of over-fried batter.

Lauren proceeded to hit 'Accept' on every pending request in his account before he could object. Before he could elucidate a response, she said, 'If nothing else, it makes you appear more human and friendly. The orchestra will respond well to that.'

He couldn't argue with her logic. She threw his phone back at him and said, 'Now be quiet. I want to hear this idiot torn apart by the judges. Be a dear and fetch another bottle from the kitchen, would you?'

SIXTEEN

SEVERAL WEEKS PASSED, WITH EACH ONE FEELING much the same as the last. Gabriel went to work at Porlington Pianos each day. The promised rush of Christmas customers never materialised, and he questioned Grant's sanity every time he beamed and said, 'We're rushed off our feet! Don't you love this time of year?' Neil was always noticeable by his absence, and Susan's coffee never improved. None of them noticed the aspidistra next to the counter slowly dying as a result of Gabriel pouring every beverage Susan ever made into its pot.

Porlington Philharmonia rehearsals didn't get any better either. Gabriel was allowed around eight minutes every other week to go over his one piece. Despite his best efforts to get the band to improve, success eluded him, and they sounded worse than a junior school recorder group led by the child with Tourette's.

Early in December, Anthea informed him that she had received confirmation from the court that Shelley's solicitors had acknowledged service of the divorce papers and they disagreed with the submission. This was substantially past the deadline set by the court, but Anthea suspected the court would allow time for a countersuit to be submitted. Apparently, courts preferred to allow time rather than stick to the letter of the law. By 9th December, nothing further had been received, and Anthea was suggesting they contact the court to request a hearing to allow the initial divorce petition to go forward.

This was all discussed at the start of the rehearsal for the Christmas concert, when Gabriel was not entirely focused on his ex-wife's (or her father's) game-playing, as he was about to debut with the esteemed Porlington Philharmonia.

'I wouldn't worry about it, my little pudding. They clearly have nothing to offer, which will become obvious to a judge once we start pushing back.'

Gabriel's confidence level wasn't so high. He knew what Mr Cole was capable of, having worked for him.

'So, is it likely this will be resolved before Christmas?' he asked, trying not to sound desperate.

'Probably not. They really should have filed something concrete by now, but I suspect they're struggling to find anything they can use. Don't fret, turnip, there's nothing you can do today.' Her words offered scant comfort.

The afternoon rehearsal went very badly. Michael appeared preoccupied throughout, frequently missing cues. Sandra didn't even glance at him throughout the entire afternoon. Elizabeth swanned in towards the end of the rehearsal and sat in the fifth pew back, staring at Michael and the orchestra with a look that Gabriel couldn't quite place—it was either boredom or hatred.

His brief moment in the rehearsal went as well as could be expected with a terrible arrangement and a below-par orchestra to play it.

They broke around 6pm, with Michael barking at the orchestra that they had to be back by 6:30pm. The sheer number of eyes rolling told Gabriel this was unlikely.

Rupert appeared at Gabriel's side before Michael had even finished speaking. 'Right, come on. Let's head over to the pub and order some steak.'

'Surely we won't have time for that?' Gabriel objected.

'Oh, who cares? The old fart won't notice if we're not back. As long as everyone is on stage when the concert begins, it's all good.'

Richard appeared nearby. 'They do the best steaks,' he opined.

Rupert suddenly lost all interest in Gabriel, muttering, 'Yes, they do...' whilst staring at Richard in a distant fashion.

Gabriel didn't even hear Anthea creeping up beside him, taking his arm. 'Come on, crumpet. Let's get some food and a pint or two before we have to suffer through this disaster.' And with that, he found himself whisked off to the pub, which did, indeed, serve extremely good steak, with a Diane sauce to die for.

Lauren didn't appear at the pub, like Gabriel hoped she would. She messaged him as he was tucking into his surprisingly large steak to say she had gone to the sushi place around the corner with Jane. Gabriel attempted to hide his disappointment, lest his divorce solicitor ask questions about the woman he was, technically, committing adultery with. It didn't work.

'Did Lauren get dragged to Madame Butterfly's with Jane and her cronies?' she asked, before Gabriel could come up with an appropriate response that didn't implicate him in any way.

'Apparently so,' he acquiesced.

'I'm sure she'll be pleased to see you later,' Anthea said, with a twinkle in her eye. Rupert barked a laugh.

Richard looked up and said, 'If you ever decide she's not for you, please let me know. I'd love to get to know her better.' Gabriel surveyed the boy sat in front of him and questioned whether he would be able to rise to the challenge of a real woman. After only the briefest moment of consideration, he decided he didn't want to think about this and shifted his thought process to his impending debut. Although the back of his mind was prompting him to ask how Lauren, who was effectively a vegetarian, would fare in a sushi restaurant.

After some particularly excellent steaks all round, they all finished their meals and headed back. Gabriel wasn't on until the start of the second half, so he sat at the back of the church through the first half, playing on his phone and trying to ignore the cacophony heading his way from the front.

Part way through the first half, he noticed a post on Facebook from one of the percussionists. It simply said, 'As I asked Delilah recently, why, why, WHY?!' He was briefly grateful to Lauren for accepting all these new people on Facebook on his behalf, and he hadn't even noticed the percussionists playing on their phones on stage. The responses were both amusing and offensive. But mostly amusing. To him, at least.

The interval arrived and all 37 people in the audience gradually rose from their places, reached for their walking sticks and Zimmer frames, paused whilst various joints slotted back into place after being sat in terribly uncomfortable pews for quite some time, and headed towards the toilets. They had no idea that the orchestra had beaten them there already, resulting in a long queue before most of the audience had achieved motion in a forward direction. The bar staff looked bored as they realised that, yet again, nobody would appear to require their services for a good ten minutes.

Except for the brass players. They had rocketed over, with the apparent sole intent of drinking the bar dry as if their lives depended on it. One of the bar staff just pointed lackadaisically at a nearby table, stocked with numerous cans of cheap lager and a stack of plastic glasses, with a bowl at the front featuring a sign which said, 'Brass players—these are for you, to stop you holding up the queue and emptying our bar. Please would you place an appropriate donation in the bowl. During the second half, we will assess if this donation is sufficient to cover our costs before deciding whether to extend you this courtesy next time.'

Henry James led the charge. 'Fellas! They've given us our own supply! Tuck in!' He grabbed an armful of cans, chucked a ten pound note in the bowl and disappeared off into the night through the south entrance. Gabriel felt a sinking feeling as he watched the 2nd trumpet, three trombones, four horn players and a somewhat geriatric tuba player who was clearly riddled with Parkinsons do the same thing, demolishing the pile of cans like the eighth plague of Egypt had passed through. How many cans could they each possibly get through before he had to conduct them during the second half, and what state would they be in?

'Sorry, coming through—has anybody seen my car keys?' yelled Menopausal Megan as she barged through the small group of people around Gabriel. As usual, she was walking purely from the knees down (with said knees being firmly clamped together, as though she hoped

159

clamping her thighs together would stop the flow of urine from her bladder). Gabriel assumed that this tensing was stemming the flow of blood to her nether-regions, resulting in a loss of sensation, which caused her not to realise that her keys were in fact hanging in mid-air next to her crotch, presumably attached to the underlying marvellous and magical menopause magnets. He thought that she might have noticed the jangling, or at least feel the weight of these as she navigated through the small crowd like an icebreaker ploughing through newly-thawed ice. Apparently not.

Eventually the queue at the solitary toilet dwindled to the point where it could be deemed acceptable to start the second half. Gabriel felt a nauseous feeling rising in his stomach, but he couldn't decide whether it was nerves or a sense of dread at inflicting the horrors of the second half on an unsuspecting audience.

He waited in the lady chapel as the applause started for Sandra to take her position as leader. As she jostled her less-than-delicate frame into the groaning chair underneath her, Gabriel went to take a step forward to cue the applause for him to take his position to conduct the first item of the second half. He got no further than a single step as Michael barged past him, beaming in his insincere way at the audience as he marched up onto the podium.

Gabriel stood in bewilderment, looking at Michael and wondering if he had the order confused. Wasn't this supposed to be him now? Had Michael had a change of heart and decided to conduct this number himself? Gabriel felt just a tiny glimmer of hope that he might have earned a last-minute reprieve.

160

'Ladies and Gentlemen,' Michael began as the applause died down. 'I am delighted to welcome our new boy to conduct the first piece in this half.' New boy? Gabriel could hear the condescension oozing onto the floor as it dripped from Michael's lips. 'He's not been with us very long, but I'm sure you'll give him the benefit of the doubt and be polite in your applause, no matter what happens.' Gabriel looked to see where the nearest exit was but realised he would have to clamber over audience to reach it. 'Ladies and Gentlemen, please welcome to the stage... Mr Flee!'

The applause was muted and polite in a way that only the English could manage. As Gabriel walked to the podium, all he could see in front of him was Anthea repositioning herself after slipping off her chair with laughter, and Rupert and Richard wiping tears from their eyes, not even attempting to stifle their guffaws.

He reached the podium, whereupon he discovered that Michael had very little intention of vacating his spot and was glaring at him with a fixed smile that close up looked more like a sneer, and eyes that radiated pure malevolence. As the applause died down, Michael grudgingly stepped off the podium, leaving his eyes fixed on Gabriel like a cat surveying a robin whose days were about to be snuffed out.

Gabriel turned to the orchestra and nervously smiled. There was a loud clinking and clattering sound from the brass section as they picked up their instruments, forgetting to be careful not to knock over the three or four empty beer cans at each of their feet. He heard one or two snorts followed by, '...ugger' as one or two of the trombones realised not all of the cans were empty and their shoes were now wet.

161

It was about this point that Gabriel zoned out and went into his own little world. When he reflected on this afterwards, he considered it might have been his mind closing in on itself in a vain attempt at self-preservation. Either way, he went to his happy place in his head and put on his favourite recording of the Glenn Gould version of Bach's *Goldberg Variations*. He managed to stay focused on this while his arms conducted Michael's excruciating arrangement of 'Joy to the World' on autopilot.

Somewhere in the seventh variation, his attention was torn away from Bach and back to Christmas as he realised there was a godawful noise coming from the brass section. This, in itself, was not unusual, but it appeared to be worse than normal. His eyes flew to the conductor score and he realised the brass weren't even supposed to be playing at this moment. He flicked furiously through the pages attempting to see what bit the trumpets thought they were on, as it appeared to be them leading the charge and dragging the rest of the section in their wake. After failing to establish what on earth they were playing, he tried to make eye contact with Henry to try and figure out what was going on via the medium of eyebrow gestures.

As he looked in Henry's direction, he realised the scores on the trumpet music stands were Lehár's 'Gold and Silver Waltz' and then he recognised what they were playing. Gabriel was so stunned, he missed two beats as his hands just fell to his side in horror. Nobody noticed. He jolted himself back to attention and continued conducting with his right hand whilst trying to wave at Henry with his left. Nothing happened as Henry's eyes (which were partially crossed owing to the eight empty beer cans at his feet) were glued to the music and he clearly had no intention of looking at the conductor.

Gabriel's flapping got wilder and before he realised what had happened, he was waving with both hands at Henry. He became aware of the ghostly faces of the percussion section staring at him, uplit by their mobile phones, their mouths slowly falling open in shock. As the brass section reached a particularly loud section of the Lehár, with the clear intention of an even bigger crescendo to come, Gabriel heard somebody scream, 'HENRY!' His surprise turned to horror when he realised it was his own throat it had come from. A few moments ago, he had been safe in the confines of his own head but this had now turned into what felt like an out-of-body experience watching one's own impending death.

Of course, only the entire audience heard him screaming at the principal trumpet. And most of the strings. And some of the woodwind. And definitely all of the percussion section who now had their phones out, filming the entire thing and probably live-streaming it worldwide. Not one of the brass players realised and they all thundered on.

Gabriel suddenly realised the end of the piece they were supposed to be playing was now imminent and the brass were likely to just keep playing the waltz. In fairness, he wasn't sure the audience had noticed, as the arrangement was so bad anyway. As they reached the closing chords, he sped the piece up, as per the score markings and did the biggest gesture he could manage to try to make it clear they were ending. The strings and woodwind ended the piece with a flourish. The percussion were still filming and howling with laughter. Amazingly, the brass section had reached a brief break in the Lehár and there was a collective intake of breath as they were about to hit the next section. Mercifully, at this

163

moment, the audience broke into applause (probably in relief that the cacophony had ended). This was just enough to make the brass players think twice and look up.

Henry, who was clearly inebriated, just saw every eye in the building on him and heard applause. Gabriel barely stifled a laugh as Henry stood and took a bow, to the amazement of everyone watching.

'Well done, chaps. That went well,' he was heard to say as he took his seat.

Gabriel turned to the audience, fighting back laughter, tears and the urge to vomit all at once, took a bow, smiled weakly and fled from the stage.

SEVENTEEN

THERE WAS NO ORCHESTRA REHEARSAL THE following Thursday as they had broken for Christmas. Even if there had been a rehearsal, Gabriel wouldn't have dared show his face, and he was grateful for the late-night opening at Porlington Pianos for a Christmas rush that still failed to materialise. He spent the next two weeks hurling himself into work and trying to forget his broken spirit whilst avoiding all contact with anyone linked with the orchestra.

On Friday 22nd December, Anthea left a message on his mobile. 'Hello my little Christmas elf, I hope you're well and not still licking your wounds after Henry caused that train wreck in the concert. Rupert has needed incontinence pants for the last two weeks due to his inability to stop laughing about it. Anyhoo, I've had a letter back from your ex-wife's solicitors and I could do with a chat. Sorry, I know it's right on Christmas, but I want to get a couple of things moving before the break. Do pop in around 4pm if you could and we can have a quick chat. Text me if you can't make it. Toodles.'

Gabriel felt a tight feeling in his stomach all day until reaching the Tallon Grey offices shorty before 4pm. Anthea was in reception waiting to meet him.

'Hello, my little cinnamon stick of Christmas joy and wonder. How are you doing? Why haven't we heard from you since that sodding awful concert?!' She swept him up in a hug that Gabriel couldn't decide was because of the disaster a few weeks before or the news she was about to impart to him.

'Hi Anthea. How are you?' he meekly offered.

'Oh, I'm just tickety-boo. Wrapped the last of our Christmas presents last night. Very difficult to know how to wrap something that shape.' Gabriel didn't dare ask what the shape was, or for whom it was intended. 'And while I think of it, you must come round for drinkies on Christmas Eve. Bring Lauren.'

It occurred to Gabriel that his divorce solicitor was taking his burgeoning new relationship awfully well, considering it could technically be counted as adultery.

'I'll mention it to her, although I think she's heading back to see her family for Christmas,' he offered.

'And what about you? Will you be staying in these parts for the festive season?'

This was a question Gabriel had dreaded anybody asking him.

'Erm, probably,' he offered, his voice quietening. He didn't really want anybody here to know that both his parents had died the previous year. Within six months of each other, both from cancer. He had no siblings or grandparents, so his Christmas was currently looking remarkably quiet and lonely.

'Not going to see your family?' Anthea asked, raising an eyebrow.

'Don't really have any left. I was thinking I'd get a Christmas lunch from Marks and Spencer, I've heard they're very good…'

'YOU WILL DO NO SUCH THING!' Anthea boomed across the office, causing the receptionist's head to briefly look up from her computer screen. 'You will be coming round to ours for Christmas lunch. We will get very drunk. We will play filthy card games and you will laugh and open presents, whether you want to or not! Do. I. Make. Myself. Clear?!'

Gabriel was somewhat taken aback by this. It hadn't occurred to him that he had made any real friends in Porlington since moving here, let alone someone he was paying to remove Shelley from his life.

'I'm not sure I could impose…'

'One more word from you and I will be forced to bitch slap you right here in front of the entire waiting room.' Gabriel looked around and realised there was nobody waiting and the receptionist had returned to her screen, resuming her bored expression. It occurred to him that this perhaps wasn't the time to argue with the force of nature stood in front of him.

'I guess that would be okay…'

'Good. The aforementioned Christmas present of strange shape is for you, so it'd be a shame for you not to have it on the day itself.'

Gabriel's mind boggled and he suddenly became somewhat nervous.

'Right, sweetie. Come with me to my office, we have boring things to discuss before we can all kick back and forget all this rubbish before getting as fissed as a part and enjoying Christmas.'

167

With that, he was swept off to Anthea's office to discover what Shelley and her father had sent back.

They sat down and Anthea was suddenly all business.

'The good news is that we've had a response. The bad news is that they've decided to contest your case. The better news is that they have no idea what they're doing, and they've made stupid demands which probably work in your favour.'

Gabriel was unsure how to take any of this, but the only words that stayed in his head were 'bad news'.

'Sweetie, don't look so downcast; they've overplayed their hand and it works in your favour.'

He wasn't so sure.

'Can I ask what they've said..?' he asked.

'The long and the short of it is: they have countersued for divorce on grounds of unreasonable behaviour.'

Gabriel felt his stomach leap out of his body and land in a pathetic mess on the floor in front of him.

'But, honestly, don't worry about it. Their grounds are bordering on farcical. They have only provided two sets of grounds, when any self-respecting solicitor knows you need at least four, preferably five, in order to make something stick. It's also worth reminding you that nobody ever really sees the grounds for divorce—it doesn't matter whether you divorce her, she divorces you, or some third party calls for an annulment. The end result is the same, and because neither of you are celebrities, this isn't going to be picked over by the press.'

'Okay…' Gabriel heard himself saying. 'So why is she trying divorce me…?'

'Right, sweetie. Take a deep breath and get a hold of yourself. Like I said, it's nothing to worry about. Can you do that for me?'

Gabriel took a lungful of air. It didn't help. He exhaled and took another. Still nothing—his heart was racing just as much. After three more attempts, and a sudden desire for a very large single malt, he began to feel his heart rate stabilising. 'Okay. Hit me with it.'

'They (and I purposefully say "they" as Shelley won't have come up with this on her own) have provided two grounds to petition for divorce on the grounds of unreasonable behaviour. The first is (and I am quoting here) that you refused to take part in her life by never socialising with her and her friends.'

Gabriel heard a number of Anglo-Saxon expletives come out of his mouth and realised that he was standing and shouting at the top of his voice. Anthea waved him down.

'Woah there, Skippy. I know, I know. I KNOW! I'm just reading what's on this stupid piece of paper; don't shoot the messenger.'

Gabriel could barely believe that his adulterous whore of an ex-wife had attempted to level that against him. He knew he was swearing; he knew his face was flushed to the point of crimson; he knew he was approaching levels of stress more commonly associated with a heart attack or a stroke, but he didn't care.

'What do you MEAN, I didn't socialise?!' he screamed. 'First off, I was never invited! I tried for years to go out with her and her stupid friends, but they didn't like me and always wanted girls-only nights!'

Gabriel heard a woman screaming in a high-pitched voice in the same room and the realisation dawned on him that it was his own voice he was hearing. He attempted to calm it down. He failed.

'And as for the majority of her social activities, they usually involved her sleeping with other men, which, funnily enough, I was never invited along to!'

Anthea just sat at her desk and waited for him to run out of steam.

'Munchkin, I am fully aware of this, and I can quite assure you that none of this will hold up in court. We have a very solid case, which they do not. I'm anticipating that we can bat this into the grass before it even reaches a judge's ears. But in the meantime, please try to calm down as if you get much more highly-strung, you're going to burst and cause a blood-splatter all over my office carpet. Those things are a bugger to try and get out.'

Gabriel stared at the desk in front of him, quietly seething and trying to unclench his jaw. 'Okay, what's the second reason she's claiming?'

'Oh boy, here we go,' Anthea muttered under her breath. Gabriel was staring so intently at her desk that he didn't notice her rolling her eyes. 'They are saying that you were financially irresponsible.'

Anthea watched Gabriel carefully and realised that, whilst he was staying quiet, his fingernails were digging into the arms of his chair so hard that she anticipated she'd need to buy a new one after he left. She jumped in before he could say anything.

'Now, from what you've told me, she didn't particularly contribute anything to the marital assets. Her father may have, but my understanding is that he also charged you rent which could be considered above the going rate and he paid you minimum wage for what was effectively a managerial position.'

Gabriel looked up, his confusion briefly overriding his fury.

'I wouldn't exactly say I had a managerial position…'

'Don't split hairs. We're going to spin it that way. Their very brief outline is that you failed to bring sufficient income into the marriage (they don't mention she brought none) and your spending was out of control. Apparently, you bought a car that you didn't need and chose a deluxe sports model when you could have opted for something cheaper.'

The hysteria finally began to take hold of Gabriel and he started laughing out loud. Anthea decided this was healthier than him damaging her furniture so let it continue.

'I bought a Nissan Primera that was ten years old, purely as a run-around. It's in your car park at the moment. It's about the only thing I walked away with.' It was Gabriel's turn to roll his eyes.

'How much did you pay for it?'

'A little under two grand.'

'And for what purpose did you buy it?'

'To get to work and back each day. And for getting around.'

'Well, they're alleging that you could have used public transport to get to work, which would have been cheaper. Apparently there is a perfectly good bus service.'

Gabriel's eyebrows raised. He didn't feel he needed to say anything beyond this gesture.

'I know, my little chocolate orange. Any judge is going to laugh that one out. Just one question, what's this about it being a sports model?'

'It's a dCi model. That just means it's a fairly high-performance car in relation to the rest of the range. That's not why I bought it; Shelley was always telling me I drive like an old man. I bought the car purely because that was

171

what I could afford and that was what the local garage had available. I wanted a Japanese car because everybody says they're reliable and I thought it would save money down the line.'

'Seems reasonable to me. Can you confirm that spending the money you did on this car in no way affected your day-to-day lifestyle? You didn't have to shop at a cheaper supermarket for food? She didn't have to give anything up in order for the marital assets to be able to afford it?'

'Ha. You've clearly never met my ex-wife. She wouldn't give anything up even if somebody else's life depended on it.'

'Just answer the question, please.'

Gabriel was slightly taken aback at Anthea's business tone. 'I can confirm we had enough money in the bank at the time that we could afford it, and we could afford to run it. Nobody lost anything by me having a car to get to work instead of taking the number 19 bus.'

'Good. You're getting the hang of this. Out of interest, did she have a car?'

Gabriel laughed out loud. 'Yeah, she has a convertible Mercedes E Class. Three years old.'

Anthea looked up from her paperwork. 'I beg your pardon?'

'Daddy bought it for her. Cost him over twenty grand.'

Anthea became aware that her mouth was hanging open and quickly closed it. 'Right, I think we can deal with that aspect fairly promptly then. Were you on the insurance for that?'

'No, of course not! She insisted on being on the insurance for mine, which I had to pay for, but I was barely allowed to ride in her car, let alone drive it.'

'They're also alleging that you lived an extravagant lifestyle. There's a claim here that your wedding got so expensive, her father had to bail you out and pay for half of it.'

Gabriel was now feeling sufficiently numb that the farcical claims were just rolling over him with no effect. 'Hardly. I was quite happy to have a registry office wedding, but she insisted that we get married at Pewley Manor, because she regarded it as being a bit grander than where her maid of honour was married the year before. She talked her father into paying for half of it as it was apparently her dream wedding venue. I had to pay for my half, even though most of the guests were theirs. I'm still paying off the £15,000 loan.'

Anthea was scribbling furiously and Gabriel was sure he heard her mutter something highly uncharitable and somewhat Anglo-Saxon.

'I think that's everything I need at this stage. I've got your financial statement already from the previous paperwork, so I'm sure I can piece together a solid enough case that we can have both of these grounds thrown out. Even if I can't, I reckon a judge will rule against her petition and in favour of yours. The fact that she is trying to counter-sue for divorce means she is consenting to the divorce, which makes things easier. Of course, getting her to admit the adultery might be a challenge, but I think it's fair to say you will find yourself divorced from her pretty easily.'

Gabriel suddenly felt a wave of emotion wash over him. There was no sorrow at the breakdown of his marriage, just relief that it might soon be over.

'One last thing. Would you mind if I instructed a private investigator to look into a couple of financial

173

affairs on her part? It will cost a bit more, but I think it might help our case and expedite things. I'd say it would be no more than a couple of hundred quid.'

'Anything to get this over with quickly. Employ who you like,' he replied without a moment's hesitation.

'Great.' And with that, Anthea put her pen down in a decisive manner. 'Now, we'll see you on Christmas Eve and Christmas Day. Don't bring anything, you can't afford it. Don't forget I know how much you're worth. Or not. Don't worry, I won't breathe a word of it to Mr Sweeney. But we have more alcohol than a Scottish distillery. And I'll be cooking my famous prune-basted sausages.'

Gabriel began to question the wisdom of attending any event at which such a thing was on the menu.

'Pop round to ours for 7:30pm on Christmas Eve. Then stay. We have a spare room as the kids won't be arriving until Christmas morning.'

'Kids..?' Gabriel asked.

'Yes, Mr Sweeney's children. We're lucky this year, all seven of them will be with us for Christmas Day.'

Gabriel desperately tried not to react to this revelation and keep his face as passive as possible.

'Their mothers will be dropping them off sometime before midday, but it does mean that you can drink on Christmas Eve and not have to worry about driving your ludicrously expensive sports car back to your mansion whilst being over the limit. As your solicitor, I would have to frown on such a thing. You can stay in the red room. That one has a mini-bar. And we can discuss the next concert!'

Gabriel's stomach sank as this reminder brought him back to the real world, a place apparently far less intriguing than Anthea and Rupert's house.

'Oh, I'm not sure I'll want to do another concert.'

'Now don't make me bend you over my desk and spank you, Tiddles. We need you, and there isn't a person in that orchestra who wouldn't agree with that. Except possibly Sandra. But she doesn't count. Besides, how could you resist the opportunity to work with the Summerton Operatic and Dramatic Society?!'

'Beg pardon?'

'That's our next concert. A week run with them at the Summerton Empire. I believe it's *Hello Dolly!* this year. They're really very good. And they're even nuttier than the orchestra. You've got to take part, just for the comedy.'

And with that, Anthea stood and ushered him to the door, parting with a peck on the cheek. 'See you Christmas Eve. Wear a silly Christmas jumper.'

EIGHTEEN

CHRISTMAS CAME AND WENT WITHOUT MUCH TO report in Gabriel's life. As instructed by Anthea, he went over on Christmas Eve and stayed over through Christmas Day. In fact, he stayed until the 28th, as Rupert was very anxious he didn't miss a moment of excitement over the festive period. Towards the end of it, Gabriel found his feelings swung between wanting to get back to his dull and boring life in his flat and a longing to stay with people who were genuinely nice and appeared to understand him. Clearly, Stockholm Syndrome was setting in.

Anthea wasn't kidding about Rupert's seven children turning up on Christmas morning. Seven children by four different mothers appeared throughout the course of the morning and Christmas lunch was a very rowdy affair. Anthea kept looking at the youngest, who was seven, and saying, 'George, don't do that...' which conjured up images of Joyce Grenfell for the rest of the day. The child's name was actually Felicity.

Gabriel noticed the various pictures they had in their house and he was convinced Anthea and Rupert had been married for at least ten years judging by their ages in their wedding pictures. Which gave rise to wondering how he had a seven-year-old daughter. Discretion got the better part of valour, though, and he didn't ask. They appeared not to notice his somewhat confused looks throughout the day.

At 4pm, Christmas presents were exchanged. Gabriel felt slightly out of place during this as he hadn't really known what to bring, so had presented Rupert with three bottles of wine upon his arrival on Christmas Eve. This had apparently been an excellent choice, as Rupert kept referring to it during Gabriel's stay at Chateau Sweeney. Gabriel had anticipated staying from Christmas Eve until Boxing Day, so he thought a bottle of Rioja per day seemed appropriate. He'd completely forgotten about Anthea's warning of a strangely shaped present that was impossible to wrap until they were part-way through the present exchange with the children and Anthea produced said shapely present from under the enormous tree.

'There you go, my little Christmas Elf. Happy Christmas,' she said.

Gabriel immediately knew what the present was but went through the pretence of unwrapping it with a look of quizzical wonder. He tore the paper from the present and scrunched it up into a ball, throwing said detritus at Rupert's head (where it bounced off with a most satisfying thwack, landing in the middle of the room, along with all the paper already waiting there from where Rupert's children had done the same thing). He was left holding a boomerang.

'Erm, thanks. I don't know what to say,' he muttered in genuine bewilderment.

177

Rupert beamed at Gabriel. 'We saw it in a flea market a month or so ago and immediately thought of you.' Gabriel couldn't even begin to fathom why.

Anthea chimed in. 'Don't you think boomerangs are a great analogy for life?' Gabriel nodded as sagely as he could. 'Whatever you throw out into life will return to you,' she continued. 'If you throw out hatred, you'll get it back. But, if you're sensible and you throw out love and hope, you'll get that back many times over. I hope you realise just how much hope you've given the members of the orchestra by being willing to turn up each week. We really do appreciate your patience, Shnookums.' Gabriel thought this was both the most profound and ridiculous thing he had ever heard. As he looked down at the young faces beaming up at him, he wondered if they were all about to break into 'Edelweiss'. They did not, much to his relief.

Richard popped in later that afternoon. 'Can't stay, got to go meet a girl in a bit.' That didn't stop him staying until 11pm and thrashing everybody at both Cluedo and Monopoly. Gabriel wondered just how long his girl was waiting for him.

The children all departed on Boxing Day morning, with both Rupert and Anthea exclaiming, 'Thank God they're gone. Let's drink!' as the last departed at 1pm. Champagne flowed for the next few hours and by the time Gabriel returned to his flat on the 28th, he wasn't sure how much of the last few days he remembered accurately, or if any of it was real.

He did remember Anthea asking some very probing questions about his ex-wife. Whilst Rupert just nodded sagely from his favourite armchair, nursing a seemingly never-ending glass of single malt, Anthea's eyes bored into Gabriel as she peeled back the layers of his last few years with Shelley. He felt slightly protective of some of the memories, and he wasn't sure quite how much he should be saying to his divorce solicitor, lest he give her cause to worry that the separation was actually his fault, but he thought he had come through it fairly unscathed.

Lauren returned to Porlington on New Year's Eve and the two of them spent the night at hers. Despite having every intention of staying up to hear Big Ben chime midnight, they were in fact working their way through the Kama Sutra at the stroke of midnight and didn't notice the year had changed until they woke the following morning. At which point, it made no real impact on their lives and they went right back to the activities they'd been engaged in the previous night.

The first week of January passed by without incident. Lauren returned to school and Gabriel returned to Porlington Purgatory, as he had come to think of the music shop. The Kings had spent a thoroughly uneventful festive period sorting VAT and tax returns for HMRC. This was apparently the highlight of their year, according to Neil. Susan just smiled and nodded whilst passing Gabriel a cup of coffee more closely resembling dishwater and Grant buffed his nails with the new electric manicure set he had received for Christmas. Shame they couldn't have run to buying him an electric toothbrush as well, as his teeth appeared even more yellowed than Gabriel remembered, with his breath able to strip paint from a skirting board at a hundred paces.

January was Sale Season in the piano shop. During this period, prices above £1,000 were discounted by five whole pounds. Anything below this was not discounted, but signs were put up with a sale price that matched the

179

pre-Christmas price and a vastly inflated Recommended Retail Price above it. Gabriel was pretty sure this wasn't legal, but he didn't want to rock the boat so kept his opinion to himself.

In the second week of January, the Porlington Philharmonia started back. Gabriel had absolutely no intention of going, despite promising Anthea and Rupert that he would. Gabriel was hiding in his flat on the Thursday evening. This was his first mistake. At 6:30pm, there was a loud knock on the door. He couldn't understand why, as he never had any visitors and he knew Lauren was going to rehearsal. He opened the door with some trepidation.

'Hello, sweet pea. We thought you'd like a lift to rehearsal,' boomed Anthea. Gabriel saw Rupert sat in the driver's seat of their car on the opposite kerb, giving him two thumbs up, at which point he realised he wasn't going to get away with his cunning plan of hiding in obscurity.

'He... hello Anthea. What an unexpected surprise. You know the rehearsal is only round the corner and I can walk it, don't you..?'

'Yes, of course I do, sweetie. But we wanted to make sure you actually travelled the few hundred yards and made it along. Grab your baton (pardon the expression). It's time to go make music. Or whatever it is that the orchestra make.'

Gabriel attempted to put up a fight and point out that Michael wouldn't let him do anything, and he was still too embarrassed to show his face after the last concert.

'Of *course* Michael isn't going to let you do anything! Which is why you need to keep turning up until he realises he has to. And why are you worrying about the last concert? That wasn't a bad one, that was just a normal one. Haven't you learned that yet?!' She was doing nothing to assuage his concerns. 'Right, come along.' And with that, she headed back over to the car where they were clearly going to sit and wait for him.

Gabriel slipped on a pair of loafers, grabbed a jacket and his keys, and followed her over to the car, climbing into the back seat like a contortionist trying to avoid the cello and double bass sticking through the other back seat.

They turned up to the rehearsal before most people arrived. Betty Brannon was laying out the chairs in her usual peculiar fashion that made no sense. She grinned at them as they arrived. Doris and Gertie walked past, carrying the box with the tea things in. Doris' son David was already sat in his usual position in the viola section, whilst Betty laid out random chairs around him, most facing the wrong way. David stared at his music stand, studying the score on it in the most intense fashion. It was only when Gabriel walked past him to go to the back of the hall to move a stack of chairs so high they might have toppled onto poor Betty and crushed her that he realised David's music stand actually contained no music whatsoever.

Debbie Greer arrived shortly afterwards and was immediately in a blind panic trying to place everybody's music on their chairs. If only the chairs were in the correct places.

Eventually, Sandra and Michael breezed through the doors. 'Oh, dear God, is it that time of year again? Must we really be subjected to musical theatre once more?' Michael yelled as he walked up the aisle of the church, with Sandra running behind him, laden down with conductor scores, a violin, a ludicrously oversized handbag and a scowl so fierce it could have stopped the Zulu army in their tracks at Rorke's Drift.

'Michael, you know that this is the biggest source of income we have each year, so we're stuck with it, no matter how much it may offend your musical sensibilities,' Sandra was heard to hiss through gritted teeth.

Anthea piped up, 'You know, if you don't want to conduct it, you could always let Gabriel do this one. Have a few weeks off. Go on holiday. Get some sun. God knows you could use it.'

A silence descended within the church as every eye turned towards Anthea, who showed no signs of backing down from her statement. Rupert's jaw dropped open, although Gabriel wasn't sure if that was in horror at what his wife had just said or in wonder at the fine figure of Richard, who had just walked through the door, his double bass perched on his back.

Michael pretended not to notice and continued muttering under his breath, whilst Sandra glared daggers at Anthea, who just returned the stare with an enigmatic smile.

Gabriel loitered near the conductor podium which Debbie had erected, waiting to hear what instructions Michael might give him. This was to no avail, as Michael and Sandra both ignored him as though he wasn't even in the room. At 7:31pm precisely, Michael began his pre-rehearsal ritual of breathing and snorting, with ludicrous arm movements, announcing shortly afterwards to the orchestra who were present that the Witching Hour had once again returned, and it was the time of year when they must endure such frivolities as musical theatre. He assured them he had made a formal complaint to the Lord

Chamberlain's office. Gabriel was pretty sure this would have very little sway as the legislation that empowered the Lord Chamberlain over performances had been revoked by an Act of Parliament in 1967 and, as they were outside of London, he would have no jurisdiction anyway.

Gabriel quickly realised that he was nothing more than wallpaper this evening, and he found a seat in the seventh row back, resigned to the fact that all he would achieve this evening would be reading the sarcastic comments from the percussion section on Facebook.

Michael struck up the opening chords of the overture and things went downhill from there. They spent the entire second half of the rehearsal playing through 'Before the Parade Passes By', and it occurred to Gabriel that at the rate the parade was passing, it would be some years hence before it passed by. He hunkered down, pulled out his phone and started a new level on the latest incarnation of Angry Birds, longing for the time to pass so that he could escape to the pub with Anthea, Rupert and a few other like-minded victims of this evening's particularly brutal brand of torture.

NINETEEN

SEVERAL WEEKS LATER AND IT WAS TIME FOR THE Porlington Philharmonia to have a joint rehearsal with the Summerton Operatic and Dramatic Society, two weeks before show week.

Gabriel arrived 15 minutes early and was somewhat taken aback to find a huge melee of people clogging up the Methodist church hall. There was shouting, there was swearing, there were knowing looks passing between the newcomers and certain members of the orchestra (this was the first time Gabriel had ever seen Henry James turn up before him). And there was a cacophony so loud that Sandra's pleas for everyone to quieten down were completely lost in the maelstrom of sound engulfing the hall.

There were singers hitting ludicrously high notes (that really didn't suit them), other singers making sounds like air raid sirens or singing 'brr' at various pitches, with other random people doing lunges and stretches in between the rows of chairs. Gabriel couldn't quite work out what this would achieve for a singing rehearsal but kept his opinion to himself.

At 7:30pm, Michael took to the podium and began his little ballet routine. Not a single eye in the building was on him with the sole exception of Gabriel, who observed that this was utterly pitiful. As Michael reached the end of his movements, he entered back into the real world to discover that he had absolutely no attention whatsoever. He attempted to call for order, to no avail. Sandra was going ever redder in the face with her barking for people to be quiet, with similar effect. Anthea caught Gabriel's eye and just stared, with eyes as dead as a shark, the left one slowly going cross-eyed. Rupert was staring at Richard, who was leaning against a wall and ever closer to a young soprano who was foolishly giggling at him.

Gabriel gradually became aware of a horrible, high-pitched sound that was grating on him, but was ever so slightly evading his consciousness. As his eyes searched around the room for where such a ghastly noise was coming from, he noticed several other people reacting to it and covering their ears in bewilderment. Eventually, a hush fell over the room as the most hideously produced Queen of the Night top F continued to waver and warble throughout the skulls of all those present.

Once total silence and confusion had been achieved, Betty Brannon closed her mouth and stopped the godawful noise that had been emitting from it. She took her seat in the second violins and beamed her gormless grin at Michael, apparently very pleased with herself that she had achieved the quiet within the room that nobody else had managed. Whilst various older members of the orchestra looked impressed, any soprano from amongst the singers just glowered in Betty's general direction with scowls aplenty.

Michael took his opportunity. 'Good evening, you lovely people, and might I say how pleased we are to have you all here tonight.' Both Michael's and Sandra's faces said otherwise. 'We do so look forward each year to working with you and...' He continued into a soliloquy worthy of Hamlet in its length, even managing to use 'Words, words, words,' during it. He summed up using the words, '...after all, all the world's a stage...' and Gabriel was genuinely concerned that after nearly fifteen minutes of drivel, Michael was going to launch into the entire Seven Ages of Man monologue from 'As You Like It'. Mercifully, he didn't. He was just winding down (Gabriel presumed, although he couldn't be sure), when a spritely man in his early fifties jumped up to wrest the limelight from Michael.

'And we're all delighted to be here to work alongside such an esteemed and experienced orchestra!' Gabriel caught the implied hint that this man meant 'old' when he said 'experienced'. He chuckled to himself in the back row of very uncomfortable Methodist chairs.

'For those of you who haven't met me before, I am Fabian Angelo, director and producer of the Summerton Operatic and Dramatic Society.' The orchestra looked utterly unimpressed. The singers sat bolt upright and applauded. The percussion section rolled their eyes and all reached for their phones to write something offensive on social media. Gabriel found himself reaching for his phone to see what this might be.

'We have been toiling hard for the last few months,' Fabian continued, with Gabriel wondering who on earth used the word 'toiling' in this day and age. 'We have sweated blood, sweat and tears...' Again, Gabriel considered whether anybody in the last hundred years had actually sweated blood or tears. Sweating sweat seemed to go without saying, but surely one couldn't ooze any other bodily fluid from sweat glands. 'We have risked life and limb in the dance routines...' Gabriel scanned the singers and decided the only risk in the dance routines would be that their enormous frames would hit the stage with such force in the event of a trip that the inertia was likely to break bones. 'We have lived and breathed this production...' Gabriel thought they all looked highly unlikely to be breathing for much longer due to either old age, stupidity or their clear consumption of forty cigarettes a day. 'And we have found ourselves here. At the orchestra call, with our dear friends from the Porlington Philharmonic.'

'Philhar*monia*,' hissed Sandra from the leader's position. Fabian's concentration was interrupted just long enough for Michael to take control again.

'So, without any further ado, shall we begin with the Overture?' Michael asked. Suddenly there was a huge crash at the back of the church. Gabriel jumped as this sound was next to him.

'Sorry, everyone! SORRY!' Menopausal Megan yelled as she breezed past the pile of chairs she had knocked over on her way in, arms laden with a horn case and a pile of at least seven ballgown bags, two of which were open with sequined dresses falling out of them, causing her to trip again several times as she fought her way up the aisle.

'Hello Roxie. How are you, darling?' Megan had stopped at two somewhat diminutive sopranos in the front row of chairs. Gabriel had somehow missed these two on his earlier scans of the room.

'Megan! Darrrrrrling!' one of them purred before standing up to hug her (Megan had to bend down a

187

considerable way). Kisses were exchanged on both cheeks before Megan leaned over Roxie (and almost landing in her lap due to the inertia of the items she was carrying) to kiss Roxie's compatriot.

'Morag, how lovely to see you.'

'Hou's it gaun?' came back the reply in a thick Scottish accent.

'Very well, thanks. How are my favourite two tiny sopranos?'

'Guid gear comes in sma' bulk.'

Gabriel was now completely confused.

'Roxie, thank you so much for lending me these dresses. They've all been dry cleaned.' And dragged up the Methodist Church Hall floor, Gabriel thought to himself.

'Not a problem, mon cherie. Did they do the trick with your gentleman friend?' With this statement, the entire brass section sat bolt upright, as did those woodwinds who were still awake.

'Well, he certainly noticed me when Tarquin and I took second place with our foxtrot!'

Roxie's eyes flared and the slightest pout appeared on her lips as she purred, 'Marvellous. I hope you left him wanting more?'

'Megan! Will you please stop interrupting my rehearsal and take your place in the horn section!' bellowed Michael. Sandra nodded furiously, glowering at the frivolity taking place before her.

'Sorry, Michael, I'll just head over…' Megan mumbled before crashing her way through the violins to reach her colleagues, all of whom looked fit to burst with questions.

Michael suddenly noticed Roxie was slowly turning towards him in the most passive-aggressively threatening manner. Her eyes locked on to his, her apparently calm demeanour clearly bristling with indignance at being told what to do. She stopped turning, hands firmly on her hips, just holding Michael's gaze until he broke and twisted round in a fluster to stare at his music stand, clearly feeling he had somehow just been scolded in front of all his friends without a word even being said.

'God, I love it when this lot turn up and keep that pompous ass in his place.' Doris had taken up residence in the seat next to Gabriel.

'Who are those two?' Gabriel asked under his breath, looking at Roxie and Morag.

'The dark haired one is Roxanne von Klausen, Countess of somewhere on the continent. Soprano. Firebrand. And cooler than Marlene Dietrich.' Gabriel could believe it. She was wearing a leopard-print fur coat that he had assumed was fake, but now upon closer inspection he began to wonder if it was actual leopard. She had jet black hair, with a pure white shock through the centre, and he could picture her stood in repose holding a cigarette in a holder. It took a brave woman to wear six-inch heels when one's calves were probably only ten inches.

'Countess...?' he enquired.

'Her third (and most recent) husband was some minor European nobility. He died last year. There was some suspicion as he hadn't been ill but was found dead in the kitchen by their maid. Nobody could ever prove anything. People talk though, especially as her previous two husbands (who had also been filthy rich) had both died.' Gabriel felt his eyebrows lifting in shock.

'Her friend is Morag McMondrian. She's Scottish. Don't expect to understand a word she says.' Gabriel's

189

gaze shifted to the similarly short woman who beamed in a manner so excitable it put him in mind of Tigger, due to her somewhat manic rocking back and forth. Or a Jack Russell, on account of her very fast breathing.

Michael struck up the overture. It did not go well. The singers got fidgety as this required none of them and the orchestra looked confused at Michael's tempo choices. When it eventually ground to a halt after three minutes, Fabian turned to the two nearest people, who happened to be Roxie and Morag. 'I've just realised that I've left all the flyers for the performance in my car. Ladies, would you mind running out and bringing them in?' He flung his keys in their general direction, landing them in Morag's lap more by chance than aim. They both looked at him with that special disdain sopranos save for when they glare at a conductor or director.

'Couldn't the tenors do it?' Roxanne asked in an almost inaudible hiss.

'They're not here yet, you know what they're like,' came back the reply, before Fabian glanced around the gathered thespians. 'Kate, you're up. Would you care to take your place here at the front?'

A figure moved serenely from her place in the seats towards the podium. Her cleavage reached the spot Fabian was indicating some time before the rest of her body.

Kate Staggs was in her mid-thirties and had long since left the West End for a quiet life in the country with her husband. She had been in a few minor productions in London and been in the chorus for Les Misérables for a whole year. Opinion was divided on whether she had left because she wasn't getting the lead roles, or because she had fallen madly in love with Jeremy, her husband, who was in middle management in banking. Pretty much everybody thought it was the former.

Fabian continued, 'Ladies and gentlemen, our Dolly!' There was a mixed round of applause, split between genuine excitement from the lower ranks of the altos, genuine hatred from the other sopranos who had been beaten to the role by this young thing, and genuine testosterone from both the straight men in the society. The orchestra just sat passively, waiting for the excitement to pass. They didn't understand excitement.

As Roxanne passed by the back row, Gabriel heard her mutter under her breath, 'It should have been *me...*'

Kate looked slightly perturbed at the front. 'Jess? Jess! Bring my ginger shot.' A slight girl appeared, rummaging in a large handbag whilst scurrying to the front. She produced a small flask and handed it to Kate, who took several sips before handing it back and waving her away.

Michael started the next number and Gabriel was shocked to hear the volume with which the assembled singers burst into, 'CALL! ON! DOLLY!' Fabian leapt to his feet and stopped the song.

'People! People! We've been over this! It's supposed to be collar vose.'

Sandra piped up, her voice dripping with feigned sagacity, 'Surely you mean colla voce, pronounced "voh-chay"..?'

Fabian looked confused. 'No, collar vose, that's what it says here in the script.' Sandra rolled her eyes and was about to continue her attempt at belittling Fabian when Michael thundered back into the start of the number, clearly irritated at having been stopped.

The chorus quietened down a touch.

191

'call. on. dolly. she's the one the spinsters recommend…'

This continued for about 60 bars before they finished with, 'Call. On…'

Kate leapt into action. 'Dolly Levi, born Gallagher—Social introductions!' Gabriel was impressed at both the American accent and the verve with which the lines were delivered. The interplay between Dolly's dialogue and the chorus' singing continued for the rest of the number until Kate launched into her next song, 'I Put My Hand In'.

'You can put your hand wherever you like, love,' piped up a distant voice from the trumpet section. Nobody could quite pinpoint who had said it, but Henry James' grin was something of a giveaway. Kate rolled her eyes and continued.

The rehearsal continued along at a snail's pace for several more hours, with Gabriel's will to live slowly oozing into the heating grill running up the central aisle. There was a brief moment of light relief during the title track 'Hello Dolly', when the moment for the high kick routine arrived and several of the middle-aged men thought this would be a good time to attempt the dance routine in the rather cramped confines of a church aisle.

As with all amateur operatic societies, there were several middle-aged men whose attested sexuality was somewhat questionable, all of whom were over the hill, all of whom had combovers, all of whom were podgy at best and none of whom could sing, act or dance. It was this particular group who decided to give the high kicks a go. As the rest of the chorus thundered through, 'It's so nice to have you back where you beloooooooong,', these unfortunate individuals hurled themselves into step, kick, step, kick, step, KICK!

There were a number of thuds, yelps and one particularly high-pitched scream that made Roxie and Morag look up to see who was hitting a higher note than them. One man had split his jeans right from the belt to under the crotch. Another had kicked a chair so hard he would have to visit Porlington District Hospital later that night for an x-ray and the unfortunate news his foot was broken (not that this would stop him going on stage and doing the high-kick routine in an airboot two weeks later) and a third had kicked so high that he had lost his balance, fallen backwards and cracked his head on a cello, causing its strings to ping in every direction as the bridge gave way. The owner of said cello looked like she was going to finish the job and stab the wannabe chorus girl (guy…) through the heart with the spike on the end of her instrument.

Michael was utterly oblivious to this and continued to conduct the number. It was unfortunate that he was attempting to conduct a piece of music written in four-four time in three-four, but it was also apparent to Gabriel that not one of the orchestra was watching him so it made not a jot of difference to the overall effect.

As the evening turned into night and 11:30pm approached, various members of the orchestra gave up, leaving their seats to pack their instruments up as everybody else continued. Gabriel guessed quite a few of them would have to get back to their care homes in the hope of receiving a belated 10pm Horlicks, whilst others probably had to leave the sight of other humans before turning back into pumpkins or mice as midnight loomed. The assembled group finally reached the closing chords and Michael and Fabian looked respectively triumphant in their somewhat mediocre achievements. A muted round of applause burst forth from the singers, aimed entirely at themselves and not the orchestra, mostly out of relief that the rehearsal was at an end and they had survived.

Gabriel was seriously worried he had put down roots into the chair he hadn't left for several hours, but briefly forgot this life-altering concern as he heard the comments from people filing past him in search of the exit and their beds.

'Honestly, Morag, that was painful. Thank God I had the foresight to bring that hip flask of gin,' Roxie said in a surprisingly loud voice.

'Tatties o'wer the side. Yer aywis at the coo's tail,' came back the reply.

'Jess! JESS! Have you picked up my bag and put my score in it?' called Kate over her shoulder. Jess didn't reply, she just ran along in Kate's wake, clutching a crazily oversized handbag and making a stabbing motion behind Kate's back that would have made Norman Bates proud.

'Ladies! I'm going to hit Mickey's Club, anyone want to join me...?' Henry called as he scurried after Kate and Jess, his tongue hanging out in a fashion reminiscent of Scooby-Doo. Neither of them acknowledged that they had heard him.

The percussion section started pushing instruments down the aisle, accompanied by various disgruntled utterances, mostly along the lines of, 'What the hell was all that about and why are we still here...?'

'Hello dewdrop. Did you enjoy that?' Gabriel suddenly realised that comment was aimed at him and he snapped back to consciousness, trying to kick his brain back into gear in order to think of an appropriate response to Anthea, who was still staring at him. All he managed was a mumble that made him sound like he had had a stroke somewhere in Act 2.

'Yup, me too. Come along Rupert, the cat needs to be taken for a walk before bed and you know that you don't put his lead on tight enough when you're tired.' Rupert's attention was wrestled away from Richard with a start.

'Yes, dear...'

'Can't stop, got to go meet a girl in the park,' Richard beamed as he ploughed his way through the bodies, heading back to his tiny car with his double bass slung across his back.

Eventually, Lauren and Jane reached Gabriel as the procession meandered along.

'Seriously, if that woman says one more thing to me...' Jane scowled.

'Honestly, I wouldn't take it to heart. But if it's upsetting you that much, why don't you have a word with her? It can't do any harm, and it might make things easier,' Lauren replied, seeming somewhat flustered.

'I've tried! She's just so stubborn! I've learned after all these years just to ignore it; she's never going to change.'

'Well, if you think that's best. Although it does seem really unfair, how she talks to you. Your bowing wasn't off, you were following what she had written in the score; I'm sure it was her that got it wrong, but then she had to blame somebody. Oh, hello Gabriel.'

Gabriel wasn't sure how to respond, as any words on his part would interrupt the flow of their conversation. 'Erm, hi. Did you enjoy that?'

'Of course not, boy! It was excruciating!' Jane barked back at him, before storming out of the church, her violin clutched so hard that her fingers were turning white.

195

'Don't worry about her, she's just crotchety because Sandra is mean to her,' Lauren explained. 'Do you want to come back to mine? I can't promise anything fun, but I like waking up with you next to me.'

Gabriel jumped at the chance and followed her through the door.

TWENTY

AFORTNIGHT LATER AND SHOW WEEK ARRIVED. Gabriel found himself in the Summerton Pavilions, questioning how such a grand title could represent a venue that really didn't live up to the promise of its name. The 600-seater theatre had clearly been designed for Victorian music hall, and apparently still displayed its original wallpaper, steeped with years of tobacco smoke, sweat and disappointment. The front of the orchestra pit had been taken out in order to fit the Philharmonia, meaning at least 100 seats had been removed and the orchestra were in full view.

Gabriel still had no function within this production, so he sat in the auditorium questioning why he was there during the first half of the tech rehearsal on Tuesday 13th February, watching what was going on. By the interval, his ears were ringing from the godawful sound coming from the orchestra; without the pit wall to contain the sound, the decibel volume was at a level somewhat akin to that of a full set of four Boeing 747 engines roaring at maximum, waiting for take-off, with about the same level of musicality. The chorus were utterly obliterated (although this was a small mercy). Principal characters were only heard because the very strange tech guy, Anthony, cranked their microphones up to stadium volume. Fabian sat in the middle of the third row, with a makeshift desk in front of him, adorned with angle-poise lights and enough sheets of paper to cover one wall of the theatre. Every 93 seconds, he would bark something at the cast, who summarily ignored him.

The cast didn't know their lines, chorus members jostled to the front in an attempt to hog the limelight, and Anthony constantly wandered around the stage, tweaking microphones and looking at lights to see if their brightness was correct from the performer perspective. Of course, this meant nobody was manning either the sound or lighting desks, resulting in both aspects being disastrously wrong.

Everyone was given a ten-minute break at the point where the interval would occur and Gabriel walked up to the orchestra to chat with Anthea and Rupert. As he was saying hello and about to express his diminishing will to live, the side doors burst open and twenty children poured into the auditorium, all screaming and running around like banshees.

'Ah, the little sods are here,' Anthea exclaimed, beaming at them. Gabriel recognised at least two of them as being Rupert's progeny. 'Hello, little sods!' Anthea cried at the top of her voice, waving furiously. Several of them waved back before going back to running around and screaming at nobody in particular.

Gabriel stared at Anthea in horror. 'Why on earth would you yell that at them?!' he asked.

'Yell what, my little Devonshire cream tea?'

'You just called them…' His voice dropped to a *sotto voce* the chorus were incapable of achieving. '…*little sods.*'

'Well that's what they are.'

'That doesn't mean you should call them that to their faces!' Gabriel's bewilderment was plastered all over his face.

'Why not? That's their name. Summerton Operatic and Dramatic Society is SODS. Their youth branch, who are joining in as penguin-style waiters in the title track in act two, are known as the Little SODS. They've been called that for years. The Charity Commission didn't even bat an eyelid when we submitted the application.'

Gabriel just stared in despair. Thankfully, his bewilderment was masked by Megan making her usual subtle entrance.

'Sorry! Sorry! Mad woman coming through! Have I missed much? I've got some great news!'

Sandra appeared from thin air. 'You've missed the whole of Act One! Nobody cares about your news. How on earth do you expect Michael to hold a rehearsal together when you can't be bothered to turn up and play?! I'm going to be suggesting to the committee that we choose another principal horn at the earliest opportunity as you are clearly utterly unreliable.' The other three horn players (who were still in their seats and listening to every word) bolted upright like meerkats, all shaking their heads furiously, clearly horrified at this suggestion.

Jane leapt from her seat and finally snapped, after weeks of tension building between her and Sandra. 'Oh for God's sake, woman! Why do you have to be such a bitch all the time? Megan told both you and Michael weeks ago that she would be late tonight, as she was in a ballroom competition. I heard her tell you both at the end of a rehearsal.' The assembled people within earshot looked back at Megan and realised she was in a very

199

skimpy outfit which appeared to be made only of red and silver sequins. Nobody noticed the most sparkling item on her as they were all transfixed by her bottom lip quivering and a single tear beginning to climb down over her right cheek.

Roxie and Morag had come over to see what the fuss was about.

'Did the dress make you feel like a princess, darling?' Roxie purred, desperately attempting to change the topic of conversation and defuse the situation. 'You look amazing. Did Graham like it?'

Sandra was about to interrupt to tell her that nobody cared when Morag glowered in her direction in a way that only the diminutive Scots can, slowly waving a tightly-balled fist, white with fury. 'Dinnae een think aboot it…' Sandra backed down as a cry burst out of Megan, who attempted to speak in between sobs and snorts.

'Tarquin and I… came first in the… foxtrot… He was so pleased that he… ran off to call his boyfriend and tell him. I was stood there all all… alone… when Graham came over and said I was the most…' There was a long pause as Megan's face scrunched up into a tight ball, going red and blotchy as more tears squirted from underneath her eyelids. '…the most beautiful woman he had ever known.' Gabriel thought that Graham had clearly never seen Megan crying, but decided not to mention this. 'And he got down on… one knee and… asked me to… ma…' At this point, her voice passed into territory where only dogs or dolphins could understand her, but she held up her left hand to show the enormous rock on her ring finger.

As one (with the exception of Sandra), all those gathered around cheered and grabbed Megan in the biggest group hug the Summerton Pavilions had ever known. Morag was sobbing, with snot pouring out of her nose. This didn't stop her landing a subtle (but painful) kick on Sandra's left shin as she hurried past her, knowing she would never be identified as the culprit in such a crowd. Rupert's shoulders were rocking back and forth and Anthea beamed a smile so bright it could have been used to search the skies during the Blitz. The other three horn players scurried forth to congratulate their leader, all eager to claim the 'minion of the month' title.

Sandra decided she didn't have a hope of getting any further with her previous argument (which she still considered to be far more important than some trifling engagement) and slipped away from the group. As she did so, she caught Roxie staring at her with eyes so dead they could have belonged to a shark. 'I know how to deal with people like you…' Roxie silently mouthed, before turning back and calling at the top of her voice, 'Megan, my darling, this calls for champagne! I shall have a bottle sent over immediately!'

Sandra skulked off to find Michael, in the hope that they could begin Act Two shortly and end this madness. She found him outside a fire exit in a heated debate with his wife, who Sandra hadn't even realised was going to be present tonight.

'For God's sake, woman, I've told you before, I'll be out as late as I need to be! Oh, hello darling.' Michael smiled at Sandra, who glossed over this greeting out of good manners.

'Hello, Elizabeth. How lovely to see you. I didn't know you were joining us this evening.'

'Aren't I allowed to come and see my own husband?' came back the curt reply.

Sandra was somewhat flustered. 'Well, of course… It's so nice to have you here with us. Will you be staying all evening?'

'I'll stay as long as I damn well want!'

'So will I!' boomed Michael. 'If I end up here into the wee small hours of the morning then I shall stay, because that is what the music demands!'

Both women said the same thing in unison. 'For God's sake, Michael, will you take your blood pressure pills?!' A silence so awkward it was practically palpable descended over the trio. Elizabeth stormed off in a silent rage. Michael and Sandra walked back into the auditorium, when they were confronted with Fabian.

'Michael! Maestro! Isn't it going so *well*?!' he enthused. 'I've just given the cast their notes and I can promise you there won't be the same cockups there were in Act One! Wouldn't want you thinking we weren't professional!' Both Michael and Sandra were dying to tell this jumped-up idiot that the SODS weren't professional, at least not as much as the orchestra, but they somehow bit their tongues. 'Are we ready to proceed with the rest of the show? Kate has to get back to relieve her babysitter and we can't very well carry on without our Dolly, can we?!'

Michael stared back at Fabian, wondering how on earth his life had brought him to this point. 'Of course. We'll carry on right now.'

Sandra thought better of mentioning the furore currently engulfing the orchestra with news of Menopausal Megan's impending nuptials. On this occasion, she was happy to let him walk obliviously into the lion's den. She watched as he marched up to the podium, unsure as to why he was so agitated or why Elizabeth had seemed so scathing towards them both. She had known about the affair since shortly after it began all those years ago, and happily released him every Thursday and Friday, probably glad of the break from him. It couldn't be that.

Michael arrived near the podium but couldn't quite reach it because of all the people crowding round Megan, who was still crying, although the tears now looked substantially happier than they had earlier. She also appeared to be holding a glass of champagne, as did Roxie, Morag, Anthea, Rupert, Richard and several others. Sandra wondered from afar how on earth Roxie had managed to summon not just several bottles of champagne in only a few minutes, but the flute glasses to go with them.

'Right! Act Two!' boomed Michael, trying in vain to push his way through the throng of people between him and his podium. This proved utterly unsuccessful as the orchestra had had many years of practice at ignoring him. 'Could we please...? Sorry. Excuse me... Can I just get through...? WHAT THE HELL IS GOING ON?!' he yelled, with no discernible effect whatsoever.

Suddenly, a voice came over the speaker system. 'Ladies and gentlemen, this is your stage manager. Please could you take your positions for the start of Act Two. Miss Staggs to the stage, please. Miss Staggs to the stage. Also, Cornelius, Barnaby, Mrs M. and Minnie to the stage. Act Two beginners to the stage. Act Two beginners.' Every eye swung to the sound and lighting desk at the back of the auditorium, where Anthony was putting a microphone back down, before checking both lighting and sound cues. Nobody seemed to notice he was doing the job of seven people. And nor did they care.

Megan slipped away from the crowd and took up her seat in the horn section whilst Roxie and Morag gathered all the champagne glasses and cheekily drained them before handing them back to a man in morning dress with a picnic hamper who could only be assumed to be Roxie's butler.

TWENTY-ONE

O PENING NIGHT CAME AND WENT WITH LITTLE incident. As opening nights go, it was average. At least 70% of the lines were not just remembered, but delivered. Mostly in the right places. The orchestra weren't terrible, at least in their minds, although several people in the front few rows didn't return for Act Two and booked hearing check-ups within a week or two.

Gabriel found himself loitering near the sound desk just before the performance started as there were no seats left for him to perch in (how on earth every seat sold out for these shows still baffled him), when Anthony called him over to the sound desk.

'Are you something to do with the orchestra?' he asked, his eyes searching for any point in the room on which to fix that didn't cause actual eye contact with another human being.

'Yes, I'm the assistant conductor.'

'What does that mean?'

'Absolutely nothing, as Michael won't let me do anything.' There was a brief pause, then they both laughed. At least, Gabriel thought Anthony had laughed; what he actually heard were several sharp intakes of

205

breath causing his vocal cords to vibrate in a strange manner at a strange pitch. It was laughing or an asthma attack, and he wasn't reaching for an inhaler.

'So you have nothing to do in this performance then?'

'Nope. Or any other performance this week.'

'Would you mind being stage manager?'

The question threw Gabriel into confusion. 'Isn't there already a stage manager?'

'Yes. Me. But I'm also technical manager, lighting person, sound person and about five other things.'

'What exactly does it entail?' Gabriel asked. 'I've not got much experience of this sort of thing.'

'Don't worry, there's not much to do. The cast always want to be on stage, so nobody is willing to be backstage crew. Fabian makes them do their own scene changes as they leave or enter the stage because of this, so you don't have to worry about that. We don't need anybody to call the show as there's only me to call instructions to and I know what I'm doing. What I really need is someone backstage on a set of cans that I can give instructions to when I can see something is going wrong.'

'Okay, that sounds easy enough,' Gabriel said, with some trepidation.

'Oh, and you need to join in the tap dance routine in Act Two. Don't worry, just follow the Little SODS and wing it.'

Gabriel went white and felt his stomach sink several inches.

'I'm kidding. There's no tap dancing. Just the ballet number.' Another long pause. 'Seriously, you musicians can't take a joke, can you?'

Gabriel laughed nervously. 'Erm, what are cans?'

206

'Sorry, theatrespeak. Headphones. There's a set back there on stage left.'

'Stage left..?'

'Instructions are from the performer perspective. Stage left or stage right are left and right as you stand on the stage looking out at the audience. Most stages are on a rake—that's an angle—towards the audience. The easy way to remember upstage and downstage is if you roll a ball from the back of the stage, it will roll down towards the audience. Make sense?'

'I think so…'

'Great. There's a little booth on stage left—you can get to it through that door over there to the right.' Gabriel was getting more confused by the moment. 'Just sit in there, pop the cans on and wait for me to tell you what to do. The first thing will be to open the curtains at the end of the Overture.'

'Isn't somebody already doing that?!'

'Yes. Me. I'm supposed to wind the curtain mechanism, then shoot through that door and run back here without the audience noticing. Then do the same thing at the end of Act One, start of Act Two, end of Act Two, and so on.'

'I'm beginning to see your problem,' said Gabriel, feeling a newfound sympathy towards this odd little fellow. 'Yeah, sure, I'll give it a go. Although I apologise now for all the things I'll get wrong.'

'Some things going wrong with more things going right creates a better scenario than nothing happening at all. You're doing me a huge favour here. Now, pop through that door, stick the cans on and wait for my instructions. There's a button on the side of them. If you press it, you can talk to me through the mouthpiece that's attached. Please don't, though. I've still got rather a lot to do.'

That was how Gabriel found himself being stage manager for a medium-sized production of Hello, Dolly! with less than two minutes warning before opening night began. His biggest disappointment was that he couldn't see Lauren from side-stage.

His duties on opening night were fairly limited to turning the lever as fast as he could manage to open or close the main curtains. As the week progressed, he learned how to open and close tabs on demand, fly hemp bars in and out, drift onto stage pretending to be part of the action to pick up props that had been dropped and left, hand inhalers to people when they thought the stage haze was making them asthmatic (despite it being medically certified as completely safe even for someone with the worst case of emphysema), help numerous beautiful women out of their costumes side stage and into new ones (whilst learning the hard way that amateur actresses apparently don't wear bras or, in some cases, knickers) and in one rather unfortunate case, how to free a man's left testicle from his rather enthusiastically closed zipper while a butch alto held her hand over said man's mouth to stop him screaming as the zipper tore both itself and a two-inch section of his scrotum open.

The show got better as the week progressed, although the orchestra still sounded pretty terrible to Gabriel's ears. Presents poured in for Megan each night, although there was still a weird atmosphere with Michael and Sandra, who appeared to be barely speaking. This probably wasn't helped by Elizabeth insisting on turning up to every performance and whisking Michael away as soon as they ended.

What didn't get better throughout the week was Gabriel's sense of self-esteem. Lauren hadn't invited him over once during the week, or come over to his flat. In fact, they had barely spoken. She appeared to be fine with him when they spoke, and he was putting the lack of contact down to a stressful week at work coupled with no time for herself due to being out every night playing the violin for the show. Gabriel accepted this, although he really didn't like it.

During the interval on the Friday evening performance, Anthea ventured backstage. 'Hello Gabriel. Can I have a moment?' He immediately knew there was a problem as she had used his name.

'Okay...?'

'Do you still have your ex-wife as a friend on Facebook, or do you have any mutual friends?'

'No, of course not. I deleted her ages ago and you know that we had very different social circles.'

Anthea paused and took a breath. 'Okay. Can you pop in for a chat next week sometime?'

'Of course, but is there a problem? You've got me worried now.'

'Not at all, my dear,' she said, placing a hand on his arm and smiling what appeared to be a genuine smile. 'There might have been a development in the case that works in your favour, but I don't want to get into it now, we've both got enough to be dealing with. But don't fret, it's good news.' And with that, she was gone.

Despite being distracted by this news, Gabriel got through the rest of the Friday performance, with Anthony giving him instructions through his headphones. He found it amusing that Anthony kept forgetting he was on a live microphone the whole time and Gabriel heard every comment he passed about the cast, the state of their singing, the quality of their costumes, the approximate size of their busts (not limited to female members of the cast) and various other little nuggets that fell out of Anthony's mouth under his breath. He was also acutely aware of the mounting tension amongst the orchestra, with various people no longer speaking or even looking at one another.

Things finally came to a head after the Saturday matinee. The cast, orchestra and crew (the latter constituting Anthony and Gabriel) were all crammed into a small room backstage to eat their sandwiches. Kate was sipping ginger and lemon water through a straw from an infuser flask which Jess was holding for her. Roxie had a hamper crammed full of champagne, caviar and foie gras which she was sharing with Morag, whilst Megan sat in another corner, munching on a Tupperware container filled with carrot sticks (her absolute favourite foodstuff) and humus, chatting to a large number of women 'of a certain age' about how she had laughed her way through the menopause, when there was an almighty crash as a chair hurtled to the floor. Every eye flew over to see Sandra glaring daggers at Michael, her lips pursed so tightly they were white and her fists shaking in rage at her side. Michael stormed towards the door and slammed it open so hard it almost came off its hinges, leaving Sandra turning ever-darkening shades of crimson, acutely aware that everybody was looking at her.

Jane stood from her chair a few feet away, walked up to Sandra and hissed at her in a voice probably not intended to be heard by anybody else but one that managed to cut through the silence anyway, 'Well what do you expect?! She's his wife and of course he's going to

210

take her side, he's got to live with her. You two seriously think nobody knows your little secret? Everybody knows! They've been laughing at you for years!'

Sandra's eyes flashed with rage and she screamed back, 'And you think nobody knows your secret?!'

Jane caught her breath and everybody in the room thought she was going to slap Sandra. Jane thought the same thing, but she managed to hold her anger in just enough to limit it to slapping Sandra's sandwich out of her hands, causing it to spread itself across a carpet that hadn't been vacuumed since Tommy Cooper performed at the Summerton Pavilions during his early years. Jane followed Michael out of the same door, hitting it so hard on the way out that the glass in its frame slightly cracked as it ricocheted off the wall behind.

Lauren looked at Gabriel across the crowded room with a look of despair. He knew she couldn't stand conflict after everything she had been through with her mother. He raised his eyebrows and puffed out his cheeks, not knowing what else to do across a crowded room. He saw her look down at Sandra's sandwich strewn across the floor, then look at the woman who suddenly seemed less fearsome and more pathetic, trapped in a relationship that would never evolve the way she wanted it to, but unable to escape from it. Gabriel saw Lauren's eyes slightly fill with tears as she watched Sandra, before walking up to her and putting her arm around Sandra's shoulders.

'Come and sit with me. No, leave your sandwich, we'll clear it up in a minute. Come and sit down here. I've got a whole flask of tea with me and you can share my salad. Do you like mushrooms?'

211

Sandra nodded, appearing to be an older woman for the first time since Gabriel had met her, rather than the battleaxe he thought she was. Morag had heard the exchange and dived over to the kitchenette drawer, finding a spare fork and bringing it over for Sandra, who smiled up at her through tired, red eyes.

As Lauren and Sandra sat on the opposite side of the room, Gabriel realised just how different she was to Shelley. He had finally found a woman who was kind and caring, thinking of other people and doing what she could to help them. He had never been so proud of someone and he beamed across the room at her, even though she wasn't looking at him. She was concentrating on Sandra, her right arm still around her shoulder, sharing her food with her, taking it in turns to eat mouthfuls.

Allegra appeared next to Gabriel, also looking over at the tableaux on the other side of the room. 'You should marry that girl, she's one of the good ones,' she said.

'Yeah, I know,' he replied, wistfully. 'I think I might just do that.'

As the closing night's performance began, Gabriel couldn't resist a sneaky glance through the tiny hole in the proscenium arch next to where he was sat, which provided him with a good view of a fair chunk of the audience and most of the orchestra pit. As Michael began his pre-concert aerobics ritual (which was apparently even more ridiculous than the one he used in rehearsals), he saw Sandra staring intently at the music stand in front of her, refusing to look at Michael, her lips pursed to within an inch of their life. Eventually, as Michael was about to start the show, he saw Sandra glare at him with one of the most murderous stares he had ever seen. Michael, of course, was oblivious to this.

The final performance happened without incident. The cast took an inordinate number of bows at the end, followed by Fabian delivering a twenty-minute speech thanking nobody in particular other than himself. There was no mention of the orchestra, Anthony, Gabriel or most of the cast. There was much lyrical waxing about the state of the world, the economy, how we can learn so much from a character such as Dolly, the importance of live performance, etc, etc. After around 50% of the audience had walked out, probably heading to hang themselves from the Summerton lifting bridge, he decided to wrap things up. Anthony instructed Gabriel to close the curtains, which he did. Fabian dived through the curtains just before they met in the middle of the stage, and delivered another twenty-minute speech to the cast. Gabriel escaped after three minutes, leaving them all to their fate.

There was no sign of Michael, Elizabeth or Sandra. Megan was locked in a passionate clinch with a senior gentleman whom Gabriel presumed to be Graham, her intended. Roxie and Morag were going round hugging the orchestra (Gabriel had no idea how they had escaped before him, as he was sure he had seen them backstage nodding at Fabian as he delivered another monologue worthy of Christopher Marlowe). Lauren caught Gabriel's eye and beckoned him over with one finger.

'Well, that went well, don't you think?' she asked.

'Nobody died, although I suspect a few members of the audience came close.'

Lauren laughed. 'Look, I need to make sure that Jane gets home okay. She's been in a state since earlier and I think she hit the bar rather hard during the interval. How do you fancy following me back to hers than following me

213

back to mine…?' Her eyebrows rose and the corners of her mouth told Gabriel everything he needed to know.

'You're on!'

He found his car keys in record time and watched Lauren carefully loading Jane (who was clearly absolutely bladdered) into her passenger seat. He followed them back to Jane's rather grand home in Porlington, then helped Lauren get her up the stairs and into her bedroom. He left the two of them to it for a few minutes and Lauren eventually reappeared.

'She's in bed and asleep. Still wearing all her makeup, but that's her problem in the morning,' she said, grinning. 'Back to mine?'

'I'll race you!'

They headed back to Lauren's, arriving a little before midnight. She poured him a large scotch and they sat on the sofa. Gabriel downed it in one and said, 'Right then. Up to bed?' before standing up and holding his hand out for hers.

Lauren laughed and took his hand. They spent the next four hours creating the most memorable night Gabriel had ever had before falling asleep somewhere between 4 and 5am.

Around 11am on Sunday morning, Gabriel stirred. He saw Lauren next to him, still fast asleep and smiled, remembering the many, many things they had tried the night before. After ten minutes of watching her breathing while she slept, he decided to slip downstairs and make her breakfast to present on a tray to her in bed.

As he eased out of the covers, still completely naked, he saw his phone flashing on the bedside drawers. There were 34 messages and texts. This seemed unusually high. The first button he hit was the missed calls icon; he saw

214

there were several missed calls from Anthea and a number of answerphone messages. After her somewhat cryptic comments on Friday night about his divorce case, he decided this was the most important thing to address first and hit the speed-dial button for his voicemail. The first message made his blood freeze in his veins.

'Hello, Maestro. I'm guessing you're still asleep after last night's performance and the ensuing bedroom acrobatics with Lauren. I'm sorry if this is a rude awakening, but you better get round to ours as quick as you can. I had the police on the doorstep an hour ago. Sandra has been found dead. Looks like it might be murder.'

TWENTY-TWO

GABRIEL AND LAUREN ARRIVED AT CHEZ Sweeney within half an hour. Morag opened the door and said, as only the Scots can, 'There's been a murrrdurrr!' before ushering the two of them into the lounge which was crammed full of people, all in a state of shock.

'Hello, you two. Come on in,' Anthea beckoned from across the room. 'I think you know everybody.' A quick glance around confirmed they at least knew who everybody was, but they hadn't spoken to a lot of them before.

There were no seats available, so Gabriel and Lauren stood awkwardly in the middle of the room. Neither liked to ask any questions as they were the two newcomers to this group and still a bit surprised Anthea had asked them over. After a few moments of painful silence, Roxie piped up. 'Anthea, darling, I know we've been over this for our benefit, but dear Gabriel and... I'm sorry, hello, we haven't been introduced. Roxanne von Klausen. And you are...?' Roxie extended a hand towards Lauren.

'Lauren. Lauren Barker. Very pleased to meet you,' came the reply in a timid voice, followed by an involuntary curtsy.

Roxie continued without skipping a beat. 'Gabriel and Lauren don't know what's happened. Perhaps you should fill them in.'

'Yes, of course. As I'm sure you noticed, Michael and Sandra had been arguing this week...'

She was interrupted by the most unlikely American accent coming out of Morag's mouth, 'Mmm-hmm, girlfriend,' accompanied by bobbing her head left and right and clicking her fingers.

'Do be quiet, dear,' Roxie said.

Anthea continued. 'Michael went round first thing this morning to talk to Sandra and clear the air. Apparently, Sandra had her nose put out of joint by Elizabeth turning up all week. She always regarded orchestra time as her time with Michael, not Elizabeth's. He found the front door open so went in. When Sandra didn't respond to him calling, he went upstairs to her bedroom and found her dead in the bed, with a pillow over her face. First thing he did was call me in a panic, clearly beside himself and not knowing what to do. I told him to calm down and call the police, which he did. Uniform turned up here within the hour.'

'Why would they turn up here?' Gabriel asked.

'Sandra had no close family and no next of kin, so I've been listed for years on her medical records as her emergency contact and primary decision maker. She was terrified of a distant cousin who she had never met deciding to leave her on life support for years in the event of a car accident, so I was listed and instructed to tell them to flick the switch at the earliest opportunity.'

Morag was getting bored, as she had heard all this before. She decided to be helpful and make drinks. 'Right, hands up who's for tea?' Most hands went up. 'And who's for coffee?' Two or three hands went up. 'Tea it is then...' she said as she headed towards the kitchen.

'So I'm guessing they don't have any idea who it was yet?' Gabriel asked, worrying this question was too obvious to ask, but wanting the answer anyway. 'Or why they would kill her?'

'Not a clue, sausage,' Anthea chimed back. 'The police tend not to give anything much away in case it prejudices a trial further down the road.'

Roxie piped up. 'Of course, when my second husband died under circumstances that weren't terribly easily explained, we had to deal with the police for months. They were ghastly. They traipsed through our house, went through every item and left the most hideous mess. My clothes were strewn everywhere and several of my best scarves were just trampled on, ruining the silk,' she said, clutching the Hermès around her throat with a look in her eye like she had lost several close friends. Nobody liked to ask how the case had turned out, although they were all itching to.

Lauren whispered to Gabriel, 'Oh god, somebody should tell Jane.'

He felt his stomach knot as she was bound to be a suspect after the arguments they'd been having all week. 'I don't think she'll be in any fit state for that conversation just yet. Perhaps we should call round on our way home later?'

The room had gone deathly quiet and what Gabriel and Lauren had thought was a private exchange had

218

clearly been heard by everyone, who had the same reaction as Gabriel.

'Poor Jane,' came a voice from the back of the room and everybody looked in amazement at Betty Brannon, these being the first words they had heard her utter in years.

There was a loud knock at the door and Richard let himself in. 'Morning Rupert! Ready for your weekly thrashing? Don't get your hopes up, I mean on the squash court! Oh, hello. What are you all doing here?'

The room returned to awkward silence. 'Perhaps you better fill him in, dear,' Anthea said to Rupert.

As Rupert began to cover the story thus far, Anthea walked up to Gabriel and said, 'You've heard all there is to hear for now, so you won't be missing much. Can I have a quick word in the parlour?' Gabriel's stomach unknotted, did a backwards flip and re-knotted.

'Sure.'

They headed through to the parlour, narrowly missing Morag heading back through with a tray laden down with crockery, cutlery, three teapots ('Who on earth owns three teapots,' Gabriel wondered, 'let alone that tea-cosy which looks like rabbits peering out from a grassy knoll.' It passed by before Gabriel could see if Lee Harvey Oswald was also depicted on it).

They reached the parlour and Anthea sat him down. She pulled up a chair very close to him and took his hand. 'Okay, dumpling. I've got some news. It works very much in our favour with the divorce, but the news itself might be a bit hard for you to hear.'

'Right. How bad is it?' Gabriel said, steeling himself and taking a deep breath. Followed by another. And another.

219

'Shelley is 16 weeks pregnant.'

Time stopped. Gabriel's mind was a blur, attempting to calculate dates and consequences all at the same time, with a mild hangover and sleep deprivation thrown into the mix. It was like a blizzard and a hurricane were happening in his brain all at the same time and he couldn't see through it.

'It's not yours.'

That news hit him as hard as the first statement. They had talked about having children eventually, but nothing serious. He had never admitted to her just how much he longed to have children, as he knew she regarded them as an inconvenience in her life. The realisation began to dawn on him that she now had the very thing he had always wished for and she wouldn't appreciate having a child. The thought process continued along and he realised that she was pregnant by another man while she was still his wife. His wife was expecting another man's child. Which would mean that everybody who knew them would know that she had cuckolded him. Of course, they would all know they had separated, they would all know that she had been sleeping with other men while they were still married, but a child provided tangible evidence of this and Gabriel suddenly felt emasculated; he felt like he was somehow a failure and not good enough to father children with his own wife.

'Take another deep breath or two, sweetie. It's okay. Whatever you're feeling right now is perfectly fine and you know you're completely safe here with me.'

Gabriel complied, and they sat in silence for a few minutes while his stomach calmed down.

'Are you okay?' Anthea asked in her most gentle voice. Gabriel nodded, still not sure if he trusted his vocal cords to produce sounds recognisable as English. 'You'll need one of these,' she said, passing him a tissue.

He took it and instinctively put it to his face, without really knowing why. As he took it away, he realised it was wet through with tears that he didn't know he had cried.

'It's going to be okay. I've had to break news like this before, and once the initial shock subsides, you'll feel numb for a while. Then angry. Then a whole load of other things. But eventually, you'll be okay again.' She smiled at him, not waiting for a response. Just wanting him to be okay. He knew that just for a few minutes, it was fine to feel whatever he wanted and continue sitting in silence.

After a while, Gabriel gathered himself and asked, 'You said this helps us?'

'Good. That's the kind of response I was hoping for. Yes, it does. I'll go into details later, but it does help us.'

'How did you find out?'

'You remember I told you I wanted to use a private investigator? This is the kind of thing he turns up. To be honest, this was an easy one as she's plastered it all over her social media, which is why I asked if you still had her or any of her friends on Facebook. I wanted to see if you'd already heard via another route. You clearly hadn't, so I didn't want to hit you with this with loads of other people around.'

Gabriel appreciated her tact, realising she was absolutely right to have taken the course of action she had.

'Does anybody else know? I mean here, in my new life,' he asked.

'No. Solicitor privilege bars me from telling anybody. I'd like to tell Mr Sweeney so that we can support you as friends, but only with your permission.'

'Yeah, sure. I don't really care who knows. Although I guess I'll have to break this to Lauren later.'

'I wouldn't worry too much about that; she knows you have no loyalties to your ex-wife anymore. I fully expect she'll be more concerned with your wellbeing.'

It occurred to Gabriel that Anthea had been very careful with her wording. When breaking the news, she had referred to 'Shelley', so there was the personal element. Now they were back in professional mode, it was his 'ex-wife' again.

Another thought occurred to him.

'Who... Who's the father?' he asked, tentatively.

Anthea waited and looked at Gabriel, assessing whether he would be ready for any new information.

'What did you say the guy's name was who she had been sleeping with when you were still together?'

'Martin. Martin Pembridge. He was her personal trainer.'

'Okay, well it's not him. Do you know someone called Dave or David Webster?'

Gabriel thought for a moment. 'No, that doesn't ring a bell.'

'Well, they're now listed on her Facebook profile as in a relationship and she's saying that they're expecting a child together. My contact says he is an investment banker working out of Surrey.'

This seemed surprising on the one hand, yet not at all surprising on the other.

'That's certainly the kind of guy she would go for. She's drawn to money and success. Can't imagine why she married me.' His wan smile gave away more than he realised. 'What happened to Martin?'

'It would appear that she has a large number of photos with Dave while she was still listed as in a relationship with Martin. Your guess is as good as mine, but I bet we're both right.'

'Bitch. She never learns. Utterly selfish bitch.'

'That's the spirit, my little Milkybar Kid. You just keep that attitude up. I know this must be hard, and it hasn't even begun to sink in yet, but you keep holding on to the anger, it'll help you. I'd be worried if you were reminiscing over what could have been.'

Gabriel had moved on from that state some minutes ago and would never return to it. He was beginning to see Shelley for exactly what she was.

Anthea turned professional again. 'I'd like to request a hearing pretty quickly, so we can start dealing with things and getting the ball rolling. Are you happy for me to do that?'

'Whatever you think best,' Gabriel replied.

'I'd also like to withhold a few things from you for the moment, if that's okay?'

This surprised Gabriel. 'Like what?' he asked.

'Well if I answered that question, I wouldn't be withholding much, would I?!'

'I suppose not. Why are you not telling me stuff? Is it like Shelley being pregnant?'

'No, not at all. I promise I will always tell you stuff like that. What I'd like to refrain from telling you is my strategy for dealing with your divorce. That way, you have plausible deniability, should it go wrong. I'm going to play a slightly high-stakes game, but one that I think will work, especially in the light of this new revelation.'

'Is it legal?'

'Completely, as long as I have your permission to be sneaky and not run everything by you. Then, if it goes wrong, you can go to another solicitor and plead ignorance. But if I'm right, this will work out beautifully.'

'Are you usually right?' Gabriel asked.

'Well, that depends if you ask Mr Sweeney or myself. But I would say yes. I wouldn't take risks in professional matters if they weren't worth it, or if I thought it would harm my client.'

'Then I guess I'll trust you and look forward to finding out what you have up your sleeve.'

'Excellent. Right, we better go and join the party again. They'll be wondering where we are.'

Anthea led him back through the catacombs of her house to the room where all were assembled. Lauren looked at Gabriel and raised an eyebrow; she had clearly seen his red, blotchy eyes.

'I'll tell you later, okay?' She nodded, the concern on her face evident.

To lighten the mood, she cast her eyes towards the far wall. Gabriel didn't quite get what she meant, so she did it again and jerked her head in its direction.

Hung on the wall was a huge framed photograph of Rupert and Richard walking through beautifully sculpted gardens in dinner jackets, carrying their double basses, both beaming at the camera. As portrait photography goes, it was a stunning shot. It also seemed a somewhat curious piece of art to have as the focal point for the main room in Rupert's house with Anthea.

Gabriel couldn't figure out how he had missed this at Christmas, until he realised that was where the enormous Christmas tree had been placed, obscuring the picture. He glanced at Rupert, who was smiling at Anthea with one

224

eye and gazing at Richard with the other. Richard was playing on his phone, no doubt messaging a girl from the previous night, or one he hoped to create a glorious night with soon. The playful smile on his lips suggested the latter.

Gabriel leaned over to whisper in Lauren's ear. 'So what on earth do you think the dynamic really is with those tw…'

He was interrupted mid-sentence by a loud rapping at the door. There was a scurrying in the distance, and within a moment or two, Morag appeared with two strangers in her wake.

'It's the police. They'd like a word,' she said, looking at Anthea.

TWENTY-THREE

TWO VERY SOBER-LOOKING DETECTIVES STOOD in the doorway, surveying the strange bunch of people in front of them. The younger, but clearly more senior of the two, stepped forward and flashed her badge around the room.

'Detective Inspector Pamela Baxter, CID, Dent Forest Division. This is Detective Sergeant Dunstan. Which one of you is Anthea Sweeney?'

Anthea looked thoroughly nonplussed, stood on the other side of the room, scanning the two officers up and down and quickly making her assessment. She paid particular attention to the rather boring shoes DI Baxter was wearing. 'That would be me,' she said, in a somewhat monotone voice, waiting for the response.

'Might I have a word?' the DI asked. 'In private.'

'Of course, my dear,' Anthea replied, immediately putting the police officer off her stride. 'I believe we were on opposing sides in the Mackenzie case last year.'

'Were we?'

Anthea bristled, clearly unimpressed that this woman didn't remember her. 'Yes. We won, and you lost, if

226

memory serves,' Anthea said with just the faintest hint of an ingratiating, patronising smile on her lips.

The Detective Inspector blinked first, nervously trying to avoid eye contact with Anthea just for a moment.

Anthea led her to the drawing room and motioned for the police officer to sit down on the opposite side of a coffee table. This was to be a professional exchange, so Anthea felt a bit of distance seemed appropriate.

'Mrs Sweeney, as you are aware after uniform branch spoke to you earlier, Miss Sandra Finley was found dead this morning…'

'Ms Finley.'

'I beg your pardon?' DI Baxter asked, thrown somewhat off guard by the interruption.

'Ms Finley. She hated being called Miss. Said it made her sound like a spinster.'

'Oh, I'm sorry, my mistake. I was under the impression she had never been married and divorced, or had a long-term co-habiting partner.'

'Is that any reason not to be able to determine one's own title?'

'I suppose not.' Baxter rallied and tried to take charge of the conversation again. 'You are listed with her GP as her emergency contact, yes?'

'Clearly, otherwise you wouldn't be here.'

Anthea surveyed the woman sat opposite her once again. Five foot nine, early forties, shoulder length dirty blonde hair that was clearly out of a bottle, a trouser suit, virtually no jewellery (notably no ring on the fourth finger of her left hand), no visible signs of a sense of humour or any lines around her eyes to suggest she had laughed in the last decade, and those godawful boring shoes.

227

Everything about this woman said 'sensible'. Or, as Anthea called it, 'boring'.

'Why were you listed instead of a family member?'

'I've been Sandra's solicitor a good many years and we knew each other in a social capacity as we played in the same orchestra. She had no close family in the area, nor any close friends to speak of. When she turned 65 three years ago, she began to consider her age and the inevitable decline which she was facing over the next couple of decades, and was terrified of decisions being taken by people who didn't know her. She had a genuine fear of being in a coma or vegetative state for a long period of time. She perceived that to hold a loss of dignity, at least in her eyes, and she was terrified of waking up and realising she had missed a passage of time. She wasn't a good sleeper from what she said, as she didn't like being out of control or in a state where somebody else could do something to her that she would be unaware of. My instructions were clear. If there was less than a 70% chance of waking up within two weeks, or if she would be faced with a life where she would be debilitated in any way, make them flip the switch and turn her off at the earliest opportunity. I have a signed document to that effect at the office.'

'Why was she more afraid of either being in a coma or having a restricted existence than she was of dying?'

'I have no idea. It wasn't up to me to ask why, as my instructions were to act in a professional capacity as opposed to a personal one. When I said we knew each other, I meant exactly that. We knew one another. We weren't friends.'

'Very well. Thank you for your candour. Look, I'm going to level with you as you're a fellow professional and an officer of the court. You know murder cases are generally drawn-out affairs and investigations can drag on for a long time.'

'So it is a murder investigation?' Anthea asked, for clarity.

'The initial indications are that it is likely to be. Finding a body of a healthy woman dead in a bed with a pillow resting on top of her face isn't usually an indication of death by natural causes. Our working theory at this time is that she was killed, although you will also be aware that we can't categorically say that until after the post-mortem. The first few hours can be critical for finding information, though, so we need to proceed along these lines just in case.'

'Of course,' Anthea said, aware that Baxter was attempting to draw her into her confidence in an attempt to shortly elicit information. She didn't mind, the woman was just doing her job and Anthea wouldn't give away anything she didn't want to.

'Can you fill me in on any information that might prove useful in this case? I'm not asking you to breach client privilege, but one of your clients is dead, potentially because of foul play. I'm asking if you can give me any background that will give us a starting point or two. Nothing incriminating, but anything that we're likely to find out anyway through the course of our investigations. Please remember that the clock is ticking.'

Anthea sat and thought for a moment.

'I'm not prepared to discuss anything privileged, for obvious reasons. But there are a good many things you're likely to turn up and out of respect to Sandra, I'll start you down some roads. However, I suspect most of them won't prove to go anywhere as I genuinely have no idea who would want her dead enough to actually follow through with killing her.'

'That's fair enough.'

'I would also like it noted that most people who knew Sandra would also know me and there is every likelihood I will be called as their solicitor in the event of police questioning, so I have to be careful what I say. I will limit anything I say to matters which are publicly known by people other than me.'

'Of course.' Baxter sat slightly further forward on her seat, waiting for what might come next.

'You can also put that notebook away and if you ever claim I gave you any information, I will not just deny it but I will use any further information I have that I don't share with you against you in court. Like I did in the Mackenzie case last year.'

Anthea saw Baxter's shoulders drop and disappointment wash across her face. 'I suppose that's fair enough.' She closed her notebook, put her pen back in the top of it and placed it back in the inside pocket of her coat.

'I have no idea how much of this you already know. I can't back up everything I have with hard evidence, but the things I tell you are things I believe to be true. I also maintain that I do not know anybody who I believe to be capable of Sandra's alleged murder, and I know of no reason why anybody would want to kill her. Other than for her dreadful violin playing and inability to stick to her own bowing markings, but that's not an offence worthy of a death penalty.'

Anthea waited for a smile or a laugh from Baxter. Neither were forthcoming. She groaned inwardly and proceeded.

'First, from a professional accountability point of view, I need to tell you that Michael Fordington rang me this morning in quite a flap. He said he had gone round to talk to Sandra after they had several arguments this week. He said he couldn't find her downstairs and she wasn't responding to him calling for her, so he went upstairs and found her in her bed. I understand he called me straight away, at which point, I told him to touch nothing and call the police immediately.'

'Do you have any idea how he gained entry to her house?'

'He told me he found the front door open when he arrived. Although he had a key.'

'Why would he have a key?'

'Because they'd been having an affair for years and he spent every Thursday with her.'

DI Baxter's eyes widened and she instinctively reached for her notebook.

'Don't even think about it, sweetie,' Anthea chastised. Baxter's hand withdrew from inside her coat. 'I'm telling you this because you will find it out soon enough and when you inevitably requisition Michael's phone records, you will see that he rang me. I'm covering myself here and providing full disclosure as Michael isn't a client of mine at the present time. I'd like that remembered when you arrest somebody and I end up representing them—I expect full disclosure from you under those circumstances, as I know how the police love to leave certain vital bits of information out.'

Baxter opened her mouth to object on professional grounds, then thought better of it and sat back in her chair.

'I would also like it noted that I have never seen anything which might suggest Michael would be responsible for Sandra's murder, and I've known them for many years. To be honest, I've not seen anything which caused alarm bells to ring from anybody I've seen interacting with Sandra, so I'm not sure what use I can be to you.'

Baxter looked visibly crestfallen, although she (unsuccessfully) attempted to hide it. 'Well, that gives us a few starting points. Thank you.'

Anthea wasn't finished. 'I'm assuming you left your sergeant in the other room with instructions to listen carefully to what people were saying. I'm afraid that I'm not terribly comfortable with undercover surveillance taking place under my roof, so I have left Mr Sweeney with instructions to take control of the conversation and steer it in any direction other than the one you hoped it would take. Shall we rejoin them?'

Baxter's face went several shades darker as she realised she had been outwitted but she politely smiled and nodded, standing and heading towards the door as this audience was clearly at an end.

As they both walked back into the room where everybody else was sequestered, they heard Rupert summing up with, '…and those are the primary differences between Windows and Apple computers.' The glazed expressions of everyone within earshot were matched only by the exasperated look DS Dunstan hurled towards his superior officer. Baxter rolled her eyes, thanked everybody for their time and headed for the door, with her slightly podgy and much older colleague in tow. As she reached the door, DI Baxter turned and addressed the gathered ensemble.

'If you could all stay around the area and be available for questioning over the next few days, we would appreciate it.'

Anthea countered with, 'And if any of you are invited to answer any questions, you all have my number to call so you're not on your own.'

Baxter scowled, Dunstan smirked, everybody else looked on nervously and Megan suddenly burst through the door past the two departing police officers, asking, 'What have I missed? I heard that something had happened!'

TWENTY-FOUR

'SO WHERE THE HELL DO WE START WITH THIS one, boss?'

It was Monday morning. Baxter and Dunstan were back at the CID offices in Porlington Police Station and Dunstan was thoroughly enjoying his superior officer's unease. Colin Dunstan was 18 months off retirement when he hit 67 years of age and objected to having had to continue beyond 65. He should be an ex-pat in Spain or Portugal by now, with his feet up on a beach lounger and a glass of Sangria in his hand, with Mrs Dunstan next to him enjoying the geographic distance between themselves and their two sons. Both offspring still lived at home, having never managed to find the right partner or the right career, or even a place of their own. Colin was very much looking forward to selling the house, kicking his two useless sons out of the nest so they could fly for themselves (despite both being in their forties) and using the capital to start a new life in the sun. In the meantime, he was going to enjoy as many moments as possible in his job. This was one such moment.

'The obvious place to start is to question Michael Fordington,' Baxter replied, her face propped up by her

234

hands on her desk with a sense of despair visibly washing over her. 'If they were having an affair, we have to begin with him.'

Dunstan took great delight in writing in a flamboyant style in his notebook, enunciating each syllable as he wrote it down. 'My. Kull. Ford. Ing. Tun. Got it. Then what?'

'Oh for god's sake, sergeant, can you take this seriously? A woman is dead.'

'That's *Detective* Sergeant to you, Ma'am.'

The look Baxter shot at him would have reduced him to cinders if he hadn't been studiously examining his notebook, purposefully avoiding her gaze. She was sure she saw a smirk hovering on the corners of his lips.

DI Baxter couldn't be more different to DS Dunstan. Career- and results-driven, she had been married in her thirties for a couple of years, before her now ex-husband had taken up with his yoga instructor, telling her, 'Pammie, it just isn't working. You're married to your job, not me. Krystal understands me and takes an interest in me.' Frankly, Krystal was welcome to him. And what sort of man did yoga, anyway? He looked bad enough in normal clothes, but his middle-aged gut attempting to burst out of lycra was just embarrassing. Since then, she had received no male attention except for a quick fumble in the stationery cupboard with a rather dishy constable two years ago. This had formed a treasured memory for her until she went to get a new highlighter some weeks later and found him *in flagrante* with a secretary in the same stationery cupboard, using the same lines on her that he had on Baxter. The panic in his voice when he begged her not to mention either indiscretion to his wife instantly negated any positive feelings she had had

235

towards him and elicited her response, 'Maybe I will, maybe I won't,' which meant he still dropped his eyes and ran away from her every time he saw her in the station.

She was attempting not to make her betrayals at the hands of various men influence her thought processes in this case, but it was a challenge.

'And after Mr Fordington?' Dunstan asked.

'Let's cross that bridge when we come to it. I think we should invite him in to answer some questions.'

'Do you want to take the risk he'll ask his solicitor friend along? If we just turn up at his house, we'd catch him unawares and we'd be more likely to get something out of him.'

'No, I don't want to risk the wife listening in. She's got to be one of the next people we talk to,' Baxter replied. Dunstan couldn't argue with her logic, although he hoped Michael wouldn't lawyer up as he was pretty sure Anthea would be quite obstructive on his behalf. As effective as her husband was at suppressing a conversation, she must be ten times more so. 'Why don't you make the call and ask him to come in this afternoon?'

'Yes, boss.' Dunstan was unimpressed at having to do the grunt work, which could easily be passed to a constable.

'Better to come from you. I trust you not to cock it up,' his superior said. 'Be friendly. Don't let him think he's got anything to worry about.'

Dunstan dutifully agreed and at 2pm, Michael found himself waiting in reception at the station. Baxter popped her head around the secure door and asked, 'Michael Fordington? Follow me, please.'

She led him through the solid metal door, clanging it behind him with a resounding thud, checking it couldn't be opened again. This wasn't necessary in the slightest, it was entirely a psychological trick to make him nervous.

Baxter led him down a labyrinth of corridors and into an interview room, where Dunstan was waiting. She gestured for Michael to sit on the opposite side of the table, with his back to the wall and with the two police officers between him and the door. Everything about this scenario was designed to intimidate.

DI Baxter opened the interview. 'Mr Fordington, thank you for coming in today to answer our questions. It helps us greatly that you have come to us, as the first few days after a crime has taken place are time-critical and it has saved us time by you coming to us rather than us having to come out to your home. I would like to confirm that you have not been arrested, therefore this is a voluntary interview and, as such, you do not need legal counsel present. Do you understand all this?'

Michael nodded, twitching, his eyes darting from one corner of the room to another.

DI Baxter continued. 'It would be really helpful to us at this stage if we could record your answers, so that we have a definitive record of what you say, in order to help us with our enquiries and catch the person that did this to poor Sandra.' She threw an ingratiating smile in Michael's direction. DS Dunstan wasn't sure whether he was more inclined to snigger at her transparent attempt to manipulate this man, or whether he might throw up a little in his mouth.

'Of course, whatever you need,' Michael said, his huge frame filling the chair opposite the officers. He was clearly nervous, although Dunstan couldn't yet work out if this was from guilt or grief. If he hadn't been the perpetrator, he clearly had one hell of a shock discovering his lover's dead body. Or it could all be a clever ruse and they were sat opposite a cold-blooded killer.

'Under the PACE guidelines—that's the Police and Criminal Evidence Act 1984—we are only allowed to record conversations if we do what is called an interview under caution. That just means that I say a few standard lines which enable us to record this interview, allowing us to gain information which may reveal further lines of inquiry. Can I reiterate that whilst the wording is similar, you are *not* under arrest and therefore do not need legal counsel present.'

Dunstan looked at his superior officer with his eyebrows rising so far he was worried they might fly off his head. She was skating on ice so thin it could be used as tracing paper, hoping to cover herself with one tiny little line that she dropped in as a technicality.

'Do whatever you need to,' Michael said, fidgeting so badly that Dunstan began to worry Baxter had covered his chair in itching powder. He wouldn't put it past her.

'Great, thank you so much. That really helps us. I'll start with the boring legal stuff at the beginning, then we can just have a friendly conversation,' she said as she reached for the tape recorder on the desk, fitted with two cassettes. She pressed the Master Record button and hurled the technical information at Michael before he had a chance to process or realise what was going on.

'Michael Fordington, you are attending Porlington Police Station today in a voluntary capacity to assist us with our enquiries into the alleged murder of Sandra Finley. My name is Detective Inspector Pamela Baxter. Also present is Detective Sergeant Colin Dunstan. You are being interviewed under caution. You do not have to say anything. But it may harm your defence if you do not

238

mention, when questioned, something which you later rely on in court. Anything you do say may be given in evidence. You have also agreed to waive your right to legal representation at this time. Do you understand what I have just said and agree to being questioned without a solicitor being present?' Baxter paused and looked at Michael, smiling and nodding to encourage his answer.

'Erm, yes,' he replied. Dunstan sat in his chair, marvelling at the woman's nerve and wondering how she got away with this stuff. She had just managed to get this entire interview recorded and could submit it as evidence against this man at a later date whilst getting him to waive his rights to a solicitor.

'Mr Fordington, could you please outline your relationship with the deceased?'

Michael looked even more nervous, but realised he didn't have any choice other than to answer their questions.

'Sandra and I have been friends for over 30 years. She was the leader in my orchestra, the Porlington Philharmonia. We have our next concert on Saturday 14th April, if you'd care to come along. An evening of Viennese Classics; tickets will be available on the door.'

He waited for a response from the police officers, but none was forthcoming.

Baxter eventually broke the silence. 'What was the precise nature of your relationship, Mr Fordington?'

Michael shifted nervously in his chair. 'I told you, we were friends and professional colleagues.'

'Nothing more than that? Might I remind you that you are under caution and if we find you have lied to us in this interview, that might give us cause to doubt anything you say.'

239

Dunstan watched Michael's eyes drop to the table, with the realisation dawning on him that he was caught in a trap and was damned if he was honest and damned if he wasn't.

'We were friends,' he said in a low, quiet voice, his eyes staring downwards. 'She was possibly the best friend I've ever had.'

'Was it a sexual relationship?' Baxter pressed. Dunstan began to feel nauseous himself at how she was pressuring this poor man.

After some time, Michael's quietest voice admitted, 'Yes, it was.'

'I'm sorry, could you speak up for the tape please.'

Michael's eyes flew up to meet Baxter's. A certain steeliness entered his gaze. 'Yes. It was.'

'Thank you. So, could you please tell us what happened on Sunday morning when you went round to Sandra's house?'

Michael seemed relieved that the line of questioning had moved away from their affair. 'We performed *Hello, Dolly!* with the Summerton Operatic and Dramatic Society last week. Sandra and I had argued on Saturday night, but we had soldiered on through the performance as we are professionals. She had left before I had a chance to talk to her after the performance, so I went round on Sunday morning to clear the air.'

Baxter and Dunstan said nothing, allowing the silence to grow sufficiently awkward that Michael would fill it himself. He fell right into the trap.

'I arrived at her house around 9am and found the front door open. This was strange, as she was always so careful about locking her doors. She didn't like her cat going out the front of the house instead of the back garden, so it

240

seemed odd to me that her front door was open. I let myself into the house and called for her. When she didn't respond, I checked downstairs, then I went upstairs and into her bedroom. That's when I saw her lying in the bed, with a pillow over her face. I ran over and took her hand, but it was stone cold. I threw the pillow off and was calling her name, but she didn't respond. She just kept staring up at the ceiling and she was blue and stiff. I tried to give her mouth-to-mouth, but nothing worked. Eventually, I realised there was nothing I could do and I rang 999 for an ambulance in the hope they could save her.'

Baxter had started taking notes. She finished a few sentences and let the silence hang in the air before looking up at Michael.

'Okay. Just a couple of quick questions on that series of events. What are you leaving out, Mr Fordington?

'Leaving out? Nothing. That's exactly as things happened.'

'Really? Because we have reason to believe other things happened yesterday morning that you're not telling us.'

'I'm telling you everything! That's exactly what happened!'

Baxter waited in the hope he would start admitting to more that he hadn't already said. His incredulous look told her this wasn't going to happen and she was going to have to probe a little deeper.

'Calling the ambulance wasn't your first call, was it? Who else did you call?'

'Nobody! I was only interested in Sandra!' Michael's vocal pitch was beginning to rise in panic.

'So if we were to requisition your phone records, they wouldn't show any other calls yesterday morning between 9am and the time you called the emergency services, which was around 9:20am?'

'Of course not!' Michael screamed.

'Mr Fordington, do you have your mobile phone with you right now?'

'Yes, of course I do.'

'Would you mind calling up your call history for us please?'

Michael fished his phone out of his jacket pocket and hit the green icon for call history. 'Oh, I called Anthea Sweeney. I'm sorry, I forgot about that. I was under a great deal of stress.'

'Could you please show me that call entry?' Baxter asked, before reading the phone log for the recording. 'Please let the record show that Mr Fordington's phone shows his first call of the day, at 0916 hours was to a number logged in his mobile phone as "Anthea Sweeney—cello". This call lasted three minutes and forty-six seconds. The next entry is a call to 999 listed at 0922 hours, which lasted for eleven minutes and twelve seconds.' She handed Michael's phone back to him.

'Why did you call Mrs Sweeney?'

Michael was beginning to unravel. 'She plays in my orchestra and she knows both Sandra and myself. She's a solicitor. In a time of crisis, that's who you call!'

'But why her first? Why not call 999 straight away?'

'I panicked! I didn't know who to call or what to do, so I called somebody who I thought could help me.'

'Precisely, Mr Fordington. You called somebody who you thought could help you. You're not saying that you called someone who could help Sandra, you were more worried about yourself than her. Why was that?'

Michael was gasping for breath and going a funny shade of puce. DS Dunstan decided it was time to pause proceedings.

'Mr Fordington, I'm DS Dunstan. Could I fetch you a glass of water, sir?' Baxter's eyes bored into her subordinate, clearly furious with him for interrupting her mid-flow when she was about to break this man and force him to confess to everything from Sandra's murder to the Lindbergh baby killing.

'Yes, thank you, that would be nice.'

'Ma'am, would you kindly pause the recording and accompany me to get this man a drink?' Dunstan said. He took great delight in watching Baxter go a darker shade of vermilion than he had ever seen her go before.

'Interview paused at 1419, DI Baxter and DS Dunstan leaving the room to fetch the interviewee a glass of water,' Baxter said through gritted teeth before hitting the big red button to pause the recording. 'Mr Fordington, please wait here. Please don't touch the machinery, you are on camera in here and that would be tampering with evidence.'

Baxter followed Dunstan out of the room to the kitchen before launching at him.

'What the *hell* do you think you're doing, Colin?!'

'Ma'am, with the greatest of respect, this man is not under arrest. He's barely here under caution and I'm attempting to save you from yourself. If you keep pushing him without legal representation and without him actually being arrested, you're leaving this whole case wide open to being blown apart.'

Baxter looked like she was chewing a lemon through an old sock, her expression growing ever more thunderous. However, she had the sense to listen to Dunstan, who had decades more experience than her.

'I suppose he will discuss this with Mrs Sweeney, who I'm sure will have something to say.'

'Quite,' DS Dunstan said, giving his superior officer a gentle look. 'Perhaps we should ask the important questions and then wrap this up?'

Baxter headed towards the interview room. 'Ma'am? Don't you think we should take the man his water?' Dunstan headed to the kitchen before he could see the look Baxter threw at his retreating back.

They returned to the interview room, where Dunstan placed the glass of water on the table in front of Michael, who downed it in one. The two police officers exchanged a glance; this man was clearly more nervous than he was letting on.

Baxter hit the red button and waited for the tape machine to emit its long beep before saying, 'DI Baxter and DS Dunstan have returned to the interview room. Interview resumed at 1423. So, Mr Fordington, would you please tell us what you did after the concert on Saturday evening?'

Michael had gathered himself slightly in their absence and thought this was a fair question, considering Sandra had been killed. 'I returned home with my wife. I didn't even see Sandra after the concert, which was unusual as we would normally go for a drink together. As I said, we'd been arguing, and because I'd been arguing with Elizabeth last week, I thought it best to go straight home.'

'Sorry, can I just confirm, Elizabeth is your wife?' Dunstan asked.

'She is.'

'Can I ask, do you have children?'

'Yes, two boys and a girl. All married with children now, and all living away from the area.'

Baxter jumped back in, the role of bad cop suiting her rather well. 'And your wife can confirm that you went home with her after the concert?'

'Yes, of course.'

'Okay, thank you. What happened after the two of you went home?'

Michael was struck by the oddness of this question, his confused expression relaying this to those in the room, although this was not picked up by the tape. 'We had our evening Horlicks and went to bed.'

'And when did you next leave the house?'

'The following morning, when I went to see Sandra.'

'What time would that have been, sir?' Baxter asked.

Michael didn't have the opportunity to answer before screaming from the corridor outside drifted through the interview room door.

'What do you mean, he's being interviewed?! Stop that at once and get my client out of there!'

Baxter and Dunstan immediately realised the game was up much sooner than they had anticipated. Furious knocking on every door in the vicinity erupted.

'Michael? *MICHAEL?!'*

DI Baxter leaned over to the tape machine and hurriedly said, 'Thank you, Mr Fordington, for coming in today and talking to us. Interview terminated at 1426.' She hit the stop button and quickly grabbed both tapes. She had had the foresight to pre-label them, and she dropped them into separate evidence bags, sealing them and thrusting them into her bag just as a red-faced constable in a state of high anxiety knocked on the door and let himself in without waiting to be invited.

'Ma'am, I think you better step out here for a moment.'

Baxter said, 'Mr Fordington, would you mind waiting here for just a moment. I have to deal with something briefly, then we'll escort you to the exit, at which point you will be free to go.' She smiled, although it came out more as a grimace.

Baxter and Dunstan scurried out of the room, pulling the door behind them.

Michael heard a number of sounds coming from the corridor outside, but at 71 years old, his hearing was all but gone. Mercifully, he (incorrectly) thought that nobody in the orchestra had noticed.

There was clearly quite an argument going on outside, which was becoming more audible as the people concerned were approaching the door.

'*WHY was he being interviewed under caution?! WHY the hell wasn't I present?! There's an almighty difference between popping round to someone's house to ask them some questions and hauling them in for questioning under the pretext that they aren't under arrest when clearly you wanted to get as much as you could on record without a solicitor present! If you try to use ANY of this in court, I will be making an IMMEDIATE application to the judge to have it struck from evidence! I'll be speaking to the IPCC about this! Where is he?! Michael? MICHAEL?!?!*'

With that, the door burst open and Anthea stormed in. 'Right! Come with me right now, and never talk to these people again without me present!'

Michael found himself dragged out of the room and towards the exit, leaving Baxter and Dunstan in their wake.

As Anthea headed towards the door of the custody suite, she screamed at the desk sergeant, 'Boy, get that door open before I reach it or you will be back on traffic duty for the rest of your career!' A rotund, middle-aged man who was clearly used to being in charge of his domain and all who entered it flew towards the huge metal door and opened it just in the nick of time.

Watching Anthea and Michael disappear into the distance, Dunstan opened his mouth to speak.

'Shut up, Colin. Just shut up,' Baxter muttered through gritted teeth, before heading off towards the other exit.

TWENTY-FIVE

TUESDAY MORNING CAME AND GABRIEL FOUND himself being interrogated by the Kings at work.

'So who do you think murdered her?' Grant asked, drumming his fingers together. Gabriel was sure he could see the nails shining in a way that suggested a clear polish had been applied, or at least a faint lacquer. Perhaps he'd just buffed them to within an inch of their life last night.

'I'm not sure it's been confirmed yet that it was a murder,' he said, wishing this line of questioning would stop.

Grant chimed in with his opinion. 'I never really liked the woman. She always seemed very sniffy whenever she came in to buy violin strings.' Susan nodded sagely, her expression appearing both interested and vacant at the same time.

'As I said, I really don't know much. I don't even know if they have a suspect. I guess it's still very early days,' Gabriel said, before trying to move away to rearrange the air guitar strings in their empty bags.

The Kings didn't seem particularly impressed by his lack of information but drifted back into the shadows, leaving Gabriel alone in the shop.

As Grant and Neil had been questioning him over the last ten minutes, he had felt his phone vibrate several times in his pocket. He took it out and saw two emails from Anthea. He opened the first one.

Dear Members of the Porlington Philharmonia,

As you will have read in the committee's email on Sunday evening, Sandra Finley was found dead at home in the early hours. Whilst it is too early to have details for a funeral yet (we have to wait for the coroner to release her body before any arrangements can be made), I would like to draw your attention to several things.

First, Michael has asked me to remind you that rehearsal will take place on Thursday evening as normal, as we only have a few weeks until our Viennese concert. This will, of course, be dedicated to Sandra. Jane Lazenby has kindly agreed to temporarily step in as leader for this concert, with auditions for the permanent post left by Sandra's departure to be held at a future date.

Secondly, I would like to inform you all that, so far, I have been less than impressed with how the police have conducted their investigations. They have shown themselves to be decidedly underhanded, and I would like to state to all of you that I will not tolerate this kind of behaviour. As a result, if they contact you, please let me know immediately. If they try to talk to any of you, please do NOT speak to them without me present. Legal Aid is only available if someone is arrested, but I would like to assure you all that I will not be charging you for being present during any questions they wish to put to you. If they ask you to attend the police station, please do NOT do so, but tell them they may

249

come and talk to you at your home, then give me a call to make sure I'm there with you before they arrive. Or, better yet, tell them they are welcome to talk to you at MY home. I'll make sure you get chocolate hob-nobs and they only get Rich Tea biscuits, which I'm already leaving out in our garden shed to go soggy.

See you all on Thursday. Please come armed with a nice story about Sandra, as we'll be taking a few minutes at the start of the rehearsal to remember her.

Best,
Anthea

Gabriel wondered how many people actually had nice stories about Sandra, thinking this may be a very short homage. He scrolled to the next email.

Hello cupcake,

I've heard back from the court. As the divorce is clearly going to be contentious, it's been slated for a hearing in front of a district judge on Tuesday 20th March at 2pm. You don't have to be present, but I'm recommending you are there. I've got something up my sleeve. Please can you put this in your diary.

See you Thursday,
Anthea

Gabriel suddenly realised he had no idea about how to take time off from work. Or even how much he was entitled to. The shop was empty, so he popped out to the cubbyhole that Neil called his office. It was more of a cupboard stacked with filing cabinets and ream upon ream of paperwork stacked in enormous piles on every inch of floorspace, shelf and cabinet top.

'Neil, do you have a moment?'

'Of course, dear boy! Have you remembered a piece of juicy information about the deceased?' Gabriel could swear Neil was actually beginning to salivate at the prospect.

'No, nothing about that.' Neil looked crestfallen. 'I was wondering how I go about taking time off?'

This appeared to stun Neil, who had clearly given no thought to this process but tried to bluster his way through it.

'Erm, if you let me know which days you would like off, I'll enter them into the computerised calendar and check them against other staff holiday to see if they're available.'

Gabriel was pretty sure Neil didn't even know where his computer was under all the documents and invoices scattered about the place, let alone how to use it.

'It's just one day. Tuesday 20th March. Anthea has just emailed to tell me that I have a hearing for my divorce and she'd like me there.'

'But of *course*, dear boy. No question, you must absolutely go!' Neil looked relieved that a month for a trip to Australia hadn't been requested. It also occurred to Gabriel that the prospect of any other staff taking a day off was a pretty remote one, as he had never known any of them take a day off other than Christmas Day, and he couldn't be completely sure they hadn't popped in anyway.

'Thanks. I've got no idea if it will all be sorted on that day or if it's just a preliminary hearing. I'm hoping it will be done and dusted pretty quickly though.'

'Yes, lad, it must be weighing on your mind. How are you holding up? Keeping that chin up?' Neil's voice dropped to a quieter level and Gabriel was sure this was as close to genuine concern as he could reach, which was touching.

'Yes, thanks. I'll just be glad when it's all over.'

'Will your ex-wife be there too?'

This thought hadn't even occurred to Gabriel and his stomach dropped at the prospect of having to see Shelley again.

'No idea,' he muttered, his thoughts drifting to a painful place for the first time in a while.

'Well, if you have a horrible shock and need some time to process it, just let me know that evening if you need the next day too. I remember what Grant was like during his divorce. He sobbed in his room for a week afterwards. Utterly inconsolable. You take all the time you need, okay?'

Gabriel wasn't sure what was more surprising: this level of concern from Neil, or the revelation that Grant had been married. The over-the-top sobbing that had just been described was less of a surprise and a very uncharitable part of Gabriel wondered if it had been at the divorce or because he had chipped a fingernail. He quickly scolded himself for being unkind and smiled back at Neil. 'Thanks. Anyway, back to work. My boss is a real nightmare, you know.'

'I've heard that. But a real charmer with the ladies, I'm told.' They both laughed.

As Gabriel reached the till in the still-empty shop, he felt his phone buzz again. A text message from Anthea.

Sunflower. Are you free tomorrow evening? Jane is flapping a bit at the prospect of stepping into Sandra's shoes (especially considering what happened to the last occupant they had). She's invited the cool kids round to hers tomorrow evening for a light supper and board games. Do come, and bring Lauren if she's available. Ax

There didn't seem to be much room for negotiation, so he resigned himself to an evening of small-talk, canapes and boring board games.

He arrived the following evening at the address Anthea had subsequently texted him, not quite sure what to expect, ringing the doorbell with some trepidation.

The door was eventually answered by a sullen girl with long, straight, jet black hair and so many studs in her face and ears it caused Gabriel to wonder if she set off airport security scanners just by being in the terminal. She stood and looked at him, without saying a word.

'Hi, I'm here to see Jane? Do I have the right address?'

The girl rolled her eyes and walked inside, leaving the door wide open. Gabriel assumed he had the right address and walked in, closing the door behind him and heading down a long hallway. When faced with numerous doors at the end which were all closed, he felt unsure what to do next. Then he heard a voice that was unmistakeably Anthea's shriek with laughter from behind the one in front of him. He tentatively turned the handle and peered into the room, desperately hoping he hadn't made the wrong choice and was about to find Rupert sat on a toilet, as he was quite sure Rupert would beckon him in for a chat while he finished his business.

Mercifully, he found himself staring into a beautifully decorated and brightly lit kitchen, with Jane, Anthea, Rupert, Richard, Debbie Greer (the orchestra librarian) and a very tall, thin man sat next to Debbie, whom Gabriel presumed to be her husband, all sat round a large table at the far end.

253

'Gabriel! Come on in! Pull up a pew and dive into nibbles! Everybody loves nibbles!' Rupert bellowed.

'Ah, nibbles,' Richard said in a wistful voice. 'He was my favourite hamster.' Despite the group (with the exception of Mr Greer) all bursting into raucous laughter at this, Gabriel still eyed up the food selection with genuine concern that what purported to be sticky chicken wings (covered in a quite delicious prune and molasses glaze, he later found out) might have been a rodent once upon a time.

'Take my seat, old boy,' Richard said. Gabriel wasn't sure how to take being called 'old' by someone in their early twenties, as he wasn't sure if it was meant ironically or because he was grouped in with Rupert in a generic anyone-older-than-me-is-ancient category in Richard's head. Dicky stood up and walked over to Rupert. 'This seat looks comfortable, if a bit well-worn,' he said, before plonking himself down on Rupert's lap.

Anthea laughed. 'Oh, you boys. You're always the same.' Rupert just grinned inanely. Richard pretended to nestle in to get comfortable, which just made Rupert's grin even wider.

Anthea turned to Jane. 'Darling, thank you for having us all round this evening. I hope you know that we're all on your side and we're willing you to succeed as orchestra leader.' The room went quiet and Jane looked down at the table in front of her.

'Thank you. It's not how I would have wished to get the position.'

'Of course not, but the position is now yours, and it's been earned over many years. Whilst I know you won't want to rock the boat for a few weeks out of respect to the dead,' Gabriel was surprised to see Richard, still perched

254

on Rupert's lap, crossed himself at the mention of the deceased, 'we all know that you will do a great job once you are able to start putting your stamp on things. At least you know how to write bowings in scores and stick to them.'

Various mumbles of 'Hear, hear' emitted from the assembled collective.

'We're all completely behind you and on your side. You know that Michael will be his normal tricky self, and he will be feeling very vulnerable without Sandra there, so expect him to be even more gruff than his usual self. But stick to your guns, you know more than he does.'

Jane smiled, touched at the show of solidarity and support from the people present.

'As long as I don't have to sleep with him like the last leader,' she said. This broke the tension and everybody laughed. 'Made that mistake once before and look at the trouble it caused over so many years.'

'Yes, that wasn't your finest moment, was it?!' Anthea said, with knowing looks from everybody else around the table. Gabriel nodded along, not quite sure how to respond to this piece of news, but it suddenly explained a lot about how Sandra used to treat Jane.

Jane didn't notice Gabriel's confusion or incredulity and said, 'Right, let's play a game. I'll get the kids,' before leaving the room.

Rupert looked at Gabriel. 'No Lauren tonight?'

'No, she's got reports to write. They're not due for another two weeks, but she hates having things hanging over her.'

'That's a shame,' Richard replied. 'Could have done with some eye candy tonight.' He shuffled on Rupert's lap to get more comfortable, causing Rupert's eyes to glaze over.

Jane returned a few minutes later with the sullen daughter who had opened the door to Gabriel and a young lad in his early twenties with a mop of curly hair that looked like it might have been permed.

'I think you all know Beatrice and Morgan. Oh, Gabriel, you probably haven't met them. Beatrice is studying physics at Durham and Morgan is doing a Masters in Fine Art at the Sorbonne in Paris.' Gabriel was somewhat taken aback that the girl had a brain. Perhaps the genes for social skills had been diverted into academic brilliance.

Morgan bounded over and shook Gabriel's hand, without looking him entirely in the eye. 'How do you do? I'm Morgan.'

'How do you do?' Gabriel responded, whilst trying to extricate his right hand from a particularly vicious handshake.

'This is my latest piece. You might be interested, as a musician. It's an artistic representation of John Cage's "4 minutes 33 seconds".' He gestured to an empty plinth in the corner of the kitchen.

Dicky jumped up from Rupert's lap to take a closer look. 'But there's nothing there.'

'Precisely. Or is there?' Morgan asked, quizzically.

'Can I take a closer look?' Richard asked, heading over to it.

'Please be careful!' Morgan shrieked in a slightly high-pitched voice. 'I don't want it damaged. I still have to put the finishing touches on it.'

Mr Greer headed over to look at the plinth with great interest. Debbie just smiled.

'Right, I thought we'd play Risk tonight,' Jane said, pulling out a large box. This wasn't just any version of Risk, it was the branded version based on the latest hit television series, which everybody except Anthea and Rupert had seen, putting them at something of a disadvantage.

Various strategies were employed over the next few hours, very few of them being legitimate ones. Jane kept topping everybody's drinks up in order to get them so drunk that it gave her an advantage. Richard and Rupert were clearly in cahoots, as Rupert would occasionally laugh very loudly, drawing everybody's attention away from the table whilst Richard would swipe cards or add pieces to his and Rupert's territories whilst the others were distracted. Beatrice and Morgan kept offering each other food items from their plates.

Somewhere around 2am, when Gabriel (who had never played Risk before) was winning by a surprising degree, Jane looked at Morgan and asked if he'd been eating the breaded mozzarella bites. Everybody looked at him and realised his face had gone a burning shade of crimson.

'Yeah, I may have had a few of the ones that Beatrice didn't want,' he said, before rubbing his hands and examining the board to see if he could come back from a highly precarious position.

'You know you're allergic to cheese!' exploded Jane.

'It's fine, Mother. It'll wear off by morning. You should be more worried about her,' gesturing towards his sister.

Everybody turned their attention to Beatrice, who had gone pale and even more quiet than before.

'Sweetie? Are you okay?' Jane asked.

257

'I'm fine, Mum. Stop worrying,' Beatrice replied.

'What have you had to eat tonight?'

'Just the stuff on the table.'

Jane shifted her attention to Morgan. 'What did you do?' she asked, in a barely audible voice through gritted teeth.

'Nothing!' came back the indignant reply.

'Morgan Lazenby!'

'What?!'

'Tell me what you did!'

'I thought the egg mayonnaise needed some zing, so I grated some garlic into it!'

Jane looked at him in horror before shifting her gaze back to Beatrice. 'Did you...?'

'It tasted so good...' Beatrice mumbled, looking pale and clammy.

'Did you know it had garlic in it?!' Jane shrieked.

'I love garlic...' was the last thing Beatrice said before slumping onto the floor.

'Morgan, I'm going to kill you! Call an ambulance! You *know* how she reacts to garlic!' Jane screamed. 'They'll have to pump her stomach which means we'll be at the hospital all night!'

'Okay, okay...' Morgan muttered, before dialling 999 on his mobile phone.

Anthea swung into action. 'Right, well, I believe Gabriel won that game. Well done, sweetie. I think it's time we were all off as it's so late, so we'll see you tomorrow night at rehearsal...'

She was too late. Beatrice, who was slumped unconscious on the floor, suddenly emitted the most enormous explosion of wind.

'Oh god, run for your lives...' Jane mumbled.

None of them moved quickly enough. The invisible fog that filled the air was so deadly it should have been on a list of substances banned by the United Nations. Tears started streaming down all their faces and at least two of the group struggled to breathe in the aftermath.

'Right, time for us to be heading off,' Anthea reiterated, before corralling any non-resident of that address to the front door and into the fresh air that would hopefully save their lives. 'Thanks, babes! See you tomorrow!' she spluttered, not quite able to see where she was walking, or breathe properly.

'Blimey,' Richard was heard to say. 'That family takes board games seriously. I've never known anybody deploy chemical weapons just to win a game.'

TWENTY-SIX

GABRIEL SPENT THE NEXT MORNING YAWNING his way through a stock check at the piano shop. He had been assigned to checking the sheet music racks. His nose still contained some of the noxious gas emitted from Beatrice's innards the previous night and, try as he might, nothing seemed to be expunging the stench from his nasal cavities.

Grant floated past, tapping his fingernails together. Gabriel thought they seemed longer than usual.

'Gone for a new style?' he asked, nodding towards Grant's hands.

'Oh, thank you for noticing. Yes, I thought I'd try going a bit longer; apparently, it's all the rage right now,' came back the creepy reply. 'I'm trying a new lacquer on them too, good for strengthening and making them shine. Do you like it?'

Gabriel inwardly shuddered and nodded in the most vague manner he could muster.

As it was stock check day, Neil had brought in a radio to boost staff morale. This apparently had zero effect as the staff consisted of Grant preening over his fingertips, Susan who was only capable of making tea more closely resembling dishwater, Neil himself who walked about with great purpose but with no apparent task to hand, and Gabriel, who was thumbing through teach-yourself-guitar-in-30-seconds books, counting all the various versions. With a plectrum. Without a plectrum. With nylon strings. With steel strings. With a ¾-sized guitar. With a full-sized guitar. With a banjo. With a ukulele. With no brain cells. With no desire to continue to live. With a foreword by Chuck Sanderson, bass player for The Cream Teas (Gabriel had never heard of them, nor did he consider the name to inspire rock and roll tendencies).

The latest number from some Britpop boy band came to a merciful end and the 11am news played on the local radio station, featuring one or two vaguely newsworthy headlines from the national centre, followed by the usual detritus of cat-stuck-up-a-tree-whilst-wearing-fishnet-stockings-and-a-bobble-hat monotony in local news. Following this, an ABBA track aired and the lunchtime presenter came on air.

'Hello, my little munchkins. I hope you've all been dancing along to that track from our Finnish favourites ABBA. This is your favourite Dancing Queen, Megan Sims, here to keep you occupied until 2pm.'

Gabriel dropped the pile of pointless music in his hands and snapped his head towards the radio. He couldn't believe that some idiot had thought it wise to unleash Menopausal Megan on the airwaves.

'As you know, today is Thursday, which means it's swap shop day. Ring in, let me know what you'd like to swap, and what you'd like in exchange. We'll try to start a bidding war that might go viral for you!'

It occurred to Gabriel that Megan clearly had no idea what any of these words meant.

As can only happen on local radio, the next two tracks were by Metallica and The Carpenters respectively. Gabriel pretended to look busy (much like any other day in Porlington Pianos) whilst hovering near the radio in order to hear whatever Megan would do next. As Karen Carpenter faded away to nothing, a long pause followed before Megan's voice suddenly appeared again, mid-sentence.

'...ame about what happened to that poor girl. I always thought she looked like she needed a good pie or two. Oh dear, I appear to have been leaning on my own mute button. Oops!' Gabriel rolled his eyes and grinned to nobody in particular. 'Well, we have our first callers for swap shop day. Hello caller number one. Who are you and what have you got to offer our viewers?' Gabriel wondered if Megan realised she was on radio and not television.

'A'right, Megs? It's Bob here, from The Oversized Turnip, Summerton's premiere organic pub, the only place for 30 miles to offer a full Vegan and gluten-free menu (don't forget Tuesday is steak and burger night).' Bob had a thick Bristol accent, which made Gabriel question if everything he had just heard was correct. Now he was beginning to get to know the locals a bit, he surmised he probably had.

'Hello Bob. How's business going since you re-opened? Terrible business that. Did they ever catch the little arse?' Megan descended into a spluttering fit and could be heard gulping down water. Or gin. One could never tell over the radio. Gabriel was beside himself, trying not to cry with laughter. 'Sorry, about that. I think I swallowed a moth. Where was I? Oh yes, did they ever catch the little arsonist?

'Nah, Megs,' Bob replied. 'The police have been useless. Little sod is still at large.'

'I'm really sorry to hear that, Bob. Glad you've got things back on track though. What would you like to get rid of today?'

'Well, as your listeners will know, we used to be The Queen Victoria, Summerton's premiere fish pub, where a pint of prawns was only a fiver. For those of you who remember, one of the great talking points of the town was the bust we had of Queen Elizabeth the First. Countless people have rubbed her nose for good luck as they passed by the bar. Anyway, it turns out old Lizzy survived the fire. We've given her a brush up and a polish with some Brasso, and most of the soot has gone. We'd like to offer her.'

'Wow, that's very generous, Bob! Ladies and gentlemen, we have a true piece of Summerton history available here! What would you like in exchange?'

'Any information leading to the capture of the little bugger that set fire to my pub. Anyone providing information leading to the capture and ultimate torture of him will be rewarded with old Lizzy. But please could you call in and let me have the information, rather than the police, as I'd like a word with him before they get to him and put him in the safety of a cell.'

'Well, folks, you've heard the man's terms. Drop the station a line and we'll put you in touch with Bob if you have what he wants. Of course, we can't condone what Bob was joking about there…'

'I wasn't joking, Megs…'

'…but if you do catch up with him, give him a good kicking from me. We'll have our next caller right after this old favourite from Bananarama.'

Gabriel could barely speak as he wiped the tears away from his eyes. If he'd known Megan had a show on Thursdays, he'd have insisted on having a radio long before now.

He continued to sift through music, just waiting for 'When We Were Young' to finish (he was also sure this was Bucks Fizz, not Bananarama). His patience was rewarded three minutes later.

'Hello viewers, this is Megan Sims on Porlington, Moleshine and Summerton FM. As we always say here, nothing cheers you up on a Thursday lunchtime like PMS FM.'

Susan came running in to find Gabriel in the foetal position amongst the music racks.

'I heard a scream! Have you hurt yourself?!'

Gabriel was gasping for breath and clutching at his chest, pointing at the telephone. Susan shot towards it to call for an ambulance before his pounding on the floor with his fist grabbed her attention and she saw him shaking his head, gesturing wildly towards the radio next to the telephone on the counter. This confused her enough to stop her. She then realised he was convulsing with laughter and assumed somebody had told a joke on the radio.

'You need a nice cup of tea, dear,' she said, a look of mock scolding on her face as she headed out the door to the kitchenette. Gabriel didn't have enough energy to stop her, accepting the consequence of his laughter would be one of Susan's dreadful cuppas.

Megan was still talking on the radio. 'And that's how Jim gets his cherry tomatoes to swell larger than any of his neighbours on the allotments. Now, we have another swap shop caller on line 2. Hello caller number two. Who

264

are you and what have you got to offer our wonderful readers?'

'Hello, Megan. It's Roxanne.'

'Ah, the Baroness von Klausen. How are you, Roxie?'

'I'm very well, thank you, Megan. And, actually, it's Countess…'

Megan seemed not to notice this correction. 'What have you got to offer the good people today?'

'Well, I've got a car I'd like to get rid of.'

'A *car?!* Good people of the Dent Valley, this might be a first! Just look at what we bring you, and all for free over the airwaves! What kind of car is it, Roxie?'

'It's a BMW 507 from 1956.'

'Oh.' Megan sounded deflated. 'Does it still go? That sounds like it'd need a lot of work.'

'It's a classic car!' Roxie's displeasure was dripping from her voice. 'It's one of the most beautiful cars ever made and extremely rare!'

Megan regrouped and pressed on, as though the last exchange had never happened. 'Marvellous! What can you tell us about it?'

'It's black and it goes like a rocket. In excellent condition, due to my late husband loving it more than he loved me.'

'Erm, okay… So what do you want for it?'

'Want for it? I just want the damn thing gone so I don't have the constant reminder hanging around the garages at my house.'

'Well, that's not quite how this works, sweetie. You need to ask for something in return. It's a swap shop.'

'Oh. I can't just give it away?'

'No, you need to ask for something in return. What's it worth to you?'

265

'I don't know! I hate the thing.' Roxie thought for a moment. 'Oh, I don't know. How about a bottle of vodka and a pot plant?'

'Any particular pot plant?' Megan enquired.

'Nope. I just need something to fill the space on the mantelpiece in the drawing room where his ashes were until I dumped them in the trash last week.'

'There you have it, folks. Our friendly neighbourhood Duchess is offering a classic German sports car in pristine condition and all she wants for it is a bottle of vodka (I assume you mean the good stuff...?)'

'Oh yes. Grey Goose with a hint of Cognac is always good.'

'...and a pot plant. Get in touch with the studio and we'll put you in touch with Roxie. Now we'll hear one of Earth, Wind and Fire's latest tunes and we'll be back with more swap shop. Oh my, that's a lot of red lights on my phone...'

Gabriel picked his jaw up off the floor and went back to checking scores in the rack, not even noticing that a cup of Susan's dishwateresque tea had appeared next to him without him noticing, blissfully unaware that, at that very moment, the first arrest was being made in relation to Sandra's murder.

TWENTY-SEVEN

'THE DATE IS THURSDAY 22ND FEBRUARY AND this interview is commencing at 1417 hours. The interviewing officer is Detective Inspector 43 Baxter, interviewing Fabian Michael Angelo. Also present are Detective Sergeant 128 Dunstan and Mrs Anthea Sweeney, Solicitor.

'I arrested Mr Angelo at 1137 hours this morning, on suspicion of murder. Can I remind you, Mr Angelo, that you do not have to say anything, but it may harm your defence if you do not mention when questioned something which you later rely on in court. Anything you do say may be given in evidence. Do you understand this?'

Fabian sat opposite DI Baxter, ashen faced, with the expression of a man whose world had just ended out of the blue, for no apparent reason. He nodded, timidly.

'For the purposes of the recording of this interview, the suspect nodded his agreement. Mr Angelo, can I advise you that if you wish to consult privately with your solicitor at any time during this interview, the interview can be delayed in order that you may obtain that advice. This interview is being recorded on three tapes

267

simultaneously for evidence. We may pause it at any time, but whenever you see this red light lit, anything you say is being recorded.'

There was a numb silence in the cramped interview room. Fabian was sat on one side of the small desk, questioning how his life had led him to this point. Anthea sat next to him, looking bored. Baxter and Dunstan were sat on the opposite side of the desk, between Fabian and the door, with acoustic tiling draining both the sound and the life out of the tiny room.

Baxter continued. 'Mr Angelo, we have given discovery of our evidence and questions to your solicitor. Has this been explained to you?'

Fabian looked nervously at Anthea, who nodded. He, in turn, nodded at Baxter.

'For the purposes of the recording, let it be known that Mr Angelo nodded his agreement.' Baxter had to resist the urge to roll her eyes. Dunstan sat next to her, seemingly interested, but quietly contemplating the following Saturday's football fixtures in his head, wondering how Sheffield Wednesday would fare.

'Mr Angelo, I arrested you this morning on suspicion of the murder of Sandra Finley. Could you shed any light on why you are a suspect in this investigation?'

Anthea sprang to life. 'I would advise my client not to answer that question due its leading nature. Might I remind the police officers present that this is not a fishing expedition. If you have specific questions to ask my client, please present them, otherwise my advice to him will be not to reply.'

Baxter visibly bristled. 'Very well, as you wish. Mr Angelo, could you please tell me what your movements were last Saturday evening?'

Fabian glanced at Anthea, who nodded at him.

'Well, erm, I, erm, was at a show.'

'What show was that?' Baxter enquired.

'I was, erm, directing, I mean, I had directed a production of *Hello, Dolly!* at the Summerton Pavilions last week. Saturday was our closing day. We had a matinee in the afternoon, then an evening performance at 7:30pm.'

'Thank you, I am aware of the performances. I understand that you had a disagreement with the deceased during the day...?'

Fabian was now panicking, his face turning whiter than his teeth. Anthea smiled at him, silently encouraging him to answer the questions that were being put to him.

'I hope you understand that I would never do anything to hurt anyone. This horrible thing that happened is nothing to do with me...'

Baxter just nodded and let the silence hang in the air, confident Fabian would fill it. Fabian couldn't understand why Anthea wasn't doing more to protect him. She was just sitting there, waiting for him to respond. He crumbled and started spouting forth.

'Oh, for God's sake, it was nothing really. Michael felt that two of the numbers should go quicker. He was only considering the musical aspects, and not looking at the wider picture. I tried to explain that my job was to look at the direction and choreography of the entire production, as well as the lighting cues—they are ever so important in such a large and notable production—but he wouldn't have it. He just kept banging on about the musicality. I *tried* to explain that this was only one aspect, and not the most important one, but he just wouldn't have it. Then

Sandra kept leaping to his defence. She was practically screaming at me in the dressing room…'

'Might I just interrupt there for a moment, Mr Angelo. I was led to believe this altercation took place in one of the corridors backstage, not a dressing room. We have several witnesses who passed by who have stated this. It would be unfortunate if you were to lie to us during interview,' Baxter said.

Anthea interjected. 'I think we can dispense with the threats, Ms Baxter.'

'That's DI Baxter please, Mrs Sweeney.'

'My apologies. Let me rephrase. I think we can dispense with the threats, Detective Inspector 43 Baxter. My client is not on trial here. Frankly, I'm only allowing this absurd line of questioning to continue in order to establish why you have arrested him in order to bring a wrongful arrest suit against you and the constabulary, as you gave me utterly insufficient information in discovery.'

'Mr Angelo, your solicitor appears to believe I was threatening you. I can assure you this was not my intent, nor what actually took place. I was just reminding you that anything you say may be taken down and you may later rely on it in court. A jury may take a dim view of you giving us false information…'

'PAMELA!' Anthea exploded. Fabian was beginning to think she might be worth having on side after all.

'My apologies. I would never wish to be accused of leading a suspect. Mr Angelo, please continue.'

Fabian suddenly felt on dodgy ground again. Anthea just nodded and smiled at him.

'Erm, it might have been in the corridor. To be honest, I think I might have been in my dressing room and they were in the corridor, talking to me through the open door.'

Dunstan interjected. 'Sir, if you don't mind me asking, why do you need a dressing room as the director? Surely you don't have any costume changes as you are not part of the cast?'

Fabian was suddenly on more solid ground. 'Well, no, of course not. But I need a base backstage. A director may observe his production from the wings, or from the audience, or he may even jump in as part of the chorus. But one always needs a space in which to be able to take people backstage to give them notes, or have private discussions.'

'I see,' Dunstan continued. 'And what sort of *private discussions* normally take place in your private dressing room?'

Anthea leapt in. 'Don't answer that.' She addressed the police officers again. 'I don't consider that to have any relevance on a murder investigation. You've already said, and my client has agreed, that a conversation took place involving him and the deceased in a semi-public forum, with the door open. Kindly don't insinuate anything else that you might later attempt to use to assassinate his character in front of a jury.'

Fabian's face once again looked like it had been bleached.

DI Baxter reluctantly picked up the line of questioning again, with a look of 'it was worth a try' passing between her and DS Dunstan.

'The thing is, Mr Angelo, this isn't the first time you've been connected with an unexplained death, is it?'

Fabian felt his face flush as the horror of a former life flooded back into his mind. He fought the descending

271

claustrophobia, knowing there was no way out of the room which suddenly felt even smaller and more menacing.

'I had nothing to do with that,' he whispered as the panic rose into his throat.

'But it was never solved was it?' Baxter pressed.

Anthea remained silent, desperately wanting to stop Baxter, but knowing she was entitled to ask her questions if they were reasonable.

'He took an overdose at a party. The police were never able to prove otherwise,' Fabian said.

'Well, that's one version of events. A healthy young man in the prime of his life, having taken a substance which wasn't tainted and of a low enough dose it shouldn't have killed him. One does have to question if that's the full set of facts,' Baxter said, raising her eyebrows and waiting for Fabian to respond.

'Is there a question here?' Anthea asked, grateful that Baxter had finally given her a chance to make her presence felt again.

'Very well,' Baxter muttered, beginning to get exasperated. 'Mr Angelo, you admitted supplying the drugs to the victim when arrested by the police at that time. Why don't you give us your version of what happened in that case?'

'Don't answer that, Fabian,' Anthea quickly said, realising he was on the verge of cracking and having an outburst that wouldn't do him any favours. 'DI Baxter, Mr Angelo clearly answered the police's questions at that time in relation to that case. He is not under arrest for that, he is under arrest for something entirely unrelated. Kindly limit your questions to the matter at hand.'

As Baxter flushed with frustration, Fabian couldn't help but say, 'I didn't supply him! He took the pill from my jacket and swallowed it before I had a chance to stop him!'

'Fabian, stop. You shouldn't answer questions which aren't about Sandra. Take a deep breath and calm down. They're trying to bait you.'

Dunstan looked up from his paperwork, briefly knocked from his football reverie by being included in collective responsibility for something he really wasn't actively taking part in.

Baxter swept in, trying to swing the momentum back in her own direction. 'But the thing is, we have Mr Angelo present at the time of, or within a few hours of two unexplained deaths. I think even you, Mrs Sweeney, would agree that we are duty bound to investigate when there is a causal link between two potential murders.'

Anthea nodded. 'I would agree that you need to investigate, however there is no causal link here, merely a tenuous one of proximity. You cannot say that a previous murder is the cause of another.'

Baxter rounded on Anthea. 'It might be if carried out by the same perpetrator for a common purpose.'

Anthea had to concede that point, but she wasn't giving up yet. 'From what I understand, you have no evidence the previous death was murder. In the absence of a solid conviction, may I remind you my client is regarded as innocent as you or me in relation to that. As such, unless you have evidence to link the two, may I suggest, again, that you limit your questions to the issue at hand. I am beginning to wonder if you have any evidence at all, other than Mr Angelo having seen Ms Finley several hours before her death, along with several

273

hundred other people, none of whom do I see in here for questioning. Unless you have something more, I would suggest our time here is at an end.'

A knock at the door interrupted proceedings. A young constable popped his head round the door, looked at Baxter and said, 'Ma'am, labs are in.'

Baxter rose from her seat, looking at the clock and saying, 'Interview paused at 1431.' She hit the pause button on the tape recorder and nodded at Dunstan, who followed her from the room.

With only the two of them left, Anthea turned to Fabian. 'Don't worry, you're doing fine. I don't think they're going to have anything else, otherwise they'd have hit us with it by now. I reckon we'll be out of here pretty soon. Now, I doubt many people have managed to say this to you since Saturday, with all the fuss, but very well done for the production. It really was good.'

Fabian was relieved to be talking about something else for a moment and the two of them shared small talk about *Hello, Dolly!* for a few minutes, whilst waiting for the officers to return.

After about five minutes, Baxter re-entered the room, with Dunstan shuffling in behind her. The door was still closing as she hit the record button on the tape recorder and said, 'Interview terminated at 1437.' She hit stop and left Dunstan to bag the tapes up.

'Mr Angelo, you are free to go. Please stay in the area as we may have some follow-up questions.'

TWENTY-EIGHT

THAT EVENING, THE ORCHESTRA FOUND themselves all present and seated by 7:30pm, with barely a word being spoken as nobody was quite sure what to say, or to whom.

Michael sat in a daze on the front row, looking very old. Events of the last few days had taken their toll. He showed no signs of moving, or that he was even aware of the time; perhaps not even where he was.

Anthea turned in her seat and smiled at Rupert, who walked forward and stood next to the podium, careful not to stand on it. When setting out the chairs, he had still put Sandra's chair in situ, which remained empty. Despite being the temporary leader, Jane stayed in her usual seat out of respect. They could all move up later, but this wasn't the time. Sandra might not have been liked much by many, but there was still a way of doing these things.

'Good evening, everybody,' Rupert began. Every eye was on him, except Michael, who hadn't moved and was still just staring into space.

Rupert continued. 'None of us would wish to be meeting tonight under these circumstances, and thank you all for coming. I'm delighted to see that I think we have full attendance tonight, which must be the first time in our history!' There were a few smiles.

'Before we begin sharing our memories of Sandra, I'm going to ask Anthea to say a couple of words.'

Anthea stood in her position and addressed the crowd.

'Good evening everyone. I'm going to keep this short as I can't say much, but I wanted to make a couple of suggestions for your own protection. You are all aware that there is an ongoing police investigation, so can I please urge you all not to gossip or speculate. This can cause immense damage and could get you in hot water, which I'd hate to see happen. I'm sure none of you would engage in either of these activities, but I'd feel bad if I didn't draw your attention to these things and somebody accidentally said the wrong thing.

'Can I also point out that, should any of you be approached by the press or media, you should not discuss anything at all. I'm sure you all saw there are one or two local reporters out the front tonight—they are not allowed on the premises, so I'm very glad that the parking here is on-site. Well done for avoiding them all thus far. If anybody approaches you, please refer them straight to me and just walk away. I've put out an official statement from the orchestra which says nothing at all. I'll just refer them back to that. Thank you.'

Rupert looked back at the assembled musicians. 'Okay, we're going to spend a little while remembering Sandra tonight, before we start rehearsing. Who would like to start us off?' He smiled at them all and inwardly begged every god he could think of to let somebody say something.

A chair at the back of the 2nd violins slowly scraped back, and people turned to see which brave soul was going first. Betty Brannon had risen to her doddery feet and she slowly moved towards the front. Rupert wondered what on earth was going to happen next as Betty had lost almost all ability to speak with the last stroke.

She reached the front and he saw she was carrying a single red rose. She closed her eyes and kissed it gently before placing it on Sandra's chair. She smiled at the empty space and shuffled back to her position. Anthea noticed through her own tears that a large number of the orchestra were silently wiping their eyes.

'Thank you, Betty… Thank you,' was all Rupert could manage.

One of the clarinet players stood. 'Okay, well, I'm just going to say it. Sandra was, perhaps, at times, not the easiest person to get on with.' Rupert opened his mouth to stop her before she made him pause with a well-placed, 'But.' Rupert closed his mouth again, worried about what might come next.

The clarinettist continued. 'She did lots of small things to help people that most folks didn't know about. In her own way, I think she viewed the orchestra as the family she never had, and I'm sure her sometimes gruff nature was only because she saw her role as the matriarch of the family.

'Years ago, she had a squirrel in her loft and she couldn't get rid of the little blighter. She tried every kind of trap going but could never get him. After a couple of months of being kept awake every night with the scurrying above her bed, she asked my John if he'd go over with our Jack Russell to sort it out. He sent Goliath up into that loft and it took less than two minutes for nature to take its course. It took longer for us to get the corpse back off him. Every Christmas after that, she always gave me a bottle of whisky for John and a big bag of treats for Goliath. Nobody else ever knew about this, but she had her ways of showing affection.' There were murmurs of agreement from around the hall.

The following 45 minutes passed by with many similar stories coming out, with people sharing about how Sandra would do their accounts for them for free when times were hard (Gabriel, sat over to the side, realised he hadn't even known she was an accountant), how she would drop round small toys when she found out people's children were sick and how she would take round trays of food for the freezer when somebody had had their appendix out. They reminisced about her favourite topics of conversation, from how she loved Italy from spending time there years before to how she could wax lyrical about an art gallery she had been to the previous week.

It was, in the end, a fitting tribute. Gabriel considered how sad it was that all these stories and sentiments never came out until after a person had died and they were unable to hear the good things people remembered about them.

At 8:20pm, Rupert drew proceedings to a close, thanked everybody for their contributions and said they would have the tea break a little early that night. Doris and Gertie had been warned about this, but were running round in a fluster nonetheless.

Everybody took their seats again shortly after 8:30pm without anyone having to ask them like usual. Even the brass were behaving tonight. Michael still hadn't moved from his place on the front row, nor had he spoken to anyone. Gabriel began to worry he might have to step in and take over running the rehearsal. As silence fell,

278

Anthea cleared her throat quietly under her breath. It was just enough to stir Michael, who took to the podium.

He looked like he was ten years older than the previous week. He was now just an old man who had lost his vitality. Gone were the usual heavy-breathing and aerobics. As he addressed the orchestra, his voice was a good five decibels lower than its normal bellow.

'Our next concert is our annual Viennese evening on Saturday 14th April. We have a professional soloist joining us for this and she has kindly agreed to come along this evening to play through her chosen piece. Daphne Maxwell is an excellent horn player and...'

He didn't get any further before Megan blurted out, 'What?! You're bringing in another horn player?!' Her section shifted uncomfortably in their seats. They were always unsettled and unpredictable when their leader was rattled.

Michael ignored this and carried on regardless, now reading from a cue card in front of him. 'Mrs Maxwell studied at the Royal College of Music and has worked with the London Symphony Orchestra. I am told her daughter is Phoebe Maxwell, who is something to do with dancing...'

This time, it was Henry James' turn. 'Phoebe Maxwell?! As in the former prima ballerina with the Royal Ballet who is now a supermodel and won last year's "Celebrities Go Wild in Ibiza"?! Is she going to be coming too? Can she wear that white bikini from the series final if she does?'

'I don't believe so,' Michael muttered in annoyance at the constant interruptions. 'Anyway, she will be playing the Britten Serenade for Tenor, Horn and Strings...'

'How's that Viennese?' piped up a voice from the percussion section.

'And why are we here if only the strings are required?' asked a brave bassoonist.

Michael continued as though neither of these things had been said. '...in the first half of the concert. Tonight, we will be rehearsing the fifth movement—Dirge.'

'Sounds about right for Britten...' was heard to drift from the percussion.

'If somebody could tell me when she arrives, I would be most grateful.'

Anthea coughed quietly under her breath again and glanced towards the back of the church.

An elegant lady in her early 50s was sat in the back row of chairs, wearing a black cape with silver thread and holding a horn on her lap. Nobody had noticed Daphne Maxwell slip in.

'Ah, here she is now, just in time,' Michael said, gesturing towards her.

Daphne stood and glided to the front of the church, with a benevolent smile on her face and a twinkle in her eye. 'Hello Michael.'

Michael seemed quite flustered by meeting her for what was clearly the first time and he barely managed to mutter out a greeting in response. Gabriel thought it was probably quite opportune Sandra wasn't here to witness this.

'Where would you like me?' she asked.

Michael was still no nearer pulling himself together, so he gestured to the usual soloist position just behind his left arm. Gabriel leapt into action and grabbed a music stand for her. 'Thank you so much,' she said, with a cheeky wink before returning to her serene position, waiting to be told what to do. She was statuesque in her repose, in stark contrast with Megan, who was shifting about in her chair like she was about to wet herself and glaring daggers at Daphne.

'And, of course, we will need our tenor,' Michael said, gesturing to the other spot to his right.

To everybody's amazement, Henry James stood from his seat and walked forwards, planting himself in said position and thrusting his hand towards Daphne. 'Hello, Henry James, international gigolo,' he said in a rumbustious voice.

Daphne took his hand and was about to shake it when he lunged forward and kissed the back of hers.

'Huge fan of your daughter's work. Is she single at the moment?'

The orchestra collectively cringed.

Daphne sidestepped with aplomb. 'Hello Henry, lovely to meet you. Tell me, how are you taking the accents in the rhythm in the Dirge when the string texture gets complex?' She thus drew him off into a brief conversation about music.

However, Henry couldn't resist a parting shot. 'This is going to be great fun. And I can see where Phoebe gets her looks from,' came out of his slightly leering mouth, followed by the most unsubtle wink since Baldrick last hatched a cunning plan.

Michael picked up his baton and was about to count the band in when the doors at the back of the church burst open, spewing forth DI Baxter and DS Dunstan, who marched up the aisle with determination.

Anthea immediately started packing her cello away, as she could tell she was going to have to swing into action at any second. She threw an apologetic look over her

281

shoulder at Rupert, who smiled back at her, correctly suspecting he was going to have to take his double bass home on the bus tonight as she'd be hotfooting it with the car.

Baxter and Dunstan reached the podium as everybody in the room froze. They could see two uniformed officers had taken up position at the back of the room, guarding the door.

Baxter spoke.

'Michael Fordington, I am arresting you on suspicion of the murder of Sandra Finley...'

TWENTY-NINE

ICHAEL WAS TAKEN TO THE STATION IN A police car and booked into custody. He was told that, after processing, he wouldn't be interviewed until the following morning. His keys, wallet, mobile phone, belt and shoes were taken from him, but they permitted him to keep his glasses. He was placed into a small cell with a metal toilet and sink, and a small bench with a foam mattress wrapped in PVC. The door slammed behind him and keys jangled in the lock, followed by footsteps disappearing away into the night.

The inside of a cell is a surreal place, but perhaps the strangest thing is to see a door with no handle. It was when he noticed that, and realised he couldn't escape, that Michael finally broke down and wept for the first time since finding Sandra's body. The sobs racked him and he felt entirely alone in the world. They eventually subsided and he realised there wasn't a chance of getting much sleep tonight.

After he had counted all the white tiles on the walls individually four times (there were 1488 of them), he was collected and taken to another room where his photograph was taken and an officer took his fingerprints on a red scanner, before a DNA sample was collected from a surprisingly painful mouth swab. They always looked like long cotton buds on television, but, in reality, the tips were metal with sharp ridges, presumably to loosen the cells they were intended to collect.

He was taken back to the sterile, white cell and left there until 8am the following morning, when he was brought breakfast. He was surprised this was something resembling an English breakfast and not just cereal, until he tasted it and realised it was clearly just a microwave meal. A particularly bland one that didn't sit well in his stomach at that.

Around 9:30am, an officer opened the cell door, handed him his shoes which had apparently been sat outside the door all night, and led him down the corridor to a room where he found Anthea waiting for him.

'Hello, Michael. How are you holding up?' she asked.

'How do you bloody think?' he retorted, purely from exhaustion and terror, without realising how aggressive he sounded.

Anthea had heard it all before and she wasn't fazed easily. 'Yes, I can imagine it was a pretty rough night. I have expressed my extreme displeasure that they took you last night, with the clear intention of making you wait overnight. Personally, I think this was just to try to wear you down by embarrassing you in front of people and then making you sweat and become sleep deprived.'

Michael internally agreed that both had been effective.

Anthea continued. 'My concern for you now is that you will be questioned whilst in a vulnerable state. They've given me a certain amount of information, which I can discuss with you before we speak to them. I'm going to suggest that you keep your answers very brief and to the point. Listen carefully to what questions they ask and don't elaborate on anything. If they ask you something that only requires you to respond with yes or no, do so. If they fall silent, don't fall into the trap of filling the silence. Just wait and play them at their own game. And don't forget that you can ask for the interview to be suspended at any point for you to ask me anything you want in private. If I think you're heading somewhere you shouldn't, I'll jump in before you get a chance to say something you don't want to.'

Michael briefly wished he had treated Anthea with a little more respect over the years. He had only ever seen her as a moderately capable cellist and had never taken the time to learn just what she did. Or just how well she did it.

Over the next twenty minutes, Anthea outlined what she had been told by the police and they discussed various strategies as to how to proceed.

Eventually, she rose from her chair and said, 'Okay, I think you're as ready as you'll ever be. I'll tell them we're ready, if that's alright with you?'

'Do I have a choice?' he asked.

'Not really, my dear. But you're not on your own.'

They were both shown into another tiny interview room, where Baxter and Dunstan were waiting for them. Baxter went through the usual rigmarole of starting the tape, waiting for the beep to finish to make sure actual magnetic tape was rolling and giving the preamble and introductions about who was there, what the time was and the arrest and caution details.

Baxter opened the interview.

'Mr Fordington, are you are aware of the evidence we have against you, as discussed with your solicitor?'

'Yes, I am.'

'Do you have anything you wish to say at this point?'

'No.'

Anthea smiled at Michael. He was doing surprisingly well so far, and following instructions.

'Why don't you have anything to say, sir?' Baxter asked. 'These are serious charges that have been brought against you, surely you wish to defend yourself?'

Anthea decided to assert her authority early on. 'DI Baxter, no charges have been brought at all. My client has been arrested, not charged. It is not for him to defend himself to you, merely to answer the questions you put to him as part of your investigation, and I haven't heard a question relating to that yet. Might I remind you of how the last couple of sessions we've had have gone and request you ask direct questions pertaining to your legal line of enquiry?'

Baxter moved on, pretending not to be bothered by Anthea's intrusion into her line of questioning.

'Very well. Mr Fordington, we have had our initial lab results back and your DNA has been found to be all over Ms Finley's house. Do you have an explanation for this?'

'I do. I was a frequent visitor to Sandra's house as we were very close. I would be surprised if you hadn't found my DNA everywhere.' Michael stopped himself from saying any more and received a smile of congratulation from Anthea.

'Yes, Mr Fordington. As you stated in our previous conversation, you were actively pursuing an extra-marital affair with the murder victim, weren't you?'

Anthea opened her mouth but Baxter cut her off before she had a chance to say anything.

'My apologies, with the deceased. I am aware your solicitor has objected to the way in which our previous conversation was carried out and she is welcome to take this up with a higher authority.'

'Sweetheart, I've already filed a formal complaint with the Independent Office for Police Conduct. I'm happy to give you the case reference number,' Anthea said.

'That won't be necessary, Mrs Sweeney,' Baxter replied, with a sickly sweet smile attempting to stick itself to her face. 'Mr Fordington, can you confirm that you were, indeed, having an affair with the deceased?'

'Yes.' Michael stated.

Baxter realised Anthea had managed to do a little more coaching with this client than the previous one. She didn't let this deter her.

'Somewhat more concerning from our point of view is the preliminary report we have received from the post-mortem. I am required,' she said, glaring at Anthea, 'to inform you that the initial post-mortem was inconclusive, and Ms Finley's body is currently undergoing further tests. However, some initial lab tests are back and we know that your blood was found under her fingernails, as though she fought you off as an attacker.'

Baxter stated this with a ring of triumph before falling silent and waiting for Michael to say something. Surely the level of sleep-deprivation he must be encountering should push him into reacting to this. What Baxter couldn't see was Anthea digging her fingernails hard into Michael's right leg under the table, silently instructing him not to say a word.

Eventually, Baxter asked, 'Do you have no reply to this, sir?'

Michael simply said, 'I don't believe you have asked me a question which requires a reply.'

Anthea was inwardly punching the air, so very proud of Michael for sticking to the plan. Oh, that every client would do as they were told so well.

Baxter was far more sure of her ground today, with DNA evidence on her side.

'Mr Fordington, can you explain how your blood was under the fingernails of the late Ms Sandra Finley?'

Michael took a few deep breaths before replying.

'No, I cannot. The only thing that springs to mind is that, on Saturday, I had a spot on my neck from where my shirt collar had rubbed during the extreme temperatures under stage lights during the run of the shows. In between the matinee and evening performances, Sandra noticed this and scratched at it to remove the flecks. As she did so, her fingernail opened the spot back up and blood started oozing again. She quickly mopped this up with a tissue so it wouldn't stain my dress shirt. I can only presume this is how she came to have my blood anywhere on her person.'

'That seems a pretty vague suggestion, sir,' Dunstan said. Michael did not reply.

Baxter jumped back in. 'Were there any witnesses to this?'

It was Anthea's turn. 'Actually, yes. I happened to be in Michael's dressing room, asking him if him and Elizabeth or Sandra would like to join Mr Sweeney and myself after the evening performance for a drink. I saw this happen for myself.'

Baxter seemed unimpressed. 'Well, that's a coincidence, Mrs Sweeney...'

'I do hope that you are not suggesting an officer of the court would be lying in a police interview, DI Baxter? I would hate to have to add an addendum to my existing complaint to the IOPC. I don't believe you have any reason to suggest I would lie in this instance and my husband can independently corroborate this chain of events as he was with me at the time.'

'I would suggest no such thing, Mrs Sweeney,' Baxter muttered, fixing Anthea with a particularly false smile.

Dunstan decided he should help his boss and he took the next question on their list. 'Sir, could you please walk me through your involvement in the events surrounding Ms Finley's death again?'

Anthea nodded at Michael, who proceeded to tell the story, once again, of how he went home with Elizabeth after the performance, where they both had their Horlicks and went to bed. The following morning, he woke and went to see Sandra, letting himself into her house via the front door, which was open, and discovering her body in her bed.

Baxter and Dunstan spent the next twenty minutes asking questions about the relationship between Michael and Sandra—how they had met, how long the affair had been carrying on for, how often they saw one another, and so on. Anthea let all these questions roll along, as the officers behaved themselves and asked pertinent and reasonable questions.

Eventually, the interview appeared to be drawing to a close. DI Baxter started her wind-down. Or so it seemed.

'Mr Fordington, thank you for being helpful and answering our questions. I have just one or two more questions. Why did you decide, at this time, to kill Sandra Finley?'

Anthea drew in a sharp intake of breath, about to object when Michael beat her to it and said, 'I did not kill Sandra. I loved her. I have no idea who killed her, but I hope that once you finish here with me today, you will go out and continue to try to find who really did this. I mourn her loss deeply and I wish nothing more than to see her killer brought to justice.'

Anthea settled back into her chair, deciding to let Michael play this out for himself as this would probably prove to be one of the most therapeutic things he did following Sandra's death.

Baxter ignored his answer. 'But the evidence we have only points towards you killing her. How do you explain that?'

Michael was building up a head of steam. 'I don't believe I have heard any evidence today. You have a DNA match with my blood underneath her fingernails, but I have provided a perfectly reasonable explanation as to how that got there, corroborated by an inscrutable witness. I haven't heard anything else put to me which would suggest I could have had anything to do with Sandra's killing, as I was with my wife throughout the entire window when Sandra was killed.'

Baxter and Dunstan exchanged a slightly nervous glance.

Baxter continued, 'But, sir, you are not putting forward any alternative explanation as to how Ms Finley may have been killed, or by whom, or for what reason.'

'That, Detective Inspector, is because it is neither my job nor my place to do either of those things. They are entirely within your remit. I have spoken the truth today. I am perfectly happy to take off all my clothes right now so you can see there are no scratches or claw marks anywhere on my body which could account for my DNA being under Sandra's fingernails.' He stood and began to unbutton his shirt. Anthea shut this down quickly by grabbing Michael's arm and pulling him back into his seat.

'DI Baxter, I can assure you that I will be having Mr Fordington examined by a medical professional to prove what he says just as soon as he is released today. If you decide to hold him in custody any further, I will be arranging for a doctor to attend this custody suite to undertake said examination. If you try to stop this, I will have you held in contempt of court for the obstruction of collection of evidence. Frankly, I'm amazed you haven't had this done already.'

Dunstan felt the shift of atmosphere in the room and looked at his boss, waiting to see how she would react. Baxter paused for a moment before replying, 'That is entirely your prerogative, and we will, of course, allow any such examination, subject to the results being shared with us.'

'I don't think so, sister. Defence don't have to share anything with prosecution. You want him examined, you sort it yourself. Just don't stand in the way of my guy.'

Baxter clenched her jaw and stopped to gather her thoughts. She thought that idiot Dunstan wasn't helping either, he was just sitting there like the gormless fool he was.

Michael suddenly went on the offensive.

'DI Baxter, might I ask a question?'

Anthea, Baxter and Dunstan all snapped their heads towards Michael, with an air of surprise.

'Of course.'

'As this interview appears to be hinging on my DNA being found at Sandra's house, might I ask how you knew it was my DNA? I haven't been asked to provide a sample.'

Baxter appeared confused by the question. 'Your DNA was taken from you last night after you were arrested.'

Michael wasn't backing down. 'Yes, I am aware of that. But that was after you arrested me. Your line of questioning has implied that my arrest hinged on my DNA being found at the crime scene. But you didn't have my DNA until after you arrested me.'

Dunstan shot his boss a warning glare, but she didn't pick up on it and thundered straight into oblivion.

'Your DNA is held in the National DNA Database after a previous arrest. When the lab samples came back after the initial post-mortem on Ms Finley, it matched with your profile held on this system.'

Anthea was wondering where this somewhat unexpected turn of events was going, but her curiosity let her watch it play out.

Michael continued. 'Can you please tell me why my DNA profile is held in your records?'

Baxter glanced down at her notes, flicking through several pages before replying.

'Yes. You were arrested on suspicion of drunk driving the Christmas before last and a sample was taken from you then.'

'I remember,' Michael said. 'Do you have the details of that case there?'

'Erm, no, I don't,' Baxter replied, with a sense of impending doom building in her stomach.

'May I fill in the blanks for you?' Michael asked.

'I don't think that's necessary,' Baxter began, before Anthea cut her off.

'Well I'd like to hear this, even if you wouldn't.'

Baxter reached for the tape recorder. 'I think our interview in relation to our questions is complete. Interview terminated at...'

Before she had a chance to finish her sentence or hit the stop button, Pamela Baxter realised Anthea's hand was clamped over hers in the tightest death-grip she had ever felt, as Anthea hissed through gritted teeth, 'Touch that tape machine and I will have you struck off for obstruction of justice.' Anthea actually had no idea where Michael was going with his story, but she decided to give him the benefit of the doubt, as he appeared remarkably in control and well-informed. She just hoped he hadn't snapped with the grief of Sandra's passing and the pressure of being back in the police station.

Anthea looked at Michael and smiled. 'Please continue.'

Baxter realised Dunstan's hand was now on hers, slowly pulling it back from the tape recorder, in a way that nobody could tell was being done from the audio recording.

'In December before last,' Michael began, 'I was pulled over by a police car on the flimsiest excuse. They said I hadn't indicated at a junction, when I had. They asked if I had been drinking that night. I said I had just half a pint of ale a few hours before. This, apparently, was sufficient excuse for them to request another car to attend with a breathalyser kit. In the interim, they rather stupidly said I hadn't indicated with sufficient time, which showed they were clearly trumping up an excuse to keep numbers up. When the other car arrived some twenty minutes later, I failed the breathalyser test and was taken into this very station where I was required to have a blood sample taken from me.'

Anthea was beginning to worry, but gave Michael the benefit of the doubt. For now.

'When the results came back, it showed I had zero alcohol in my blood, as I had metabolised the half-pint I'd enjoyed quite some hours before. Whilst waiting for the results, I had my fingerprints, mug shots and DNA taken and I was treated like a common criminal, despite having committed no crime. I am assuming that it is that DNA profile that you have on your system. Am I correct, Detective Inspector?'

Baxter could see where this was heading and decided to hedge. 'I'm not entirely sure, Mr Fordington, I'd have to check.'

'You do that,' came back Michael's response. 'You will also discover that the breathalyser unit used in that test was faulty, following your officer's unlawful decision to pull me over for no reason, presumably just to keep his statistics up for that day. I was released with no charge or prejudice.'

Anthea realised she was beaming from ear to ear and she decided to take up the narrative from this point.

'Is this correct, DI Baxter?'

'I'm really not sure, I'd need to check.'

'I'm pretty sure it's all there in front of you, Pamela.'

Baxter was, by now, at screaming pitch, but she couldn't see a way out of this and she knew exactly where both Michael and Anthea were heading.

Michael beat Anthea to the punchline. 'Now, I'm not a legal person, but, as I understand it, any fingerprint or

DNA records taken from me at that time should have been destroyed immediately..?'

Baxter attempted to head this line of conversation off, whilst Dunstan just hunkered down in his seat and waited for the inevitable to happen. 'I think you'll find we are entitled to hold records for up to three years, which we are still well within…'

Anthea exploded in the passive-aggressive way only the English can. 'I think you'll find, DI Baxter, that you are only entitled to hold those records if there is a good reason, such as a person being charged or being under suspicion for another crime. In this instance, they should have been destroyed immediately, unless ordered otherwise by the Biometrics Commissioner. Has that authorisation been granted in Mr Fordington's case, because I fail to see why it would have been?'

'I don't have that information to hand…'

'I think you do, but you don't want to admit it, my dear,' Anthea pushed. 'Now, I suspect that this has occurred due to some ridiculous police oversight, or laziness, but it doesn't negate the fact that your constabulary are in breach of Article 8 of the European Convention on Human Rights, enshrined in the Human Rights Act of 1998.'

Baxter felt sick. Anthea felt triumphant.

'So, let me recap the situation for you. You used a DNA profile on my client that you should not legally have had. You arrested him based on this, and subjected him to questioning. During this, he passed your questions with flying colours, but by being arrested, it gave you the opportunity to gather his DNA profile once again, which I am sure is what you intend to present to the Crown Prosecution Service and, ultimately, the courts. However, this whole scenario relies on evidence that was obtained illegally, thus negating the entirety of the last 13 hours. Do I really need to explain how easily I'm going to have this thrown out by the first judge I get this in front of?'

Baxter realised the game was up. She looked at Dunstan for support, only to see his eyes were firmly fixed on a spot on the table in front of him and he wasn't for turning. Pamela opened her mouth to speak but had no idea where she could go next, so she closed it again. Then opened it. Then closed it. This process was repeated several times.

At that moment, the clouds parted and the sun shone through as there was a knock at the door to give her an excuse to flee the scene. She paused the interview tapes and stepped outside with Dunstan.

The young constable, looking utterly bemused at how this case was panning out just stared at Baxter, as the elderly woman next to him spoke.

'I understand you are the detective in charge of the Sandra Finley case?'

'Yes, I am,' Baxter said.

'My name is Elizabeth Fordington. You can let that stupid old bastard go, he had nothing to do with it. I'm the person you want. I killed Sandra.'

THIRTY

ELIZABETH SAT IN THE INTERVIEW ROOM, waiting for Baxter and Dunstan to come in and start the interview, some hours later. She had a duty solicitor who appeared to be aged twelve years old sat with her. She had briefly spoken with Anthea in the immediate aftermath of her bombshell.

'Elizabeth, I'm so sorry, I can't represent you. As I represented Michael in his interview following arrest, I'm afraid it means both I, and anybody from my firm, would have a conflict of interests in representing you. However, I've instructed Brandon Marlborough from Diffney Whyatt Solicitors to attend your interview with you. I know him well, I trained him when he was on his training contract with us, and I have absolute faith in him.'

Elizabeth wasn't so sure, looking at the child next to her, whom she was sure was still pre-pubescent. But she was also past the point of caring.

It had been tremendously tempting to let Michael take the fall for Sandra's murder after all the years of putting up with their affair. Granted, it had suited Elizabeth to be shot of Michael for a day or two each week, as it had meant she could get on with her own life without him constantly getting in the way, but that didn't negate the fact she had no say in the situation, nor did it take away the pain of knowing she had never been enough for the man she had married and had once loved.

Baxter and Dunstan had discussed things up in their office.

'Okay, boss. Nobody saw this coming, but it would appear this case may have just solved itself. Possibly not a bad thing, considering how things were going,' Dunstan said.

'Oh, do shut up, Colin. If things were overlooked, they were done so by you too. Perhaps if you'd paid a little more attention to the case and done your job, rather than just running down the clock to retirement, we might not have dropped the ball on so many things,' Baxter countered.

Dunstan let this slide. 'So how are we going to play this?'

Baxter had thought long and hard about this, as well as running the unexpected turn of events up the chain of command.

'I think the only thing we can do is sit there and listen. At the moment, we don't know if this is her way of trying to get her husband off the hook, or if she wants to grind the axe she's clearly got and somehow land him in it further. We've got time on our side, so I think we just listen to what she's got to say and then discuss things before going back in with further questions.'

Baxter was aware that a confession was the strongest lead the case had so far, and their actions were under constant scrutiny from higher up. She would never admit it to anyone, but, so far, they had only been clutching at straws. This might just make it all okay and get the result they wanted.

Elizabeth had been arrested on the spot, and held in custody ever since. It was an old trick, to leave someone in a cell for a while to unnerve them, but when somebody wanted to confess, it was sometimes better to get that on tape sooner rather than later.

To keep their options open, Michael also remained in custody, in a different cell, as they didn't have to make a decision on him just yet. Anthea Sweeney would, no doubt, have something to say on this subject, but the police officers were still within their rights to hold him for now.

A little after 3pm, Baxter and Dunstan were loitering around the desk sergeant's desk, biding their time until Elizabeth's solicitor came out to tell them they had spoken and were ready. Eventually, Brandon Marlborough came out and informed them that his client was ready to speak to them.

They went through the motions of prepping the tape, reminding everybody that an arrest had been made and a caution provided, before DI Baxter opened proceedings.

'Mrs Fordington, you voluntarily came to the station today to confess to the murder of Sandra Finley in the early hours of last Sunday, the 18th February. You have been arrested on suspicion of this murder and are now being questioned by myself and DS Dunstan. Do you understand everything so far?'

'I do,' Elizabeth replied, firmly.

'First, I'd like to thank you for coming in to speak to us, that can't have been easy,' Baxter continued. 'Could you please tell us, in your own words, what happened?'

Elizabeth picked up the narrative.

'I assume you want me to start from the very beginning, to explain my reasons?' Elizabeth asked.

Baxter smiled her first genuine smile for quite some time and nodded, wondering what had happened in this woman's life to push her to finally snap.

'Very well. My husband started having an affair with Sandra years ago. I'm still not entirely sure of exactly when this began. My best guess is that it was a little over 30 years ago, although I've never been able to get him to commit to an answer, as he never wants to discuss it and tells me to stop asking questions. Frankly, I'm not sure I ever wanted to know the answer, so I stopped trying to find out many years ago.

'I found out about the affair about 29 years ago. He was acting very strangely. He was clearly preoccupied and was acting furtively—more so than usual—and he would disappear off frequently, not wanting to tell me where he was going, what he was doing, or who he was meeting. I tried to talk to him about this, but he always brushed off my questions.

'One morning, he was even more distant than normal. I couldn't get any sense out of him, so I decided to follow him that day and find out what he was up to. This wasn't easy, as he always took our car, so I wasn't entirely sure where he would be. I dropped our son off at pre-school and took a guess as to where Michael might be, taking the bus to Moleshine. I walked around the entire village, trying to find him, but I couldn't. A few days later, when he left, I took the bus to Fawlham, walking around again. Still no sign.'

Baxter interrupted her. 'Sorry to interject, you and Mr Fordington live in Summerton, correct?'

'Yes, that's right. We have done since we got married,' Elizabeth said.

'Over the next few days, I tried various villages and towns, but I couldn't track him down. I was always limited with my time, as I had to get back to pick up our son from pre-school. Eventually, one Thursday, I decided to try Porlington, as I knew he had orchestra that night. I walked around the town for an hour or two, but I still couldn't see any sign of him. This seemed strange, as I knew he must be there, but I didn't know where. I knew one of his committee, Sandra, lived in Porlington, so I decided to walk down her road.'

Dunstan decided to ask a question. 'How did you know her address?'

Elizabeth continued, 'She was listed as the secretary for the orchestra. Michael has never been good with admin, so I used to type his letters for him at home, get him to sign them, then post them. I had typed her address numerous times, so I knew it.

'On this particular day, I was determined to stay until I got some answers, so I had arranged for my neighbour to pick up our son from pre-school when she picked up her own son. The two boys were great friends, so this would be a treat for them.'

Baxter jumped in with a question, not wanting to interrupt Elizabeth, but needing to make sure her timelines were correct. 'This was when you only had one child, correct?'

'Yes, that's right. I was pregnant with our second at the time, about five months along.'

'Sorry to interrupt, please continue,' Baxter said.

'It was beginning to get late by the time I walked to Sandra's road. As I turned the corner, I saw the two of

301

them come out of her house. They were both clearly flustered and had had an argument. Sandra checked and re-checked she had locked her house, and Michael appeared on edge. It looked like they had both been crying, although I was some distance away so I couldn't be sure.

'As they walked out to our car, Sandra stopped and just waited. Michael walked back from the car and hugged her. Then they looked at one another, and he kissed her. On the lips. In a way that means only one thing. At that moment, I knew what had been going on for some time.'

Dunstan jumped in. 'Did you confront them?'

'No. I watched them kiss for a minute or two, then hug, then cry together. In all the years I have been married to Michael, that is the only time I've ever seen him cry, and it was with another woman, not me.'

Baxter felt herself begin to feel empathy with this woman, but desperately tried to suppress it. 'What did you do next?'

'I hid in a neighbour's front garden with high hedges, so they didn't see me. They drove off, presumably to the orchestra rehearsal.'

'And then what?'

'I caught the bus back home and collected my son from my neighbour.

'I didn't know what to think or feel, so I said nothing for days. This turned into weeks, with Michael disappearing off all the time and being evasive about where he was going.

'Eventually, after a few weeks, I confronted him. Of course, he denied everything and started yelling at me that this was all my fault, everything was in my head, I didn't understand what he was going through, etc. I knew from his reaction that I was right, and both him and Sandra had been having an affair.

'It was the next day that I lost our baby. The doctors were never able to tell me exactly why, they just put it down to being "one of those things", but I knew it was from the pain and stress I was under.'

Baxter reached across the table and put her hand on Elizabeth's. 'I'm so sorry, I really am.'

Elizabeth bristled and pulled her hand back. 'Well, that was all a very long time ago.

'Of course, I wouldn't let it go. I kept pressing Michael about Sandra, but he always denied everything, and got very angry with me. I told him that he had to choose between the orchestra or me and our remaining child. He would always side-step and tell me I didn't understand what he was going through. He would say that I didn't understand the pressures he was under trying to run a major orchestra. I genuinely think he believed he was running a major orchestra, not some tinpot, half-arsed bunch of musicians who can't play the most basic symphony.

'A week or two later, I guess the two of them had got the message. One day, Michael came home and was furious with me for no discernible reason. We had the most almighty row and I thought he was going to kill me—he had me against the kitchen wall with his hands around my throat, screaming at me about how I ruined everything and everything was my fault.

'I had no idea what had sparked this off and kept begging him to tell me. Eventually, he yelled at me that Sandra couldn't take the guilt anymore and had moved away. I believe she went out to Italy, which she loved and often holidayed there throughout her life.'

Baxter and Dunstan both independently thought how well Elizabeth was doing telling this story. She was clearly still caused pain by what had happened in her life, but there was also a resignation that had presumably set in years before. They waited while Elizabeth took a sip of water.

'Michael was completely indifferent to us losing a child. But then, he was never overly impressed when we had one, either.'

Baxter jumped in. 'That must have been hard for you,' she said.

'It was,' Elizabeth replied. 'But I just resigned myself to it. He was never going to change that much.

'About a year later, I noticed that his mood had improved. He was more attentive towards me, and things appeared to get better. I became pregnant again with our next child. The orchestra seemed to be going well, from what he told me, and things were improving. I was nearly full-term with Daniel when I went to a concert and saw Sandra was back in the orchestra and playing. I ran to the nearest toilet and was sick. Mercifully, I didn't lose Daniel. I don't think I could have faced losing another child. I was determined not to let the two of them rob me of anything else.

'When we got home that evening, I confronted Michael and he admitted that Sandra had returned a few months before and they had been seeing each other again. There appeared to be no room for discussion on the topic, and we never spoke of it again. That was nearly 30 years ago. I've known what has gone on with the two of them throughout this time, but I was always too scared to raise this, after the time he had his hands around my throat. Daniel was born, then a couple of years later, we had our daughter. I wish I could say she wasn't his, but there was one night when we were all away on holiday in Devon that nature took its course. That was the last time he and I ever had relations.'

Baxter, Dunstan and Marlborough all looked at her in amazement. She had managed to last over 25 years without being intimate with her husband, out of either duty, fear or loathing. The tape missed all this, but Elizabeth noticed, and was grateful that somebody else maybe finally understood her pain.

Dunstan's curiosity got the better of him. 'Please carry on.'

'I have tolerated those two making me a laughing stock for decades. Over the last two years, his doctor and I have been trying to persuade him that he isn't up to the pressure of running the orchestra each week any more. I've tried to discuss it with him on so many occasions, but he just won't have it. We've argued more and more over the last year, but I wouldn't let it go. I've stuck by him, no matter what he's put me through. I've put up with having to see Sandra and pretend to be friends with her for years, but when Dr Fry told him that he had to scale back or risk an early grave, I upped the pressure on him. He might have been awful to me, but I don't really fancy being stuck here on my own without anybody to talk to for the remaining years I have. Our children live away now, so the only person I have here is him. I guess I also thought that if I could get him away from the orchestra, I might have him back to myself and tear him away from Sandra. I waited most of my life to be able to do that.

'Over the last couple of months, he appeared to come round to the idea that he might have to scale back, but it was grudgingly. He was getting more and more stressed with the most recent concert, and he promised me he'd think about handing over more to the new conductor the orchestra had. We reached an agreement that he would be home by 11pm each night of the recent run of *Hello, Dolly!*, but he didn't manage this at all. I confronted him about this, but he wouldn't have me interfering. In hindsight, I don't think he had any intention of stepping down at all.

'The arguments got worse as the week went on, and Sandra was always there, putting her point of view forward and defending my husband to me. As the week went on, I realised that the real problem was her interfering all the time. If she wasn't around any more, I'd have him back and he might see sense and retire.'

Baxter and Dunstan could see the inevitable coming, but they had to let Elizabeth play the scenario out.

'Michael, Sandra and I had several blazing rows throughout the week. Eventually, I just gave up, as it wasn't worth the effort. But after the last night, I told him that he was coming home with me. I don't often put my foot down, but he knows that when I do, I mean it. He was sulking the entire time, as I know he'd rather have gone back to hers, then return to me the next day.

'We went home and I prepared our usual Horlicks. However, I put a healthy glug or seven of liquid Night Nurse in his. I told him that I'd put a whisky in it, and he believed me. He was so euphoric after the performance, and so full of his own self-importance, that he didn't even question the fact his Horlicks was semi-green. I didn't actually have Horlicks, I had coffee, to stay awake.

Around 3am, I realised he was completely out of it and I got dressed, got in the car and drove to Sandra's. I had taken Michael's keys, which included a key for her front door. I went upstairs quietly and found her asleep in bed. I took the spare pillow from next to her, presumably the one Michael would normally use, and placed it over her face. I leaned down on it with all my might and held it there for ten minutes. My arms were aching by the end of it, but I knew she couldn't possibly come back from this. I left the pillow on her face, as I didn't ever want to see her again. I checked her wrist for a pulse and found there wasn't one.

'I went back downstairs, got in the car and drove home. I climbed back into my bed, next to Michael's, and went to sleep, not waking until the following morning. Somehow, killing somebody just didn't make that much of a difference to me.

'I don't care what I did. I just couldn't take it all any more, and I would do it again. After everything she put me through over the years, I don't care now.'

Baxter ended the interview. Marlborough hadn't said anything. Dunstan looked at his boss with a sadness in his eyes.

Baxter waited a few seconds after the tape had finished recording before saying, 'Mrs Fordington, I am so sorry for what you have gone through. We're going to need some time to discuss this, if that's okay with you?'

Elizabeth had resigned herself to her fate. 'Of course.'

Baxter and Dunstan exited the room, and Elizabeth was shown to a cell by a constable.

Around 7pm, Michael and Elizabeth were both called to an interview room, with Anthea and Brandon

307

Marlborough. Baxter and Dunstan sat across from all of them and Baxter took up the conversation.

'Thank you all for your patience. This is a somewhat unusual set of circumstances, and we wouldn't normally discuss these things with two suspects present, but seeing as you two are married, we've decided to talk to you both at the same time. I've discussed this situation with my superior officers and we have reached some decisions. This is all based on the information we have from the post-mortem and the coroner's office.

'Michael, we are releasing you on conditional bail. This will all be explained to you at the custody sergeant's desk as we book you out. Basically, you need to attend this station each day at 1pm for the foreseeable future, until we tell you otherwise, to sign in as part of your bail conditions. Before you ask, we don't require money to be held as part of bail in this country, we take your word for the fact you won't skip the area. You will, however, need to surrender your passport and then bring your driving licence each day as identification. You will also have to stay at your home address and not spend a night anywhere else.'

Michael opened his mouth to say something, but Anthea placed her hand on his arm to stop him. He closed it slowly, and nodded.

Baxter continued.

'Elizabeth, you are free to go and are no longer a suspect in the murder enquiry.'

Four mouths dropped open. Dunstan did his usual trick of staring at the table. Baxter waited a moment before replying.

'Based on the post-mortem results, Sandra's cause of death was not asphyxiation. I have no doubt that you did the things you described to us, but it would appear that Sandra was already dead when you did them. We are still holding open the possibility of charging you with interfering with a human body, but, frankly, this is a very minor charge, and I'm not inclined to pursue it, as it is not material to finding the actual killer.'

THIRTY-ONE

BAXTER AND DUNSTAN SAT ON OPPOSITE SIDES of the desk in the CID offices the following Monday morning, not quite sure what to say or do. They had both spent the weekend going over the case in their minds and being completely preoccupied, despite not being on duty since Friday evening's bombshell conversation.

'The problem we've got is that Elizabeth's testimony is very believable,' Baxter said.

'Mm-hmm.' Dunstan wasn't known for being verbose at the best of times. Baxter was more verbalising her internal monologue and didn't need much of an input from him anyway.

'I'm inclined to believe what she said. Although this gives us two problems. First, it means two people tried to kill Sandra Finley in the same evening. What are the odds of that happening? Secondly, it gives Michael, who is still (in my opinion) the most likely suspect a cast-iron alibi.'

'Mm-hmm.'

'For heaven's sake, Colin, can you try to help a bit?!'

'Sorry, boss. I agree with everything you've said.'

'That's not much help!' Baxter hurled back.

'Would you rather I didn't agree with everything you said..?'

Baxter thought to herself that Dunstan had no idea just how close he was to being a murder victim himself.

She continued her train of thought. 'So do we think the two of them cooked it up between themselves?'

Dunstan thought he better make an effort. 'Seems unlikely, ma'am. I can't see her wanting to help him after a lifetime of torment.'

'No, I'd agree. Although I've seen stranger things and I'm not entirely sure Stockholm Syndrome wouldn't play a part here.'

'True. But she seems just a little too together for that. And the anger she felt towards both of them does seem pretty genuine.'

'Yes, it does,' Baxter agreed. 'So if he was bombed out of his brain on sleeping medication and she had the car anyway, that rules him out. Don't ever tell Anthea Sweeney this, but I'm not entirely sure he'd want to bump off his mistress anyway, so I don't know what motive he'd have, other than the two of them having lots of arguments. Killing her whilst drugged and without transport does seem a bit extreme.'

'Mm-hmm…'

'COLIN!'

'Sorry, ma'am. Couldn't resist.'

'Try harder.'

'I shall, boss.'

Baxter couldn't work out if he was intentionally trying to wind her up, or if it was just his unique personality.

Her thought patterns shifted somewhere else.

'So who on earth else could it be?'

'Honestly, ma'am, I have no idea. The list of people who didn't particularly like the deceased is quite extensive, but nobody appears to have enough of a grudge to even stop having anything to do with her. They were all still happy to attend events she was at. If you hated someone enough to want to kill them, I'd have thought you'd have done everything you could to avoid seeing them.'

'Yes, that's a fair point. So should we be looking for somebody not on our list?'

'Well, one always keeps the list open, but I don't know where else we'd start. Ms Finley didn't seem to have much outside of the people who are already on it. Perhaps a disgruntled client from years before, when she was more active as an accountant?'

'God, where would we even begin?' Baxter wondered. 'I suppose we could ask HMRC for a list of people whose accounts she'd submitted which resulted in charges, but that wouldn't include people who felt she hadn't done a good enough job, people who submitted their accounts themselves after she prepared them, people who felt she missed something that later got them in trouble through the courts. The list of possibilities is endless. And from what I can see, she's been winding down her list of clients for some years now, heading into retirement.'

This line of enquiry seemed like a mammoth task which would be insurmountable without a major break early on, and those never happened.

'So who do we have on the list so far?' Baxter asked.

'Hold on, just let me find it here,' Dunstan said, rifling through a mountain of papers on his desk. 'Okay, there's Gabriel Lee. New conductor at the orchestra. Apparently he's been side-lined since he joined by both Michael and Sandra.'

'Doesn't seem like a motive to kill someone, and surely he'd have gone after Michael?' Baxter said. 'From what I understand, he's a bit wet and preoccupied with a divorce.'

'Yes, that's the impression I got,' Dunstan agreed. 'Then there's Jane Lazenby. Her and Sandra apparently didn't like each other and frequently had arguments in public. She would be the next in line to move into Sandra's position as leader of the orchestra, whatever that means.'

'Okay.' Baxter went along with the suggestion for a moment. 'Do we know why they hated each other?'

'Orchestra gossip suggests Jane and Michael had a one-night fling years ago. No idea if Sandra knew about it, but there was no love lost,' Dunstan said.

'Seems a bit unlikely that Lazenby would kill Sandra though. Surely the other way around. Unless she was hoping to get Michael to herself if Sandra wasn't around any more.'

'From what my source tells me, Jane didn't really like Michael and the two aren't close.'

Baxter couldn't resist the opportunity to pry. 'Who *is* your source in the orchestra?!'

Dunstan deflected. 'I couldn't possibly say, ma'am. All strictly hush-hush and off the record.'

'I'm guessing it's a man and his wife plays bridge with your wife each week, Colin?'

'You might say that, ma'am. I couldn't possibly comment.' Dunstan was rather enjoying having more information than his superior. 'A good journalist never reveals his sources.'

313

'You're not a journalist and, even if you were, you wouldn't be a good one! You can barely make a list of who wants tea and coffee accurately.'

'Fair point, ma'am. Fair point.'

'Okay, who else do we have?'

'Debbie Greer, the orchestra librarian, who was shouted at on a weekly basis by both Michael and Sandra.'

'Thoughts, Colin?' Baxter asked.

'The woman is afraid of her own shadow. And I'd think she'd be more likely to go for Michael than Sandra anyway.'

'This is getting us nowhere. Next.'

Dunstan decided to play with his boss's head. 'Well, there's always one Anthea Sweeney. Apparently she's not the most invested person in the orchestra and nobody can figure out why she still bothers with it.'

Baxter laughed out loud for what Dunstan thought was probably the first time since the turn of the millennium. 'I'm going to suggest that route of enquiry will land both you and I in a gulag somewhere.'

'Quite probably, ma'am.'

'Next on the list?'

'There's not really anybody else who sticks out. None of the orchestra appear to have particularly liked Sandra, but nothing that would suggest murder. I'm beginning to think it might be more likely that we're looking for an ex-client.'

'Oh god, don't say that,' Baxter groaned. 'I wouldn't even know where to begin. Has nobody else shown any murderous tendencies recently?'

Baxter rifled through his papers again. 'Apparently one Jessica Carlin was seen to make a stabbing motion

314

behind somebody's back in the run-up to the show the other week.'

'Was it Sandra's?' Baxter suddenly got excited.

'No,' came back the response. 'It was the girl playing the lead in the show, who is in SODS, not the Porlington Philharmonia. Apparently it was deserved, but nothing to do with the deceased.'

'Great,' Baxter said, her stomach sinking into her rather boring size 5 flat shoes. 'So where do we go from here?'

'My advice, ma'am, is to look busy and have the appearance of activity. I've been doing that to you for years. It'll be at least a month before the extended tests and toxicology results come back from the post-mortem and Lord knows how long it'll take after that for the coroner's office to pass them on to us. You know what they're like.'

'Dear god, so we've got to sit on our hands for a month and pretend to look like we're actively pursuing a case with no leads, no witnesses, no motive, no obvious cause of death and no chance of being solved?'

Dunstan smiled up at his boss. 'It would appear so, ma'am. A whole month nearer retirement with nothing concrete to go on. Won't that be fun?'

Baxter looked at her subordinate. 'Colin, bog off.'

THIRTY-TWO

THURSDAY 15TH MARCH ARRIVED AND GABRIEL found himself back on the podium for the orchestra rehearsal. The intervening two and a half weeks had proved uneventful in the murder investigation and things had gone worryingly quiet. Rupert had called Gabriel over the weekend after Elizabeth's confession and filled him in on the events Anthea had been able to share, which weren't many. Michael was apparently in a complete state and was refusing to leave the house, except for his daily trips to sign in at the police station. He kept referring to himself as being under house arrest.

Elizabeth had gone to stay with their daughter and nobody had heard from her. Including Michael. A team of the older people from the orchestra were taking food round to Michael each day and keeping an eye on him.

The one thing Michael was adamant about was that the concert should happen on 14th April. It was looking increasingly unlikely that he would be able to conduct it, and he certainly wasn't making rehearsals in the meantime, so Gabriel suddenly found himself in the position of having to hold everything together. This was a somewhat terrifying prospect, as the programme was ludicrously long and Gabriel didn't really know half of it.

Nevertheless, he spent his days at Porlington Pianos learning the scores and getting up to speed (he had nothing else to do there). Neil and Grant kept pestering him for information that he didn't have, but also turned a blind eye to him spending most of his days poring over the pieces he needed to memorise. Susan kept him well supplied with beverages of an unspeakable nature.

This week's rehearsal was somewhat paramount in his mind, as Daphne Maxwell was back for an intermediate rehearsal. He wouldn't see her again until the week of the concert, so he wanted to make a good impression. They had spoken on the phone a couple of times to discuss how certain sections of the Britten should go, and she had been lovely and very understanding of his predicament. She had also sent him a video of her performing the piece once before. That was with a real tenor, though, not Henry James. And a real orchestra. Gabriel was worried about how well he'd be able to whip the Philharmonia into playing to a similar standard.

Whilst he had managed phone calls with Daphne, Henry had insisted on taking him for a pint to discuss how he wanted the work to go, which was completely at odds with Daphne's perspective. Very early on, Gabriel decided Daphne would win. And it wasn't one pint with Henry, it was many. The conversation was laden with playground innuendo that just made Gabriel cringe, but it all appeared to keep Henry amused.

The first half of the rehearsal was spent blasting through some of the waltzes and polkas. Gabriel was impressed with how the orchestra managed to make these pieces sound so boring that nobody would want to dance to them and, even if they did, they wouldn't know how to follow the beat, which kept shifting depending on when the trombones stopped playing everybody else's lines.

Gabriel told the orchestra part-way through the first half that he wanted to take out all repeats. This was mostly to keep the concert under five hours in length, although he didn't admit that. The cheer he got from the band stunned him into silence. He even saw smiles being thrown in his direction. Although, in Betty Brannon's case, he couldn't tell if it was a smile or if she had wind.

Over the last couple of weeks, having seen how wound up Doris and Gertie got in previous rehearsals when Michael was in charge, he made sure he said to them in advance that he was absolutely sure he would finish the first half on the dot of 8:30pm. The first week, he was halfway through the Blue Danube when said time occurred, so he stopped the players and told them to take their break. Of course, Doris and Gertie hadn't believed him or been ready, which threw them into a panic. From the second week, they were ready for this though, and tonight they threw him beaming smiles for being so considerate.

The orchestra filed out to the foyer area where insipid tea and chocolate digestives waited for them. Gabriel found himself chatting to Lauren and Jane.

'Thank you so much for bowing up all the string scores, Jane. We're getting through much quicker, and it sounds and looks great. Well, it would do if the players followed your bowings, but it's a start!' he said.

'That's okay. I've always been a bit of a stickler for that sort of thing. Sandra never was, but I like to have standards,' Jane replied.

The conversation paused, as nobody was quite sure what to say next whenever somebody inadvertently mentioned either Sandra or Michael. As usual, the elephant in the room was ignored and the conversation moved on with no further mention.

Anthea came up to Gabriel and took his elbow, before saying under her breath, 'Could I just have a quick word?'

Gabriel found himself outside the church in somewhat chilly climes. Even the brass section weren't out there smoking.

Anthea dived straight in. 'Okay, my little lotus flower. We've got your divorce hearing on Tuesday. How are you feeling about it?'

'Is it the actual hearing, or is it just a preliminary thing to get the ball rolling?' he asked.

'Oh no, this is the hearing. Very often, these things are dealt with purely on papers, with the judge just rubber-stamping whatever us legal beagles say. But, in this instance, I have a trick up my sleeve, and I'd like you there in person to hear it.'

'Okay. Should I be worried?' Gabriel asked, with a hint of nervousness in his voice.

'God, no. I've got this. I just want you to hear it all for yourself,' Anthea quickly replied. 'Just act surprised. It'll make for a much more fun hearing.'

Gabriel considered that he didn't have much of a choice in this matter, as he really didn't know what Anthea had up her sleeve.

As he headed back to Jane and Lauren, he heard snippets of various conversations between people. Two percussionists were discussing Daphne's background. 'Well, I'd heard that her husband Ernst is something very high up in MI6. We probably ought to get this one right, in case we're taken out by snipers.'

As Gabriel passed by Daphne, who had arrived early, he realised she was talking to Megan. 'Yes, it's a German horn. It's an Alexander. Would you like to try it?'

Megan was sobbing and itching her crotch with what looked like a magnet malfunction. 'Oh, may I?! I've never even held one, let alone tried one!' She proceeded to blow snot and spittle into Daphne's horn, producing a godawful sound, which was unlike Megan who, despite being certifiable and in desperate need of HRT, was actually a pretty good player. 'It's a beautiful instrument!'

Daphne replied, 'Why don't you come over sometime for a lesson? You've got a lovely tone and your instrument isn't dissimilar. It would only take a couple of tweaks for you to achieve that on your own horn.'

Megan leapt on Daphne and hugged her tightly, not even attempting to wipe away the various fluids pouring from every one of her facial orifices. 'You must come on my radio show sometime.'

'I'd love to! We could chat about all sorts.'

'Yes, we could talk about what life is like for horn players going through the change—I'm sure there would be lots of listeners who could relate.'

Gabriel wasn't sure anybody could relate to Megan, but he smiled as he walked past and was very grateful to Daphne for humouring her.

The second half of the rehearsal passed by without anybody dying. This seemed like an achievement in itself. The Britten wasn't hideous and Gabriel felt he hadn't left too bad an impression on Daphne. The percussion and wind sections were most grateful when Gabriel gave them the option of either leaving early or going into a back room to go over the other things in the programme. Most shot straight to the pub (Henry James looked highly unimpressed at being unable to do the same as his voice was required for the Britten), but a few intrepid woodwind players took the opportunity to slip off to the back room to go over their parts, feeling like the kids who had persuaded the supply teacher they were allowed to go to the computer room to work on their non-existent projects.

Once the rehearsal had finished and Gabriel had thanked everybody, he found himself back at Lauren's place.

'I thought that went well tonight, darling,' she said as she hung her coat on the hook by the door.

'Yeah, I was pleased,' he agreed.

'What did Anthea want in the break?' she asked.

'Just prepping me for the divorce hearing on Tuesday.'

'How are you feeling about it?'

'Honestly, I don't know. I have no idea what to expect. Anthea seems to have something up her sleeve, but I'm not sure what. Babes, do you have any beer?'

Lauren glared at him. 'You know I've given up drinking. If you want alcohol, you'll have to go drink my mouthwash!'

'Aww, man!' Gabriel replied, with a mock action of stabbing himself through the chest with an imaginary knife. 'I've just had to sit through that rehearsal and you expect me not to need a drink?!'

'I'm sure I could think of something to take your mind off things,' Lauren said, with a wink.

'Race you upstairs.'

THIRTY-THREE

TUESDAY ARRIVED AND GABRIEL MET ANTHEA in the car park outside the court. He was shaking with nervousness.

'Are you ok, my little cherub?' Anthea asked, noticing that Gabriel was as white as a sheet.

'In all honesty, no,' was all he could manage.

Anthea put her hand on his arm and smiled. 'It's okay, it's to be expected. I sometimes forget that because I'm so used to being here, clients who aren't used to this sort of thing are gibbering wrecks. We've got time, shall we grab a coffee?' she asked.

They headed up to the coffee shop on the 2nd floor of the court building and sat opposite each other, Gabriel with his Americano and Anthea with a cup of something with a name so long Gabriel was amazed she remembered it or that the barista had got it right first time.

Anthea decided to keep Gabriel's mind occupied.

'Right, my lovely, there is nothing to worry about. You won't be called on to say anything, this is entirely on me today. The judge has had the papers and will have read them already, so all we're doing today is asking for the decree nisi to be granted and a financial order to be made.

Then, in 43 days' time, I will apply on your behalf for a decree absolute. This is just a rubber stamp of what takes place today and the only reason it wouldn't be granted is if the court is informed in the interim of a legal reason why the marriage should not be dissolved. The hard work is done today and whatever the outcome of today, nothing is likely to change between now and the decree absolute being issued. I don't even attend for the later hearing, it's dealt with on papers, and it really is just a formality. Once today is over, you will pretty much be guaranteed to be divorced in around 50 days.'

Gabriel was beginning to calm down and having an end date to look forward to helped.

'So are we expecting any nasty surprises today?' he asked, nervously.

'No, I don't think so. I suspect we'd have heard by now. There are a few procedural things to go through, but I expect the judge to rubber stamp whatever I ask. He's a golfing buddy and he doesn't like solicitors from out of town who he doesn't know,' she said, with a wink.

'So why am I here?'

'Oh, you'll see, petal. You'll see.' Anthea pushed her chair back and indicated for Gabriel to stay in his. 'Give me two ticks. I'm just going to go and have a word with the clerk's office and find out what time they realistically expect us to go in.'

She disappeared off for a few minutes before arriving back at the table and taking her place again.

'Right, they reckon we'll be called in about 15 minutes.'

Gabriel felt his stomach knot again at the prospect of having to wait. This was worse than the dentist. Anthea saw his face blanch and jumped back in.

'Well, if we've got all this time on our hands, we better fill it, and not with talk of the divorce. Let's talk about something else. What do you fancy?'

Gabriel's mind went blank and all topics of any form of conversation flew out of his head. He floundered, his eyes wandering around the room for any form of inspiration. They settled on Anthea's hand, holding her coffee cup in front of her face, and he noticed a beautiful engagement ring with a rock that would shame Gibraltar nestled next to her wedding ring.

'I've been meaning to ask you something. Rupert's children. None of them are yours, but several of them are definitely young enough that they must have been born since the two of you were married, judging by the wedding picture in your house.'

The question was out of his mouth before he realised that was something that should very much have stayed as part of his internal monologue. Anthea's mouth fell open in shock and Gabriel thought he was going to be sick.

He was saved by Anthea throwing her head back and laughing hysterically.

'Well! Nobody's been brave enough to broach that subject in a while! Good for you.'

Gabriel felt the relief wash over him, although he still wanted to melt into the industrial lino flooring.

'Okay, we're friends, so I'm perfectly happy to answer that.

'Mr Sweeney and I got married 15 years ago. I was already a solicitor and I had quite a large client base in family law. Him and I had discussed having children many times over the years and it always came back to two problems. I have never wanted children. He, on the other hand, did want children, but didn't really want the hassle

324

of having them around all the time; he always used to joke that children who lived with their mother and just visited on Christmas would be an ideal solution.

'Due to all this, we went for several years without ever reaching a conclusion, and no children appeared in the meantime as I'm really very careful.

'A couple of years in, one of my clients, a delightful woman named Jeanette—you met her at Christmas when she dropped Toby and James off—had a problem that she confided to me about. Sad story.

'I had dealt with the restraining order against her ex-partner. They had split many years before and he had been sent to prison for attacking her. How he didn't get sent down for attempted murder, I will never know. After he was released, he tracked her down, confronted her and poured boiling water onto her. Apparently, it was all her fault that he had been sent to prison. She had some pretty horrific burns on her body and one side of her neck, and the guy she was with at the time didn't stick around.

'About a year after this happened, I bumped into her in the supermarket car park and was asking how she was. She completely broke down on me, so I took her for a drink. By now, I wasn't her solicitor any more, and I was more concerned about her wellbeing. She had lost all confidence in her body and really struggled to start new relationships or trust a man. Understandable, really.

'What she was more upset about was that she was heading for 40 and was desperate for a baby, but she didn't want a partner because she was too afraid. I offered Mr Sweeney's services on the spot.'

Gabriel gasped.

'Not like that! As a sperm donor. All above board and tickety-boo. She seemed open to the idea, as he's got all his own teeth and there are no congenital diseases in his immediate family. Plus, she knew that if I said he was a good guy, he was. I went home and mentioned this all to him and we had several meetings with Jeanette over the coming months. Agreements were all drawn up, although we've never needed them, and a turkey baster somewhere in the hospital was put to good use. She's now got Toby and James by Mr Sweeney.

'The others were very similar situations, although all different scenarios. Two others were ex-clients of mine, and one was another lady whom Jeanette had become friends with when she was in a women's refuge some years before.'

Gabriel didn't know whether to laugh or cry. He didn't get the opportunity as the television screen started flashing, "COLE V LEE, COURT 2".

'Ah, we're up. Come along.'

Gabriel ran along in Anthea's wake, down a flight of stairs and into a sterile court room with an enormous coat of arms above the judge's position. They took their seats.

Gabriel looked at the bench to his right and realised Shelley was sat there with her father and their solicitor, Martin Brady. He felt nauseous and thought he was going to pass out when Anthea shoved a glass of water in front of him and whispered, 'Drink it. Drink it all. And take deep breaths.'

He did as he was told. It was only on the third gulp that he realised it was gin with nowhere near enough tonic. He managed not to splutter it out and went to put the glass down when he heard Anthea hiss under her breath, 'I said drink it all! Can't leave evidence lying around now, can we.' He knocked back the rest and within 30 seconds, the world suddenly seemed a little calmer. 'Good boy,' Anthea muttered without moving her lips.

'All rise,' the clerk boomed. Thankfully, the gin hadn't reached Gabriel's legs yet and he managed this. The judge walked in and sat at his very high desk. Everybody sat, except Gabriel, who more collapsed as his legs involuntarily decided to stop working.

'Good morning everybody. I see we have the marital parties with us today. May I remind you all that you should not speak and leave all discussions to just your solicitors and myself. I have the papers from both sides in front of me and I see that both parties are suing for divorce. That should make this nice and simple as nobody is contesting. I will begin with the side who submitted the first application for divorce. Mrs Sweeney.'

'Thank you, Your Honour,' Anthea said, rising to her feet and snapping into a business-like mode that defied anybody to get in her way. 'This shouldn't take long. You can see from our application that we are requesting a divorce on grounds of adultery. As you can see from our submission, this would be virtually impossible to dispute, as Mrs Lee is currently pregnant by another man.' Gabriel loved that Anthea had decided to call Shelley 'Mrs Lee' rather than 'Ms Cole', which she preferred.

Anthea continued. 'We filed our application on the 7th of November, at which point Mr Lee was already convinced of Mrs Lee's adulterous behaviour, probably with multiple partners. However, as you can see in my addendum, on the 18th of January, Mrs Lee posted that she was in a relationship with one David Webster and that they were expecting a baby. She posted a picture of her twelve-week scan. Now we are not sure of whom the father is, whether it is Mr Webster, or Martin Pembridge, who she was previously having an affair with, or any other unnamed man with whom she may have had sexual intercourse.'

Gabriel looked over at the Cole bench and saw the three of them shifting very uncomfortably at having Shelley's predilections boomed out to total strangers in open court. Mr Cole was already a shade or two nearer beetroot than normal and his moustache was twitching like a mouse that had been glued to his face and was trying to make its escape from this sweaty, oversized little man.

Anthea was still in full flood. 'What we are sure of is that Mr Lee is not the father, as he has not seen Mrs Lee since the 24th of September. I suppose we should give Mrs Lee the opportunity to confirm that Mr Lee is, indeed, not the father…'

The judge looked over at Martin Brady. 'Well?' Brady was on the back foot and didn't realise he had been asked a question. 'Mr Brady, is Mr Lee the father of Mrs Lee's baby?'

Brady stood, opened his mouth, checked himself that he ought to confirm this, leaned down to Shelley and whispered in her ear, before she was heard to hiss, 'Of course he's not!'

Brady stood upright again. 'Your honour, I can confirm that Mr Lee is not the father. However, if I may just raise…'

'No, you may not,' the judge said. 'Mrs Sweeney, please continue.'

'Thank you, Your Honour. As there had been no direct communication during this time between Mr and Mrs Lee, my client could not possibly have known that Mrs Lee was pregnant. I would also draw your attention to the dates involved. Mrs Lee's twelve-week scan was ten

328

weeks after the date on which we filed for divorce, meaning, unbeknownst to us, she must have been pregnant at the time of filing, thus providing irrefutable evidence of the adultery.'

'Thank you, Mrs Sweeney. That all seems to be in order and I would agree with your assessment of the dates. Mr Brady, I have just one more question—was this baby conceived naturally, through the course of sexual union, or was it by in vitro fertilisation?'

Brady was clearly embarrassed at having to ask Shelley these questions. He had known her since she was a child and, whilst he was probably well aware of what she was like, having to ask her these questions in front of her father can't have been easy.

Brady conferred with Shelley and replied, 'It was conceived naturally, Your Honour.'

'Very well, I think that answers everything I need to hear on that subject. Mrs Sweeney, do you have anything to add at this time before I hand over to Mr Brady?'

'One or two things, Your Honour. I would next like to address the counter-application for divorce made by Mrs Lee's solicitors. As you can see from the addendum I submitted last week, we are applying for this to be thrown out. They have submitted insufficient grounds and the two they have submitted have both been refuted by me on paperwork. I would humbly suggest to the court that this very weak application on their part does not hold up and the divorce should proceed only along the lines of Mrs Lee's adultery.'

Brady was ready for this and clearly had a mountain of paperwork to support their case. He was beginning to rise to object to ensure he was heard when the judge waved him back into his seat.

'Yes, Mrs Sweeney, I am inclined to agree with you. Mr Brady, this is a pitiful submission on your part and I will not allow the dignity of my court to be sullied with something that an A-Level Law student could have done a better job of writing. Your application for divorce on grounds of unreasonable behaviour is hereby denied and that case is thrown out. I find Mr Lee's application to be convincing and uncontested, so I am inclined to grant a decree nisi with immediate effect.'

Brady dropped back down into his chair, not quite sure what had just happened and even less sure how to counter it.

'Mrs Sweeney, anything else to add?'

'One last thing, Your Honour. Mrs Lee's application for ancillary relief. We'd like it thrown out as this is an article that hasn't existed for quite some time.'

'Agreed,' responded the judge. 'So ordered.'

Brady was straight on his feet. 'Your Honour, if that is the case, then we would request that any financial order as to the division of marital assets follows the usual principle of equal division.'

Gabriel was beginning to feel happier as things seemed to be going their way. Then he heard Anthea mutter under her breath, 'I'll bet he does,' before standing to say, 'We have no objection to that, Your Honour.'

The Cole bench looked utterly triumphant. Brady continued, 'If it pleases Your Honour, we would like to deal with this today.'

The judge looked at Anthea. 'Fine by me,' she said. Gabriel was starting to wonder what was going on, as the Coles were appearing happy and Anthea didn't seem bothered.

'Your Honour, if I may?' Brady asked. The judge waved at him to continue. 'Since Mr Lee abandoned my client, she has been left destitute, with no income and only the generosity of her parents to keep her afloat.' Anthea, now back in her seat, rolled her eyes at Gabriel. 'Mr Lee was the sole earner of the household…'

'Because she wouldn't get a job!' Gabriel hissed at Anthea, receiving a pat on the arm and a look that told him to pipe down and let this play out.

'…and when he left, he took all their money and his sports car. She currently has no assets and some considerable debt to her parents. We understand that Mr Lee found immediate work in Porlington but refused to send any money to his penniless wife. I have detailed Mrs Lee's finances in this document, if I may approach?' The judge nodded and Brady handed two copies to the clerk, who handed one up to the judge, whilst Brady handed another to Anthea.

Gabriel was on the verge of going nuclear when he felt Anthea kick him under the bench.

'Mrs Sweeney, do you have Mr Lee's current statement of finance there?'

'I do, Your Honour.' Anthea handed two copies to the clerk and one to Brady. It was modest, but with far more on it compared to the document where Brady was claiming Shelley was on the verge of bankruptcy.

The judge looked back at Anthea. 'And you say you're happy with an equal division of assets..?' he asked, somewhat surprised.

'I am, Your Honour.' Anthea sat back down and started studying the piece of paper Brady had handed her very intently.

'Very well then. In that case, if I take the bottom lines from these two documents and add them together…'

'Sorry, Your Honour, just one thing,' Anthea said whilst still sat and looking at the sheet of paper.

'Yes, Mrs Sweeney?'

Anthea looked up and over the rims of her glasses. She stood. 'My apologies, it would appear that Mr Brady has left a sheet or two off this statement.'

The judge looked over at Brady, who appeared confused. He stood. 'No, it's just the one sheet, that's everything.'

The judge looked back at Anthea.

'There appears to be a sizeable amount of Mrs Lee's finances missing from this document, which, if done intentionally, would be grounds for contempt of court,' she responded.

All eyes shifted back to Brady, who was looking nervous and confused. 'I can assure you that is everything I was given by my client and is an accurate reflection of her finances today.'

Attention shifted back to Anthea. 'Really, Mr Brady? I'm pretty sure you are entirely aware of just what Mrs Lee's net worth is.'

Brady flustered but no coherent words came out.

'I had a private investigator do some digging—all perfectly legal before you object. Your Honour,' Anthea said firmly, putting her attention back on the judge. 'Over the last two years, Mr Cole, Mrs Lee's father, has been trying to diversify his business interests and move into the property market. Around a year ago, he went into business with a company called Ground Up Buildings. Things appeared to be ticking along quite nicely, until Mr

Cole became distrustful of Ground Up and realised their accounting practices were slightly less than ethical.

'Rightly so, he had the sense to protect himself, although not enough to cease working with them, which gave a tacit approval of their shady dealings. However, in order to protect his grocery company, currently valued at £5.2million, he became nervous that the creditors the new venture was building up might come after him.

'On 28th August last year, one Martin Brady submitted an amendment to Companies House, transferring 80% of Mr Cole's shareholding in Cole's grocery business into Mrs Lee's name, presumably to protect the family business in the event of the property business going down the swanee.'

Shelley jumped to her feet. 'I don't know anything about that! I don't own any shares!'

'Take your seat at once, Mrs Lee! Communicate through your solicitor!' the judge barked.

'Actually, my dear, according to these documents, you do.' Anthea handed piles of paper around like before. 'And if you don't, the solicitor sat next to you certainly did, as it was him who submitted the documents. Your Honour, after checking Cole's annual return at Companies House in the interim, and checking one last time with Companies House this morning, I can assure you that this is still the case.'

The judge managed to keep his face passive. 'Well, this certainly changes things. Mr Brady, what do you have to say for yourself?'

Brady was a whiter shade of pale. 'Your Honour, I'm going to need some time to consult with my clients,' he began.

'I think not. I see nothing here to prevent me from making an order right now, as you yourself requested. I hereby grant a decree nisi to Mr Lee on the grounds of Mrs Lee's adultery. I further order that the finances of Mr and Mrs Lee be divided in equal parts between the two of them. Just to clarify…' The judge looked firmly at the Cole bench. '…that means this court is ordering that 40% of the shares in Cole's Ltd pass immediately to Mr Lee. I further order that each side are responsible for your own costs. Let's be honest, you can all afford it. Mr Brady, I will see you back here two weeks from today, along with both your clients, at which point I will expect some answers. Somebody is going to be held in contempt of court, so I suggest the three of you figure your stories out by then, lest I decide to share the blame equally amongst you all. The papers confirming all of this will be drawn up and posted to all of you. Court is adjourned.' He banged his gavel.

Everybody in the room was staring at the judge, mouths open; except for Gabriel, who was staring at Anthea. He alone saw her mouth, 'Thanks, Tufty,' at the judge, followed by a wink. She looked down at Gabriel. 'Congratulations, my dear. You are now a very rich man. Somewhere in the region of £2.08million, by my reckoning. And, you own a sizeable chunk of Cole's, which will no doubt annoy all of them greatly. Let's go.'

THIRTY-FOUR

G ABRIEL FOUND HIMSELF SAT IN HIS CAR IN THE car park of the court building, not quite sure what the hell had just happened. He had arrived with the sole intention of getting rid of Shelley and her family, but was now apparently a major shareholder in their business, with a net value of some considerable worth.

This was going to take some time to get his head around.

Once they had left the courtroom, Anthea had told him to do nothing for the time being, and to refer any communication he received from Shelley, her family or anybody representing them (as she guessed Martin Brady wouldn't be around for much longer after today) to her. She said that they could meet in a week or two in order to discuss his future options and whether he wanted to retain his shares in the company or sell them. Either way, she was happy to advise him and act on his behalf. Gabriel thought she had more than earned this and completely trusted her to act in his best interests, based on what he'd seen today.

He drove around the town for some time, not quite sure where he was heading. He didn't really have anywhere to go. Going back to his flat seemed a bit of an anti-climax. Going anywhere else seemed pointless. He had messaged Lauren, but he knew she would be teaching and busy until at least 3:30pm.

He decided they needed to celebrate that night, so he called *Nessun Dorma* and booked a table for that evening at 7:30pm. He sent Lauren a message saying he'd be at hers for 5pm so they could talk through things and then they had dinner plans.

Gabriel spent the next few hours walking round the charity shops of Porlington (of which there were many), looking at nothing in particular, just trying to come to terms with being free of Shelley. And having somehow ripped an extremely large chunk of their business away from them. The more he thought about it, the more he realised he had earned it. All the years of kowtowing to the whole family for nothing suddenly seemed to have been worth the while. Especially after the emotional abuse they had all put him through.

He called into the local supermarket and picked up a bottle of champagne. It seemed entirely reasonable to do so after the day's events. As he was stood in the wine and spirits aisle, he thought he should probably also pick one up for Anthea.

He found himself stood at the checkout. The sullen, spotty teenage checkout assistant said, 'That'll be £49.98,' in between chewing gum. Gabriel happily put his card into the machine to pay for this.

'They're not both for me, although I am celebrating tonight!' he said.

'Great. Would you like a receipt?' the checkout operator asked in the most bored, uninterested monotone Gabriel had ever heard.

'I've just got divorced!' he found himself saying.

'Great. Would you like a receipt?' It was like Groundhog Day.

Lauren had replied while he was negotiating the perils of the local supermarket and wanted to know everything. He said he'd fill her in when he got to hers tonight, but that it was good news.

He went out to his car and decided to go exploring, as he didn't really know the neighbouring towns very well yet. He went back to his to shower and change ready for the evening, as well as putting the champagne in the fridge. He then spent an hour wandering around Fawlham (which was mostly filled with even more charity shops) before heading back to his place to pick up the champagne and head over to Lauren's.

She was just arriving as he got there and was struggling with several large boxes with books that needed marking. He ran over, threw the champagne into the top one and grabbed it so she could open her front door.

'Hey, how was it? Are you okay? Are you divorced then?!' she asked.

'Effectively, yes. Just got to wait for the paperwork to go through over the next few weeks,' he replied as she fought her way through the front door.

They dumped the boxes in her hallway and she hugged him really tightly. 'I'm so pleased for you. I've been worried all day that there would be some nasty shock involved.'

'There was a nasty shock, but it was for them, not me.'

He put the champagne in the fridge, moved to the lounge and they sat down on her sofa so he could give her the highlights. This turned into 90 minutes of him filling her in on events (which was considerably longer than the hearing itself lasted, but he kept repeating the exciting bits, jumping up and demonstrating what Anthea had done).

Gabriel got to the end of the story. Lauren sat next to him in shock.

'Sorry, how much did you say you're worth?!' she asked, her mouth agape.

'Ha! Trust you to focus on that!'

'Oh god, sorry, no, that's not what I meant at all. God, now I sound like a gold-digger! I wanted to make sure, so I know you're going to be okay financially. That's a life-changing amount of money!'

'Well, I'm not sure how it all works, but I guess once it's all sorted it means I can give up working at the music shop.' This did not disappoint him. He had grown somewhat fond of the Kings, but not enough to stay there for minimum wage.

'Will you keep your shares in Cole's?' Lauren asked.

'I don't think so. I had a brief chat to Anthea afterwards. We'll talk properly in a couple of weeks once it's all finalised, but she said it probably wouldn't be worth it as they'd make sure they ran at a loss just to make sure I never got any dividends and didn't actually see any money. She reckons I'd be better off selling up to them and she reckons they'll happily buy me out just to get rid of me. Although heaven knows how they'll raise the money to do so.'

'That's what you get for shafting people. They took advantage of you from day one,' Lauren said, with a look of disgust.

'Yeah, I'm beginning to realise that.'

'And I am *so proud* of you for getting out. I can't tell you how pleased I am things have worked out for you.'

He smiled and hugged her. He started to kiss her neck, but she pushed him away.

'You, mister, are just going to have to wait for that. I need to have a shower as I've been at work all day. Take me for dinner and you can have your way with me when we get back here after.'

Gabriel fell back onto the sofa, pouting.

'Don't give me that look. You'll enjoy it even more if you have to wait for it!' Lauren said over her shoulder as she got up and headed for her bathroom.

Gabriel turned the television on and hopped between the channels. There was nothing worth watching. He sat on the sofa and contemplated how different his life was compared with just a few hours ago. He really must find a way of thanking Anthea.

He suddenly realised he was hungry. He hadn't had breakfast as he was too nervous and was worried it would just come back up again in court. He'd been in such a state of shock after the hearing that he'd forgotten to get a sandwich in the supermarket. As such, he headed for Lauren's kitchen to see what he could sneak a bite of. They were going out in half an hour, but by the time they got to *Nessun Dorma*, ordered and waited for the food to arrive, it would probably be heading for two hours before he got any food.

Gabriel reached the kitchen. He took two champagne flutes from the cupboard and placed them on the worktop. He opened the fridge and took out the champagne. He saw the half-eaten plastic container of salad Lauren had put back in the fridge that she clearly hadn't finished at lunchtime and took that out too, grabbing a fork from the cutlery drawer and digging in. It was only rabbit food, but it would keep him going until they got fed at the restaurant. He was starving.

He unwrapped the foil on the champagne and popped the cork, taking each flute in turn and partially filling them until the bubbles reached the top. He let them settle, then filled them both up to the brim.

He grabbed the plastic container with the salad and the fork lying in it and thought it would be fun to drink straight from the champagne bottle like they did on Formula 1 racing.

He took the bottle with his other hand and lifted it to his lips, about to take a sip when Lauren appeared in the doorway, wrapped in a towel.

'Darling, I was thinking, once the money comes through, will you…?'

She stopped mid-sentence, staring at him.

He pulled the bottle away from his mouth and said, 'Bottoms up!' lifting it back to his lips when she screamed and ran at him, hitting the bottle out of his hand. It flew into the two glasses on the side, smashing them and itself, sending glass and fizz flying in all directions.

'How much have you had?!' Lauren screamed at Gabriel.

'Nothing! I was about to take my first sip!' he yelled back at her, confused as to what was happening.

'GABRIEL! HAVE YOU DRUNK ANY OF IT?!' Lauren shrieked, clutching his face in her hands.

'No! I didn't have a chance before you smashed it! Do you have any idea what that cost me?!' he shouted back, not quite sure why they were screaming at each other.

It was only then that he noticed she was bleeding from where some of the glass had scratched her and she was shaking uncontrollably. Tears were running down her face and she was pure white.

'Lauren, what the hell is going on?' he asked, trying to defuse the situation.

She was hysterical in his arms and was now beating him trying to get away. Her feet were cut from the glass on the floor and she slipped on the champagne spreading across it. He caught her and righted her back onto her feet.

'God, look at you. We need to get you to a hospital to get those cuts checked out, you're bleeding all over the place.'

She looked at him in horror and said, 'We need to get you to a hospital and get your stomach pumped.'

Gabriel was completely confused. 'What are you talking about?'

He didn't see she had reached to her side and taken a large kitchen knife until it was too late. Lauren stood in front of him in her towel, bleeding all over the floor, clutching a knife which was aimed at him. It began to dawn on him that this wasn't normal behaviour and he might be in danger.

Lauren just shook, barely able to hold the knife. She took a small step forward and aimed the knife at him, before crying as a piece of glass went deep into her foot. Gabriel moved backwards but realised he was pinned against the sink. He looked in horror at Lauren who was standing on one foot and holding the knife at him. He saw anger pass across her face, then fear, then pain. And with that, she turned the knife on herself and stabbed it towards her neck. She caught the side, but her aim was off because she was shaking so much. She pulled it back and tried again, digging it into the flesh, just above her collarbone.

Gabriel lunged forwards, his shoes crunching on the glass on the floor. He grabbed the blade of the knife and tore it from Lauren's hands, hurling it across the kitchen out of her reach. She was bleeding from her neck and sobbing. He picked her up and carried her into the lounge, feeling her trying to resist. He threw her onto the sofa and grabbed his phone from his pocket, managing to dial 999. She tried to get up, but he was too quick. He dropped his phone onto the glass table in front of the sofa and held her down.

He could hear the voice in the distance coming from the tiny speaker. 'Emergency, which service?'

Gabriel screamed at the phone, whilst wrestling Lauren into staying on the sofa. 'Police! Ambulance! I don't care! Just get me help right now! My girlfriend just tried to kill herself and I think she's bleeding out!' He yelled the address at them, at which point Lauren went limp in his arms and started sobbing.

She kept whimpering, 'I'm sorry, I'm so sorry…' as he held her down for her own safety, bleeding all over her furniture and Gabriel.

THIRTY-FIVE

I T WAS THE FOLLOWING DAY. LAUREN, BAXTER and Dunstan were in an interview room at the police station, with a duty solicitor who was even nearer retirement than Dunstan. Baxter went through the usual preamble with the tape recorder.

Lauren was sat opposite Baxter and Dunstan, wearing basic custody clothes—tracksuit bottoms and a T-shirt, her hair falling loosely around her shoulders.

The police had arrived at Lauren's flat within seven minutes. Gabriel had refused to let Lauren go in case she did something stupid, so the officers had kicked the door in and found the two of them in the lounge, surrounded by blood. They saw Lauren was bleeding from the neck and pulled Gabriel back, in case he had inflicted the wound on her. As one held Lauren down, the other held Gabriel against the wall with one hand whilst shouting into his radio that they needed a priority ambulance.

Lauren had been rushed into hospital, where she was kept overnight. The cuts from the glass had been patched up. The stab wound to her clavicle had needed stitches, but there was nothing life-threatening.

Gabriel had been questioned at the hospital by two more officers and he had tried to give as much information as possible. When he said she had told him he needed to have his stomach pumped, one of the officers had grabbed a passing doctor and made them check Gabriel out. There were no signs of anything life-threatening, but they ran numerous tests anyway. Nobody could understand why taking a sip from a bottle of champagne could be a problem, but they weren't taking chances.

He hadn't been allowed to see Lauren again, as the police were still worried that Gabriel might have attacked her. It was only when an officer spoke to her later that night that she had said she'd tried to kill herself and she needed to speak to DI Baxter. Mentioning Baxter's name had set alarm bells ringing with the uniform officers and one of them called through to CID, who called Baxter at home. She was at the hospital within 20 minutes. She listened to Lauren for about two minutes, then told her not to say anything else until the following day. Baxter knew this was going to have to be handled correctly and she didn't dare step out of correct procedure. It was a risk, in case Lauren changed her mind in the interim.

The hospital had insisted on keeping Lauren overnight, so Baxter had placed two uniformed police officers to guard her door, not letting anybody who wasn't medical personnel with ID in or out. Lauren was patched up and released the following day, at which point she was arrested by Baxter, who was on hand, and driven to the station.

'Okay, Miss Barker. Can you tell us your story in your own words please?' Baxter began once the tape machine had finished its initial whine. 'We'll try not to interrupt unless we need clarification on something, okay?'

Lauren nodded. She was sat opposite them in a daze, her eyes seemingly vacant and her body language slumped and resigned.

She began by telling them about her life, much as she had told Gabriel all those months before. An emotionally abusive mother, a father too scared to interfere or stand up for her. Her mother's constant disappointment in her. And, finally, how they died within a few months of one another during her final year at university.

Lauren continued. 'After they died, I had to go through their house and clear everything out. I discovered a locked metal file box in their loft. I had no idea what was in there, but I was trying to be meticulous in how I dealt with things, so I grabbed a metal pole from the garden and forced it open. I found piles of letters in there from my grandmother, and a few other documents.

'My maternal grandparents were Italian. They lived over there all their lives. My mother couldn't wait to escape, so she came here to the UK to go to university. That's where she met my father, in an amateur dramatic group at Exeter University; they got married two years after they graduated. Reading the letters between my mother and grandmother, it became evident that they tried for a baby for years, never successfully.

'From what I could work out, at some point, my grandmother contacted them to say she knew of somebody who wanted to put a baby up for adoption over in Italy. It seemed to be a private affair, not through official channels, so I guessed it was somebody my grandmother knew.

'My grandmother had arranged it all and paid a sum of money. That baby was me. She had taken me in until my parents could get there. They went over, collected me and registered my birth in Italy, which apparently hadn't been done. The Italians believed my mother had been pregnant with me when she arrived. The British authorities believed her when she came back with an official birth certificate from Italy.

'When I was going through the documents, I found several letters from the woman who was obviously my birth mother—Sandra Finley. There were letters to my grandmother, which I guess my mother took when Grandmama died. I can only assume Sandra was under the impression my grandmother had kept me and raised me.

'Judging by Sandra's letters, my grandmother never replied. Sandra was clearly begging for information about me for the first couple of years, but I don't think any was ever forthcoming. The letters seemed to peter out eventually and there were no more after when I would have been about five years old.'

Lauren paused to take a sip of water. Baxter and Dunstan sat opposite her, neither saying anything, and allowing her to continue her story.

'I did nothing for some years. I think initially the shock of realising I wasn't related to the people I thought were my parents was too much for me to take in. That eventually turned to anger that nobody had ever told me. Eventually, the anger turned towards Sandra. Why had she abandoned me? Why didn't she want me? Who and where was my father? Why had she left me with somebody in another country? Why did she eventually stop writing to ask about me—even if she wasn't getting responses, I don't understand how she could just let me go and forget me. Thinking I was still in Italy, why didn't she fly out to see me and take me home with her?

'I still have no idea how her and my grandmother came to meet, or how they agreed my grandmother would take me. I know she worked as a midwife in her village, so I can only assume she delivered me and realised Sandra didn't want me. I guess I'll never know, not that I care anymore.'

Baxter ventured a question. 'So why did you choose to find Sandra?

'After some years, the anger had turned into rage. All the questions I've already said, and more, were eating away at me. Mostly, I think it was anger at how awful my mother was to me, not just as a child, but even when I was at university. I guess she'd never formed that bond with me because I wasn't actually hers. Maybe she felt guilt at taking somebody else's baby. I think, in the end, she just raised me and kept up the pretence out of duty and because she was trapped in the lie with no escape.

'Two years ago, I decided to look Sandra up. Maybe she would be the nice mother I never had. And perhaps she could give me answers.

'Initially, I was too scared to contact her and tell her who I was; I had no idea how she would react. Then one day in the Times Education Supplement, I saw a teaching job advertised at Porlington Primary. I knew where Sandra lived, and the name immediately jumped at me. I applied, got it and moved here.

'That was 18 months ago. When I first moved here, I just wanted to settle into my new life, and being a teacher kept me busy. I found Sandra's house and would sometimes walk past. One day I saw her in the front garden and it felt like my heart stopped. She had just arrived home with shopping and she was wrestling several bags. She eventually got her key in the lock, opened the door and went inside. I kept walking, although my heart was racing by now.

'Every now and again, I'd walk past her house. Occasionally I'd see her, but I had no idea how to approach her.'

Baxter intervened again. 'How did you end up making contact with her?'

'Completely by accident. Last summer, it was all getting too much for me and I decided I needed to find some friends here, as I knew nobody outside of my colleagues at school. I did a search for a local orchestra to join and came across the Porlington Philharmonia.

'I emailed the address on their website and it was Sandra who emailed me back, telling me to go along to any Thursday rehearsal and be prepared to audition. I had been going to start with the new term in September, but when I realised she was part of them, I was too nervous. After term was well underway and I was more settled with my new class, I decided to try it in October. I'd waited long enough and she wouldn't know who I really was.

'It was horrible. As the evening went on, I realised just what an awful person she was. Pompous, arrogant and horribly full of her own self-importance. It was just like looking at my adoptive mother. I just wanted to get out of there.'

'So why did you go back?' Dunstan asked, gently.

'During that week, I thought it might be unfair to judge her based on only one rehearsal. Everybody deserves a second chance, right? Plus, several of the violinists were texting me constantly, begging me to go back, so I went along the following week. It wasn't much better, but the other violinists were lovely and I thought it might be worth making friends. Perhaps just watching Sandra from afar would be enough; maybe I never needed to tell her who I was. However, I still wanted answers to my questions, so I decided to stick it out.

'Over the next couple of weeks, the girls started to tell me the orchestra gossip and I realised that Michael must be my father. This came as a huge shock, as I think I'd thought it would be some time before I discovered who my real father was, sometime after I'd told Sandra who I was. I didn't know how to take the news, as he seemed as awful as she was. I just couldn't get away from the thought that these two seemed worse than my parents and I should never have tried to find anything out. I became more miserable and couldn't reconcile coming from them.

'It was at the end of the first concert I did with them that things changed for me. Sandra decided to turn on Jane and myself,' Lauren said.

'Sorry, who's Jane?' Baxter asked.

'Jane Lazenby. I sit with her in rehearsals.'

'Thank you,' Baxter said, writing the name down and remembering it from their earlier enquiries. 'Please continue.'

'Earlier in the day, I had found out from the girls that Michael had a wife, and I realised she probably didn't know about me. I felt immense guilt, even though my existence was nothing to do with me and was entirely on Michael and Sandra.

'When we were leaving at the end of the concert, Jane said something disparaging about Michael's conducting. Sandra heard this and turned on both of us. I was only stood next to Jane and hadn't said anything, but Sandra just spat venom at me. My heart broke. It suddenly dawned on me what these two people had done. To Michael's wife. To each other. To me. That they had abandoned me to a woman who abused me so much throughout my life was bad enough, but I realised in that moment that they were even worse and life with them would be horrible. It was like something snapped inside me as I ran away and I just decided they had to pay for what they'd done to cause so much pain to so many people. I felt more alone than I had after I lost both my parents and had nobody left in the world. Now I had people in the world, but they were monsters. I've never felt so unloved.

'That was also the night I got together with Gabriel. I was sobbing in my car, rocking back and forth, not knowing how to face this new world I was in when he appeared at my car door. He'd parked in the same car park and saw me when he went back to his car. He was so nice, and just hugged me. When I was at my most broken, he was there and gave me the love that I had always wanted.'

Lauren began to cry. Not at what she had done to Sandra, but at what she had done to Gabriel.

After a while, she calmed down and was able to speak again.

'Last night, when I knew he would discover what I'd done, I panicked and nearly went for him with the knife. Then I saw his eyes and knew I could never hurt the one person who had given me something beautiful. So I tried to kill myself. Standing there at that moment, I would have been happy to go because, just briefly, I had know what it was to be happy.'

Baxter felt sympathy for Lauren, but she needed to get a lot more information recorded if they were going to get this to stand up in court, even with an admission of guilt.

'So how did you kill Sandra? We're still waiting for final results from the post-mortem. How did you even get into her house? There were no signs of a break-in,' Baxter asked.

'I didn't go to her house. And, in one sense, I didn't kill her, she killed herself. I took Jane home after the performance with Gabriel and spent the night and next day with him. He can corroborate that.'

Baxter and Dunstan exchanged a nervous glance.

'Don't worry,' Lauren continued. 'I take responsibility for what I did, because I knew what the outcome would be.

'It didn't really take much planning at all. I just had to wait for the right opportunity, which took some months. It could have taken years, but I was prepared to be patient.

'My degree is in biochemistry. I specialised in mycology as I've always been fascinated by fungi. Living organisms that more closely resemble plants than animals. Being a vegetarian, I've always enjoyed mushrooms, which is what I think led to my interest in them.

'*Coprinopsis atramentaria*, more commonly known as the inky cap mushroom, is common, harmless and has a nice flavour. I usually have it in salads a couple of times a week. It would have been far too obvious to invite Sandra over for dinner, or to go to hers in order to get her to eat them, so I had to wait. In between the two performances, Sandra and Jane had a blazing row, resulting in Jane knocking Sandra's food from her hand. I was able to go over to Sandra to comfort her and share my salad with her, which was full of these mushrooms. We both ate it in full view of everybody.'

Dunstan chimed in, 'So did you just avoid the mushrooms and leave them for her?'

'No,' Lauren said. 'I ate them too. Like I said, they're harmless.'

Baxter was confused. 'So how did you kill her?'

'I just told you,' Lauren said.

'But if the mushrooms are harmless and you ate them too, why is Sandra dead and you're not?' Baxter asked.

'Because *Coprinopsis atramentaria* is, on its own, entirely harmless. However, when you combine it with alcohol anytime up to five days later, it creates a binary poison. Either ingredient on their own is harmless, but in combination, these two create a disulfiram syndrome.

'Sandra was well known for having a very large whisky when she went home after concerts, usually several. The reaction would have taken around ten minutes to kick in, which I reckon was enough time for her to knock back the first one and be well into the second or third.

'At that point, she will have felt like she had a hangover setting in. The severity of the symptoms depends on the amount of alcohol consumed. Whisky has an extremely high percentage and she probably had a fair bit. It's not always fatal, but it can do severe damage if the victim does survive.'

Dunstan interjected. 'So why did you choose this method if it's not always fatal?'

Lauren looked at him coolly. 'Because Jane had let slip once that Sandra had a heart condition and the doctor was waiting for her to have a heart attack. *Coprinopsis atramentaria* coupled with a lot of alcohol in a short space of time and someone primed for a myocardial infarction will almost certainly kill them. I would imagine she drank when she got home, felt like hell itself within ten to twenty minutes and staggered up to bed, where she died.'

Baxter looked at Lauren. 'And that's why you freaked out yesterday when you saw Gabriel stood at your fridge holding your lunchtime salad and about to drink champagne.'

Lauren's eyes fell. 'Yes. I thought I might already be too late, although because champagne has less alcohol than whisky, if he had digested the mushrooms and the champagne, he'd probably have lived.'

The room fell silent. Eventually, Baxter said, 'Thank you, Miss Barker. I'm going to stop this interview here as we need to consult with a lot of people. As I'm sure you're expecting, we are going to have to remand you in custody, and we may come back to you with further questions over the next few hours.'

Lauren nodded her understanding.

'Interview terminated at 1655 hours.'

THIRTY-SIX

LAUREN WAS SUBSEQUENTLY CHARGED WITH Sandra's murder. She pleaded guilty at the first hearing, so no trial ever took place. As a result, much of her story never came out in public.

She wrote to several people from prison to explain. Her letter to Gabriel was long and was virtually the only one which contained an apology. Lots of them, in fact. She wrote to Jane and the two of them stayed in touch for the rest of their lives. She also wrote to Michael as she wanted him to know everything.

Lauren was given a life sentence with a minimum term of 17 years. As usually happens with parole boards, her first few attempts to get released were refused and she ended up serving 25 years in prison.

The news that he had another daughter broke Michael. He had always wondered whether the child had been a boy or a girl, but Sandra would never tell him, keeping that one piece of information for herself. He had always assumed the child had grown up in Italy. He never recovered from the knowledge that his own child had been the one responsible for taking Sandra away from him.

He wrote to Elizabeth to tell her the news, as she had never even known there was a child. She sent no reply and Michael never heard from her or any of his children again.

Elizabeth died three years later, having spent the remainder of her days with their daughter. Shortly after she left Porlington, her daughter realised she was behaving a little strangely and Elizabeth was subsequently diagnosed with dementia. Due to this possibly explaining some of her stranger actions and erratic behaviour around the time of Sandra's death, she was never charged with interfering with a human body.

Michael, finding himself all alone in the world, suffered a breakdown. He lived another twenty years, but as a shell of himself. He never met anybody else romantically and became one of those strange old men who never leaves their house, peering out of his windows and being mocked by the neighbourhood children. He never conducted an orchestra again.

DS Dunstan retired a little over a year later, with a commendation from the Chief Constable for his work on the Finley case. This always somewhat irked DI Baxter, who felt he hadn't contributed enough to deserve one. Pamela Baxter was promoted to Detective Chief Inspector, where she supervised cases and other officers rather than actively investigating them herself. She had a long and somewhat unmentionable career.

Porlington Pianos continued to be a thriving business and nobody ever found out that it was just a front for a drugs empire, run by the Kings. Despite being investigated by HMRC several times over the years, nobody ever managed to turn anything up, mostly down to Neil's brilliance at creative accounting. Nobody ever looked closely enough to realise that the violin rosin they shifted thousands of units of was actually cannabis resin. Their cover for sending so much 'rosin' into deprived areas was that they were supporting local education and the arts in schools.

The only time they came close to getting caught was when a block of rosin and a block of resin got muddled up. Jemima Hicks, a rather uninspiring and talentless eight-year-old violin student left what she thought was rosin on the kitchen worktop one day after she couldn't be bothered (yet again) to pack her violin away. The family schnauzer, Boggle, sniffed this out and ate the lot, thus destroying the evidence. Mrs Hicks, Jemima's mother, then had to pay over two thousand pounds for Boggle to be weaned off cannabis by a mixture of canine counselling and psychiatric treatment, with a few charcoal stomach rinses. Mrs Hicks blamed Jemima's 14-year-old brother, Mickey. This was unfair, as, whilst Mickey was a pothead, on this occasion, he wasn't to blame.

Boggle was never quite the same after this and spent the rest of his days furiously sniffing the skirting boards of every room he was in, looking for a fix. Mickey spent the rest of his days wondering how the hell Boggle had managed to get hold of better stuff than he could.

Henry James eventually found love, two years later. A quite beautiful brunette called Krystal asked for his number in a club one night, and things went from there. Within six months they were married and blissfully happy. Nobody could quite believe it, and it still didn't stop him from making innuendos at every opportunity.

Two years into the marriage, and Henry brought up the subject of having children, only to be told by his new wife that she couldn't have children. When Henry pressed the matter further, Krystal finally told him that she had been born male and was known as Anthony until she was 24 years old. Henry opened his mouth to question her further and only the words, 'Meh. Fair enough. Let's go upstairs, love,' came out. They both died within a year of each other, shortly after celebrating their golden wedding anniversary.

Roxie was cast as the lead in the SODS production of *Turandot* six months after *Hello, Dolly!* Her top C registered each night on a seismograph in a weather station a mile away and caused some concern amongst the meteorologists that there may be a minor earthquake coming. Purely by chance, there was a minor tremor registered in Fawlham a week later, but it was entirely unrelated to Roxie.

Roxie and Morag remained firm friends for the rest of their lives, getting up to far more hijinks as the years went on. Shortly after Roxie's fifth husband died, some years later, Roxie and Morag set up the Foundation for Fallen Sopranos, as a home for aging and ailing sopranos who had fallen on hard times. They always thought they would eke out the remainder of their days here, but they never had the chance as they both died in a freak speedboat accident off the coast of Monaco in their early 80s. Roxie was survived by her ninth husband, Elmer. He had been her butler for decades prior to becoming lucky number nine. For the rest of Morag's life, nobody ever understood more than 50% of any sentence she said in her Scottish drawl, but they all loved her anyway.

Megan Sims married Graham the following year and they moved to an ex-pat ballroom dancing community on the Costa Brava where Graham read books while Megan danced her way through life. She felt it was probably time to stop using the magnets as she must be through the menopause. As it turned out, she had only ever been pre-menopausal and the magnets had delayed it all—once she stopped using them every day, she fell pregnant immediately and gave birth to their daughter, Minim, (Megan's third child) nine months later. After a few years, Megan decided she didn't like the heat as it reminded her too much of having a permanent hot flush (and, by this time, she actually *was* going through the menopause), so they moved back. She led counselling and group therapy sessions for those struggling with going through the change at Roxie and Morag's Foundation for the rest of her life. Megan and Daphne Maxwell remained firm friends for the rest of their lives, frequently appearing as a double act on Megan's radio show.

After she died, Graham donated Megan's horn to the Foundation, having no idea that she had acted on Daphne's advice and bought a new one without telling him. He never knew that he gave away an Alexander Model 301 Full Triple French Horn with a hand hammered, detachable bell and gold and lacquer finish, worth well over £17,000. The horn spent many years in the front garden of the Foundation, with petunias growing in it.

Minim became a brain surgeon. On rabbits.

Rupert and Anthea ended up taking over the running of the Porlington Philharmonia. The Viennese concert took place on 14th April, as they had already booked Daphne and sold tickets. Seventeen of them, to be precise. Over 350 people turned up to the concert, mostly out of morbid curiosity as gossip had spread like wildfire throughout the area.

Anthea ended up becoming a judge some years later. Rupert fathered another five children, none of them by Anthea, and all for the best possible reasons.

After the Viennese concert, Rupert and Anthea decided the orchestra needed a break over the summer to regroup. During this time, they asked Gabriel to be the permanent conductor when it all started back in September.

Gabriel spent most of those months unsure what he would do. The Cole family practically demanded to buy his shares in their business within a week of the divorce hearing. Anthea brokered a deal on Gabriel's behalf, sensing she could push this matter due to their desperation and on 11th May, Anthea presented Gabriel in person with his decree absolute and a cheque for £2.75million (and that was after her fees). 'There you go, my little purple mountain flower, don't spend it all at once!'

Gabriel never heard from Shelley or any of the Cole family again, although Anthea told him some months later that Martin Brady had been held in contempt of court, receiving a two-week prison sentence, suspended for two years. As a result, the Solicitors Regulation Authority instigated an investigation against him, and he was subsequently struck off.

Gabriel was heartbroken over Lauren, but, as usually happens, time allowed him to heal. The two of them kept in touch via letter throughout her years in prison, although he never went to visit her. This was by mutual agreement on both their parts, as they both felt it would be too painful and wouldn't allow either of them to ever move on. They did occasionally meet for coffee many years later, after her release, and continued to do so as friends for the rest of their lives.

Over the summer following the Viennese concert, Gabriel considered his future. As soon as he had his cheque, he gave notice of one month at Porlington Pianos, but occasionally popped in to see them. He never did find out what was really going on there, although, in a strange twist of fate, he did have his crotch sniffed by Boggle the schnauzer in the park one day as Boggle was desperately trying to find another hit.

Eventually, as tempted as Gabriel was to leave the area and the memories attached to it, he found that he didn't want to leave the friends he had made.

That summer, he hurled himself into a new fitness regime, running every day and going to the gym. Henry James rather let himself go after he got married, and Gabriel was quite pleased some years on that he was in considerably better shape than the trumpeter.

Gabriel found himself taking to the podium on 6th September as the new principal conductor of the Porlington Philharmonia. Having had some months off, there was a good turnout at this rehearsal, with some new faces having joined over the summer break.

As he stepped onto the podium, he felt a twinge in his right calf from running earlier that day, so he grabbed his foot and stretched his calf out. His neck was quite tense from weight training earlier, so he thought he better get rid of the clicks before beginning and moved his head from side to side.

As he realised the task he had ahead of him of uniting this bunch of people in the aftermath of the events of the last year, he closed his eyes and took a deep breath.

'Oh god, not again…' was heard to drift over from the percussion section.